# A WITCH'S PRINTING OFFICE

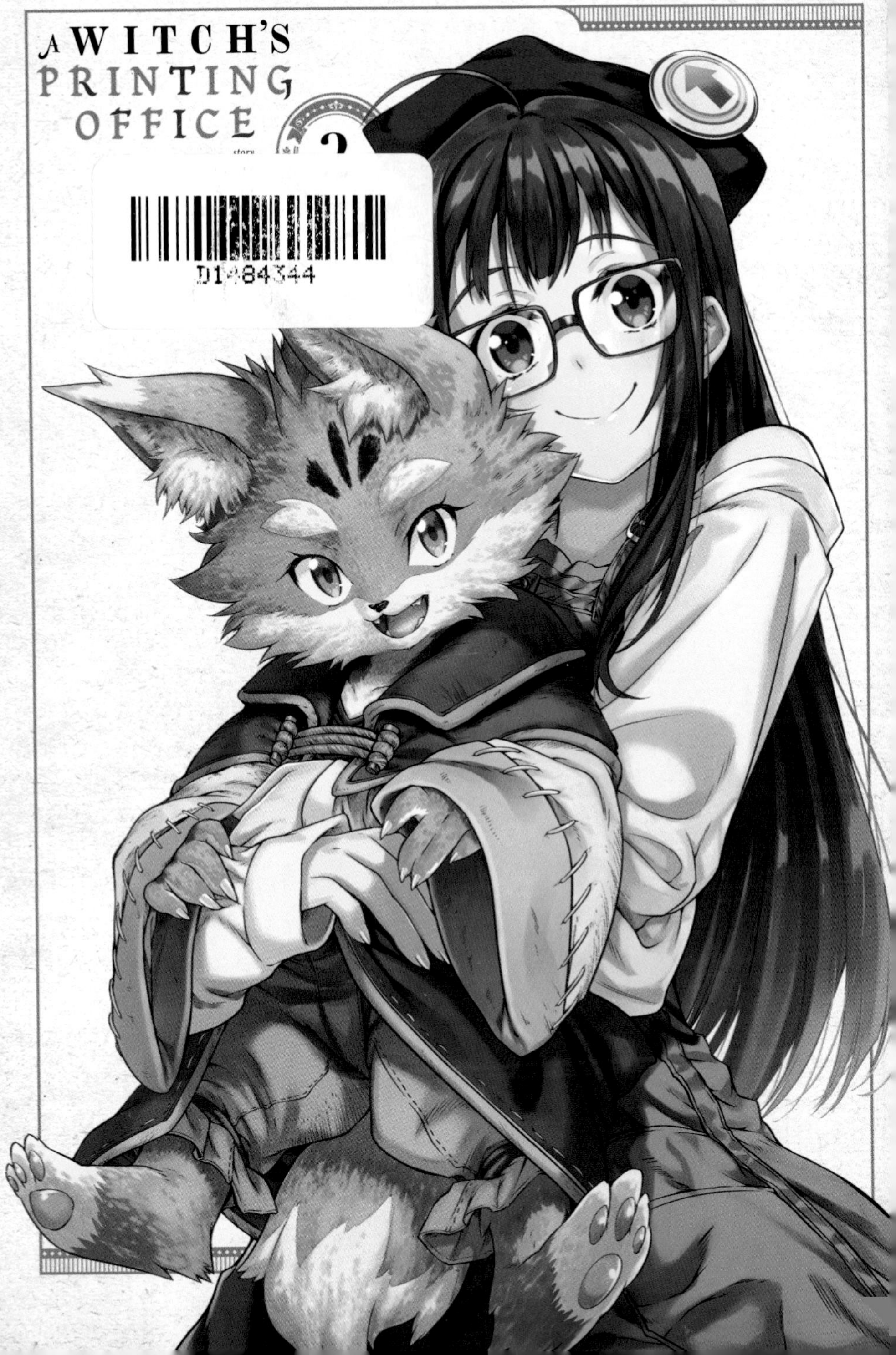

# CONTENTS

✴

Chapter

# 7
[003]

Chapter

# 8
[031]

Chapter

# 9
[051]

Chapter

# 10
[079]

Chapter

# 11
[107]

Chapter

# 12
[133]

✴

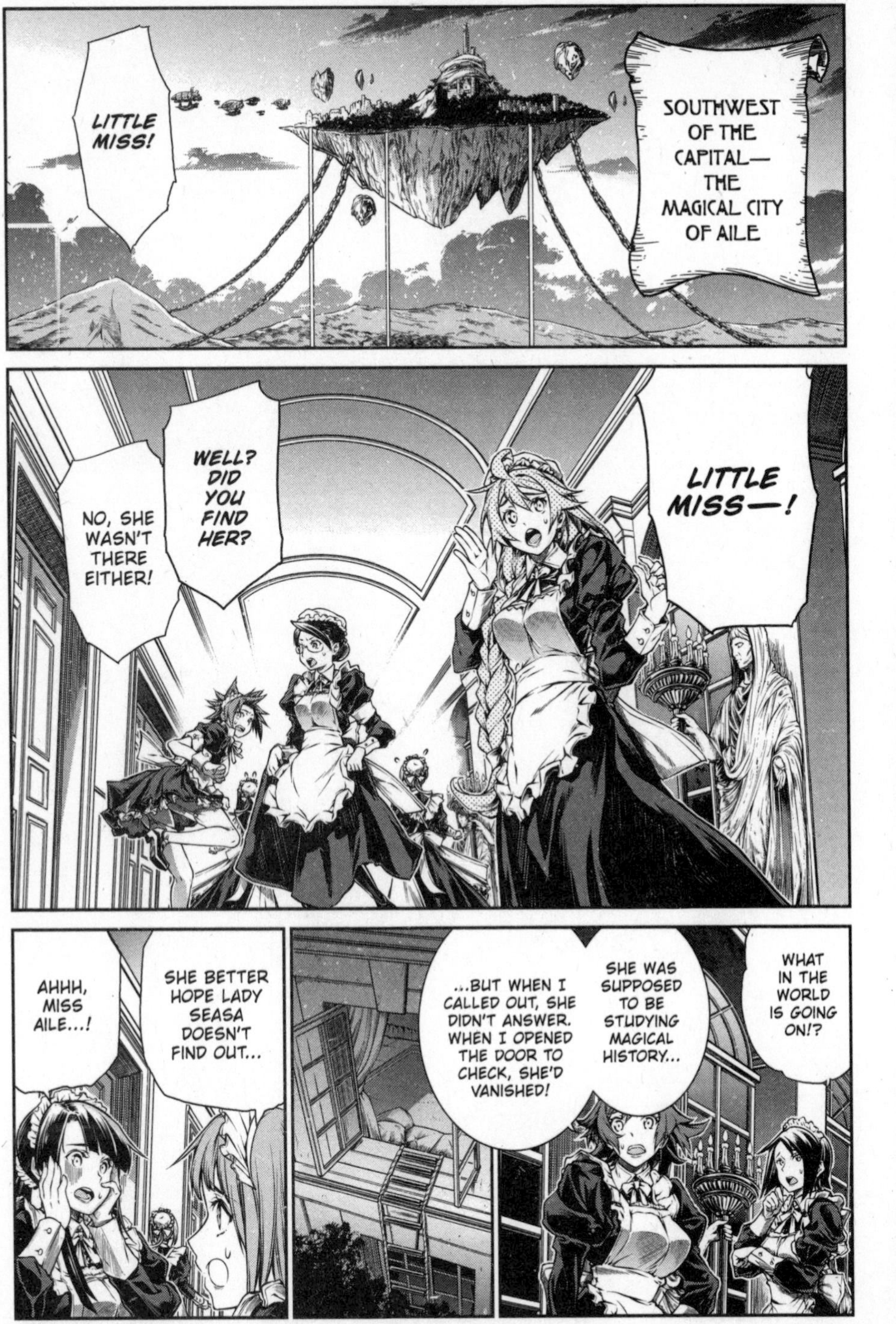
SOUTHWEST OF THE CAPITAL— THE MAGICAL CITY OF AILE
LITTLE MISS!
LITTLE MISS—!
WELL? DID YOU FIND HER?
NO, SHE WASN'T THERE EITHER!
WHAT IN THE WORLD IS GOING ON!?
SHE WAS SUPPOSED TO BE STUDYING MAGICAL HISTORY...
...BUT WHEN I CALLED OUT, SHE DIDN'T ANSWER. WHEN I OPENED THE DOOR TO CHECK, SHE'D VANISHED!
SHE BETTER HOPE LADY SEASA DOESN'T FIND OUT...
AHHH, MISS AILE...!

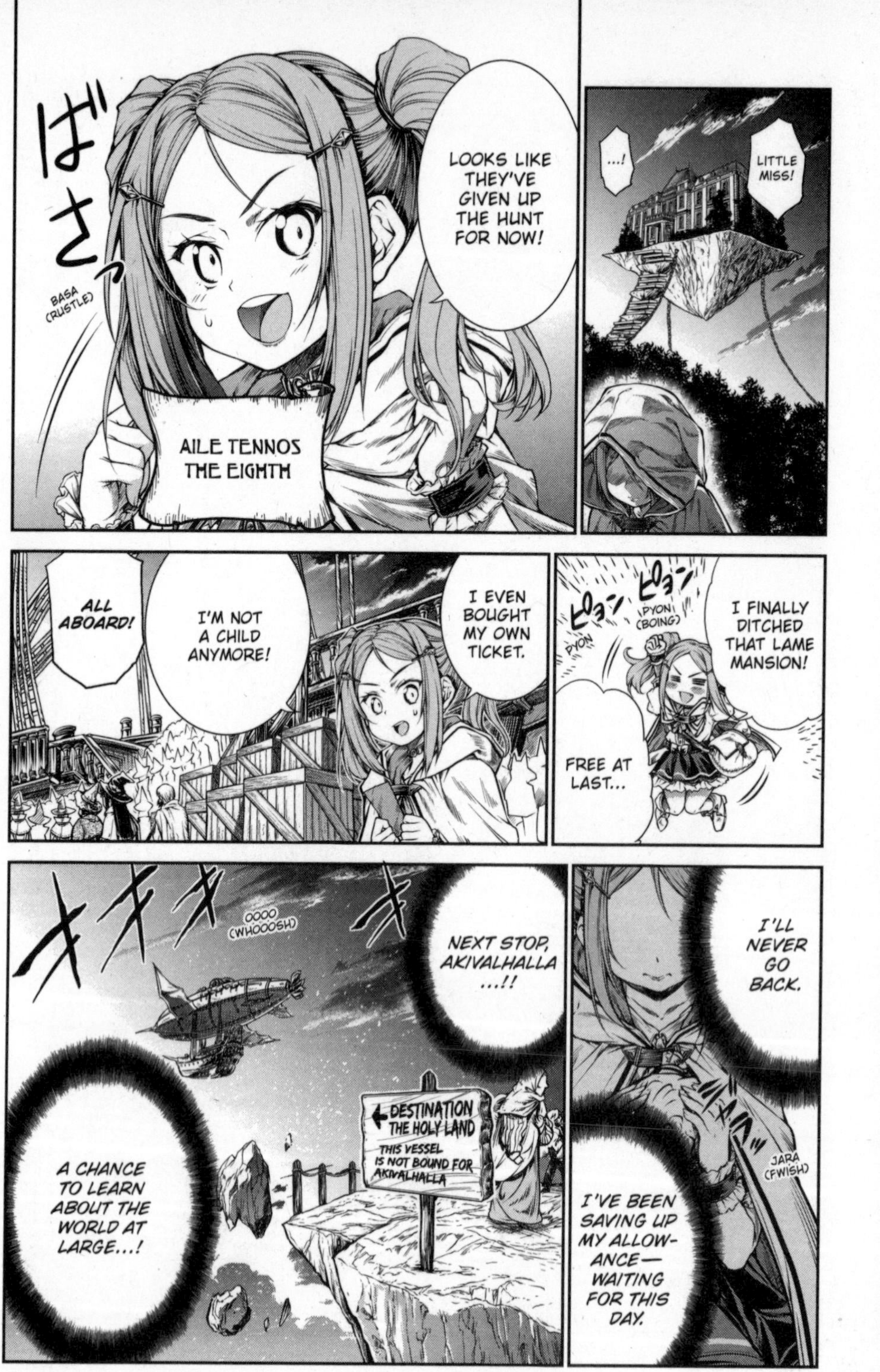
LITTLE MISS!
...!
LOOKS LIKE THEY'VE GIVEN UP THE HUNT FOR NOW!
ばさっ
BASA (RUSTLE)
AILE TENNOS THE EIGHTH
I FINALLY DITCHED THAT LAME MANSION!
PYON (BOING)
PYON
FREE AT LAST...
I EVEN BOUGHT MY OWN TICKET.
I'M NOT A CHILD ANYMORE!
ALL ABOARD!
I'LL NEVER GO BACK.
JARA (FWISH)
I'VE BEEN SAVING UP MY ALLOW-ANCE— WAITING FOR THIS DAY.
NEXT STOP, AKIVALHALLA ...!!
OOOO (WHOOOSH)
← DESTINATION THE HOLY LAND
THIS VESSEL IS NOT BOUND FOR AKIVALHALLA
A CHANCE TO LEARN ABOUT THE WORLD AT LARGE...!

# Chapter 7

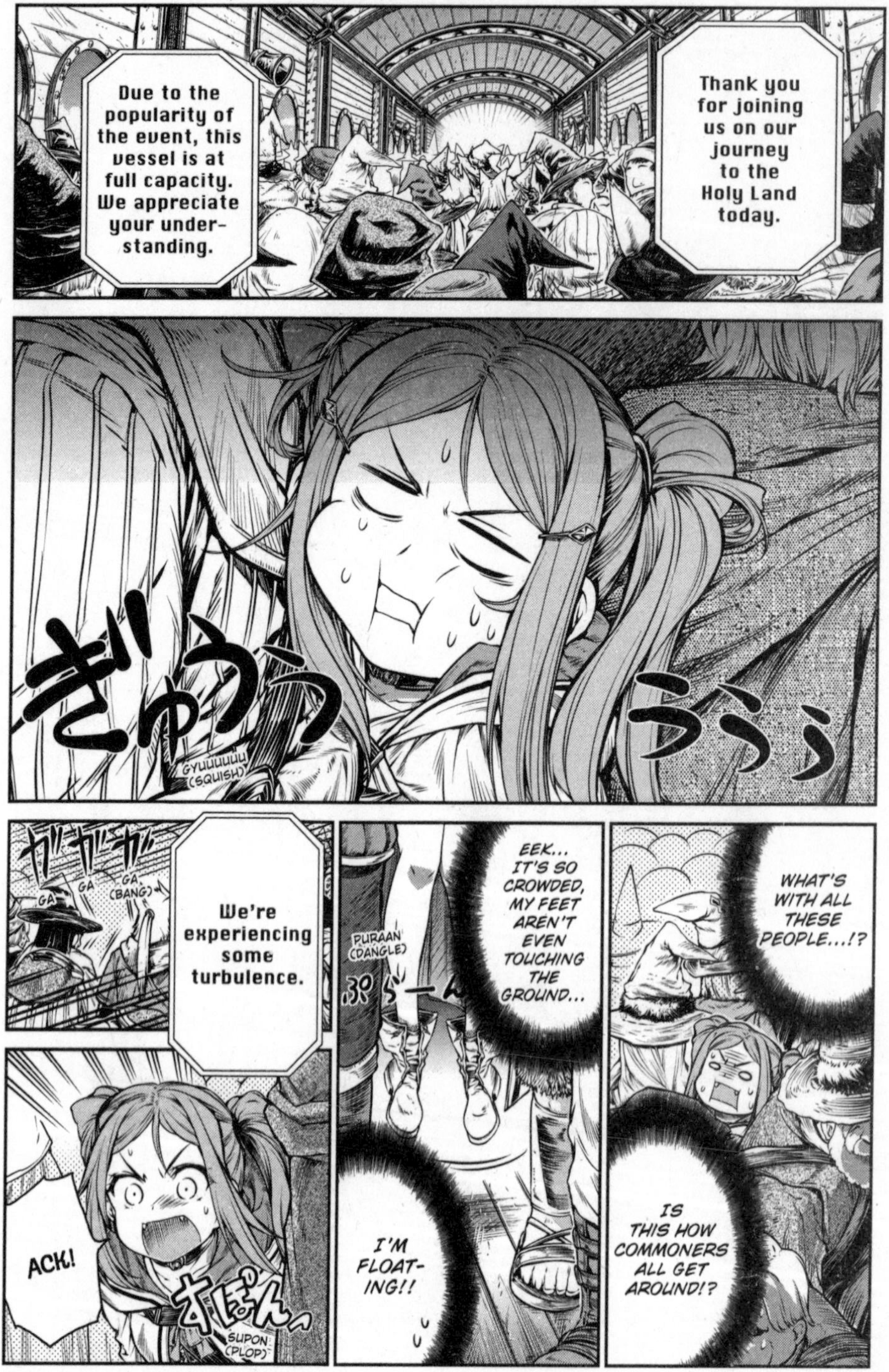

Thank you for joining us on our journey to the Holy Land today.
Due to the popularity of the event, this vessel is at full capacity. We appreciate your understanding.
GYUUUUUUU (SQUISH)
WHAT'S WITH ALL THESE PEOPLE...!?
IS THIS HOW COMMONERS ALL GET AROUND!?
EEK... IT'S SO CROWDED, MY FEET AREN'T EVEN TOUCHING THE GROUND...
PURAAN (DANGLE)
I'M FLOAT-ING!!
GA GA GA (BANG)
We're experiencing some turbulence.
ACK!
SUPON (PLOP)

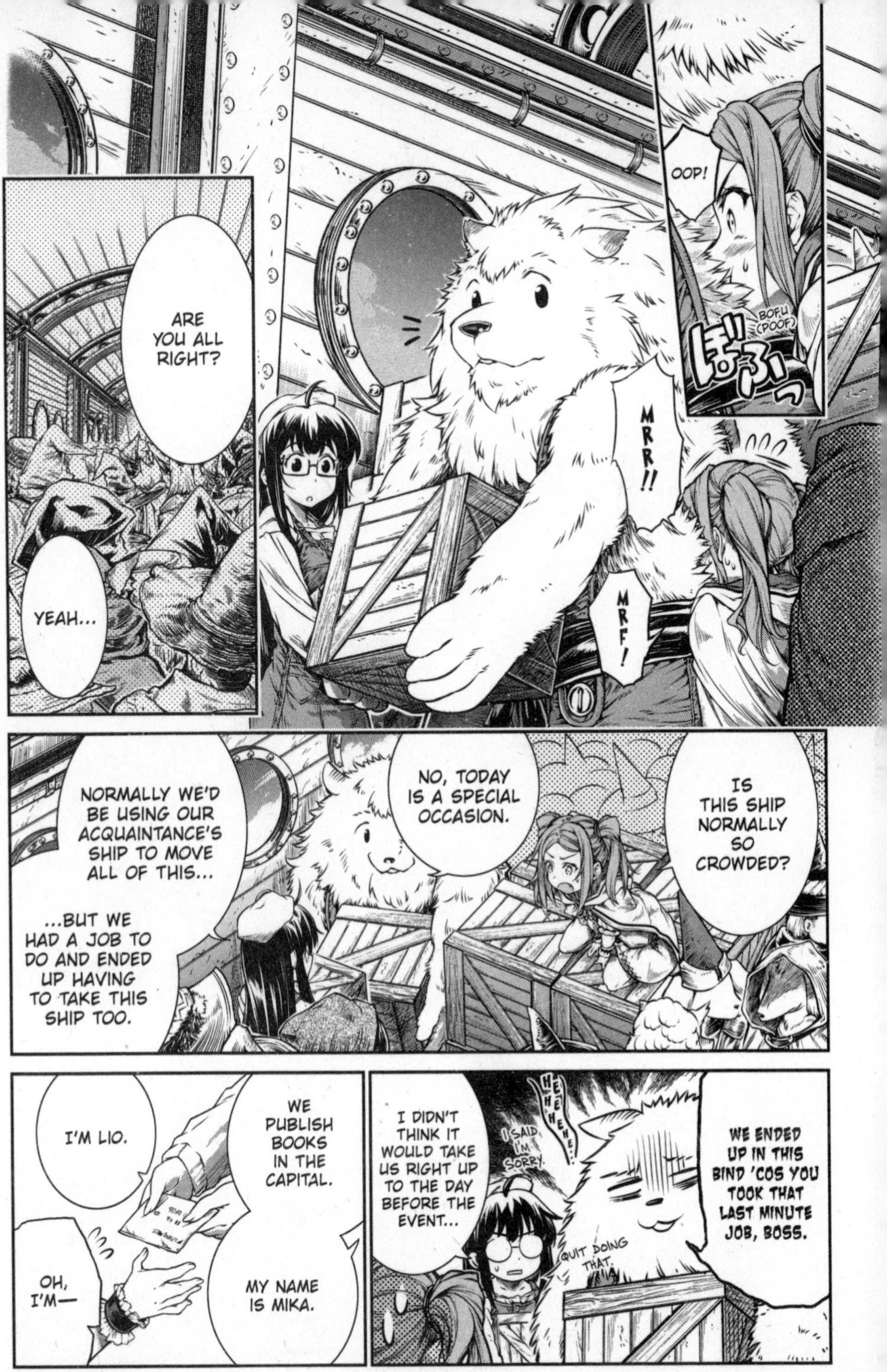
OOP!
BOFU (POOF)
ぼふっ
MRR!!
MRF!
ARE YOU ALL RIGHT?
YEAH...
IS THIS SHIP NORMALLY SO CROWDED?
NO, TODAY IS A SPECIAL OCCASION.
NORMALLY WE'D BE USING OUR ACQUAINTANCE'S SHIP TO MOVE ALL OF THIS...
...BUT WE HAD A JOB TO DO AND ENDED UP HAVING TO TAKE THIS SHIP TOO.
WE ENDED UP IN THIS BIND 'COS YOU TOOK THAT LAST MINUTE JOB, BOSS.
HEHEHEHE...
I SAID I'M SORRY.
I DIDN'T THINK IT WOULD TAKE US RIGHT UP TO THE DAY BEFORE THE EVENT...
QUIT DOING THAT.
WE PUBLISH BOOKS IN THE CAPITAL.
MY NAME IS MIKA.
I'M LIO.
OH, I'M—

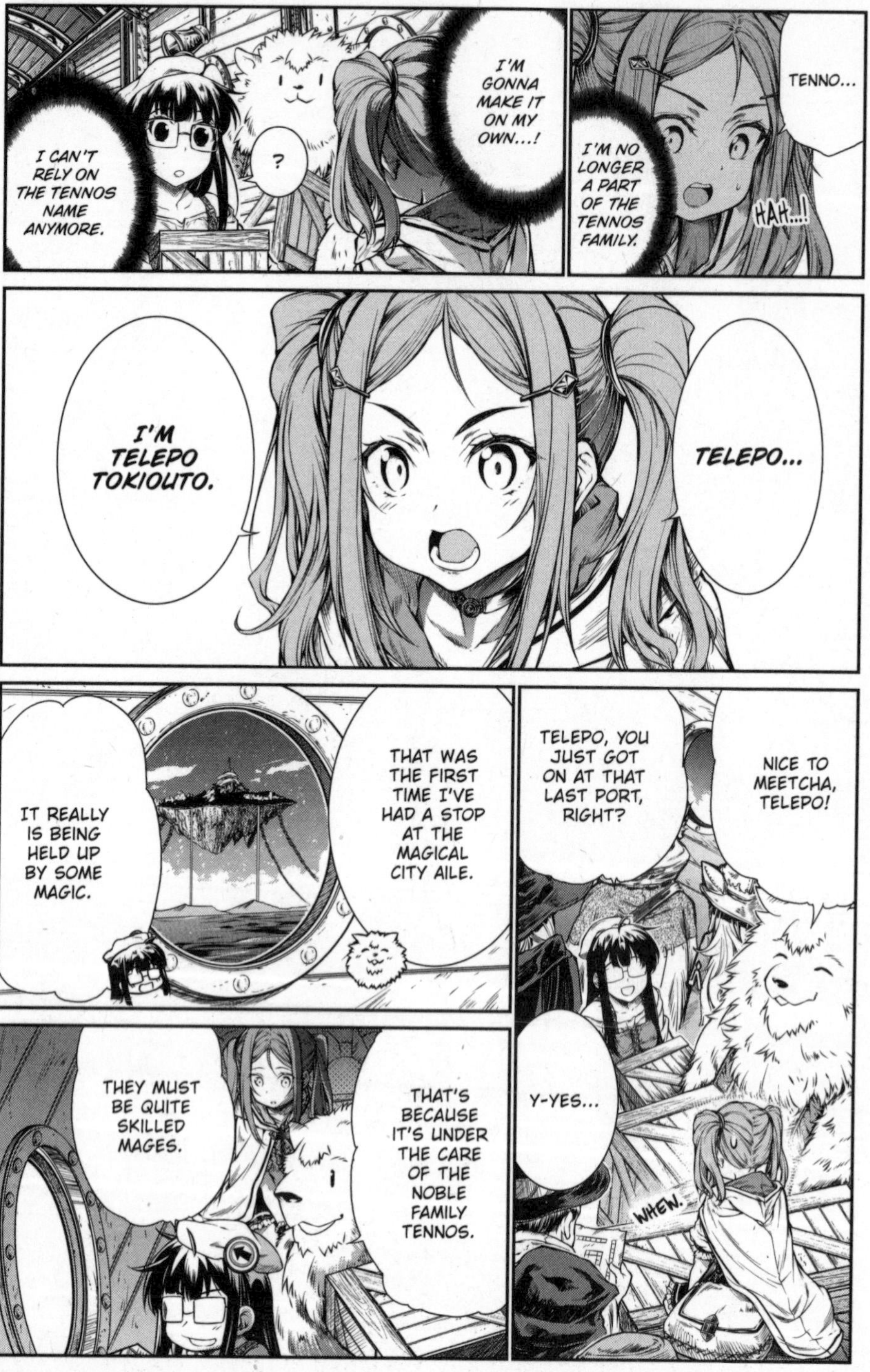
TENNO...
I'M NO LONGER A PART OF THE TENNOS FAMILY.
HAH...!
I'M GONNA MAKE IT ON MY OWN...!
?
I CAN'T RELY ON THE TENNOS NAME ANYMORE.
TELEPO...
I'M TELEPO TOKIOUTO.
NICE TO MEETCHA, TELEPO!
TELEPO, YOU JUST GOT ON AT THAT LAST PORT, RIGHT?
Y-YES...
WHEW.
THAT WAS THE FIRST TIME I'VE HAD A STOP AT THE MAGICAL CITY AILE.
IT REALLY IS BEING HELD UP BY SOME MAGIC.
THAT'S BECAUSE IT'S UNDER THE CARE OF THE NOBLE FAMILY TENNOS.
THEY MUST BE QUITE SKILLED MAGES.

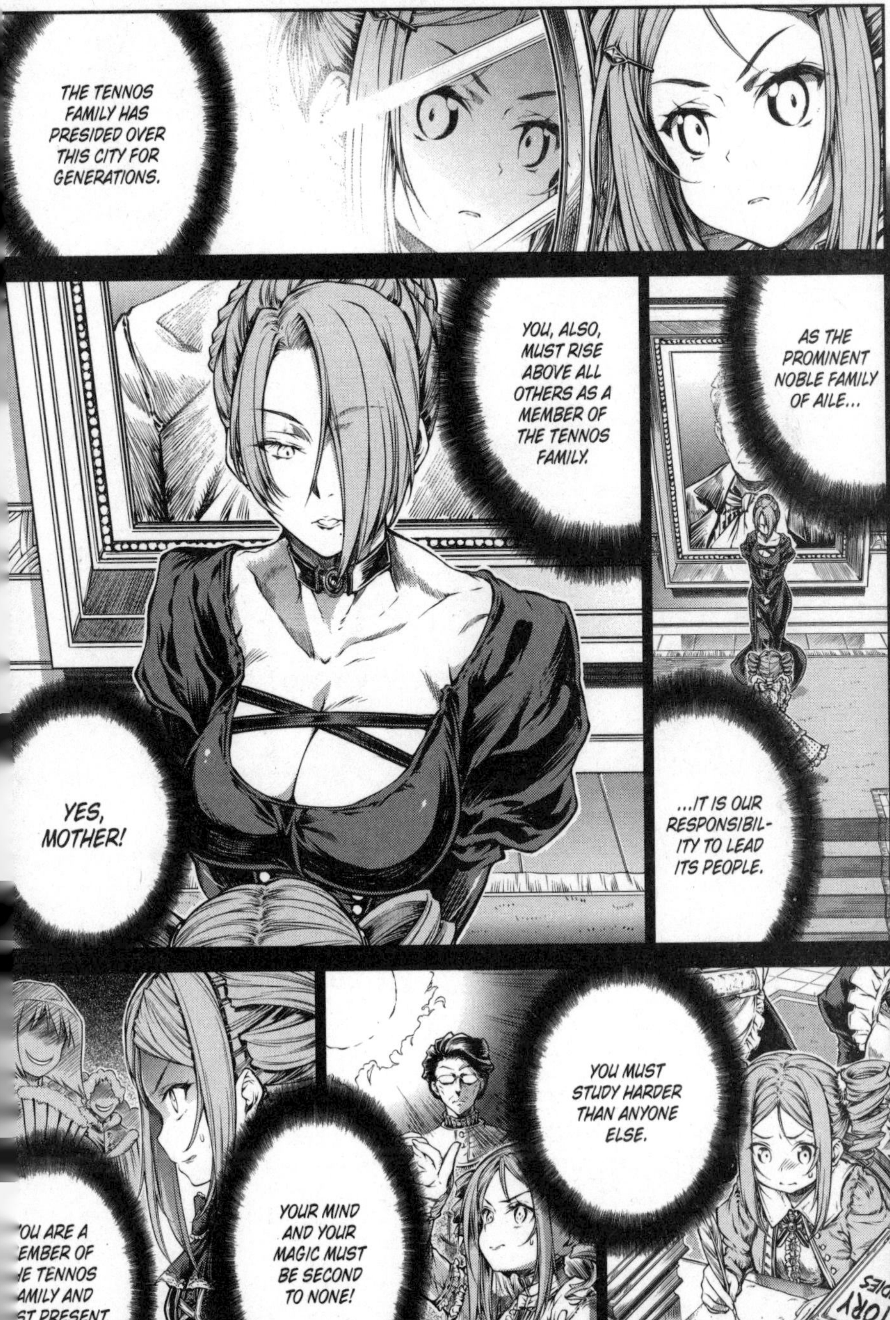
THE TENNOS FAMILY HAS PRESIDED OVER THIS CITY FOR GENERATIONS.
AS THE PROMINENT NOBLE FAMILY OF AILE...
...IT IS OUR RESPONSIBILITY TO LEAD ITS PEOPLE.
YOU, ALSO, MUST RISE ABOVE ALL OTHERS AS A MEMBER OF THE TENNOS FAMILY.
YES, MOTHER!
YOU MUST STUDY HARDER THAN ANYONE ELSE.
YOUR MIND AND YOUR MAGIC MUST BE SECOND TO NONE!
OU ARE A EMBER OF E TENNOS AMILY AND ST PRESENT URSELF AS SUCH.

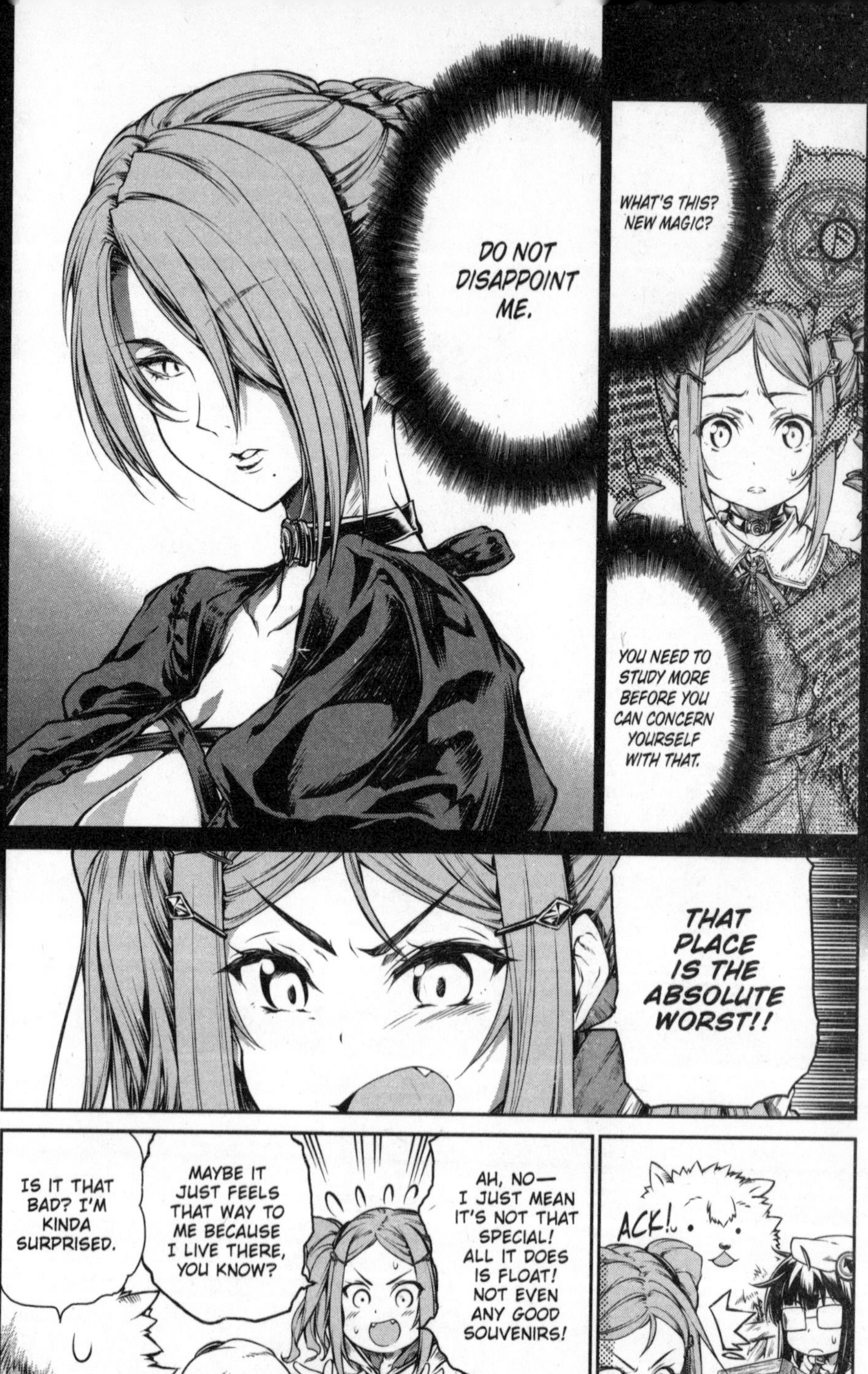
WHAT'S THIS? NEW MAGIC?
YOU NEED TO STUDY MORE BEFORE YOU CAN CONCERN YOURSELF WITH THAT.
DO NOT DISAPPOINT ME.
THAT PLACE IS THE ABSOLUTE WORST!!
ACK!
AH, NO— I JUST MEAN IT'S NOT THAT SPECIAL! ALL IT DOES IS FLOAT! NOT EVEN ANY GOOD SOUVENIRS!
MAYBE IT JUST FEELS THAT WAY TO ME BECAUSE I LIVE THERE, YOU KNOW?
IS IT THAT BAD? I'M KINDA SURPRISED.

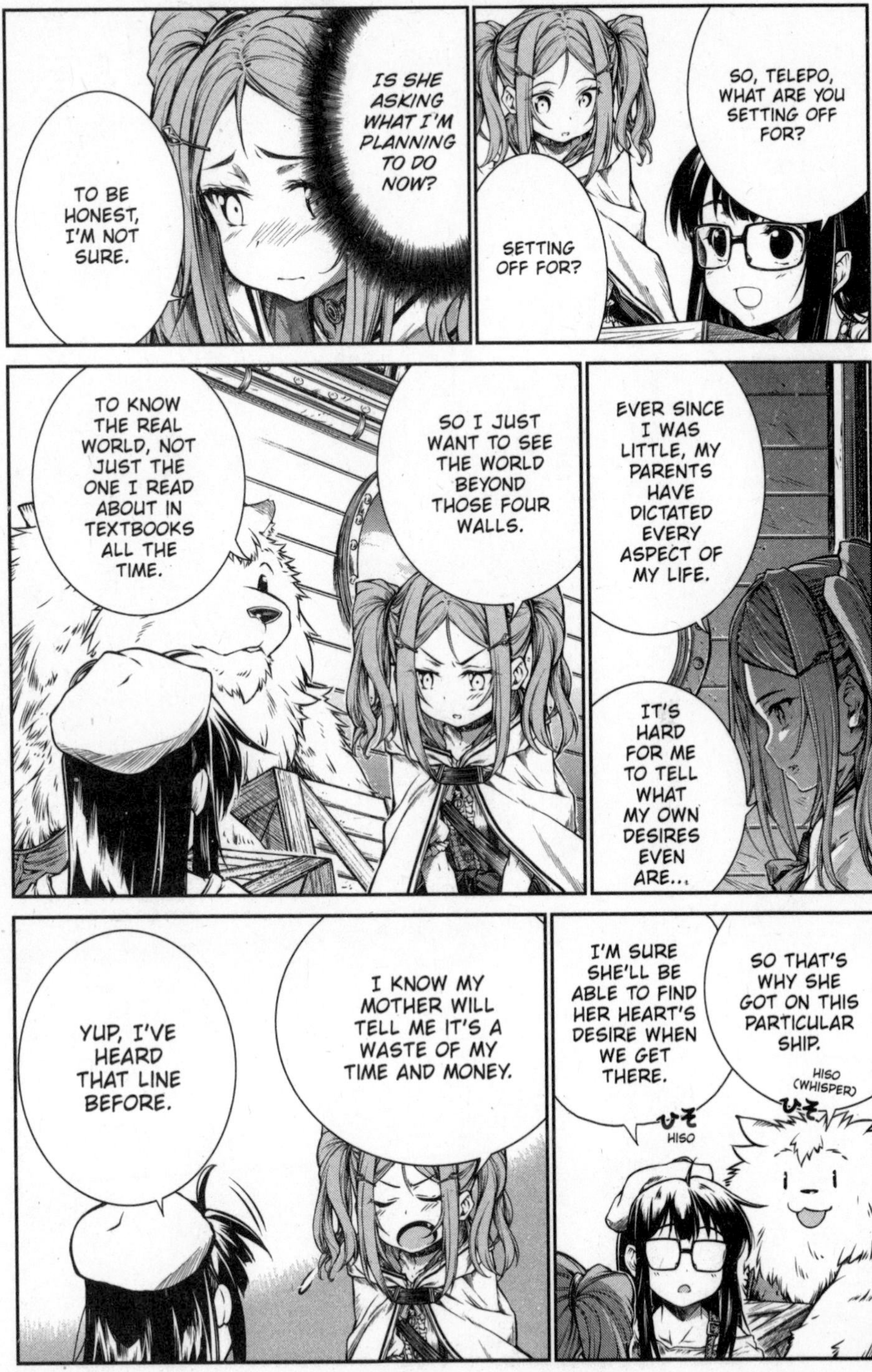
SO, TELEPO, WHAT ARE YOU SETTING OFF FOR?
SETTING OFF FOR?
IS SHE ASKING WHAT I'M PLANNING TO DO NOW?
TO BE HONEST, I'M NOT SURE.
EVER SINCE I WAS LITTLE, MY PARENTS HAVE DICTATED EVERY ASPECT OF MY LIFE.
IT'S HARD FOR ME TO TELL WHAT MY OWN DESIRES EVEN ARE...
SO I JUST WANT TO SEE THE WORLD BEYOND THOSE FOUR WALLS.
TO KNOW THE REAL WORLD, NOT JUST THE ONE I READ ABOUT IN TEXTBOOKS ALL THE TIME.
SO THAT'S WHY SHE GOT ON THIS PARTICULAR SHIP.
ひそ HISO (WHISPER)
I'M SURE SHE'LL BE ABLE TO FIND HER HEART'S DESIRE WHEN WE GET THERE.
ひそ HISO
I KNOW MY MOTHER WILL TELL ME IT'S A WASTE OF MY TIME AND MONEY.
YUP, I'VE HEARD THAT LINE BEFORE.

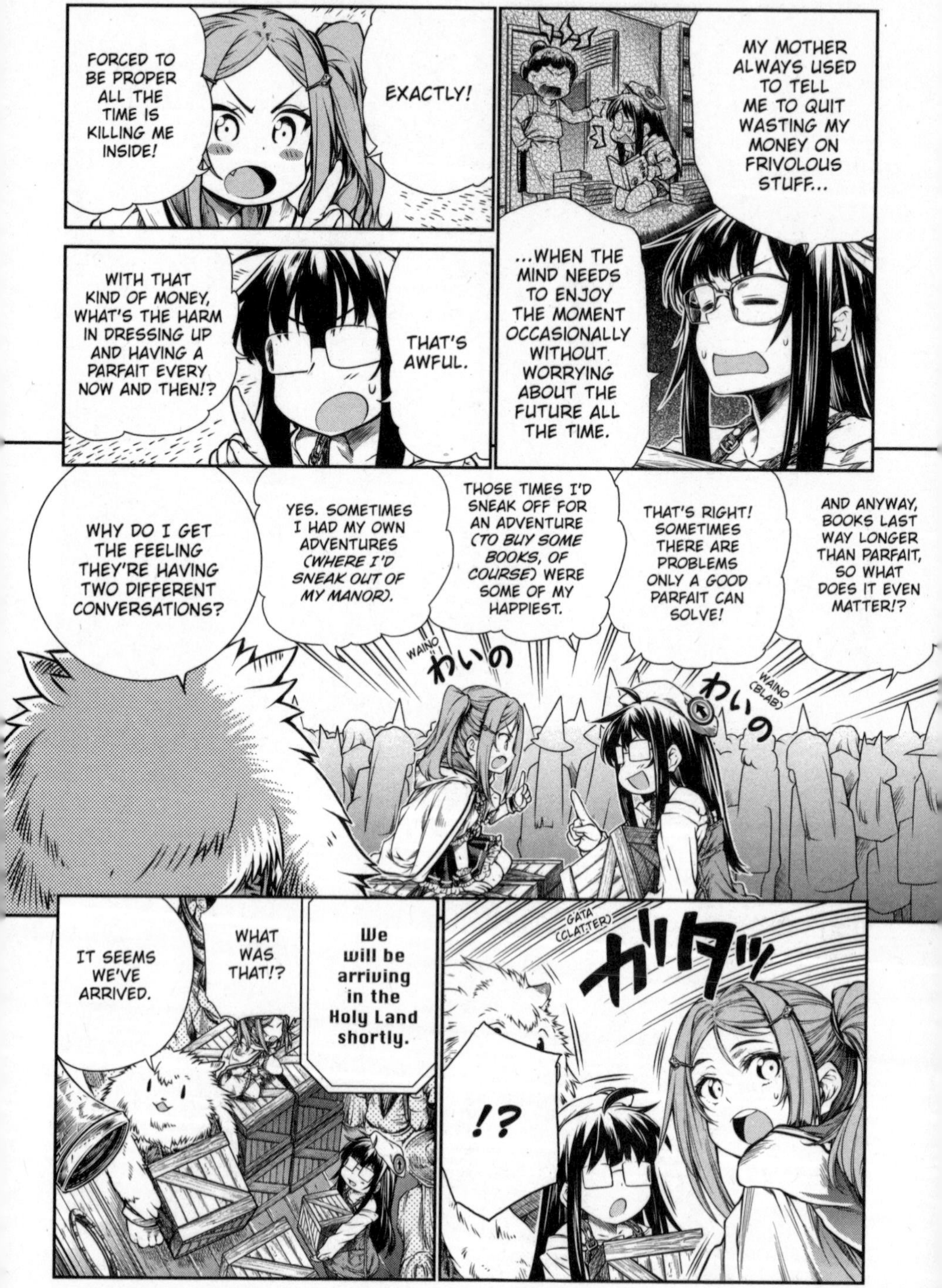
MY MOTHER ALWAYS USED TO TELL ME TO QUIT WASTING MY MONEY ON FRIVOLOUS STUFF...
...WHEN THE MIND NEEDS TO ENJOY THE MOMENT OCCASIONALLY WITHOUT WORRYING ABOUT THE FUTURE ALL THE TIME.
EXACTLY!
FORCED TO BE PROPER ALL THE TIME IS KILLING ME INSIDE!
THAT'S AWFUL.
WITH THAT KIND OF MONEY, WHAT'S THE HARM IN DRESSING UP AND HAVING A PARFAIT EVERY NOW AND THEN!?
AND ANYWAY, BOOKS LAST WAY LONGER THAN PARFAIT, SO WHAT DOES IT EVEN MATTER!?
THAT'S RIGHT! SOMETIMES THERE ARE PROBLEMS ONLY A GOOD PARFAIT CAN SOLVE!
THOSE TIMES I'D SNEAK OFF FOR AN ADVENTURE (TO BUY SOME BOOKS, OF COURSE) WERE SOME OF MY HAPPIEST.
YES. SOMETIMES I HAD MY OWN ADVENTURES (WHERE I'D SNEAK OUT OF MY MANOR).
WHY DO I GET THE FEELING THEY'RE HAVING TWO DIFFERENT CONVERSATIONS?
わいの
WAINO (BLAB)
わいの
WAINO
ガタッ
GATA (CLATTER)
!?
We will be arriving in the Holy Land shortly.
WHAT WAS THAT!?
IT SEEMS WE'VE ARRIVED.

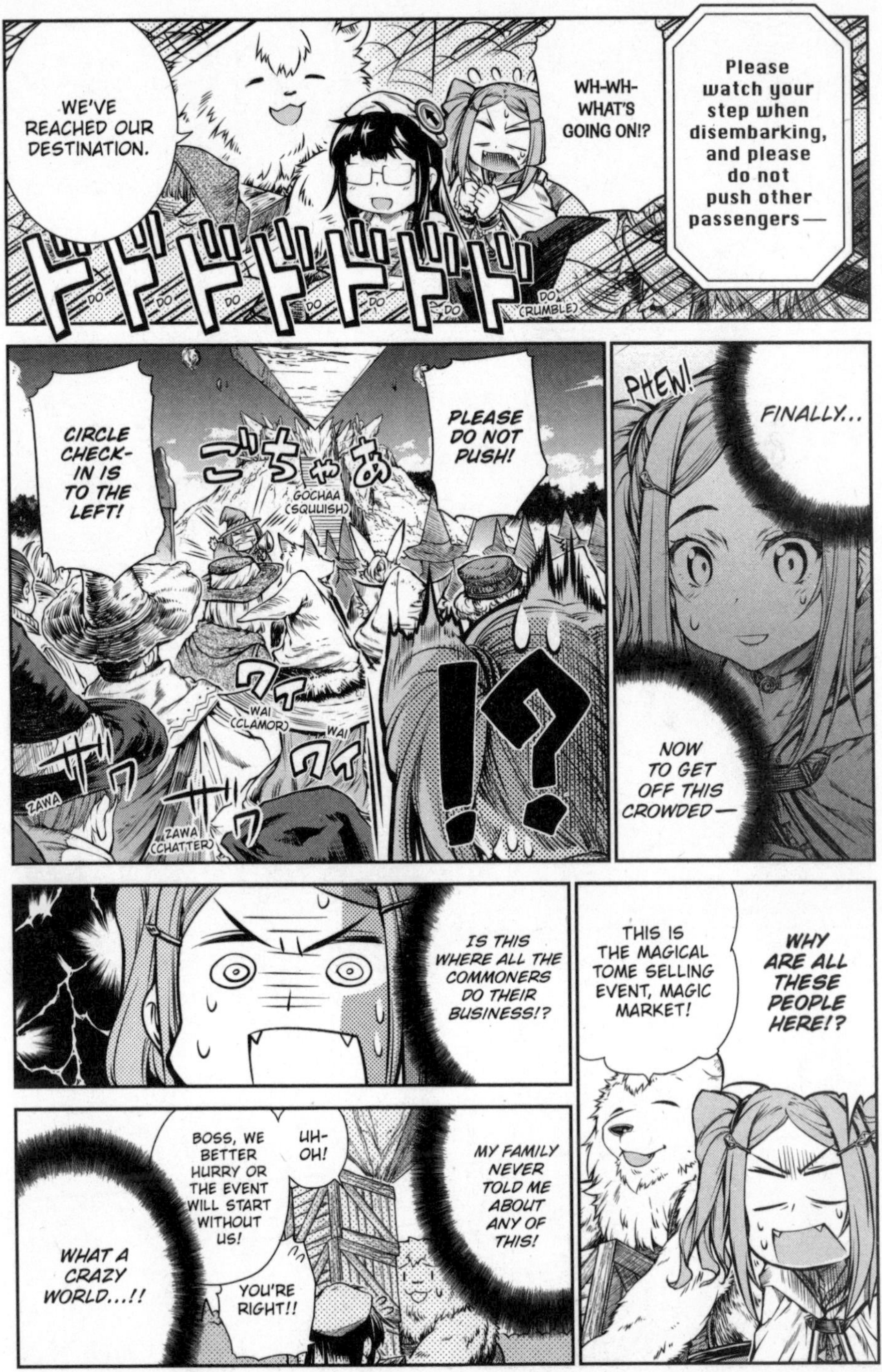
Please watch your step when disembarking, and please do not push other passengers—
WH-WH-WHAT'S GOING ON!?
WE'VE REACHED OUR DESTINATION.
DO DO DO DO DO DO DO DO (RUMBLE)
PHEW!
FINALLY...
NOW TO GET OFF THIS CROWDED—
PLEASE DO NOT PUSH!
GOCHAA (SQUISH)
CIRCLE CHECK-IN IS TO THE LEFT!
WAI (CLAMOR) WAI
ZAWA ZAWA (CHATTER)
WHY ARE ALL THESE PEOPLE HERE!?
THIS IS THE MAGICAL TOME SELLING EVENT, MAGIC MARKET!
IS THIS WHERE ALL THE COMMONERS DO THEIR BUSINESS!?
MY FAMILY NEVER TOLD ME ABOUT ANY OF THIS!
UH-OH!
BOSS, WE BETTER HURRY OR THE EVENT WILL START WITHOUT US!
YOU'RE RIGHT!!
WHAT A CRAZY WORLD...!!

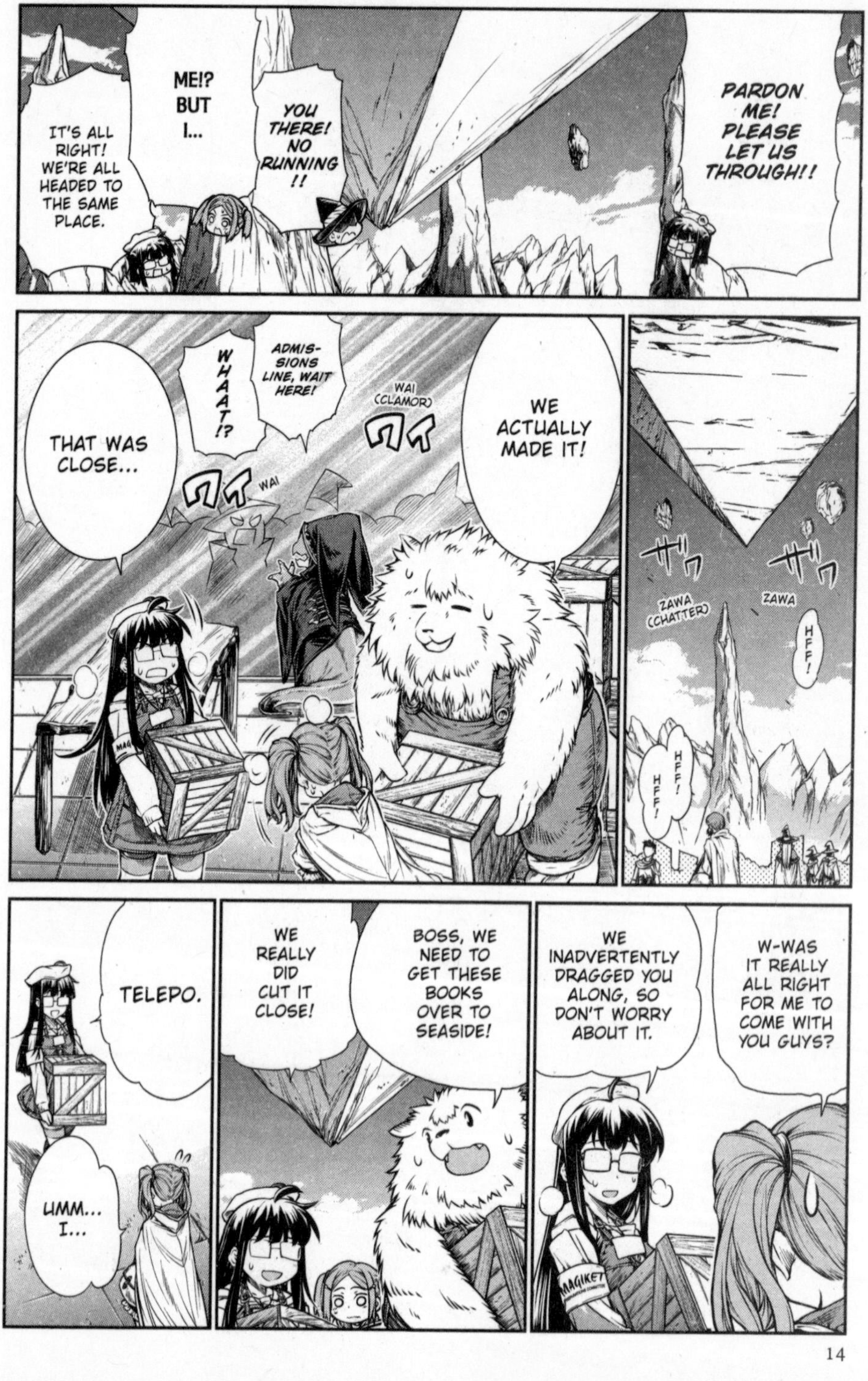
PARDON ME! PLEASE LET US THROUGH!!
YOU THERE! NO RUNNING!!
ME!? BUT I...
IT'S ALL RIGHT! WE'RE ALL HEADED TO THE SAME PLACE.
ザワ
ZAWA
ザワ
ZAWA (CHATTER)
HFF!
HFF! HFF!
WE ACTUALLY MADE IT!
ワイ
WAI (CLAMOR)
ADMISSIONS LINE, WAIT HERE!
WHAAAT!?
ワイ
WAI
THAT WAS CLOSE...
W-WAS IT REALLY ALL RIGHT FOR ME TO COME WITH YOU GUYS?
WE INADVERTENTLY DRAGGED YOU ALONG, SO DON'T WORRY ABOUT IT.
BOSS, WE NEED TO GET THESE BOOKS OVER TO SEASIDE!
WE REALLY DID CUT IT CLOSE!
TELEPO.
UMM... I...

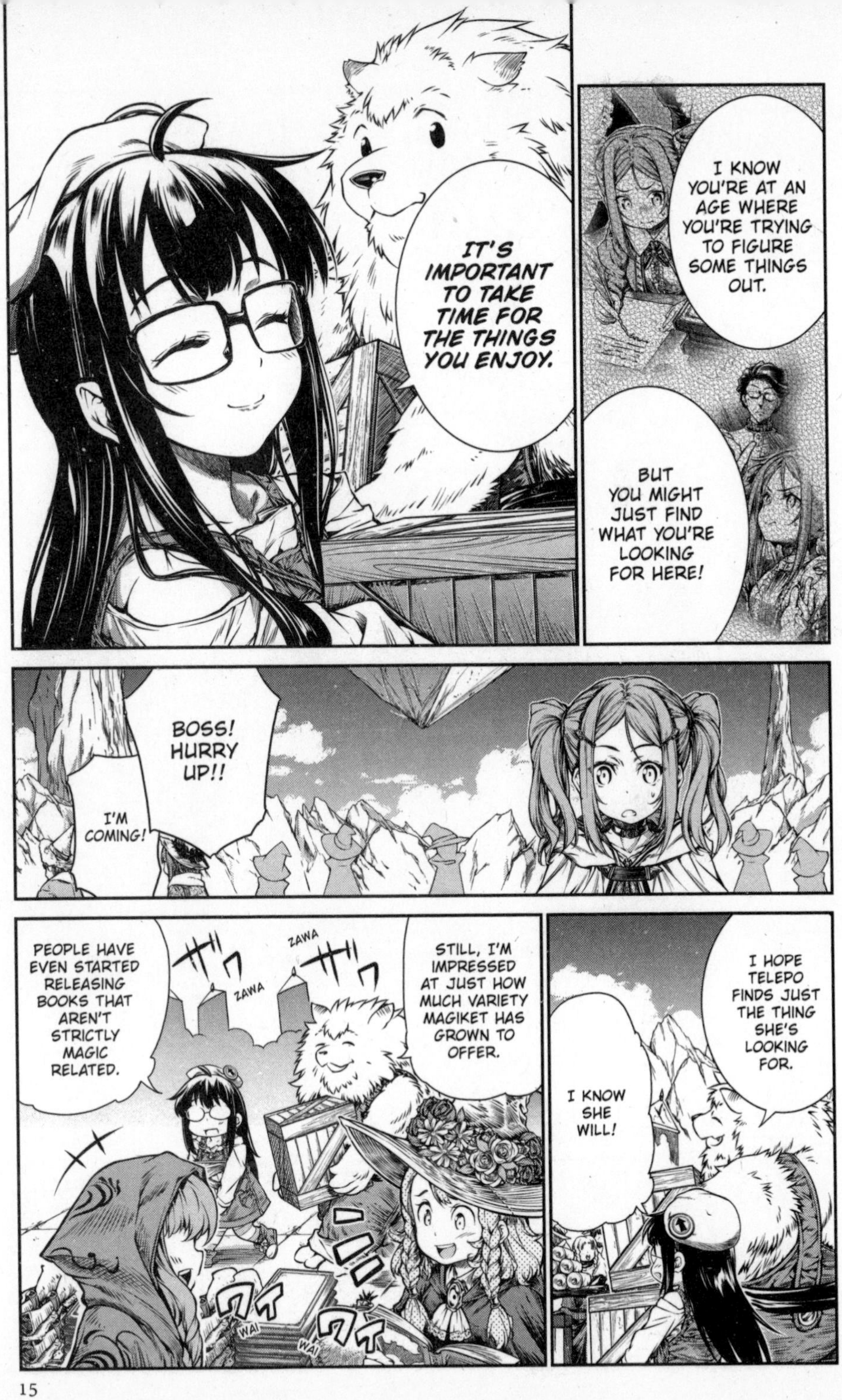
I KNOW YOU'RE AT AN AGE WHERE YOU'RE TRYING TO FIGURE SOME THINGS OUT.
BUT YOU MIGHT JUST FIND WHAT YOU'RE LOOKING FOR HERE!
IT'S IMPORTANT TO TAKE TIME FOR THE THINGS YOU ENJOY.
BOSS! HURRY UP!!
I'M COMING!
I HOPE TELEPO FINDS JUST THE THING SHE'S LOOKING FOR.
I KNOW SHE WILL!
STILL, I'M IMPRESSED AT JUST HOW MUCH VARIETY MAGIKET HAS GROWN TO OFFER.
ZAWA
ZAWA
PEOPLE HAVE EVEN STARTED RELEASING BOOKS THAT AREN'T STRICTLY MAGIC RELATED.
WAI
WAI

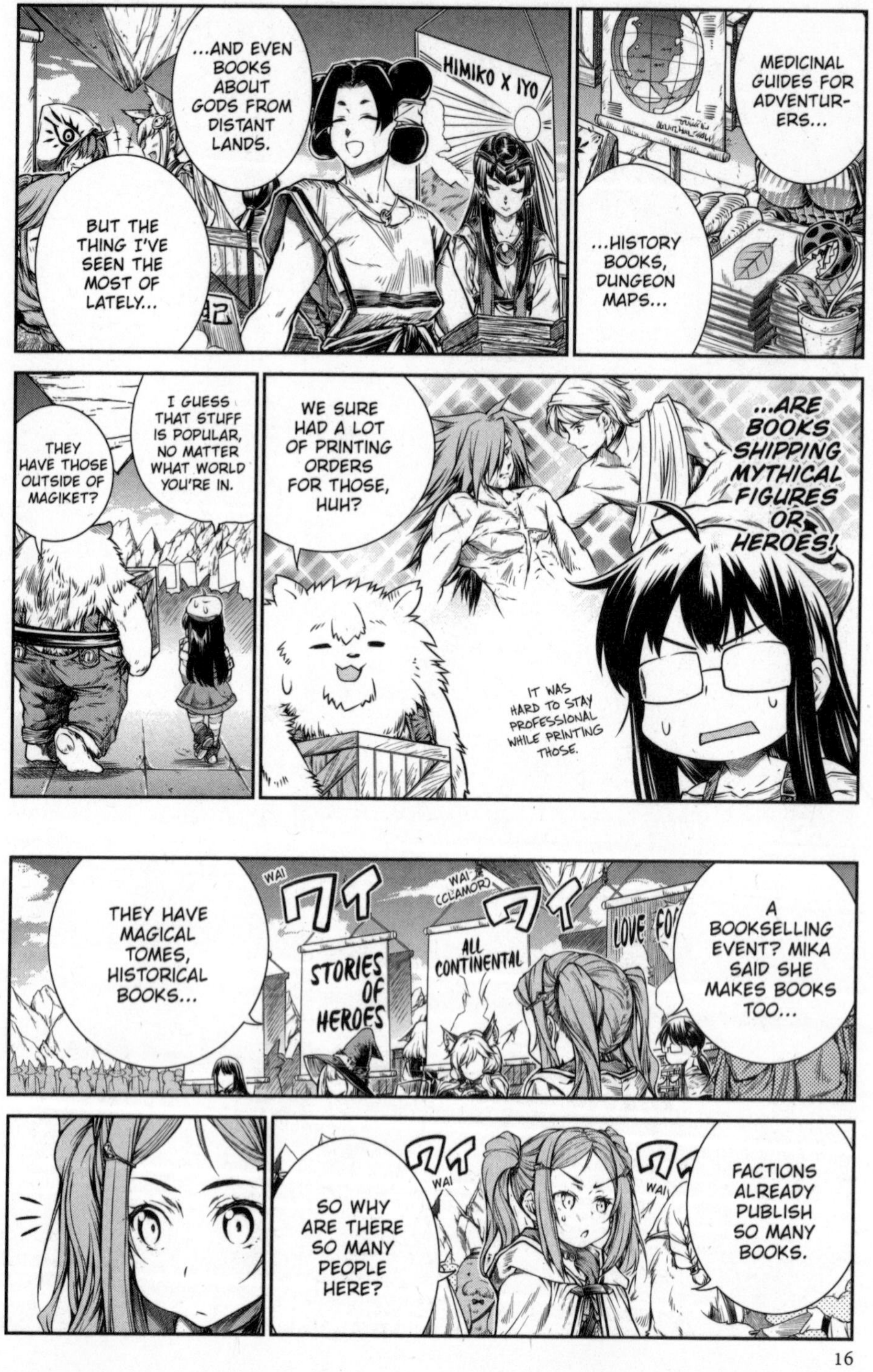
MEDICINAL GUIDES FOR ADVENTURERS...
...HISTORY BOOKS, DUNGEON MAPS...
...AND EVEN BOOKS ABOUT GODS FROM DISTANT LANDS.
HIMIKO X IYO
BUT THE THING I'VE SEEN THE MOST OF LATELY...
...ARE BOOKS SHIPPING MYTHICAL FIGURES OR HEROES!
WE SURE HAD A LOT OF PRINTING ORDERS FOR THOSE, HUH?
IT WAS HARD TO STAY PROFESSIONAL WHILE PRINTING THOSE.
I GUESS THAT STUFF IS POPULAR, NO MATTER WHAT WORLD YOU'RE IN.
THEY HAVE THOSE OUTSIDE OF MAGIKET?
A BOOKSELLING EVENT? MIKA SAID SHE MAKES BOOKS TOO...
WAI (CLAMOR)
ALL CONTINENTAL
STORIES OF HEROES
WAI
THEY HAVE MAGICAL TOMES, HISTORICAL BOOKS...
FACTIONS ALREADY PUBLISH SO MANY BOOKS.
WAI
WAI
SO WHY ARE THERE SO MANY PEOPLE HERE?

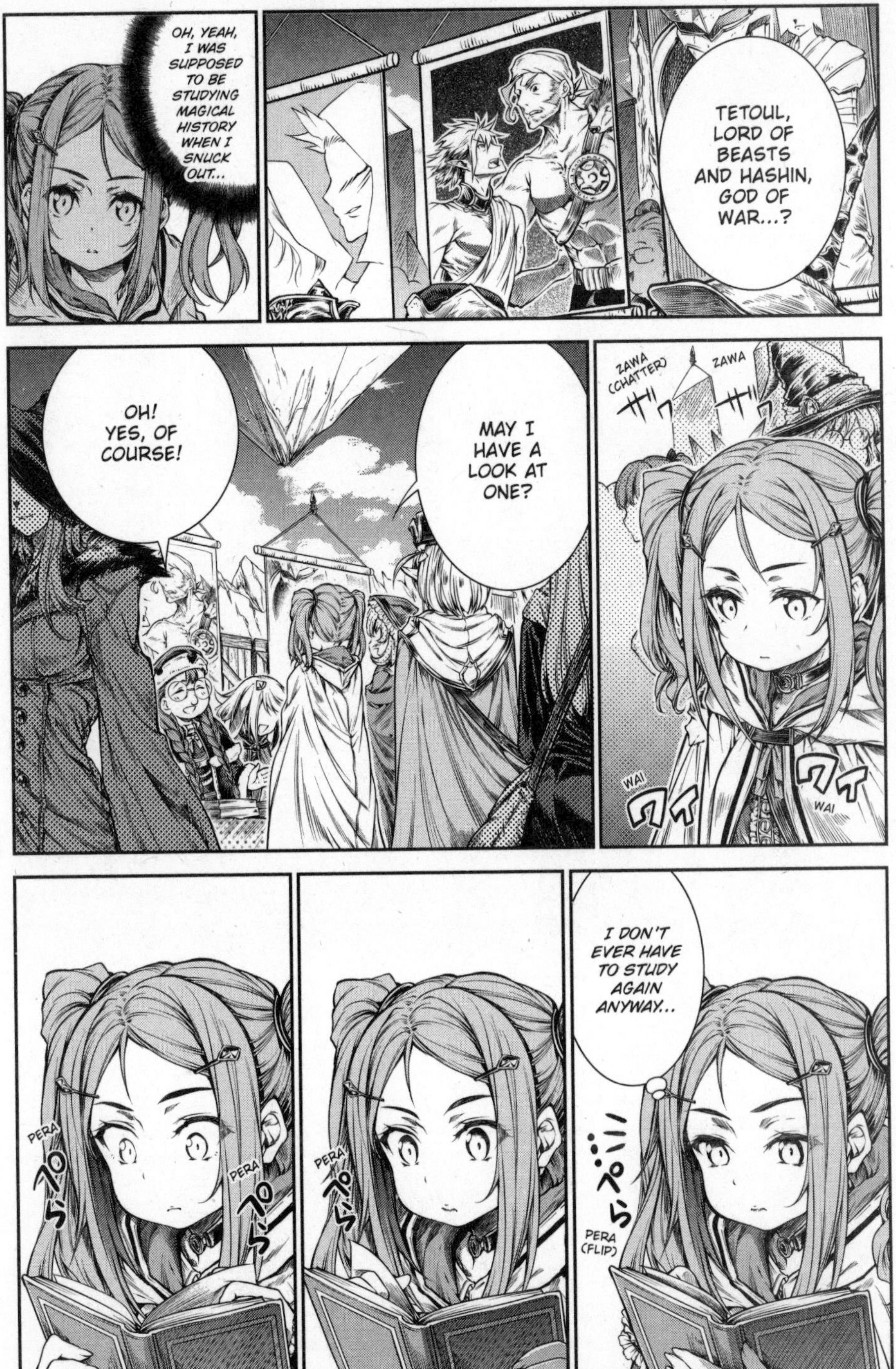

TETOUL, LORD OF BEASTS AND HASHIN, GOD OF WAR...?
OH, YEAH, I WAS SUPPOSED TO BE STUDYING MAGICAL HISTORY WHEN I SNUCK OUT...
ZAWA (CHATTER)
ZAWA
WAI
WAI
MAY I HAVE A LOOK AT ONE?
OH! YES, OF COURSE!
I DON'T EVER HAVE TO STUDY AGAIN ANYWAY...
PERA (FLIP)
PERA
PERA
PERA

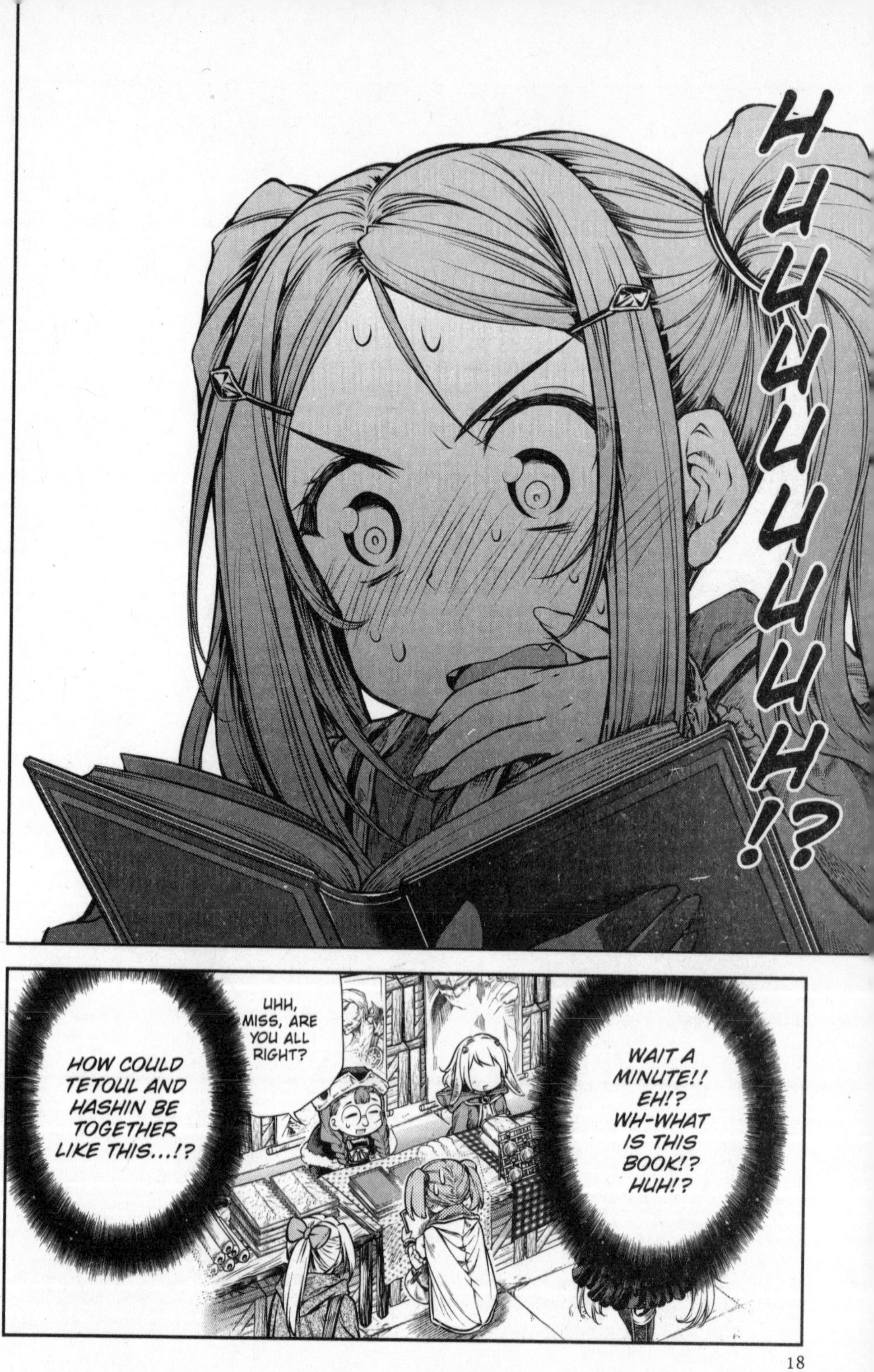
HUUUUUUUH!?
WAIT A MINUTE!! EH!? WH-WHAT IS THIS BOOK!? HUH!?
UHH, MISS, ARE YOU ALL RIGHT?
HOW COULD TETOUL AND HASHIN BE TOGETHER LIKE THIS...!?

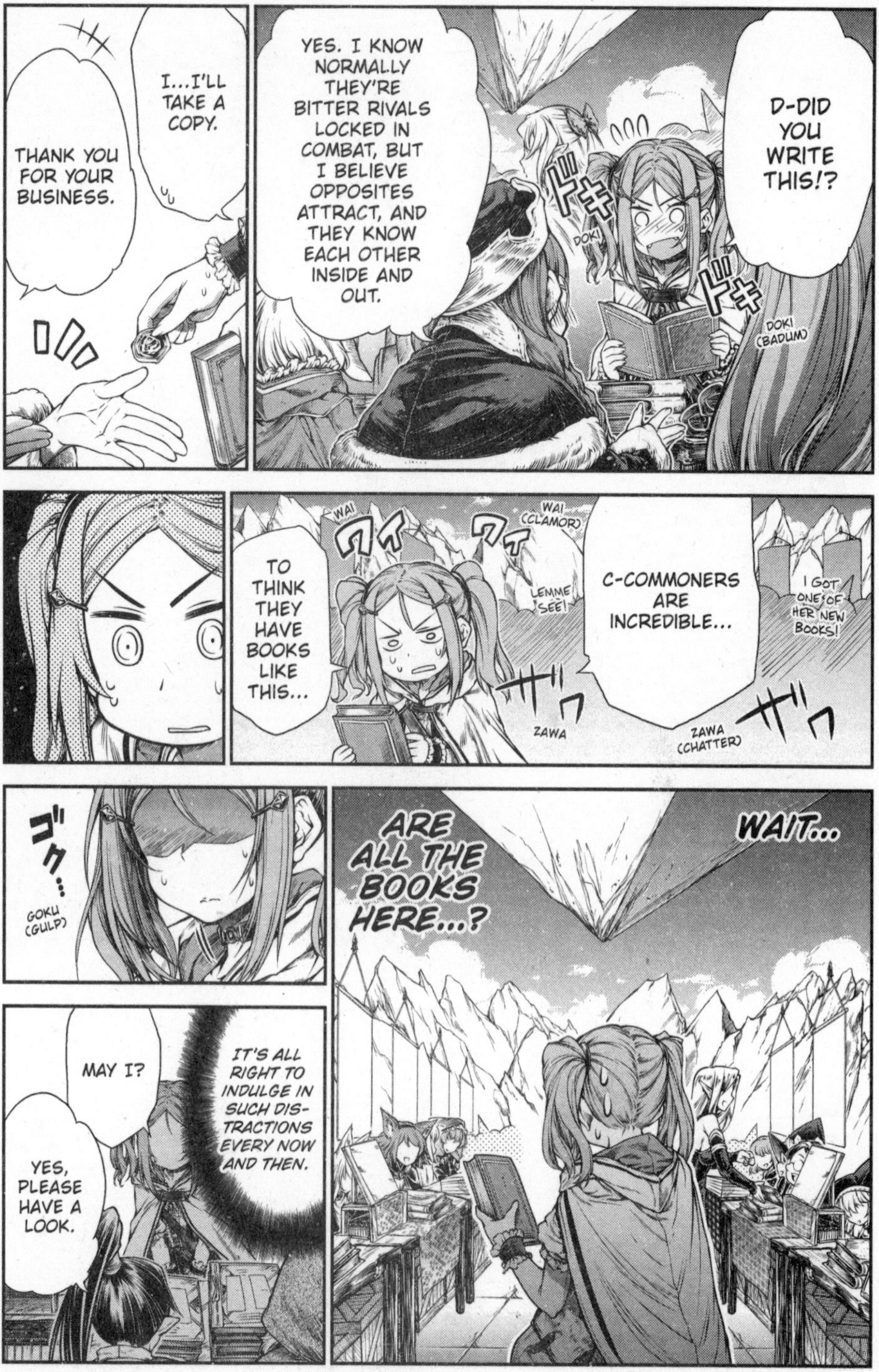
D-DID YOU WRITE THIS!?
DOKI
DOKI (BADUM)
YES. I KNOW NORMALLY THEY'RE BITTER RIVALS LOCKED IN COMBAT, BUT I BELIEVE OPPOSITES ATTRACT, AND THEY KNOW EACH OTHER INSIDE AND OUT.
I...I'LL TAKE A COPY.
THANK YOU FOR YOUR BUSINESS.
I GOT ONE OF HER NEW BOOKS!
C-COMMONERS ARE INCREDIBLE...
ZAWA (CHATTER)
WAI (CLAMOR)
LEMME SEE!
WAI
TO THINK THEY HAVE BOOKS LIKE THIS...
ZAWA
WAIT...
ARE ALL THE BOOKS HERE...?
GOKU (GULP)
IT'S ALL RIGHT TO INDULGE IN SUCH DISTRACTIONS EVERY NOW AND THEN.
MAY I?
YES, PLEASE HAVE A LOOK.

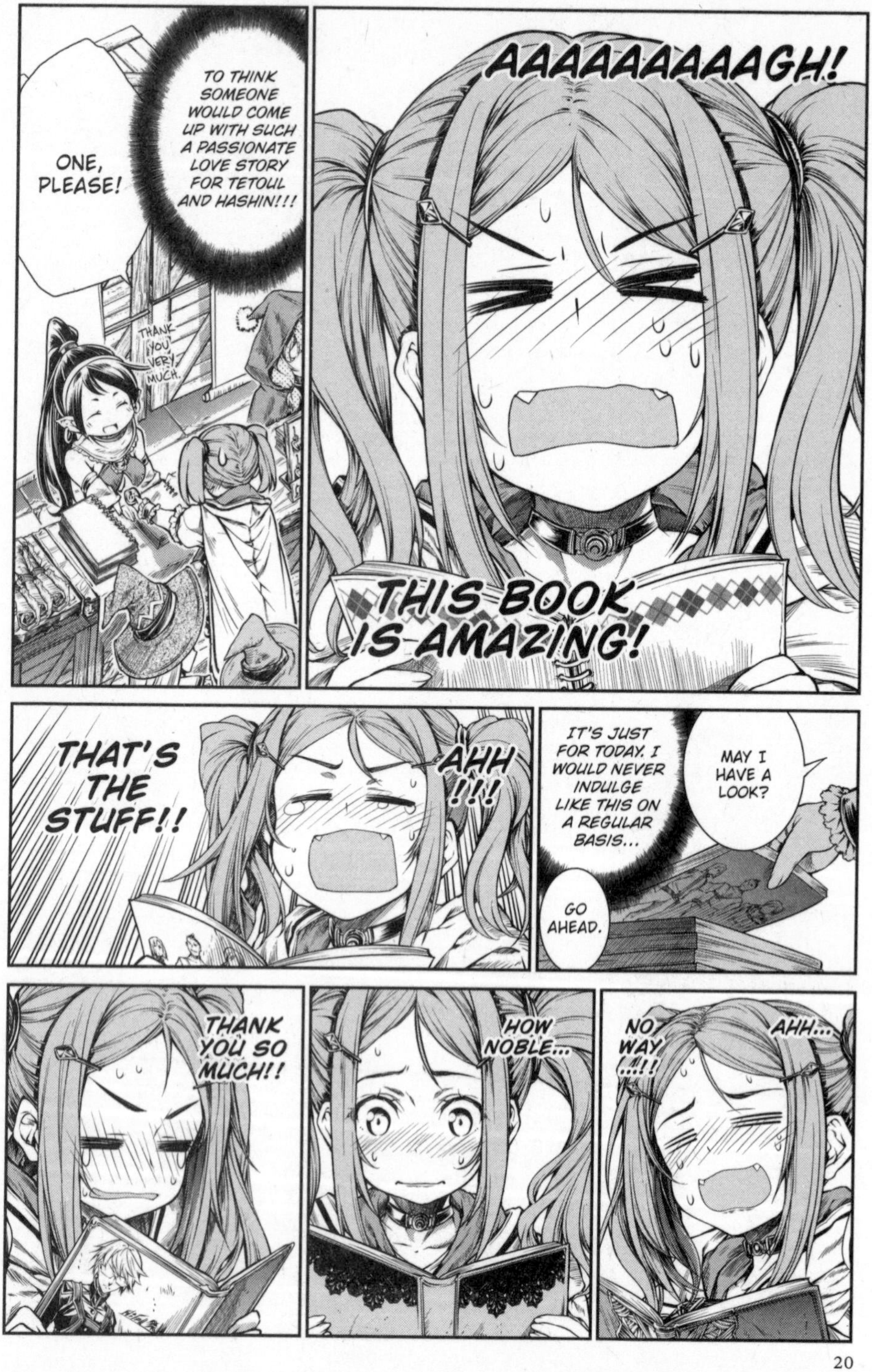
AAAAAAAAAGH!
THIS BOOK IS AMAZING!
TO THINK SOMEONE WOULD COME UP WITH SUCH A PASSIONATE LOVE STORY FOR TETOUL AND HASHIN!!!
ONE, PLEASE!
THANK YOU VERY MUCH.
MAY I HAVE A LOOK?
IT'S JUST FOR TODAY. I WOULD NEVER INDULGE LIKE THIS ON A REGULAR BASIS...
GO AHEAD.
AHH!!!
THAT'S THE STUFF!!
AHH...
NO WAY...!!
HOW NOBLE...
THANK YOU SO MUCH!!

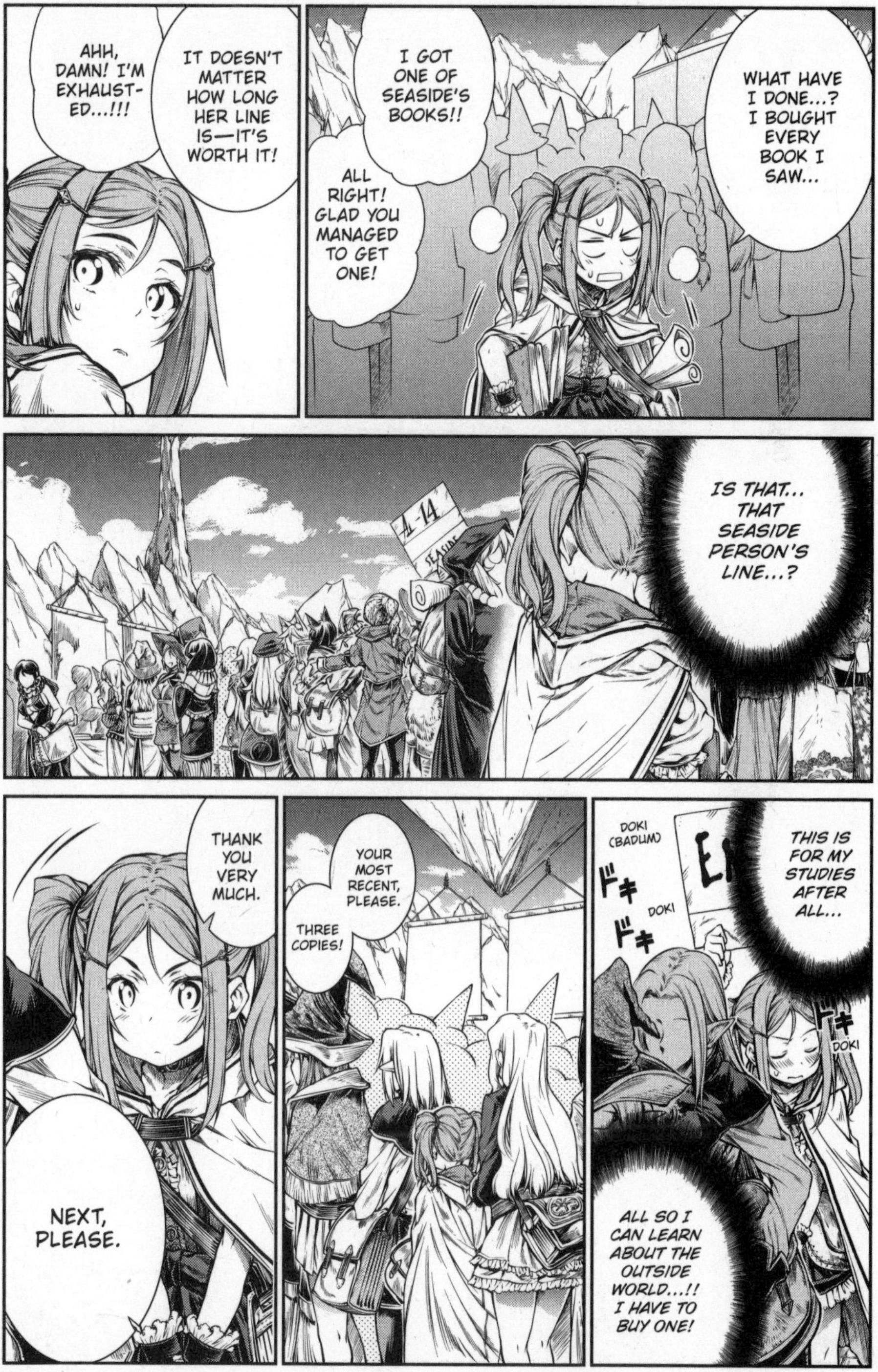
WHAT HAVE I DONE...? I BOUGHT EVERY BOOK I SAW...
I GOT ONE OF SEASIDE'S BOOKS!!
ALL RIGHT! GLAD YOU MANAGED TO GET ONE!
IT DOESN'T MATTER HOW LONG HER LINE IS—IT'S WORTH IT!
AHH, DAMN! I'M EXHAUST-ED...!!!
IS THAT... THAT SEASIDE PERSON'S LINE...?
THIS IS FOR MY STUDIES AFTER ALL...
DOKI (BADUM)
ドキ
DOKI
ドキ
ドキ
DOKI
ALL SO I CAN LEARN ABOUT THE OUTSIDE WORLD...!! I HAVE TO BUY ONE!
YOUR MOST RECENT, PLEASE.
THREE COPIES!
THANK YOU VERY MUCH.
NEXT, PLEASE.

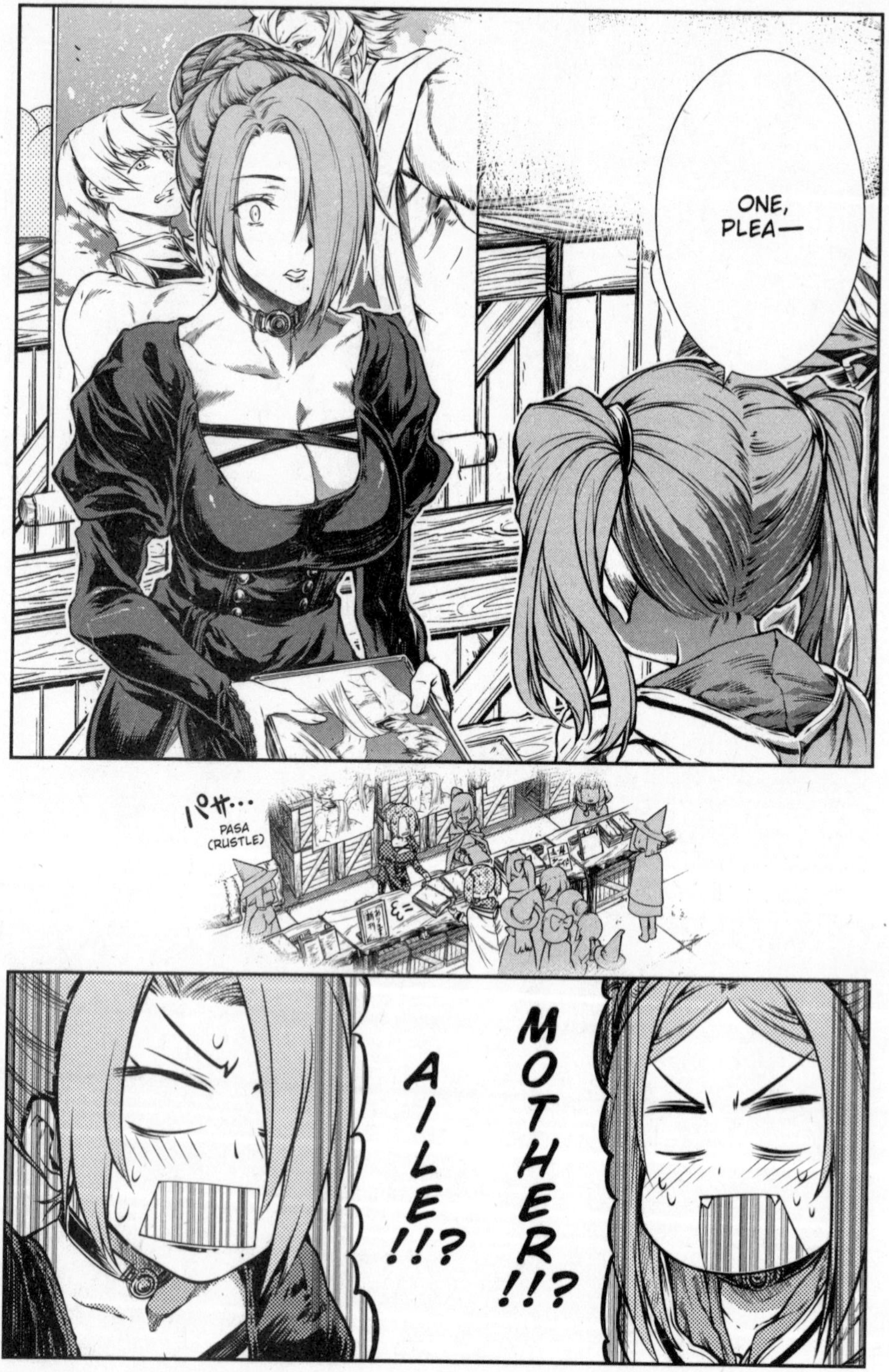
ONE, PLEA—
パサ…
PASA (RUSTLE)
MOTHER!!?
AILE!!?

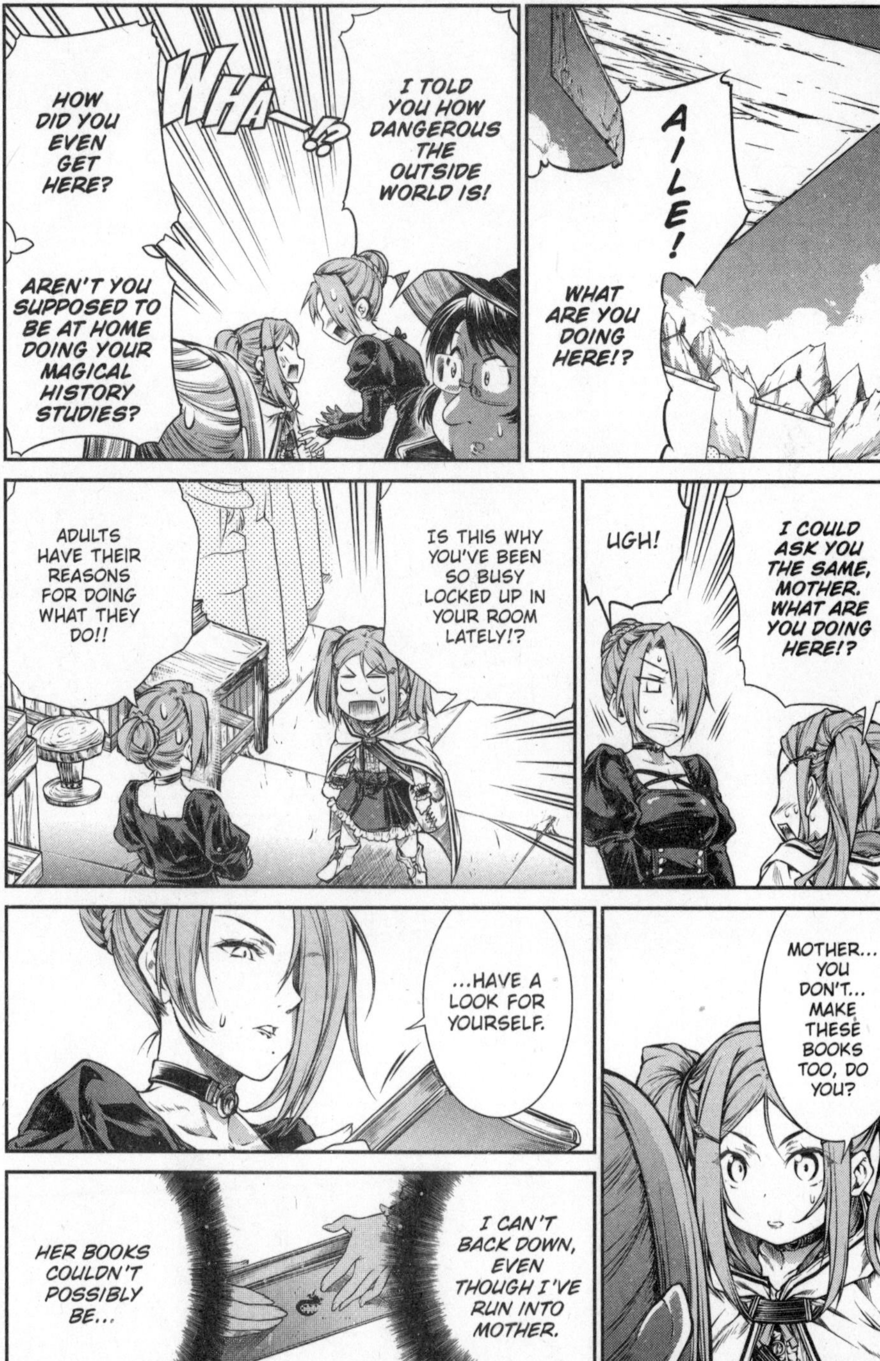
AILE!
WHAT ARE YOU DOING HERE!?
I TOLD YOU HOW DANGEROUS THE OUTSIDE WORLD IS!
WHA—!!?
HOW DID YOU EVEN GET HERE?
AREN'T YOU SUPPOSED TO BE AT HOME DOING YOUR MAGICAL HISTORY STUDIES?
I COULD ASK YOU THE SAME, MOTHER. WHAT ARE YOU DOING HERE!?
UGH!
IS THIS WHY YOU'VE BEEN SO BUSY LOCKED UP IN YOUR ROOM LATELY!?
ADULTS HAVE THEIR REASONS FOR DOING WHAT THEY DO!!
MOTHER... YOU DON'T... MAKE THESE BOOKS TOO, DO YOU?
...HAVE A LOOK FOR YOURSELF.
I CAN'T BACK DOWN, EVEN THOUGH I'VE RUN INTO MOTHER.
HER BOOKS COULDN'T POSSIBLY BE...

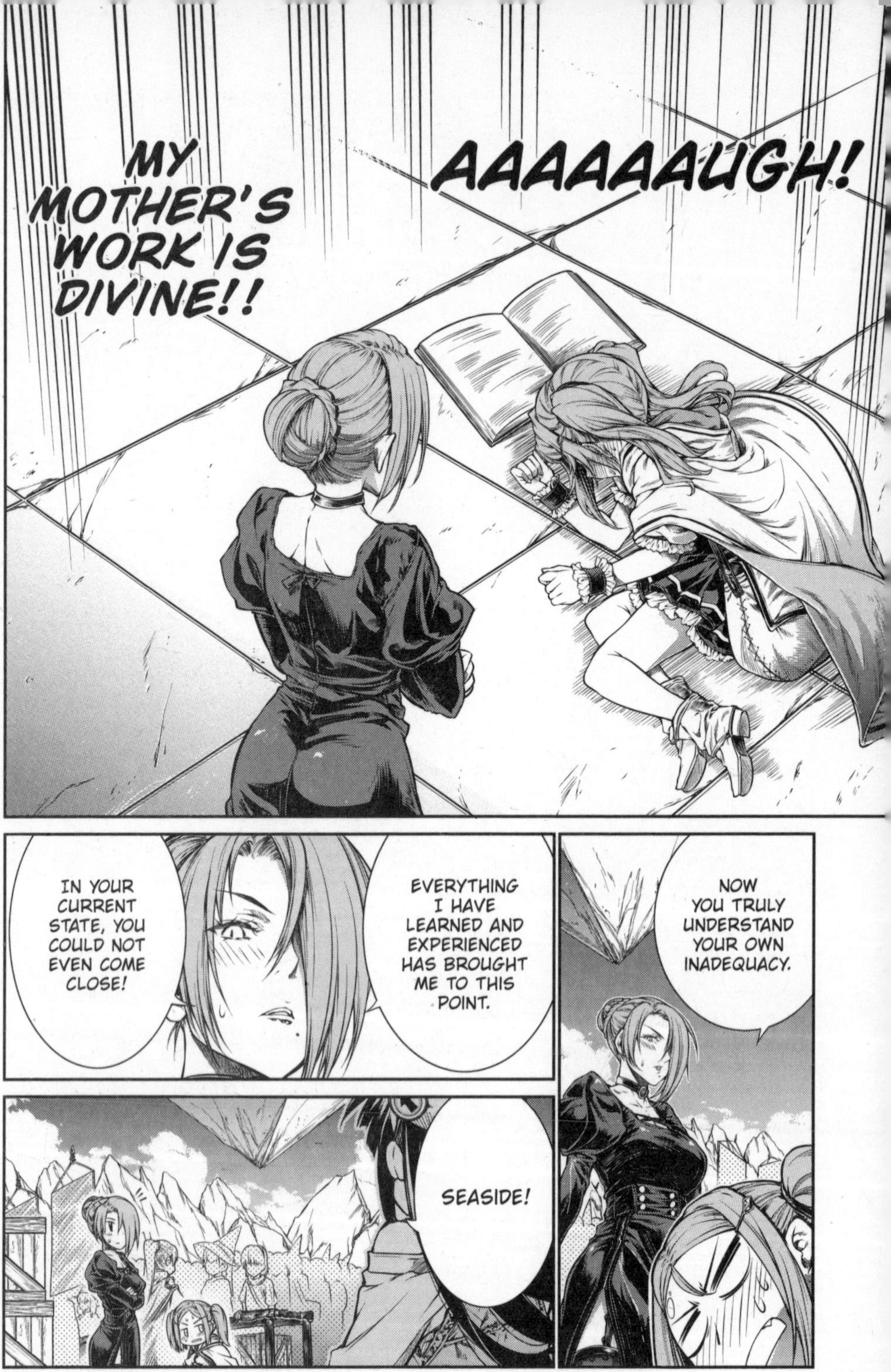

AAAAAAAUGH!
MY MOTHER'S WORK IS DIVINE!!
NOW YOU TRULY UNDERSTAND YOUR OWN INADEQUACY.
EVERYTHING I HAVE LEARNED AND EXPERIENCED HAS BROUGHT ME TO THIS POINT.
IN YOUR CURRENT STATE, YOU COULD NOT EVEN COME CLOSE!
SEASIDE!

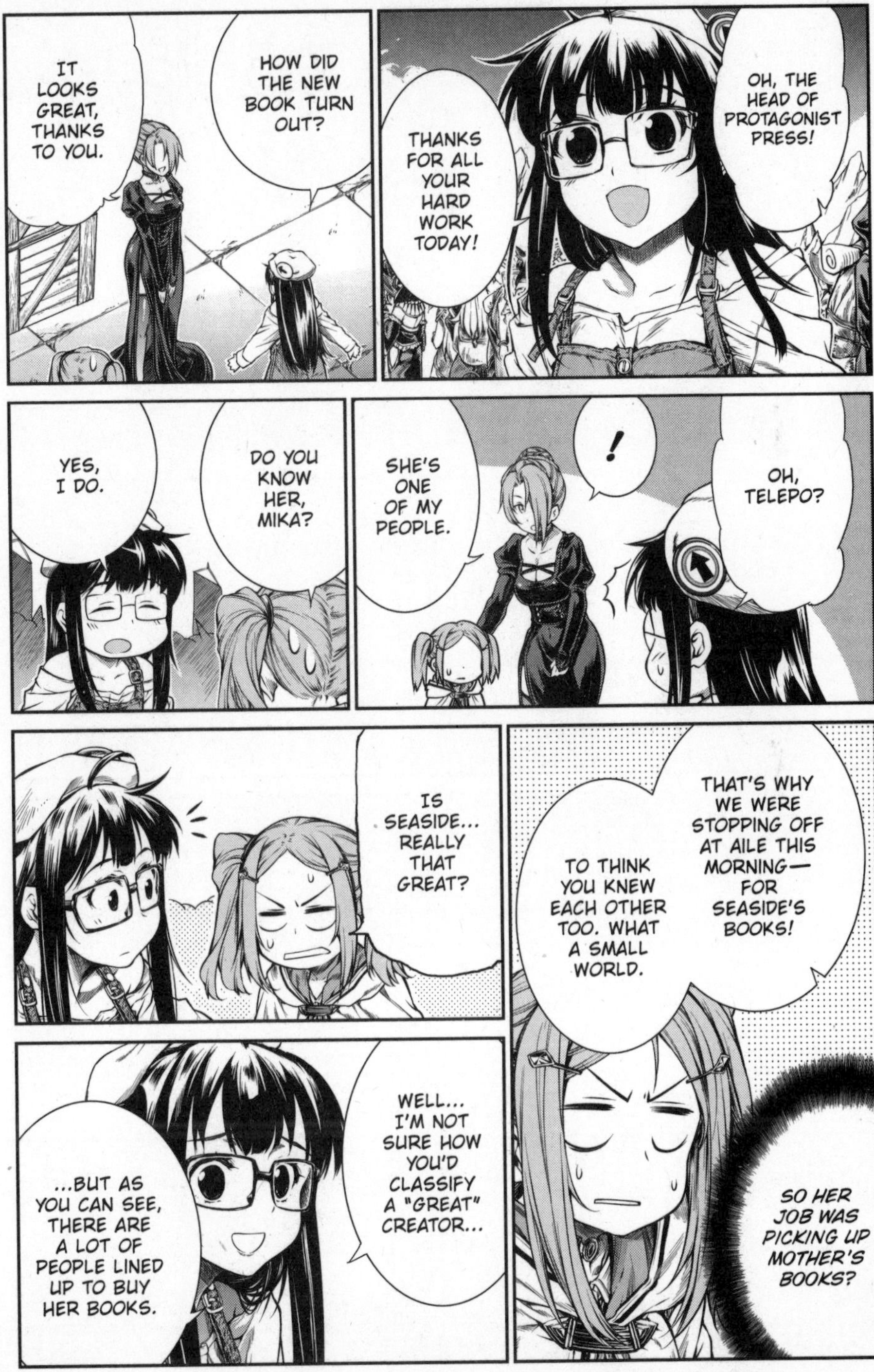
OH, THE HEAD OF PROTAGONIST PRESS!
THANKS FOR ALL YOUR HARD WORK TODAY!
HOW DID THE NEW BOOK TURN OUT?
IT LOOKS GREAT, THANKS TO YOU.
OH, TELEPO?
!
SHE'S ONE OF MY PEOPLE.
DO YOU KNOW HER, MIKA?
YES, I DO.
THAT'S WHY WE WERE STOPPING OFF AT AILE THIS MORNING—FOR SEASIDE'S BOOKS!
TO THINK YOU KNEW EACH OTHER TOO. WHAT A SMALL WORLD.
SO HER JOB WAS PICKING UP MOTHER'S BOOKS?
IS SEASIDE... REALLY THAT GREAT?
WELL... I'M NOT SURE HOW YOU'D CLASSIFY A "GREAT" CREATOR...
...BUT AS YOU CAN SEE, THERE ARE A LOT OF PEOPLE LINED UP TO BUY HER BOOKS.

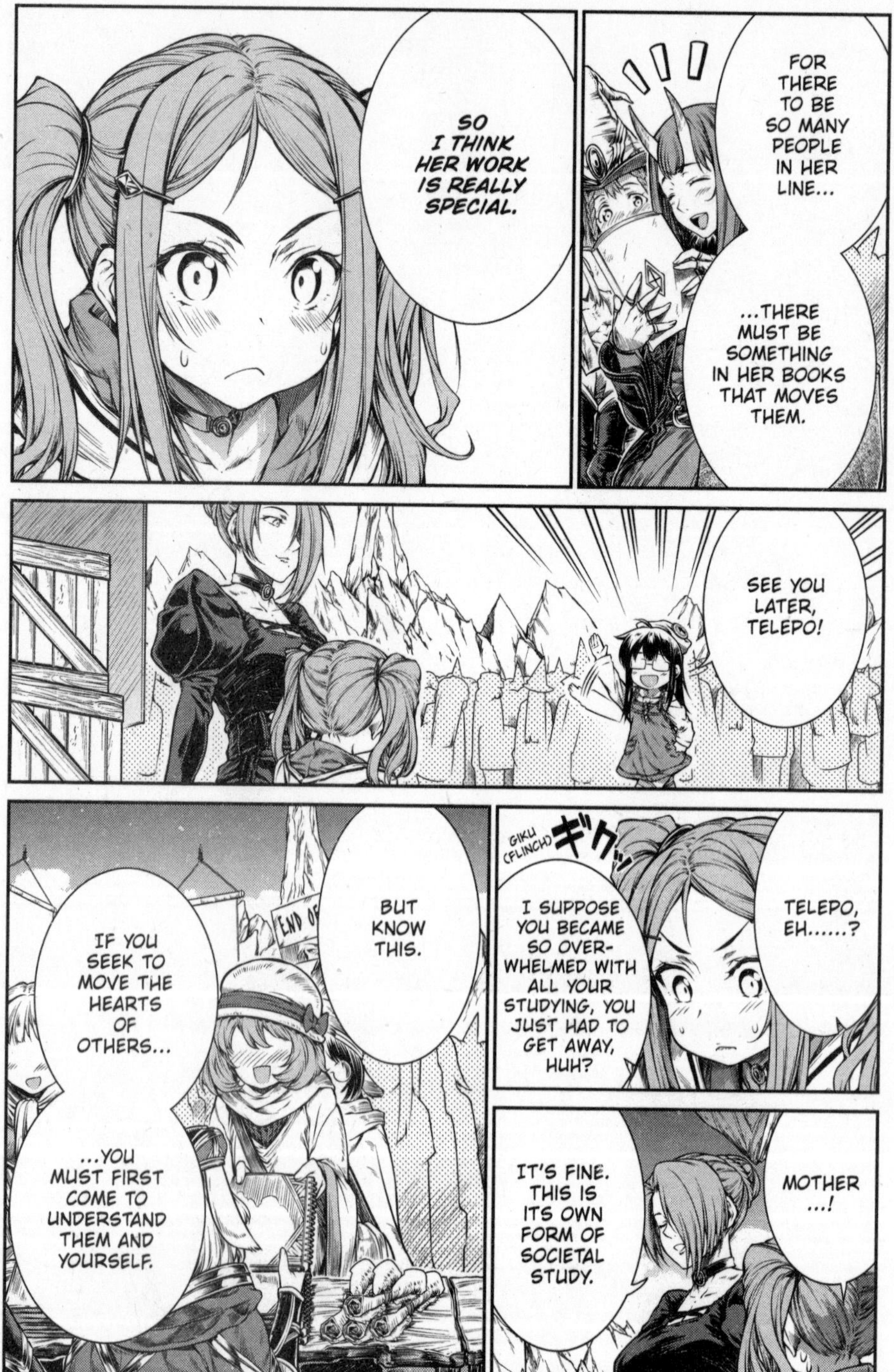
FOR THERE TO BE SO MANY PEOPLE IN HER LINE...
...THERE MUST BE SOMETHING IN HER BOOKS THAT MOVES THEM.
SO I THINK HER WORK IS REALLY SPECIAL.
SEE YOU LATER, TELEPO!
TELEPO, EH......?
GIKU (FLINCH) ギクッ
I SUPPOSE YOU BECAME SO OVER-WHELMED WITH ALL YOUR STUDYING, YOU JUST HAD TO GET AWAY, HUH?
MOTHER ...!
IT'S FINE. THIS IS ITS OWN FORM OF SOCIETAL STUDY.
BUT KNOW THIS.
IF YOU SEEK TO MOVE THE HEARTS OF OTHERS...
...YOU MUST FIRST COME TO UNDERSTAND THEM AND YOURSELF.
END OF

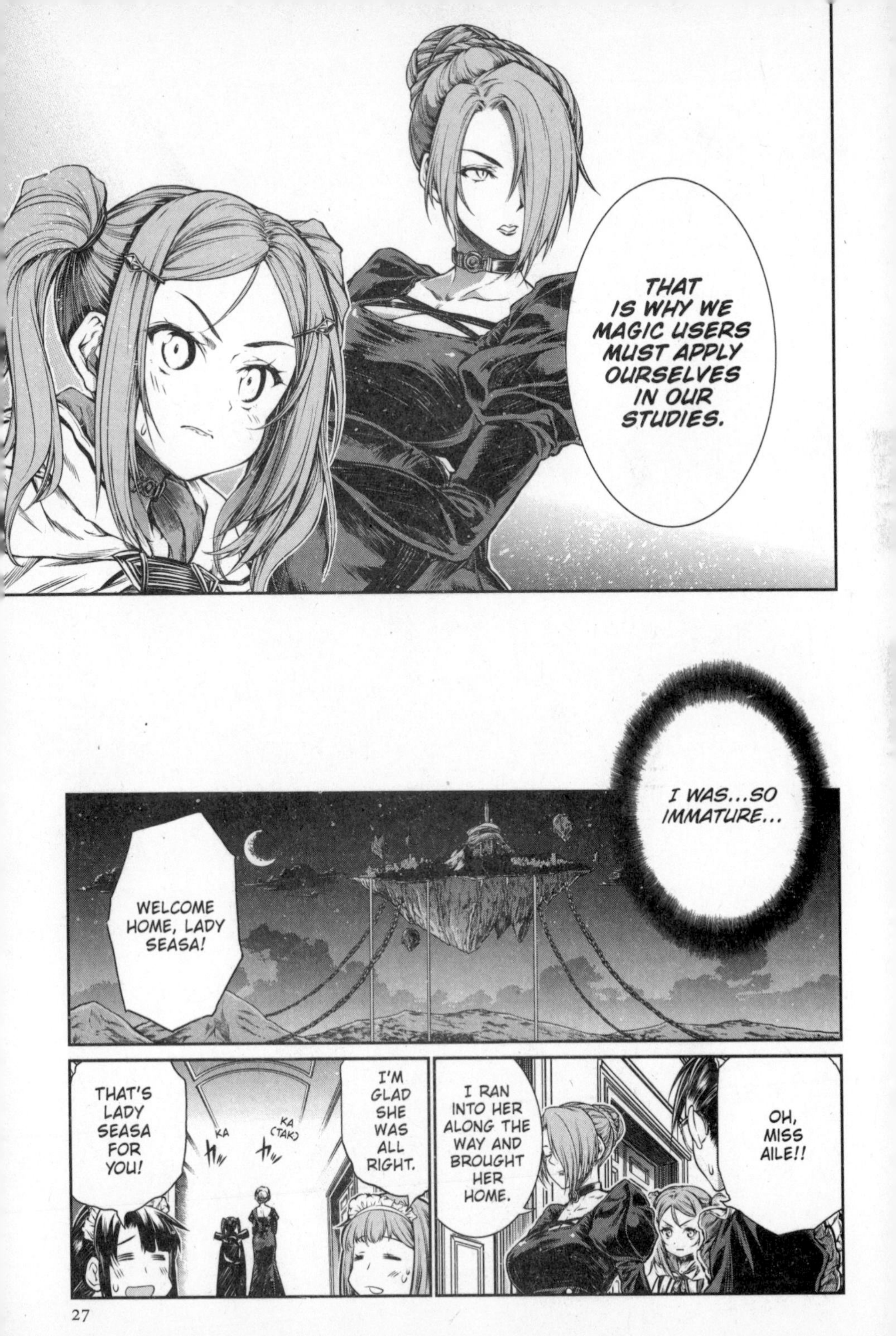
THAT IS WHY WE MAGIC USERS MUST APPLY OURSELVES IN OUR STUDIES.
I WAS...SO IMMATURE...
WELCOME HOME, LADY SEASA!
OH, MISS AILE!!
I RAN INTO HER ALONG THE WAY AND BROUGHT HER HOME.
I'M GLAD SHE WAS ALL RIGHT.
KA (TAK)
KA
THAT'S LADY SEASA FOR YOU!

I MUST KEEP STUDYING, MORE AND MORE...

...SO I CAN ENJOY ALL THAT THE OUTSIDE WORLD HAS TO OFFER!!

WHY DOES SHE HAVE SO MUCH LUGGAGE?

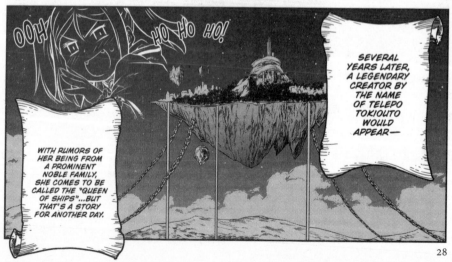

OOH! HO HO HO!

SEVERAL YEARS LATER, A LEGENDARY CREATOR BY THE NAME OF TELEPO TOKIOUTO WOULD APPEAR—

WITH RUMORS OF HER BEING FROM A PROMINENT NOBLE FAMILY, SHE COMES TO BE CALLED THE "QUEEN OF SHIPS"...BUT THAT'S A STORY FOR ANOTHER DAY.

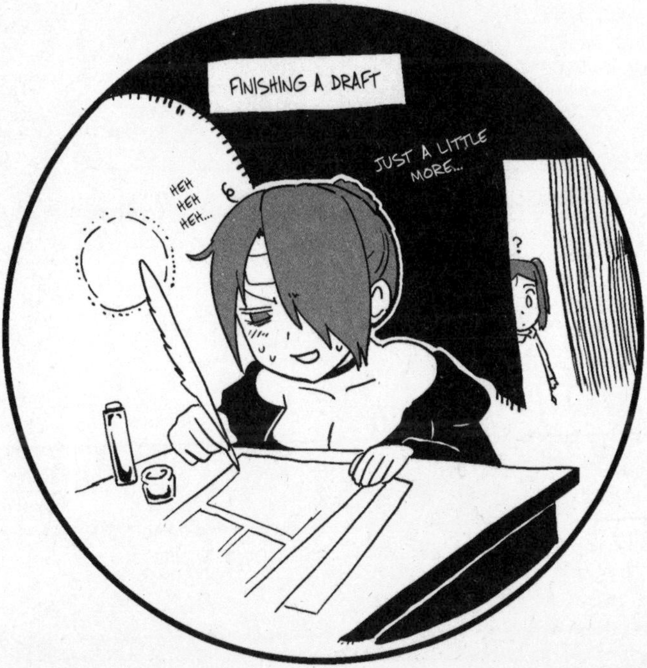
FINISHING A DRAFT
JUST A LITTLE MORE...
HEH HEH HEH...
?

# TRANSLATION NOTES

### Page 3 – Aile
Aile's name is pronounced like "isle," which her name is a reference to. "Seasa" is a reference to "seaside."

### Page 8 – Telepo Tokiouto
The fake name Aile has pulled for herself sounds suspiciously like "Teleport Tokyoutou," in which "Teleport" refers to a train station in the city of Tokyo (*Tokyoutou*).

### Page 16 – Himiko x Iyo
Queen Himiko was a ruler of Japan in the third century who is something of a legend due to her name being absent from historical records, though she is mentioned in Chinese histories. She was succeeded by her daughter, Iyo.

### Page 28 – Queen of Ships
In the Japanese version, Aile is referred to as a *kifujin*, which means "noble lady." In this case, the *fu* has been swapped with the *fu* character from *fujoshi*, which means "rotten," implying she's a woman who enjoys stories about male characters in romantic relationships (BL stories).

### Page 34
All of the characters attempting to pull the Holy Blade are given slightly off-brand versions of names of video game characters from *Street Fighter* and *Final Fantasy*.

### Page 37 – The Holy Blade
The name of the Holy Blade (Dwayne-kigai) is a play on the word *denkigai*, or Electric Town, which is another name for Akihabara.

### Page 52 – Demon Lord
The names of Satziiko and other denizens of the underworld are references to singers of *enka*, a genre of traditional-sounding Japanese music. Satziiko's name is likely a reference to renowned singer Sachiko Kobayashi, who has also been given the nickname "Final Boss" by her fans. Some of the other singers referenced include Hibari Misora (Misra) and Akiko Wada (Akko).

### Page 76 – Spirit of Storms and the Ageless Twin Witches
Continuing the theme of the demon lords being references to famous singers, Spirit of Storms Takanori is a reference to Takanori Nishikawa, stage name T.M. Revolution. (On the facing page you can even see him rendered in the outfit from his "Hot Limit" music video.) The Ageless Twin Witches Ka and Noh are likely meant to reference the group Double U (W). Kago Ai and Tsuji Nozomi made up the duo and debuted together at age twelve in the group Morning Musume。, where they were known as the "twins." Their first single was a cover of a Peanuts song—another duo known for being a twin act.

### Page 129 – Shou Wadley
Wadley's name is another play on places in Akihabara. In this case, "Shou Wadley" is a play on *showa-doori*, or Showa Street, which is the eastern entry point to *Chou-dori*, the main street in Akihabara.

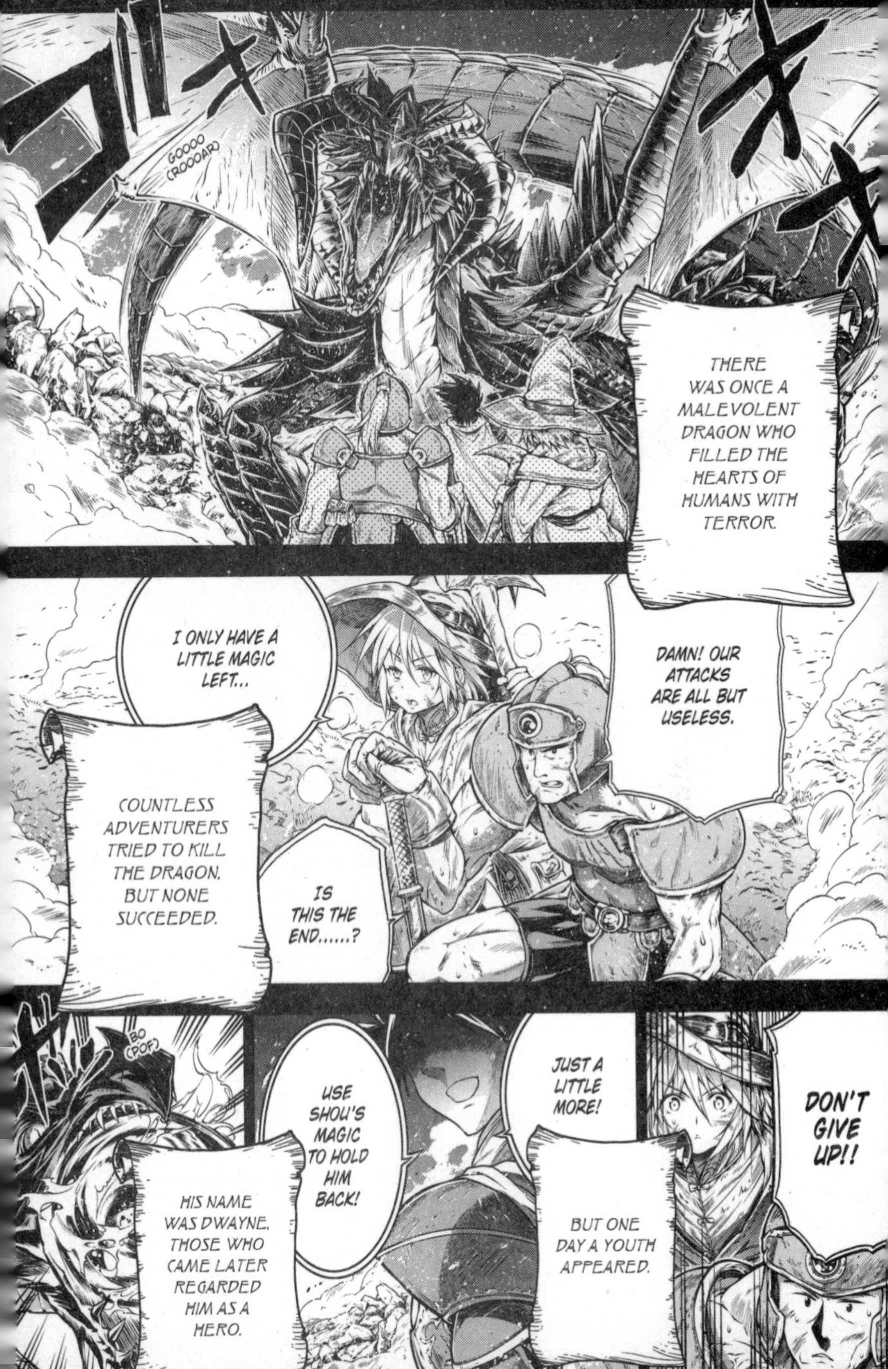
GOOOO (ROOOAR)
THERE WAS ONCE A MALEVOLENT DRAGON WHO FILLED THE HEARTS OF HUMANS WITH TERROR.
DAMN! OUR ATTACKS ARE ALL BUT USELESS.
I ONLY HAVE A LITTLE MAGIC LEFT...
COUNTLESS ADVENTURERS TRIED TO KILL THE DRAGON, BUT NONE SUCCEEDED.
IS THIS THE END......?
DON'T GIVE UP!!
JUST A LITTLE MORE!
USE SHOU'S MAGIC TO HOLD HIM BACK!
BUT ONE DAY A YOUTH APPEARED.
BO (POP)
HIS NAME WAS DWAYNE. THOSE WHO CAME LATER REGARDED HIM AS A HERO.

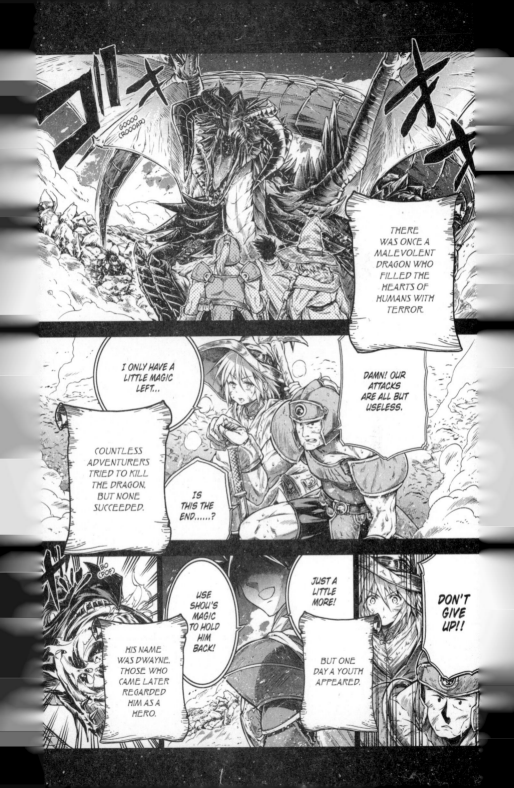

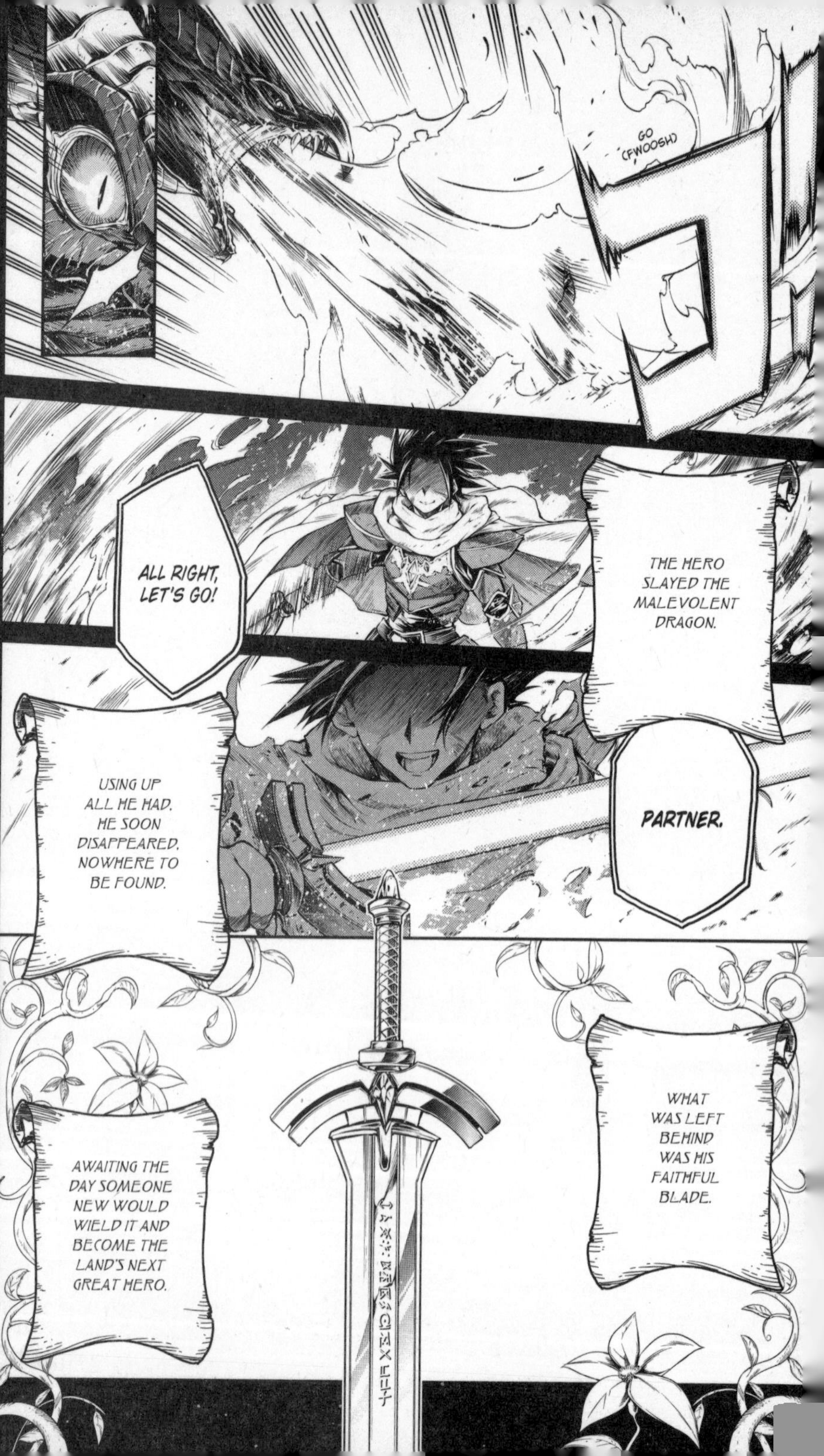
GO (FWOOSH)
THE HERO SLAYED THE MALEVOLENT DRAGON.
ALL RIGHT, LET'S GO!
PARTNER.
USING UP ALL HE HAD, HE SOON DISAPPEARED, NOWHERE TO BE FOUND.
WHAT WAS LEFT BEHIND WAS HIS FAITHFUL BLADE.
AWAITING THE DAY SOMEONE NEW WOULD WIELD IT AND BECOME THE LAND'S NEXT GREAT HERO.

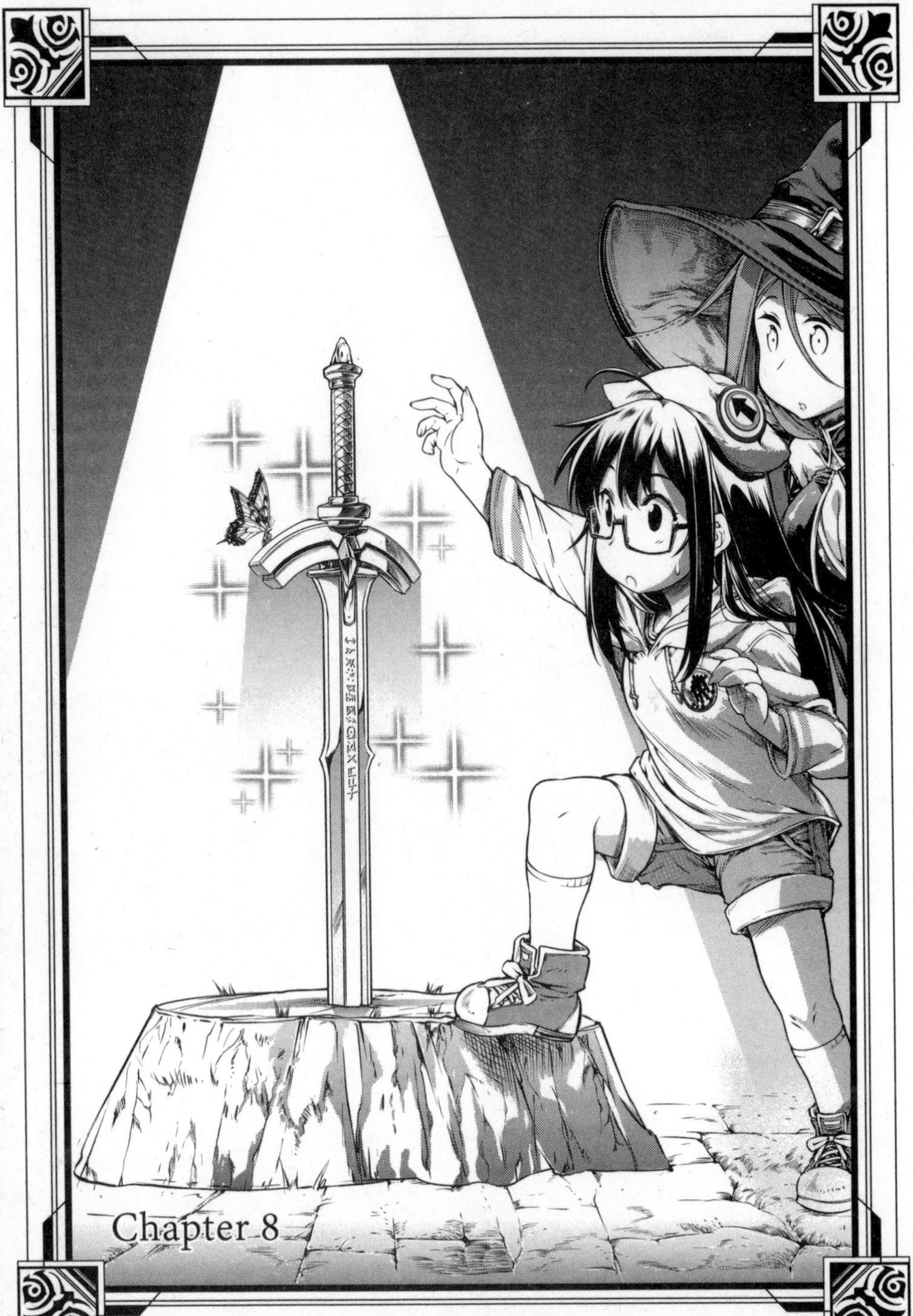
Chapter 8

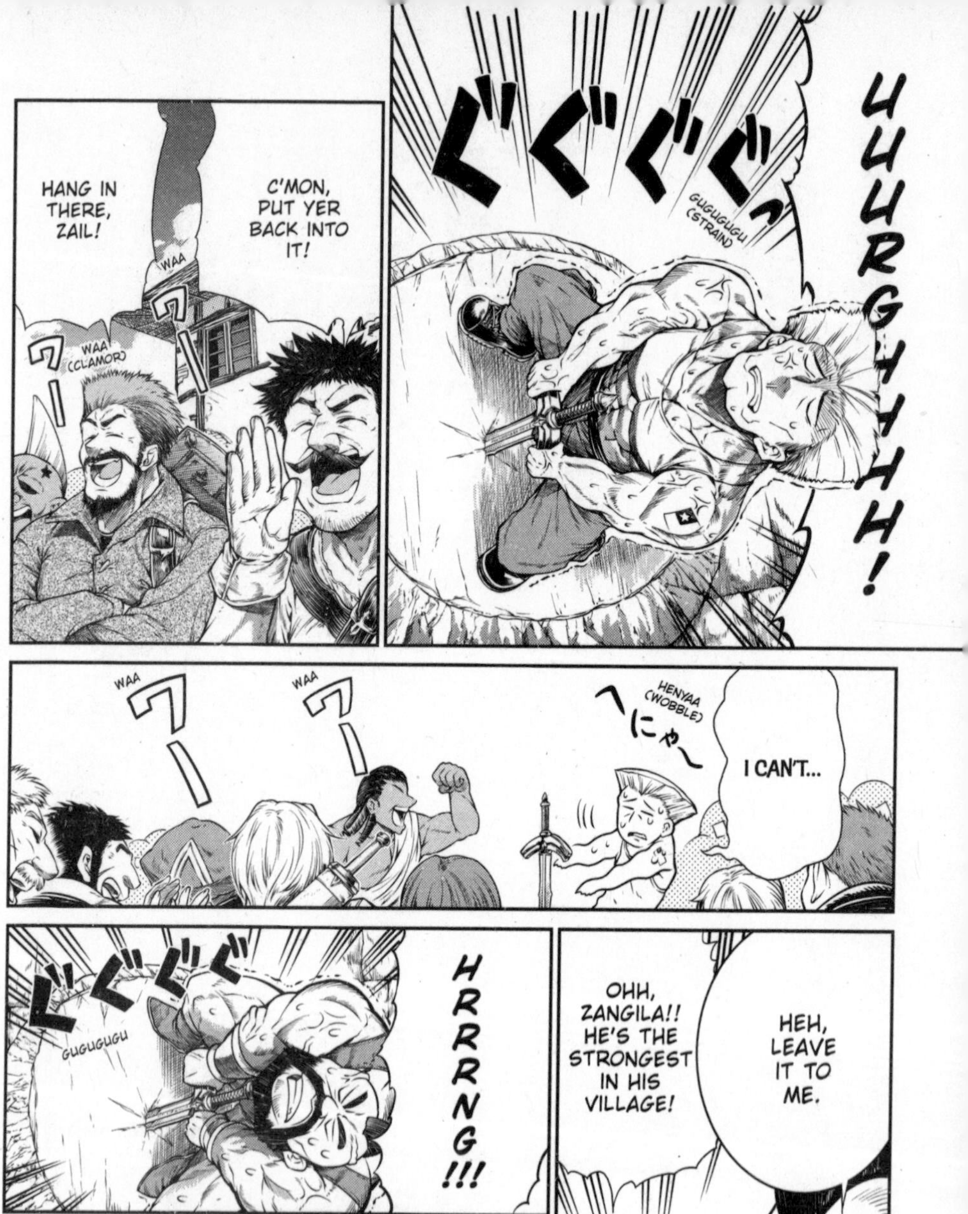
UUURGHHHHH!
GUGUGUGU (STRAIN)
C'MON, PUT YER BACK INTO IT!
HANG IN THERE, ZAIL!
WAA
WAA (CLAMOR)
I CAN'T...
HENYAA (WOBBLE)
WAA
WAA
HEH, LEAVE IT TO ME.
OHH, ZANGILA!! HE'S THE STRONGEST IN HIS VILLAGE!
HRRRNG!!!
GUGUGU
OKAY, THAT'S ENOUGH...
WHOA...
WHAT'S ALL THAT ABOUT?

SFX: BAKI (CRACK) BOKI (CRICK)

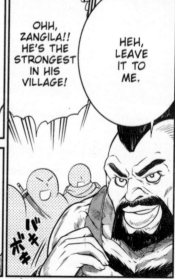

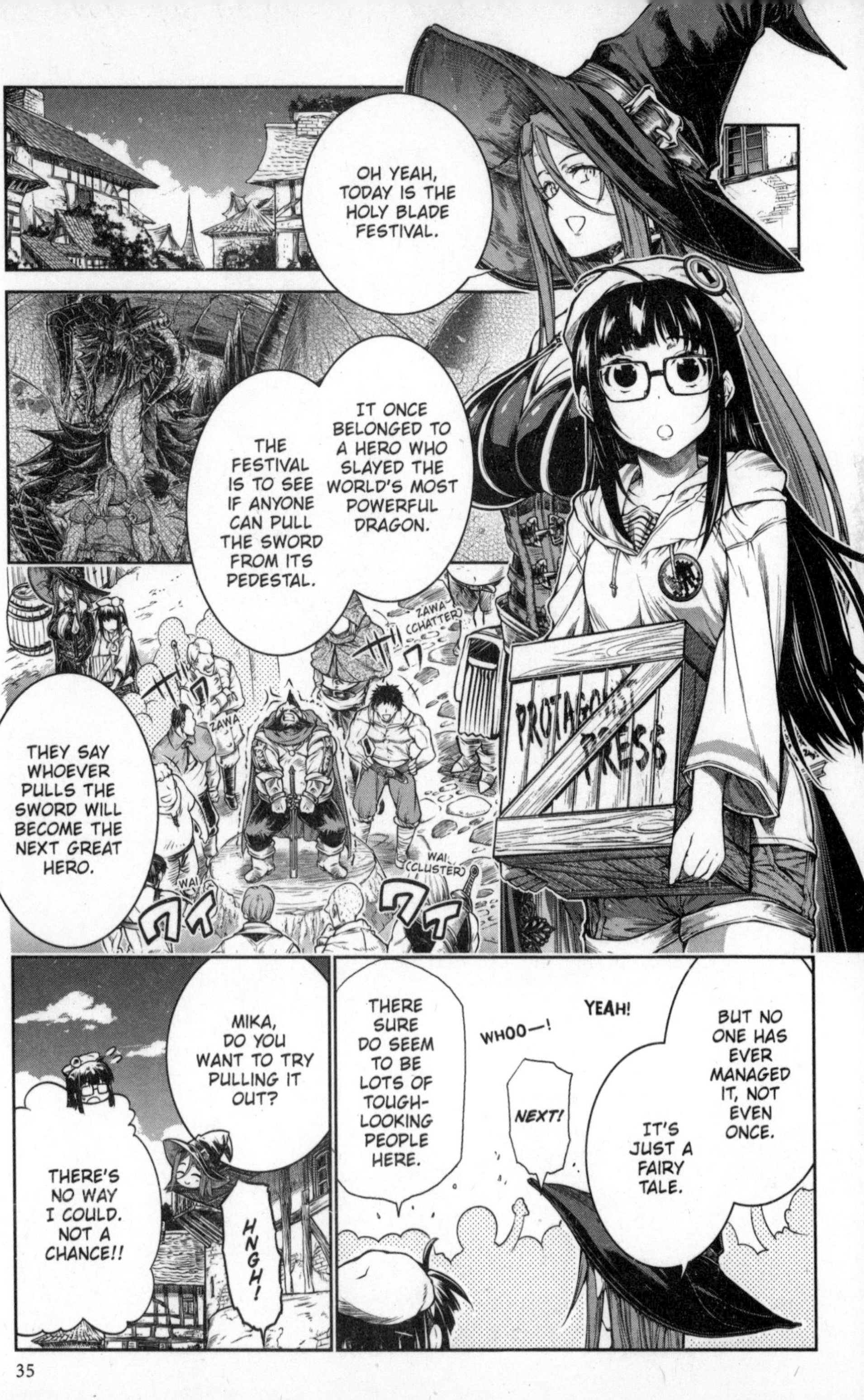
OH YEAH, TODAY IS THE HOLY BLADE FESTIVAL.
IT ONCE BELONGED TO A HERO WHO SLAYED THE WORLD'S MOST POWERFUL DRAGON.
THE FESTIVAL IS TO SEE IF ANYONE CAN PULL THE SWORD FROM ITS PEDESTAL.
ZAWA (CHATTER)
ZAWA
PROTAGONIST PRESS
THEY SAY WHOEVER PULLS THE SWORD WILL BECOME THE NEXT GREAT HERO.
WAI (CLUSTER)
WAI
BUT NO ONE HAS EVER MANAGED IT, NOT EVEN ONCE.
IT'S JUST A FAIRY TALE.
YEAH!
WHOO—!
NEXT!
THERE SURE DO SEEM TO BE LOTS OF TOUGH-LOOKING PEOPLE HERE.
MIKA, DO YOU WANT TO TRY PULLING IT OUT?
THERE'S NO WAY I COULD. NOT A CHANCE!!
HNGH!

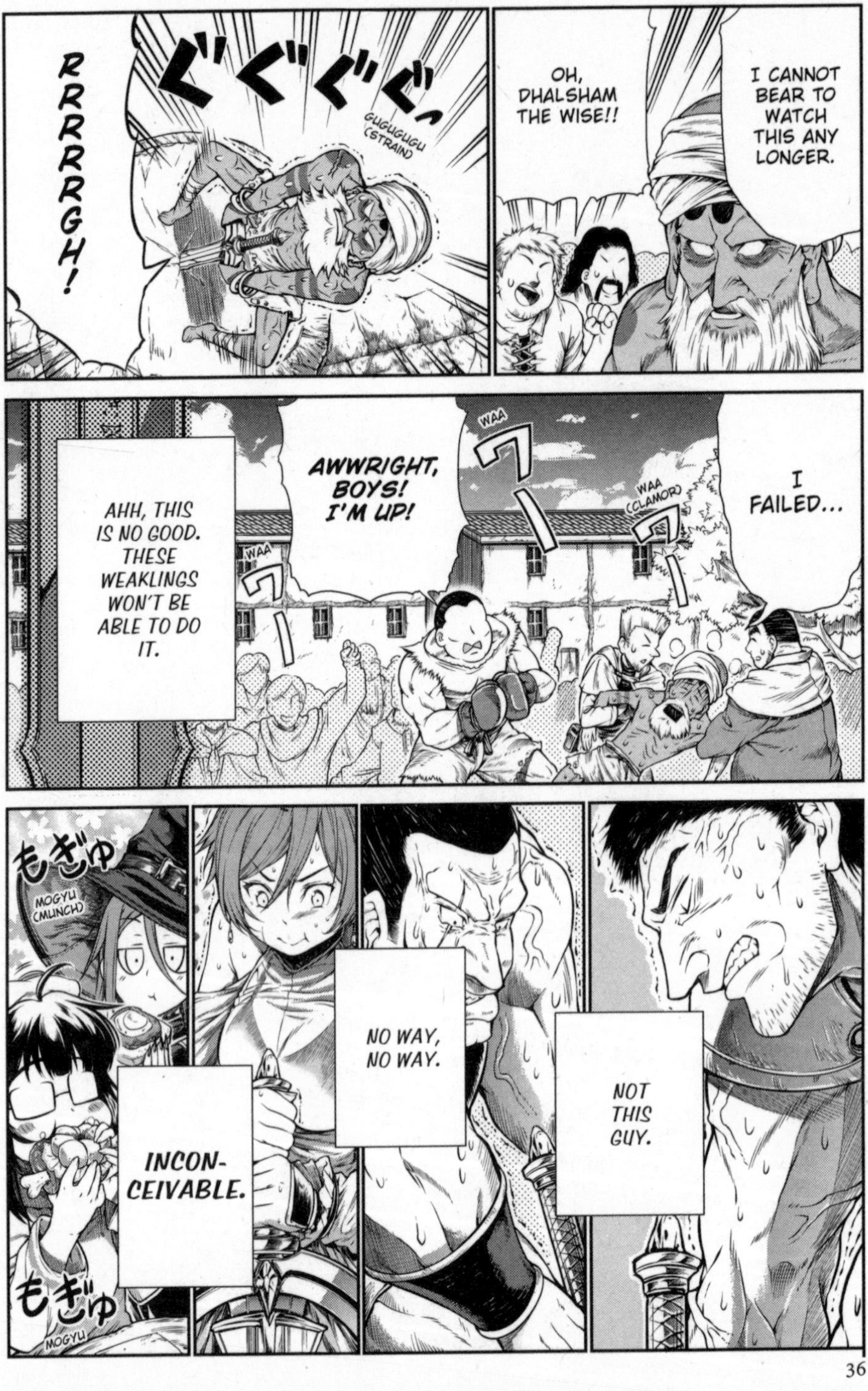
I CANNOT BEAR TO WATCH THIS ANY LONGER.
OH, DHALSHAM THE WISE!!
ぐぐぐぐ
GUGUGUGU (STRAIN)
RRRRRGH!
I FAILED...
ワー
WAA (CLAMOR)
ワー
WAA
AWWRIGHT, BOYS! I'M UP!
ワー
WAA
AHH, THIS IS NO GOOD. THESE WEAKLINGS WON'T BE ABLE TO DO IT.
NOT THIS GUY.
NO WAY, NO WAY.
INCON-CEIVABLE.
もぎゅ
MOGYU (MUNCH)
もぎゅ
MOGYU

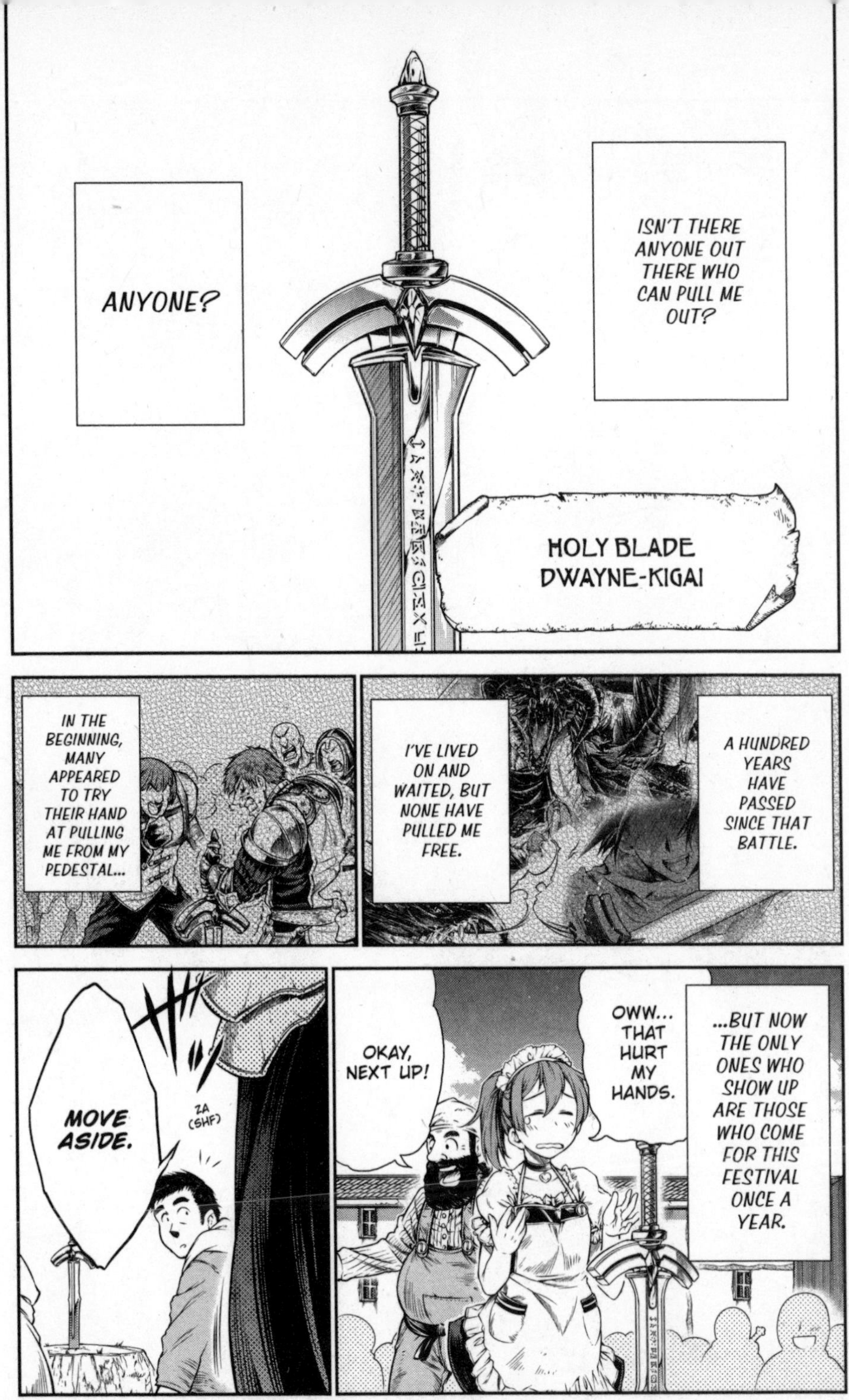

ISN'T THERE ANYONE OUT THERE WHO CAN PULL ME OUT?
ANYONE?
HOLY BLADE DWAYNE-KIGAI
A HUNDRED YEARS HAVE PASSED SINCE THAT BATTLE.
I'VE LIVED ON AND WAITED, BUT NONE HAVE PULLED ME FREE.
IN THE BEGINNING, MANY APPEARED TO TRY THEIR HAND AT PULLING ME FROM MY PEDESTAL...
...BUT NOW THE ONLY ONES WHO SHOW UP ARE THOSE WHO COME FOR THIS FESTIVAL ONCE A YEAR.
OWW... THAT HURT MY HANDS.
OKAY, NEXT UP!
ZA (SHF)
MOVE ASIDE.

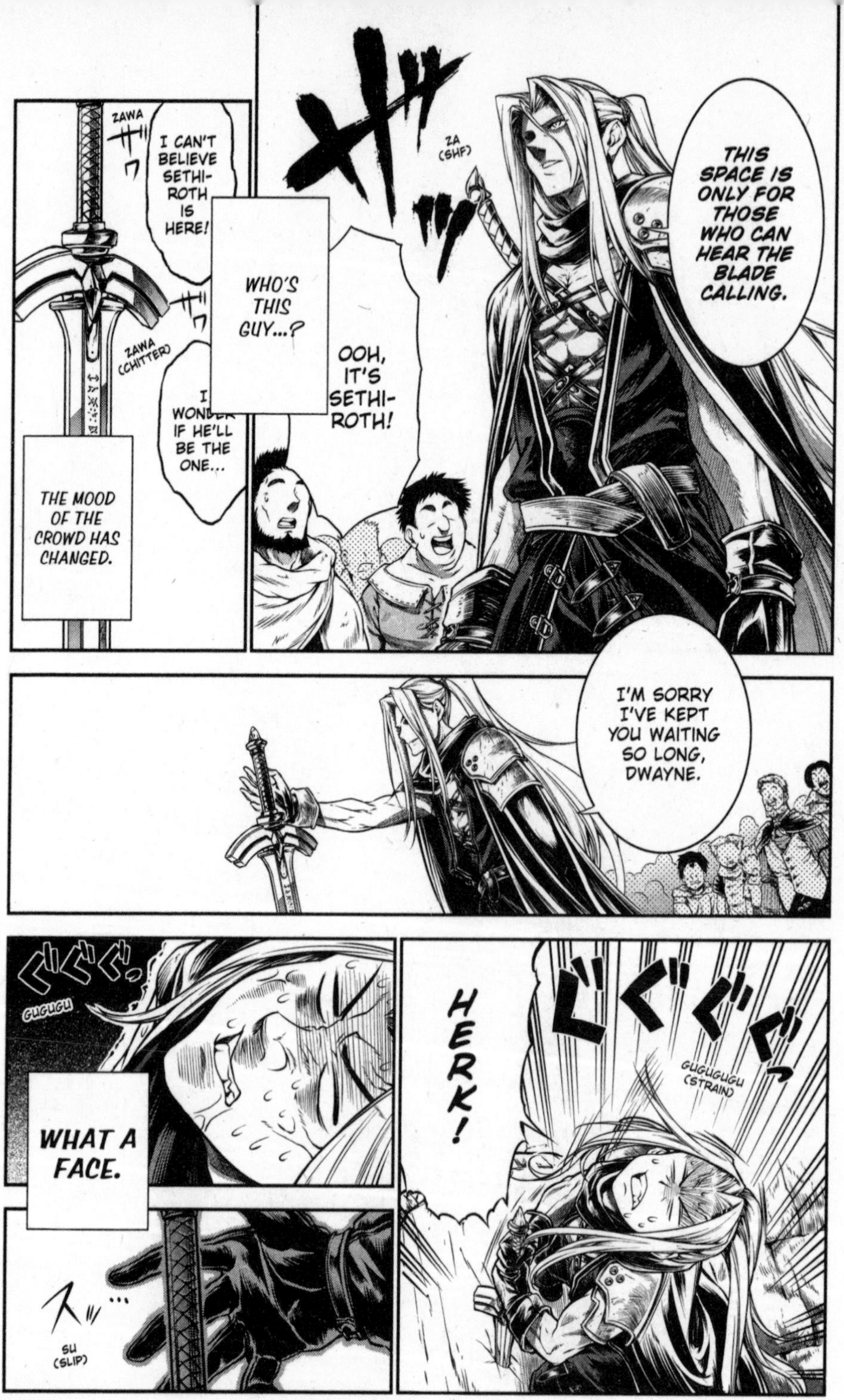
ZA (SHF)
THIS SPACE IS ONLY FOR THOSE WHO CAN HEAR THE BLADE CALLING.
OOH, IT'S SETHIROTH!
WHO'S THIS GUY...?
ZAWA
I CAN'T BELIEVE SETHIROTH IS HERE!
ZAWA (CHITTER)
I WONDER IF HE'LL BE THE ONE...
THE MOOD OF THE CROWD HAS CHANGED.
I'M SORRY I'VE KEPT YOU WAITING SO LONG, DWAYNE.
HERK!
GUGUGUGU (STRAIN)
GUGUGU
WHAT A FACE.
SU (SLIP)

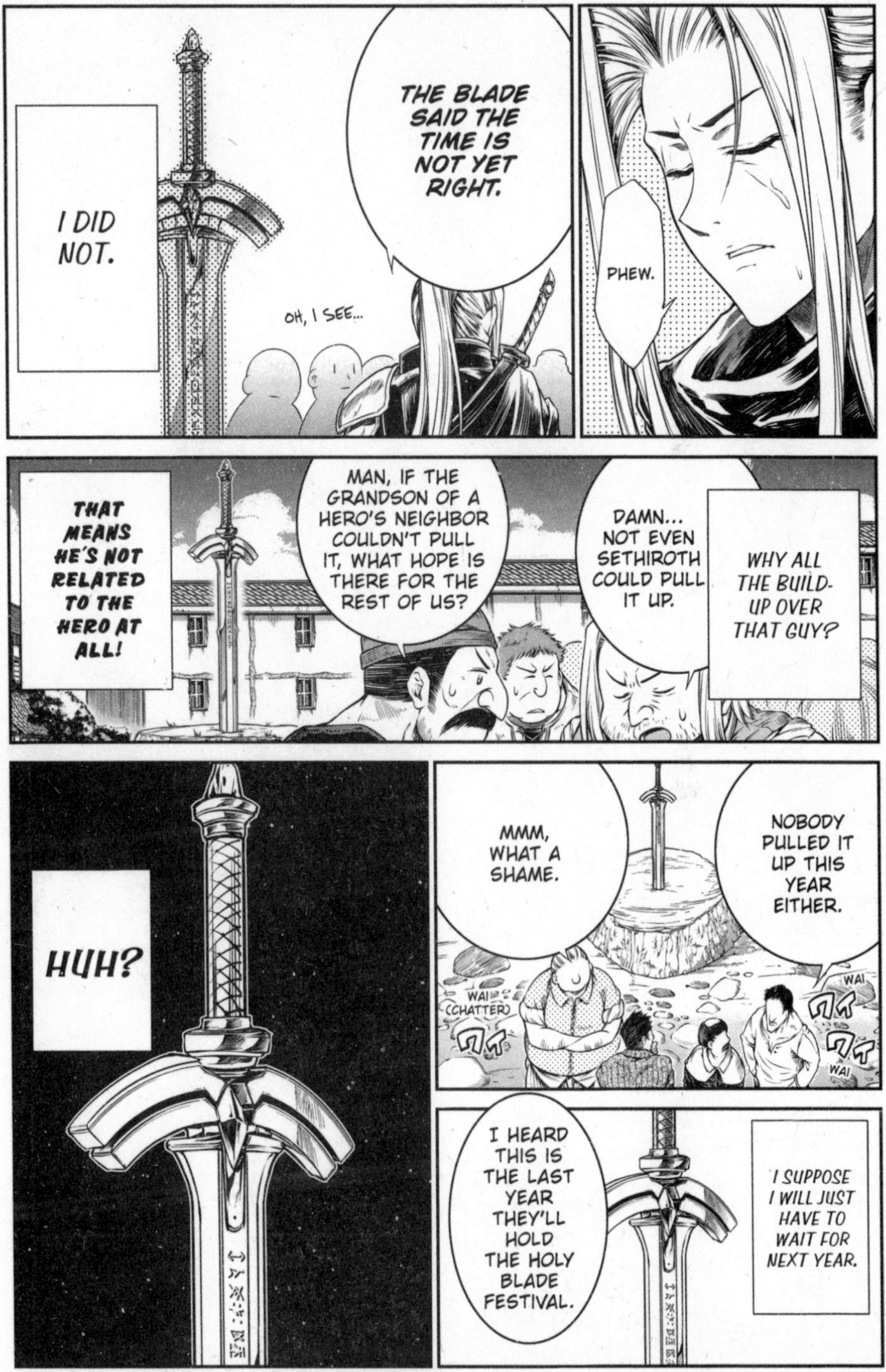
PHEW.
THE BLADE SAID THE TIME IS NOT YET RIGHT.
I DID NOT.
OH, I SEE...
WHY ALL THE BUILD-UP OVER THAT GUY?
DAMN... NOT EVEN SETHIROTH COULD PULL IT UP.
MAN, IF THE GRANDSON OF A HERO'S NEIGHBOR COULDN'T PULL IT, WHAT HOPE IS THERE FOR THE REST OF US?
THAT MEANS HE'S NOT RELATED TO THE HERO AT ALL!
NOBODY PULLED IT UP THIS YEAR EITHER.
MMM, WHAT A SHAME.
WAI
WAI (CHATTER)
WAI
I SUPPOSE I WILL JUST HAVE TO WAIT FOR NEXT YEAR.
I HEARD THIS IS THE LAST YEAR THEY'LL HOLD THE HOLY BLADE FESTIVAL.
HUH?

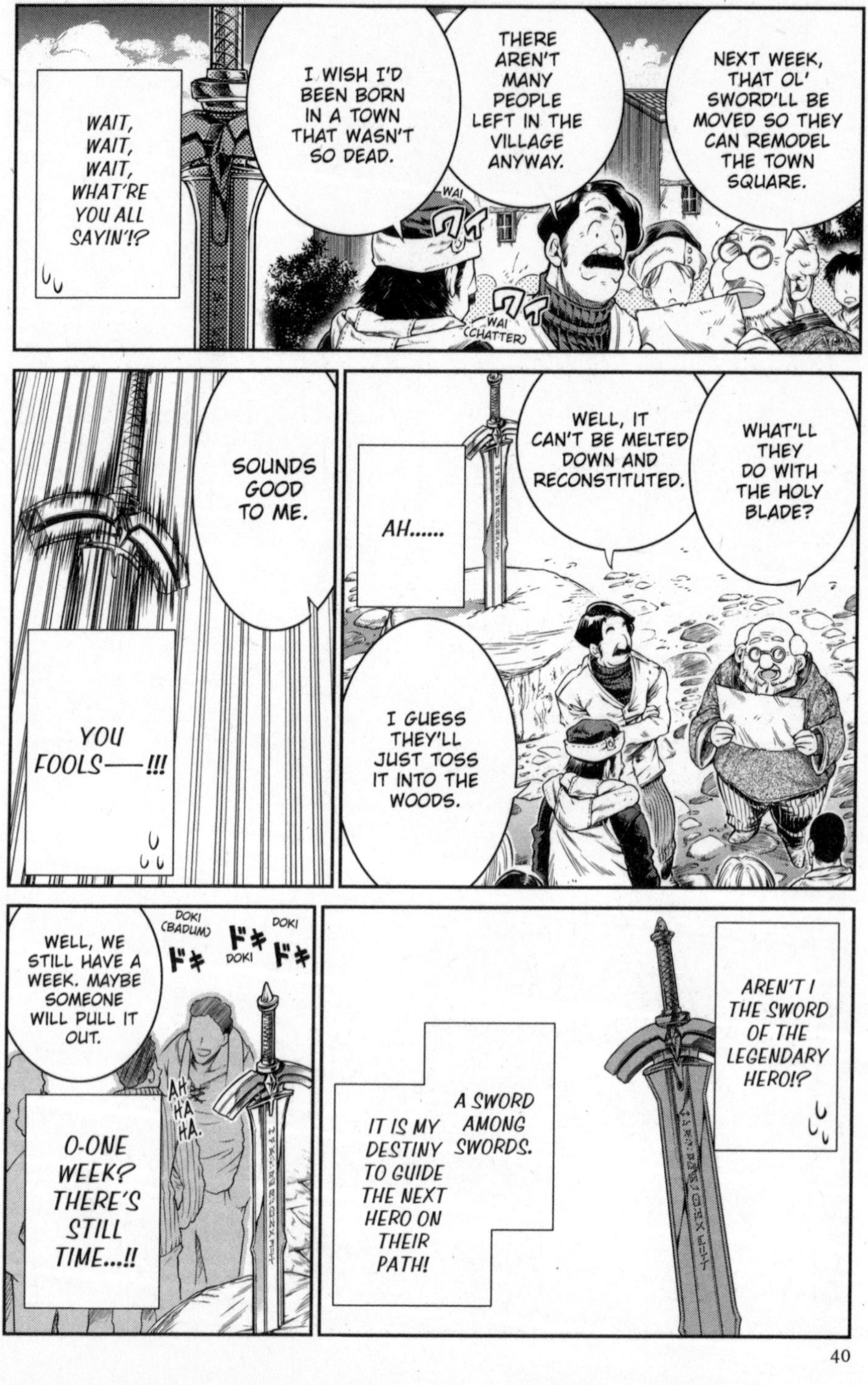
NEXT WEEK, THAT OL' SWORD'LL BE MOVED SO THEY CAN REMODEL THE TOWN SQUARE.
THERE AREN'T MANY PEOPLE LEFT IN THE VILLAGE ANYWAY.
I WISH I'D BEEN BORN IN A TOWN THAT WASN'T SO DEAD.
WAI WAI (CHATTER)
WAIT, WAIT, WAIT, WHAT'RE YOU ALL SAYIN'!?
WHAT'LL THEY DO WITH THE HOLY BLADE?
WELL, IT CAN'T BE MELTED DOWN AND RECONSTITUTED.
AH......
I GUESS THEY'LL JUST TOSS IT INTO THE WOODS.
SOUNDS GOOD TO ME.
YOU FOOLS——!!!
AREN'T I THE SWORD OF THE LEGENDARY HERO!?
A SWORD AMONG SWORDS.
IT IS MY DESTINY TO GUIDE THE NEXT HERO ON THEIR PATH!
WELL, WE STILL HAVE A WEEK. MAYBE SOMEONE WILL PULL IT OUT.
DOKI (BADUM) DOKI DOKI
AH HA HA.
O-ONE WEEK? THERE'S STILL TIME...!!

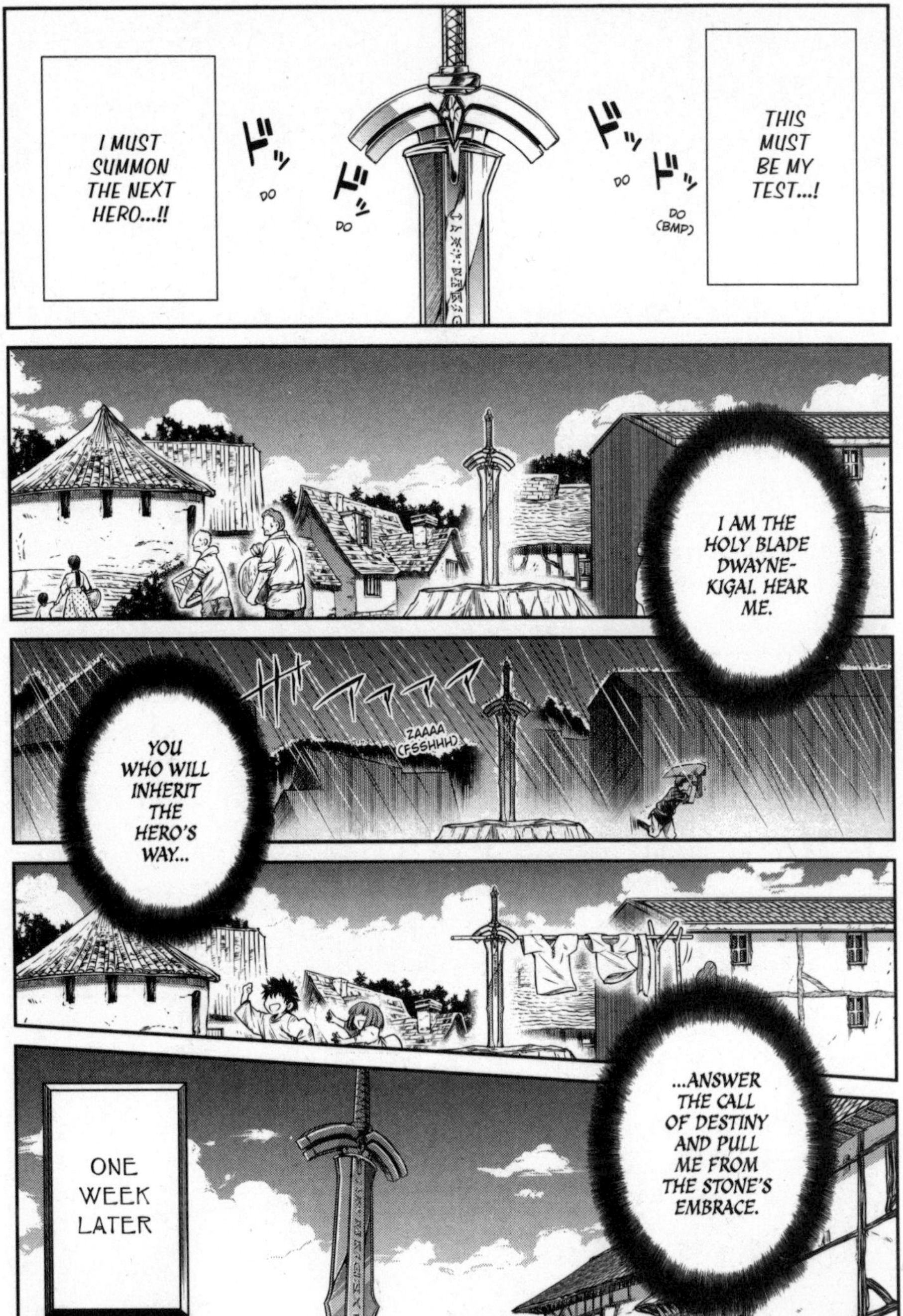
THIS MUST BE MY TEST...!
DO
DO (BMP)
DO
DO
I MUST SUMMON THE NEXT HERO...!!
I AM THE HOLY BLADE DWAYNE-KIGAI. HEAR ME.
ZAAAA (FSSHHH)
YOU WHO WILL INHERIT THE HERO'S WAY...
...ANSWER THE CALL OF DESTINY AND PULL ME FROM THE STONE'S EMBRACE.
ONE WEEK LATER

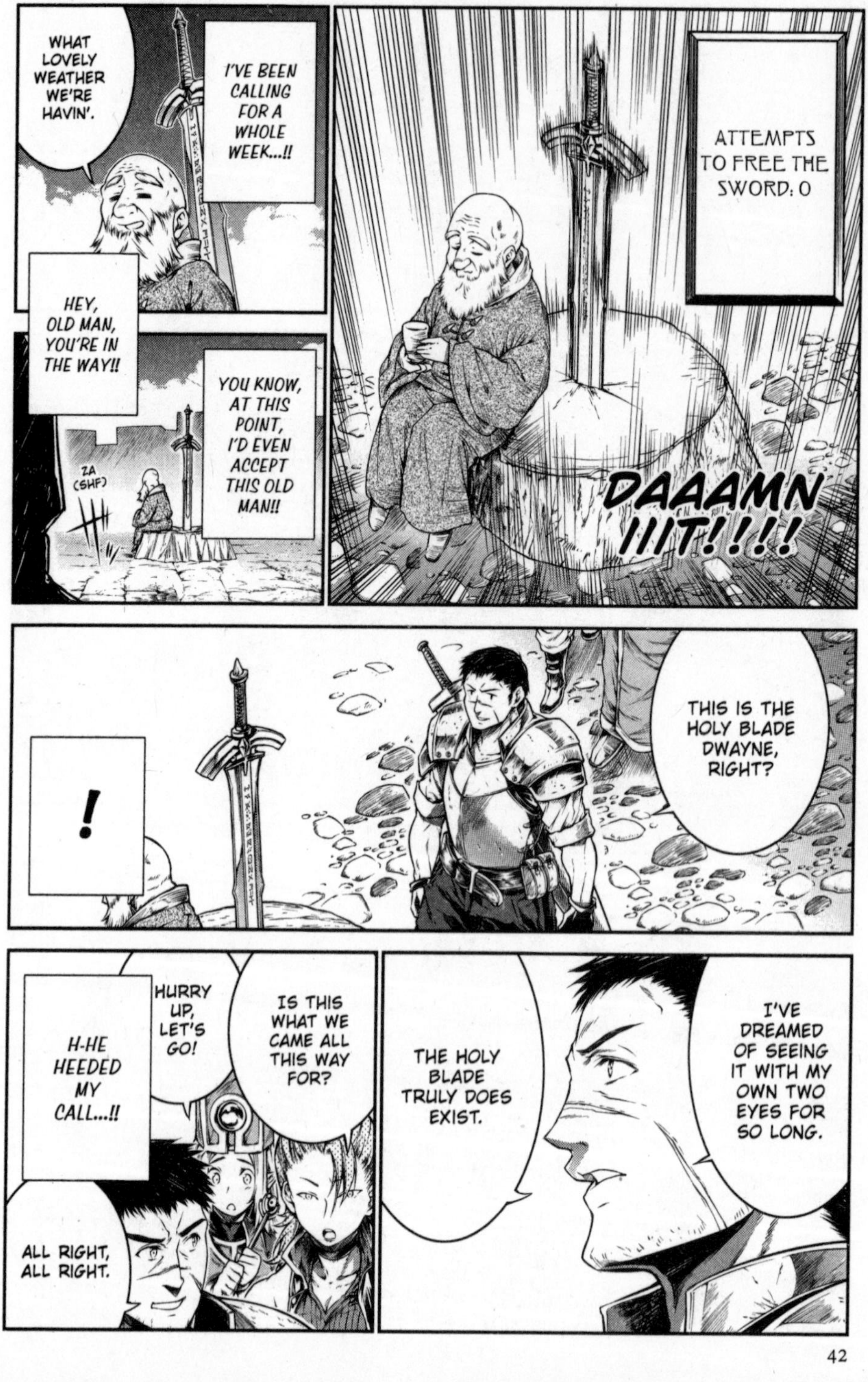
ATTEMPTS TO FREE THE SWORD: 0
DAAAMN IIIT!!!!
I'VE BEEN CALLING FOR A WHOLE WEEK...!!
WHAT LOVELY WEATHER WE'RE HAVIN'.
HEY, OLD MAN, YOU'RE IN THE WAY!!
YOU KNOW, AT THIS POINT, I'D EVEN ACCEPT THIS OLD MAN!!
ZA (SHF)
THIS IS THE HOLY BLADE DWAYNE, RIGHT?
!
I'VE DREAMED OF SEEING IT WITH MY OWN TWO EYES FOR SO LONG.
THE HOLY BLADE TRULY DOES EXIST.
IS THIS WHAT WE CAME ALL THIS WAY FOR?
HURRY UP, LET'S GO!
H-HE HEEDED MY CALL...!!
ALL RIGHT, ALL RIGHT.

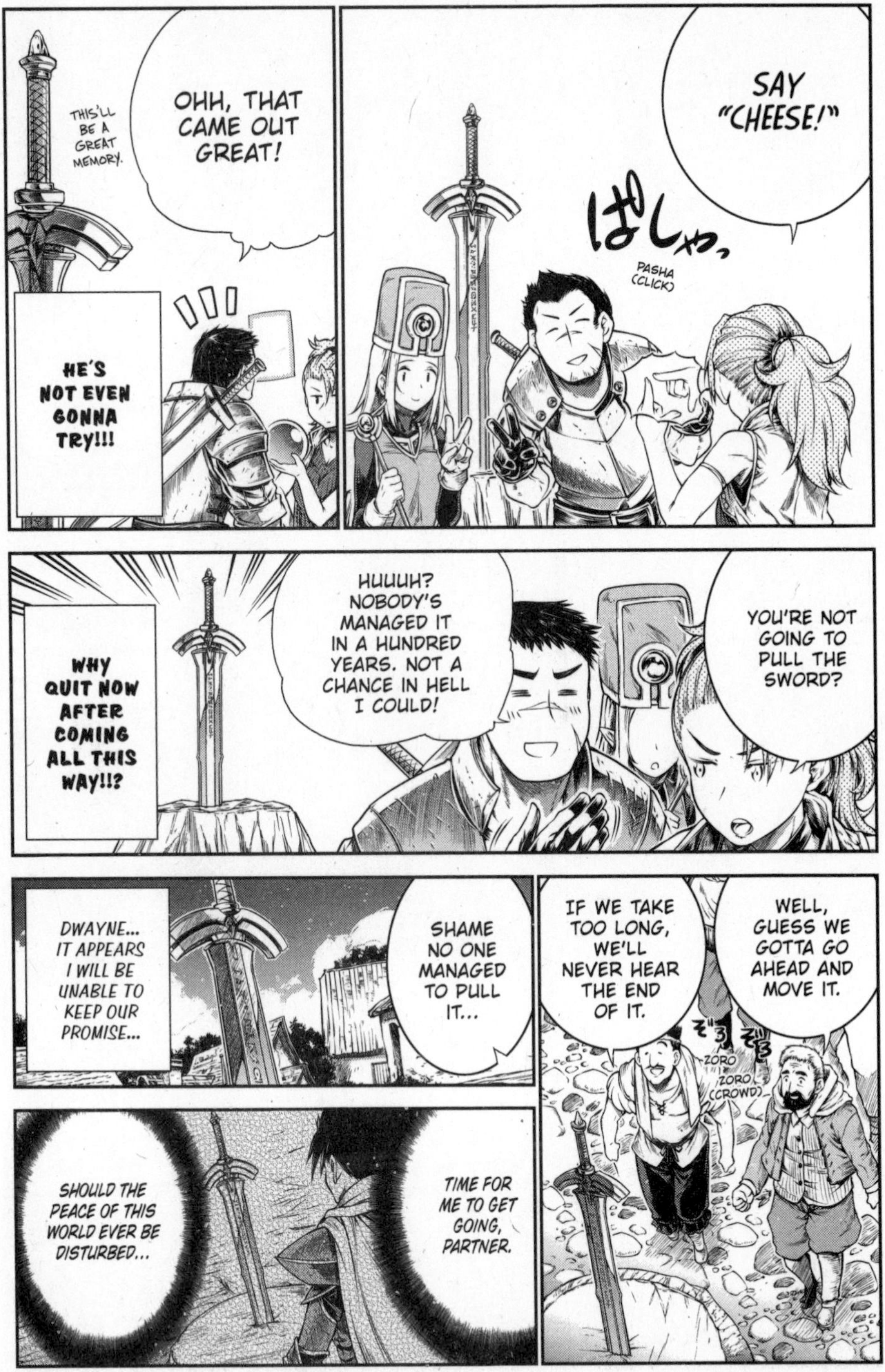
SAY "CHEESE!"
ぱしゃっ
PASHA (CLICK)
OHH, THAT CAME OUT GREAT!
THIS'LL BE A GREAT MEMORY.
HE'S NOT EVEN GONNA TRY!!!
YOU'RE NOT GOING TO PULL THE SWORD?
HUUUH? NOBODY'S MANAGED IT IN A HUNDRED YEARS. NOT A CHANCE IN HELL I COULD!
WHY QUIT NOW AFTER COMING ALL THIS WAY!!?
WELL, GUESS WE GOTTA GO AHEAD AND MOVE IT.
IF WE TAKE TOO LONG, WE'LL NEVER HEAR THE END OF IT.
ぞろぞろ
ZORO ZORO (CROWD)
SHAME NO ONE MANAGED TO PULL IT...
DWAYNE... IT APPEARS I WILL BE UNABLE TO KEEP OUR PROMISE...
TIME FOR ME TO GET GOING, PARTNER.
SHOULD THE PEACE OF THIS WORLD EVER BE DISTURBED...

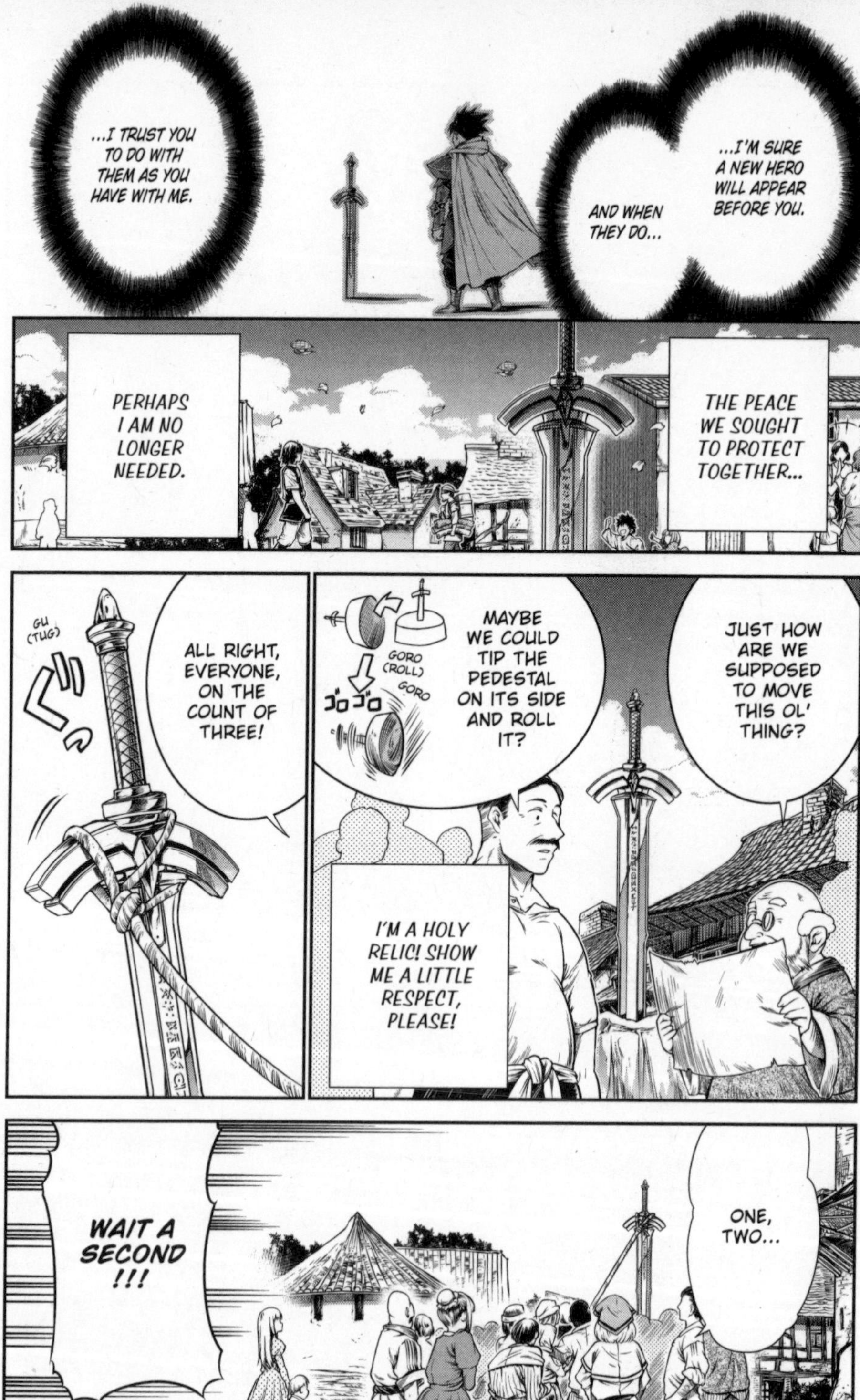
...I'M SURE A NEW HERO WILL APPEAR BEFORE YOU.
AND WHEN THEY DO...
...I TRUST YOU TO DO WITH THEM AS YOU HAVE WITH ME.
THE PEACE WE SOUGHT TO PROTECT TOGETHER...
PERHAPS I AM NO LONGER NEEDED.
JUST HOW ARE WE SUPPOSED TO MOVE THIS OL' THING?
MAYBE WE COULD TIP THE PEDESTAL ON ITS SIDE AND ROLL IT?
GORO (ROLL) GORO
ゴロゴロ
I'M A HOLY RELIC! SHOW ME A LITTLE RESPECT, PLEASE!
ALL RIGHT, EVERYONE, ON THE COUNT OF THREE!
GU (TUG)
グッ
ONE, TWO...
WAIT A SECOND !!!

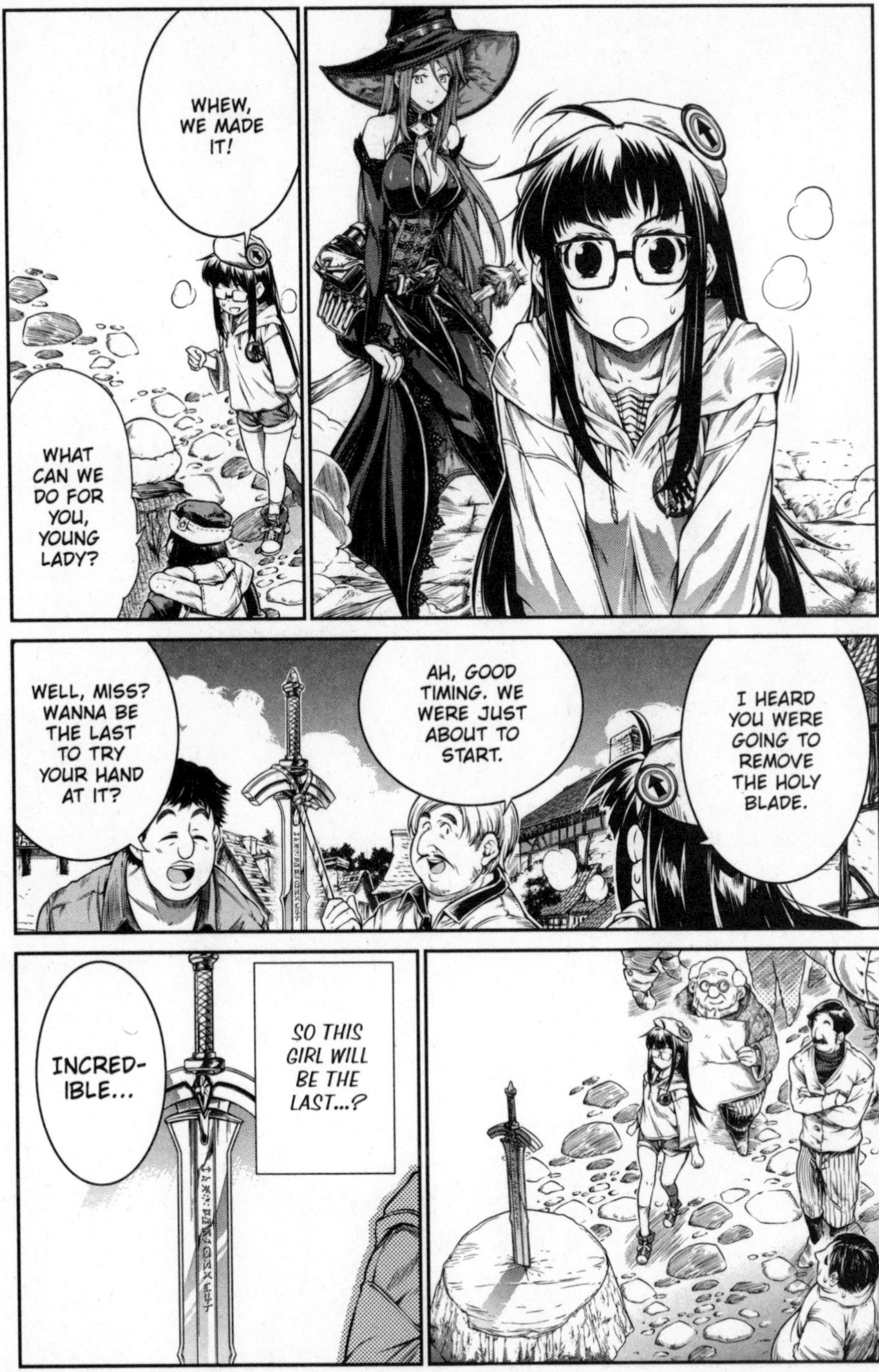
WHEW, WE MADE IT!
WHAT CAN WE DO FOR YOU, YOUNG LADY?
I HEARD YOU WERE GOING TO REMOVE THE HOLY BLADE.
AH, GOOD TIMING. WE WERE JUST ABOUT TO START.
WELL, MISS? WANNA BE THE LAST TO TRY YOUR HAND AT IT?
SO THIS GIRL WILL BE THE LAST...?
INCRED-IBLE...

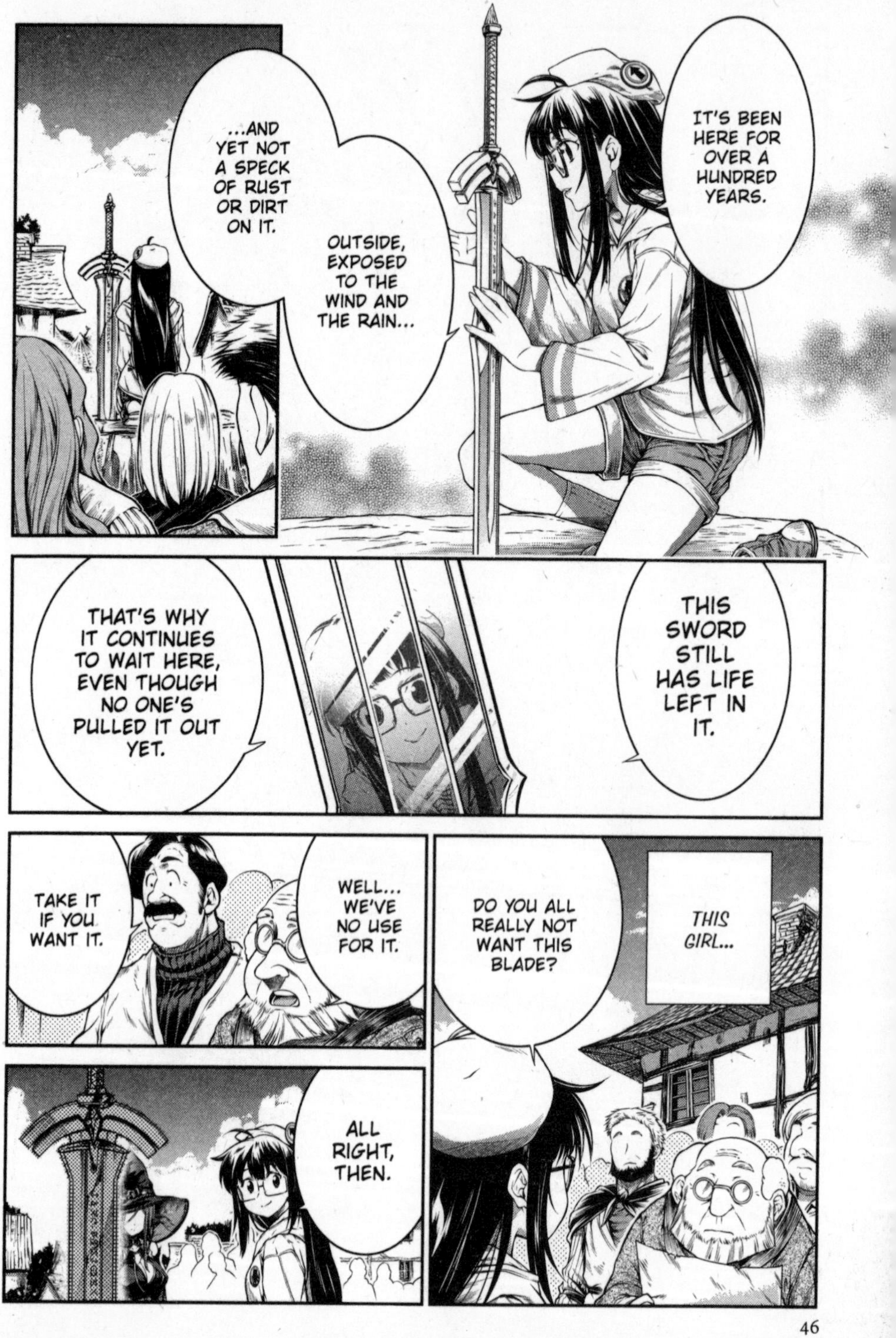
IT'S BEEN HERE FOR OVER A HUNDRED YEARS.
OUTSIDE, EXPOSED TO THE WIND AND THE RAIN...
...AND YET NOT A SPECK OF RUST OR DIRT ON IT.
THIS SWORD STILL HAS LIFE LEFT IN IT.
THAT'S WHY IT CONTINUES TO WAIT HERE, EVEN THOUGH NO ONE'S PULLED IT OUT YET.
THIS GIRL...
DO YOU ALL REALLY NOT WANT THIS BLADE?
WELL... WE'VE NO USE FOR IT.
TAKE IT IF YOU WANT IT.
ALL RIGHT, THEN.

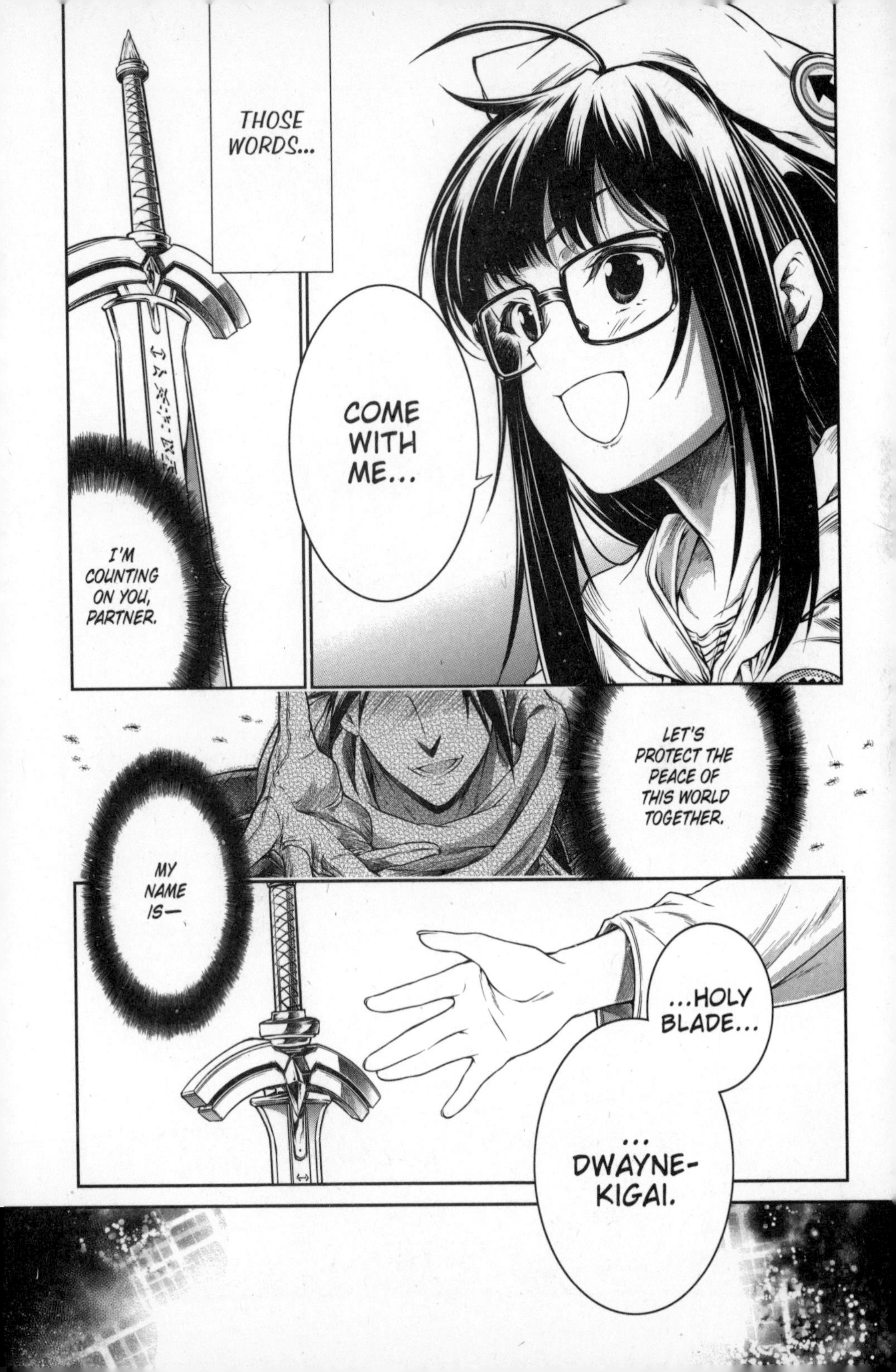
THOSE WORDS...
COME WITH ME...
I'M COUNTING ON YOU, PARTNER.
LET'S PROTECT THE PEACE OF THIS WORLD TOGETHER.
MY NAME IS—
...HOLY BLADE...
... DWAYNE-KIGAI.

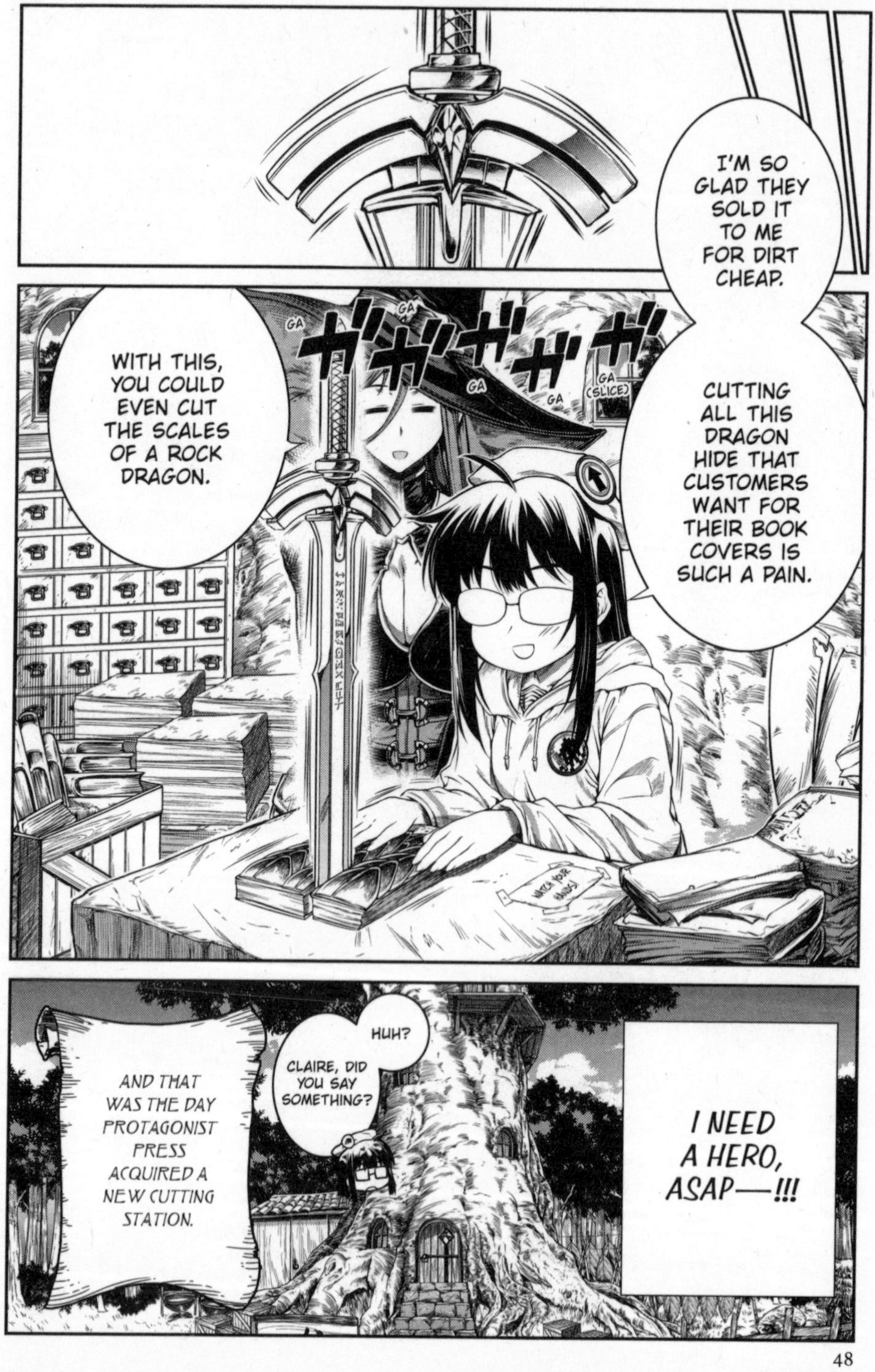
I'M SO GLAD THEY SOLD IT TO ME FOR DIRT CHEAP.
CUTTING ALL THIS DRAGON HIDE THAT CUSTOMERS WANT FOR THEIR BOOK COVERS IS SUCH A PAIN.
GA GA GA GA GA GA (SLICE)
WITH THIS, YOU COULD EVEN CUT THE SCALES OF A ROCK DRAGON.
WATCH YOUR HANDS!
I NEED A HERO, ASAP—!!!
HUH?
CLAIRE, DID YOU SAY SOMETHING?
AND THAT WAS THE DAY PROTAGONIST PRESS ACQUIRED A NEW CUTTING STATION.

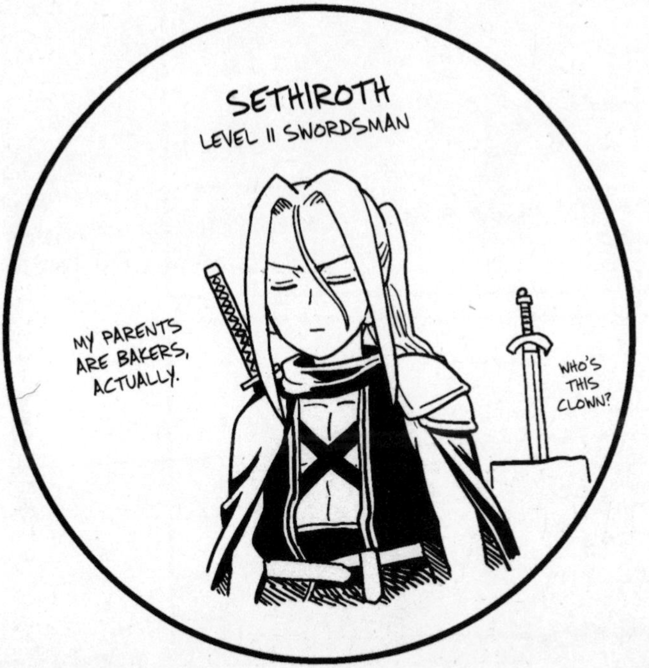
SETHIROTH
LEVEL 11 SWORDSMAN
MY PARENTS ARE BAKERS, ACTUALLY.
WHO'S THIS CLOWN?

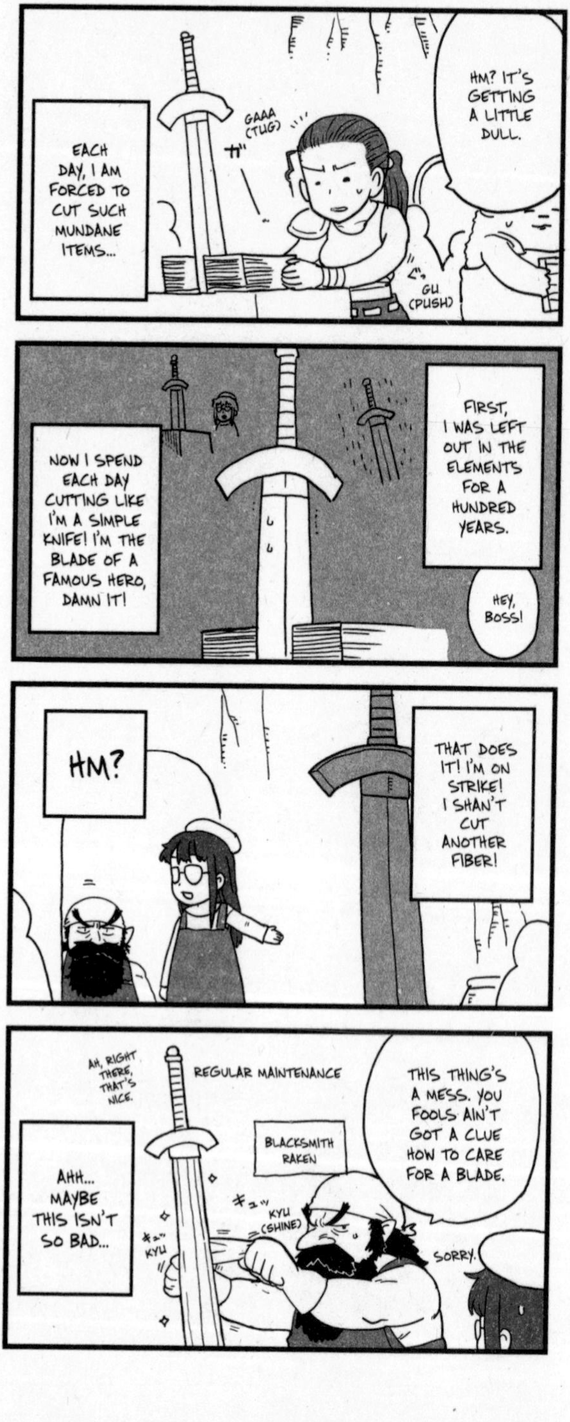
HM? IT'S GETTING A LITTLE DULL.
GAAA (TUG)
EACH DAY, I AM FORCED TO CUT SUCH MUNDANE ITEMS...
GU (PUSH)
FIRST, I WAS LEFT OUT IN THE ELEMENTS FOR A HUNDRED YEARS.
HEY, BOSS!
NOW I SPEND EACH DAY CUTTING LIKE I'M A SIMPLE KNIFE! I'M THE BLADE OF A FAMOUS HERO, DAMN IT!
THAT DOES IT! I'M ON STRIKE! I SHAN'T CUT ANOTHER FIBER!
HM?
THIS THING'S A MESS. YOU FOOLS AIN'T GOT A CLUE HOW TO CARE FOR A BLADE.
REGULAR MAINTENANCE
AH, RIGHT THERE, THAT'S NICE.
BLACKSMITH RAKEN
KYU (SHINE)
SORRY.
KYU
AHH... MAYBE THIS ISN'T SO BAD...

# Chapter 9

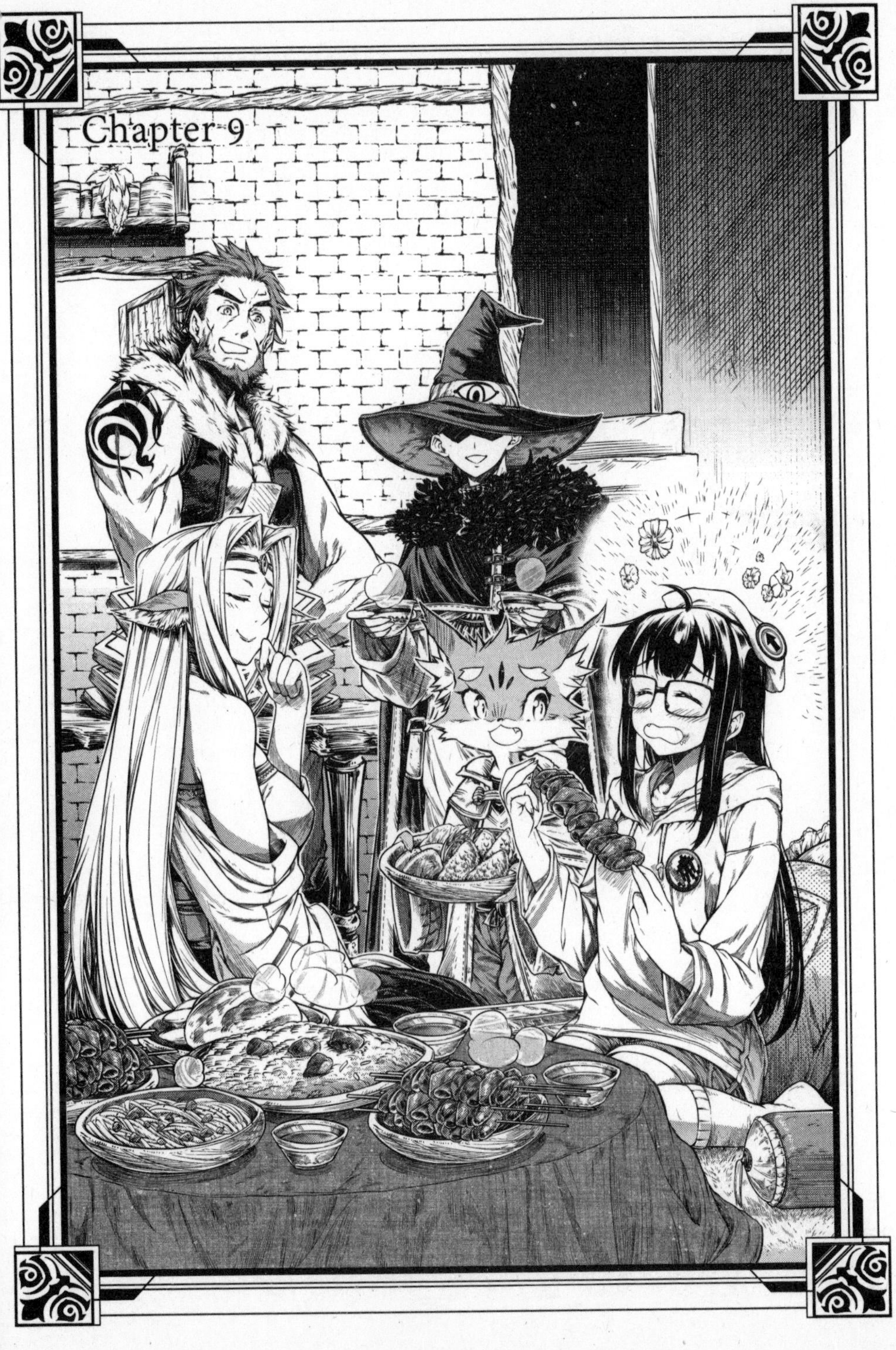

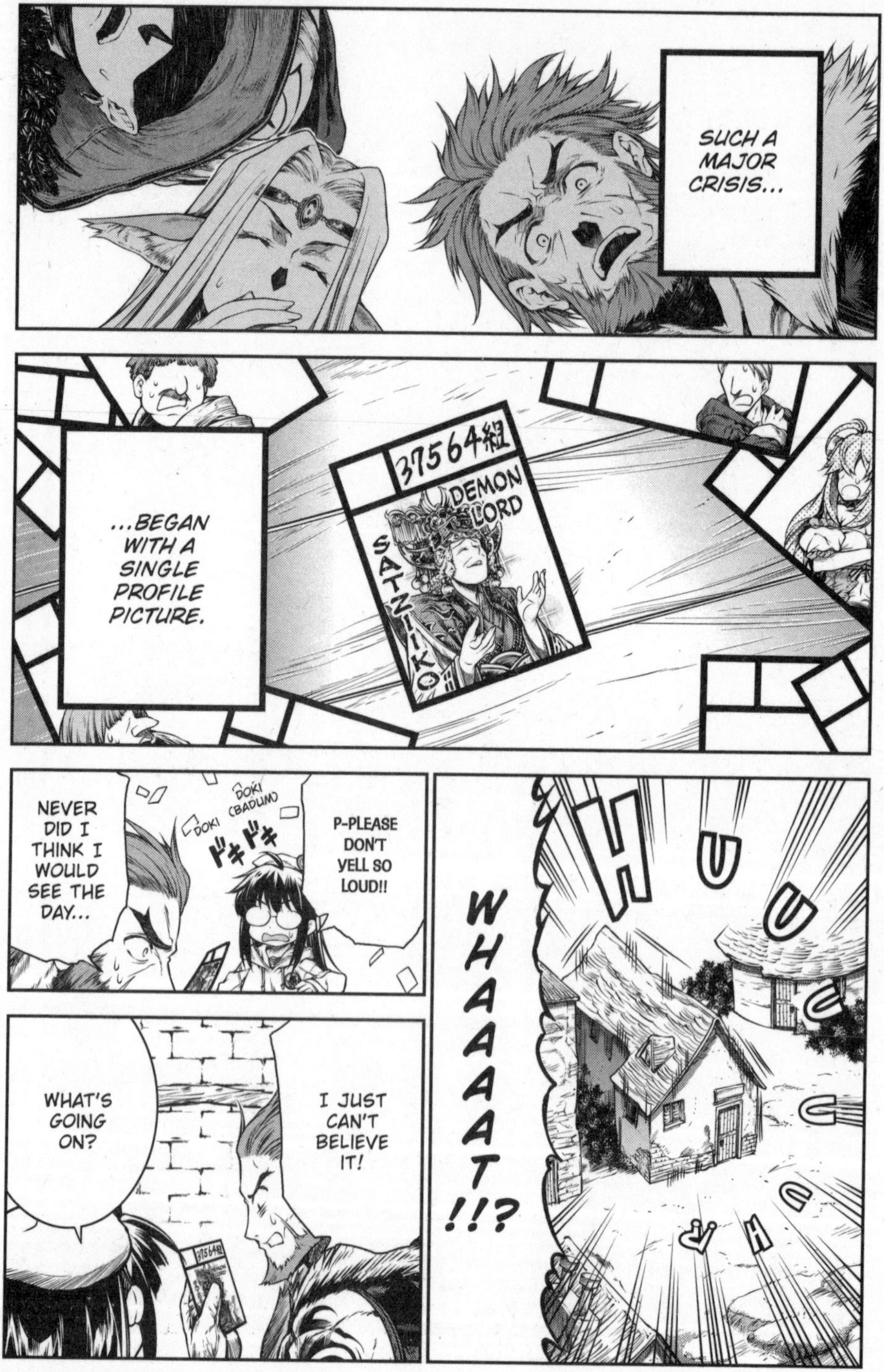
SUCH A MAJOR CRISIS...
37564組
DEMON LORD
SATZIIKO
...BEGAN WITH A SINGLE PROFILE PICTURE.
HUUUUUH?!
WHAAAAAT!!?
P-PLEASE DON'T YELL SO LOUD!!
ドキドキ DOKI DOKI (BADUM)
NEVER DID I THINK I WOULD SEE THE DAY...
I JUST CAN'T BELIEVE IT!
WHAT'S GOING ON?

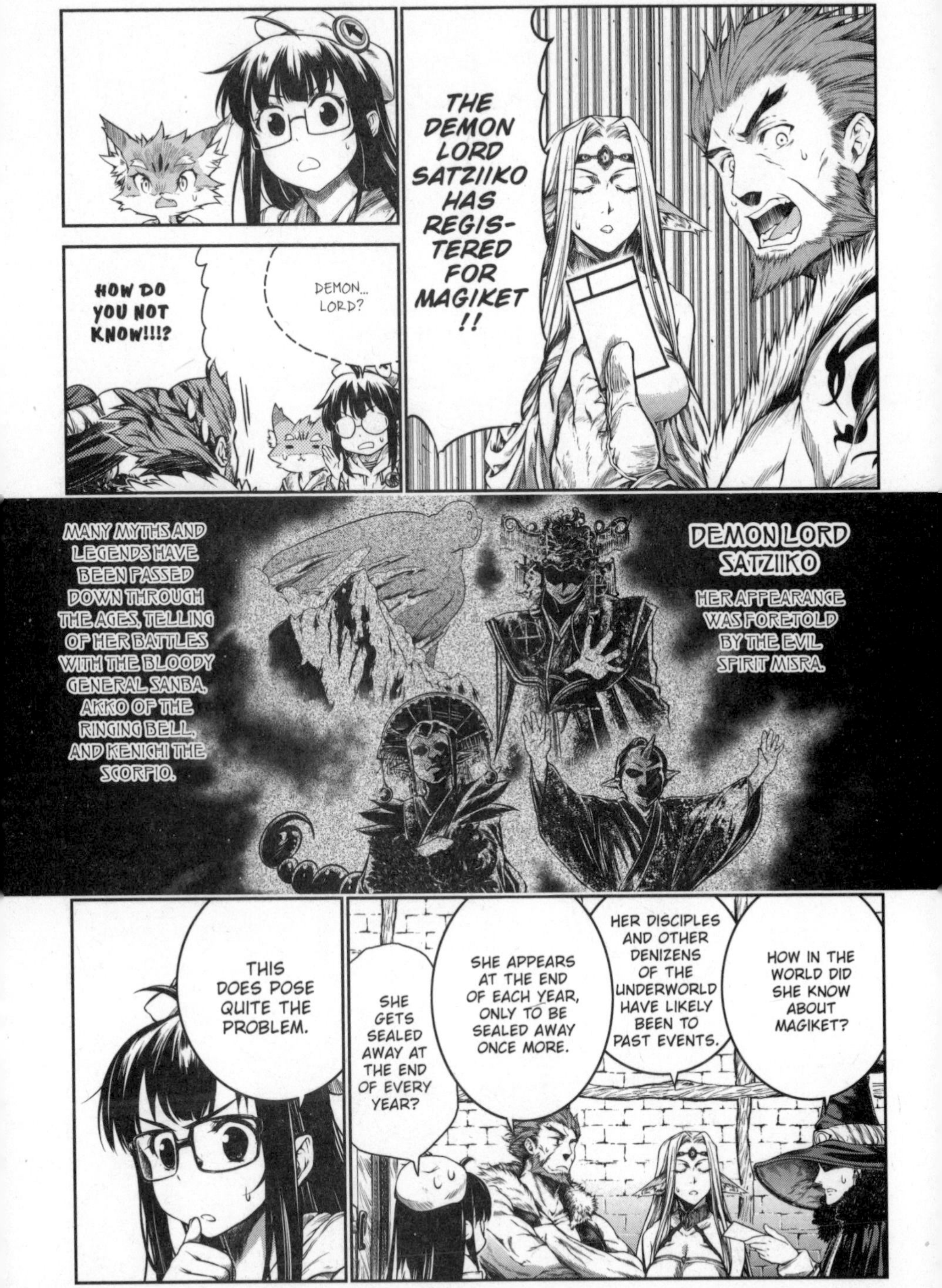
THE DEMON LORD SATZIIKO HAS REGISTERED FOR MAGIKET!!
DEMON... LORD?
HOW DO YOU NOT KNOW!!!?
DEMON LORD SATZIIKO
HER APPEARANCE WAS FORETOLD BY THE EVIL SPIRIT MISRA.
MANY MYTHS AND LEGENDS HAVE BEEN PASSED DOWN THROUGH THE AGES, TELLING OF HER BATTLES WITH THE BLOODY GENERAL SANBA, AKKO OF THE RINGING BELL, AND KENICHI THE SCORPIO.
HOW IN THE WORLD DID SHE KNOW ABOUT MAGIKET?
HER DISCIPLES AND OTHER DENIZENS OF THE UNDERWORLD HAVE LIKELY BEEN TO PAST EVENTS.
SHE APPEARS AT THE END OF EACH YEAR, ONLY TO BE SEALED AWAY ONCE MORE.
SHE GETS SEALED AWAY AT THE END OF EVERY YEAR?
THIS DOES POSE QUITE THE PROBLEM.

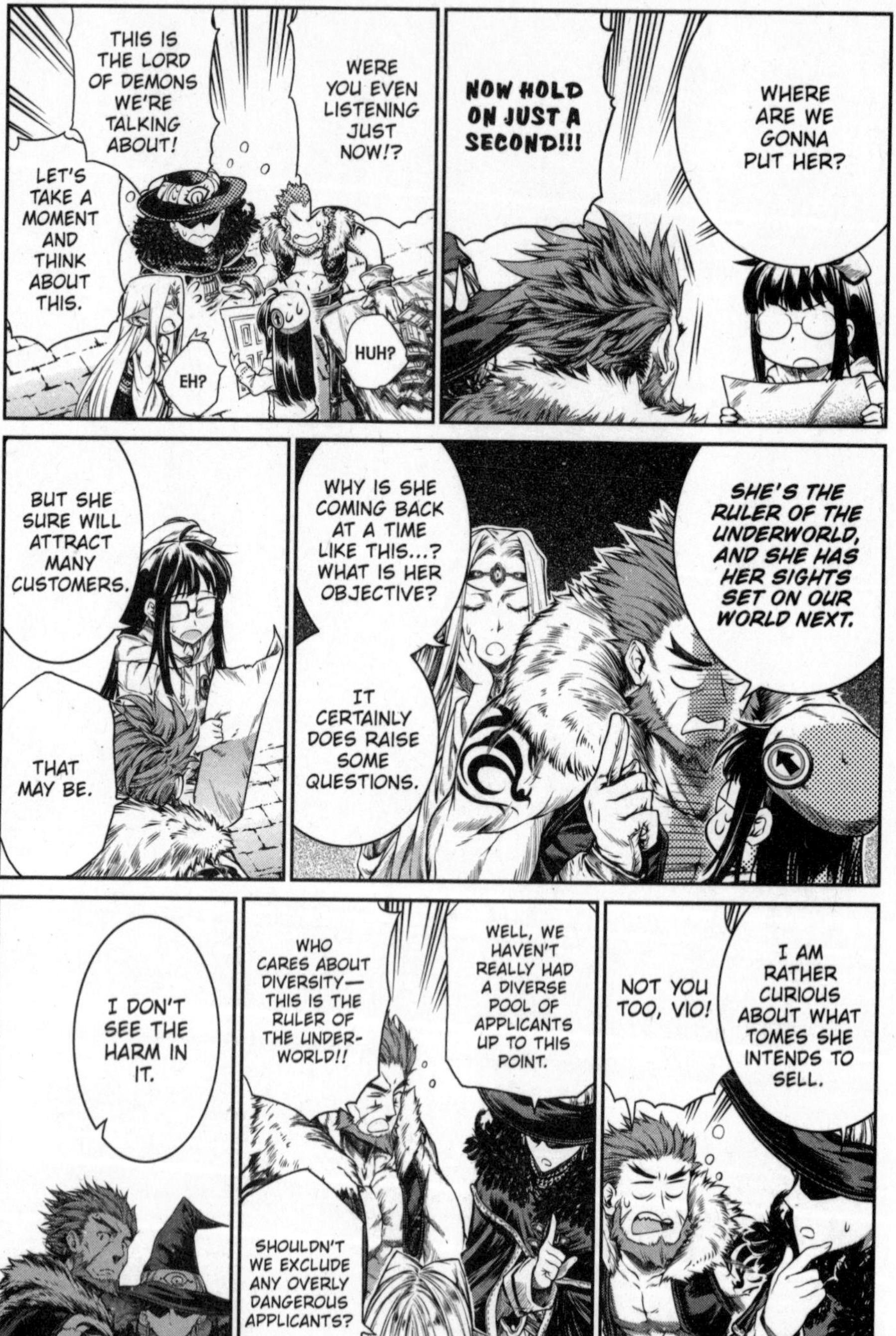
WHERE ARE WE GONNA PUT HER?
NOW HOLD ON JUST A SECOND!!!
WERE YOU EVEN LISTENING JUST NOW!?
THIS IS THE LORD OF DEMONS WE'RE TALKING ABOUT!
LET'S TAKE A MOMENT AND THINK ABOUT THIS.
HUH?
EH?
SHE'S THE RULER OF THE UNDERWORLD, AND SHE HAS HER SIGHTS SET ON OUR WORLD NEXT.
WHY IS SHE COMING BACK AT A TIME LIKE THIS...? WHAT IS HER OBJECTIVE?
IT CERTAINLY DOES RAISE SOME QUESTIONS.
BUT SHE SURE WILL ATTRACT MANY CUSTOMERS.
THAT MAY BE.
I AM RATHER CURIOUS ABOUT WHAT TOMES SHE INTENDS TO SELL.
NOT YOU TOO, VIO!
WELL, WE HAVEN'T REALLY HAD A DIVERSE POOL OF APPLICANTS UP TO THIS POINT.
WHO CARES ABOUT DIVERSITY—THIS IS THE RULER OF THE UNDER-WORLD!!
SHOULDN'T WE EXCLUDE ANY OVERLY DANGEROUS APPLICANTS?
I DON'T SEE THE HARM IN IT.

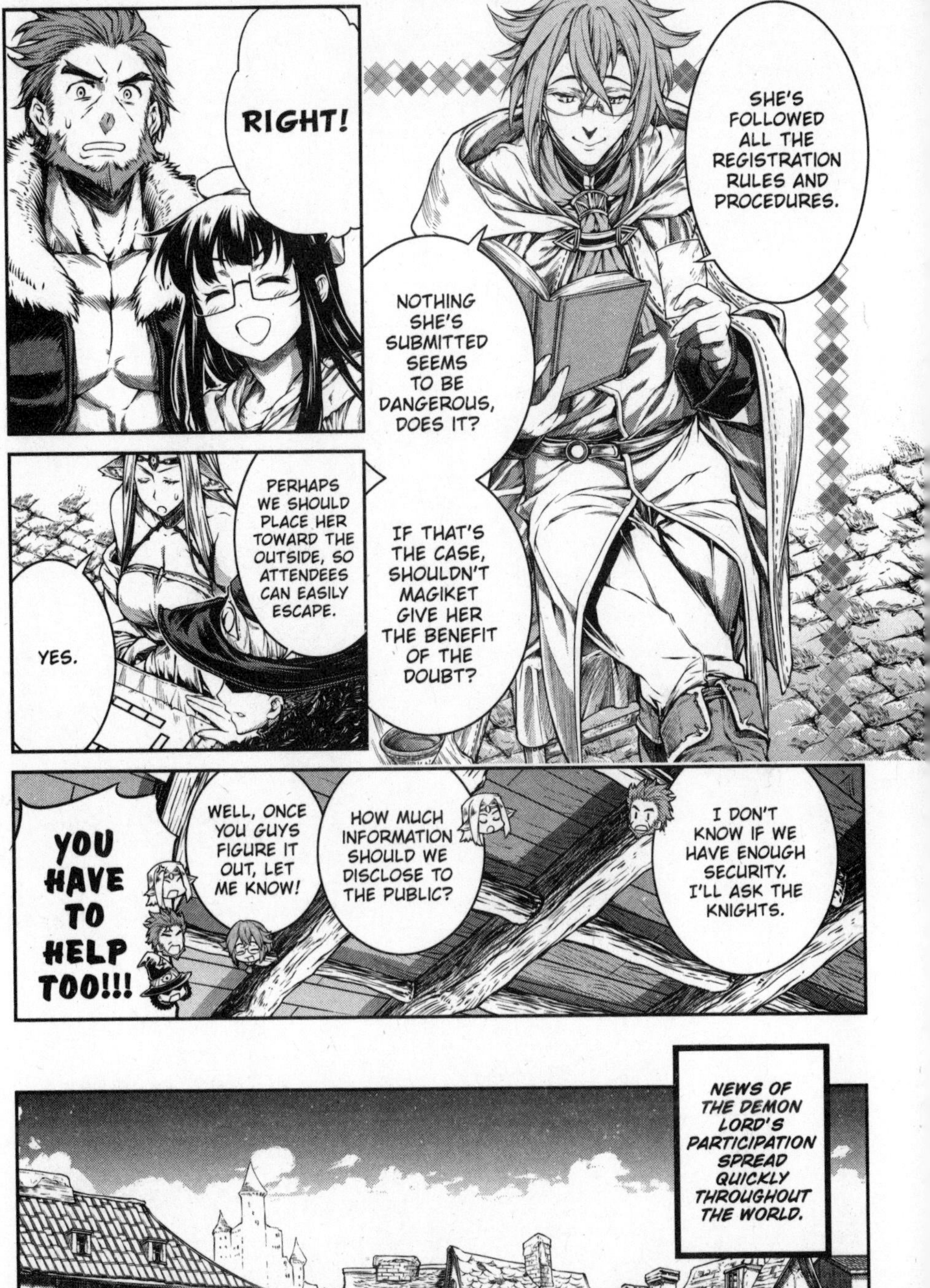
SHE'S FOLLOWED ALL THE REGISTRATION RULES AND PROCEDURES.
NOTHING SHE'S SUBMITTED SEEMS TO BE DANGEROUS, DOES IT?
IF THAT'S THE CASE, SHOULDN'T MAGIKET GIVE HER THE BENEFIT OF THE DOUBT?
RIGHT!
PERHAPS WE SHOULD PLACE HER TOWARD THE OUTSIDE, SO ATTENDEES CAN EASILY ESCAPE.
YES.
I DON'T KNOW IF WE HAVE ENOUGH SECURITY. I'LL ASK THE KNIGHTS.
HOW MUCH INFORMATION SHOULD WE DISCLOSE TO THE PUBLIC?
WELL, ONCE YOU GUYS FIGURE IT OUT, LET ME KNOW!
YOU HAVE TO HELP TOO!!!
NEWS OF THE DEMON LORD'S PARTICIPATION SPREAD QUICKLY THROUGHOUT THE WORLD.

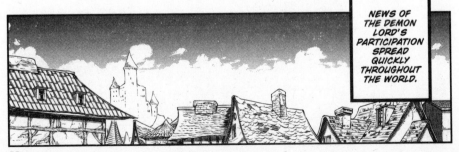

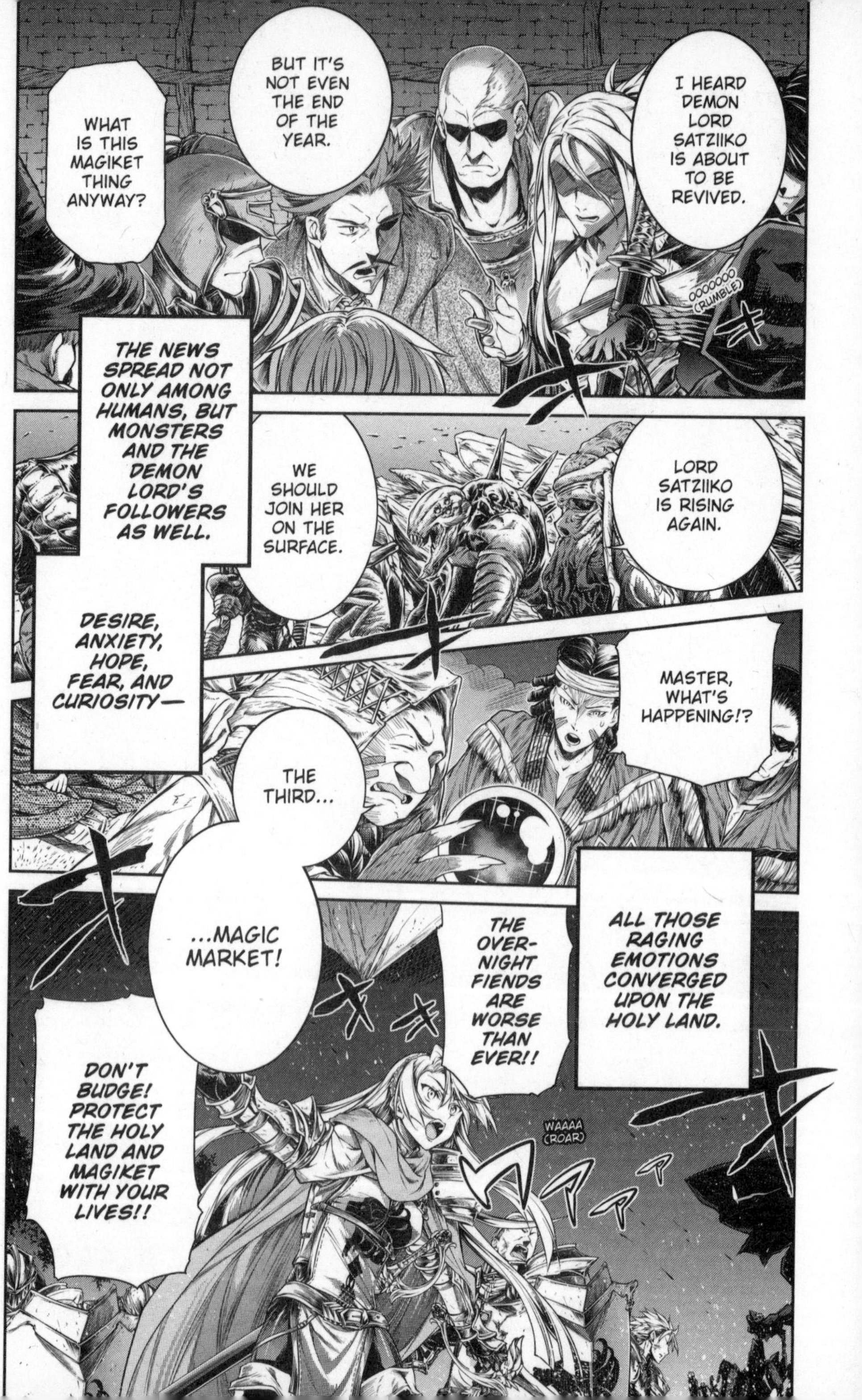
I HEARD DEMON LORD SATZIIKO IS ABOUT TO BE REVIVED.
BUT IT'S NOT EVEN THE END OF THE YEAR.
WHAT IS THIS MAGIKET THING ANYWAY?
OOOOOOO (RUMBLE)
THE NEWS SPREAD NOT ONLY AMONG HUMANS, BUT MONSTERS AND THE DEMON LORD'S FOLLOWERS AS WELL.
LORD SATZIIKO IS RISING AGAIN.
WE SHOULD JOIN HER ON THE SURFACE.
DESIRE, ANXIETY, HOPE, FEAR, AND CURIOSITY—
MASTER, WHAT'S HAPPENING!?
THE THIRD...
...MAGIC MARKET!
ALL THOSE RAGING EMOTIONS CONVERGED UPON THE HOLY LAND.
THE OVER-NIGHT FIENDS ARE WORSE THAN EVER!!
DON'T BUDGE! PROTECT THE HOLY LAND AND MAGIKET WITH YOUR LIVES!!
WAAAA (ROAR)

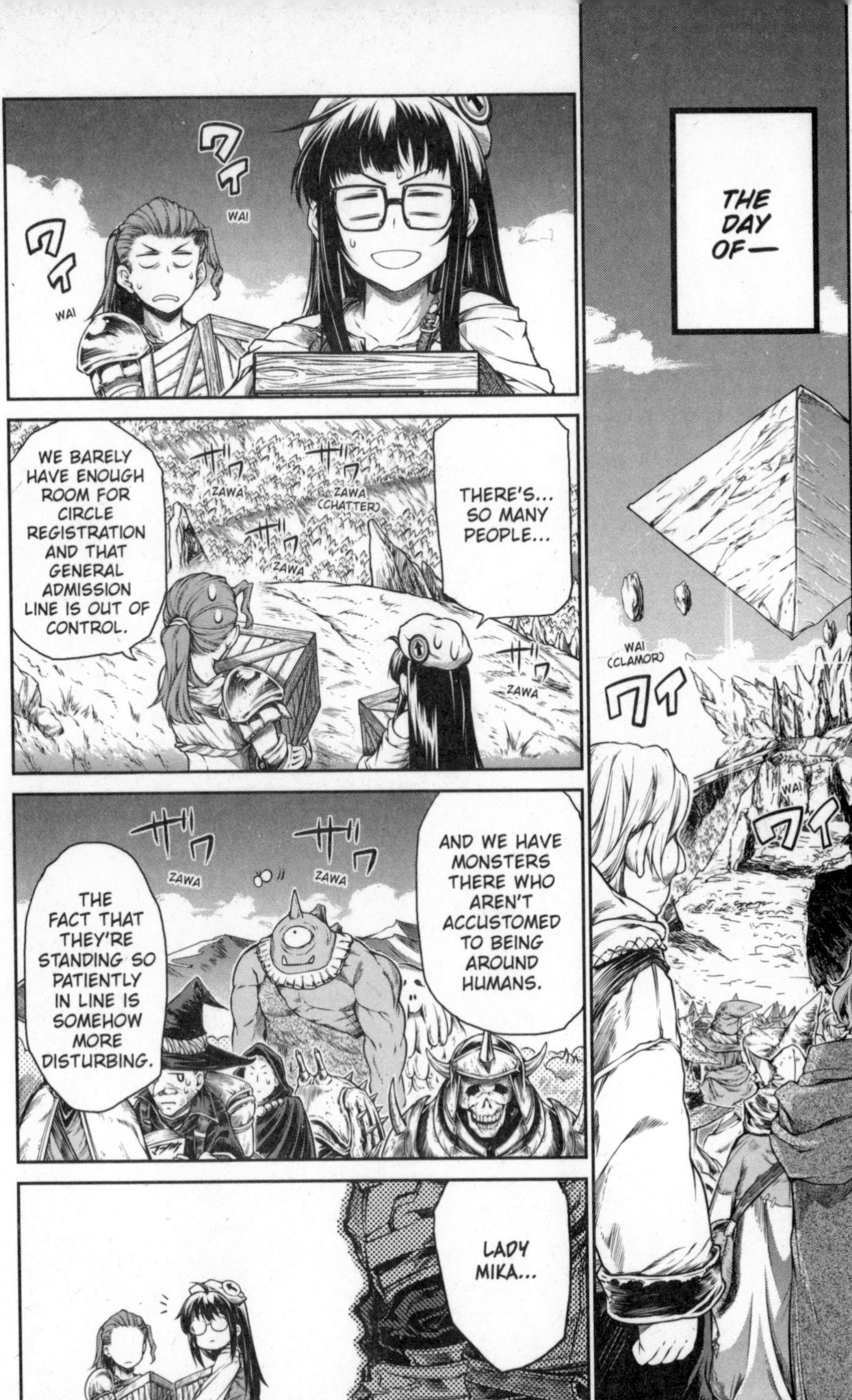
THE DAY OF—
WAI (CLAMOR)
WAI
WAI
WAI
THERE'S... SO MANY PEOPLE...
ZAWA (CHATTER)
ZAWA
ZAWA
ZAWA
WE BARELY HAVE ENOUGH ROOM FOR CIRCLE REGISTRATION AND THAT GENERAL ADMISSION LINE IS OUT OF CONTROL.
AND WE HAVE MONSTERS THERE WHO AREN'T ACCUSTOMED TO BEING AROUND HUMANS.
ZAWA
ZAWA
THE FACT THAT THEY'RE STANDING SO PATIENTLY IN LINE IS SOMEHOW MORE DISTURBING.
LADY MIKA...

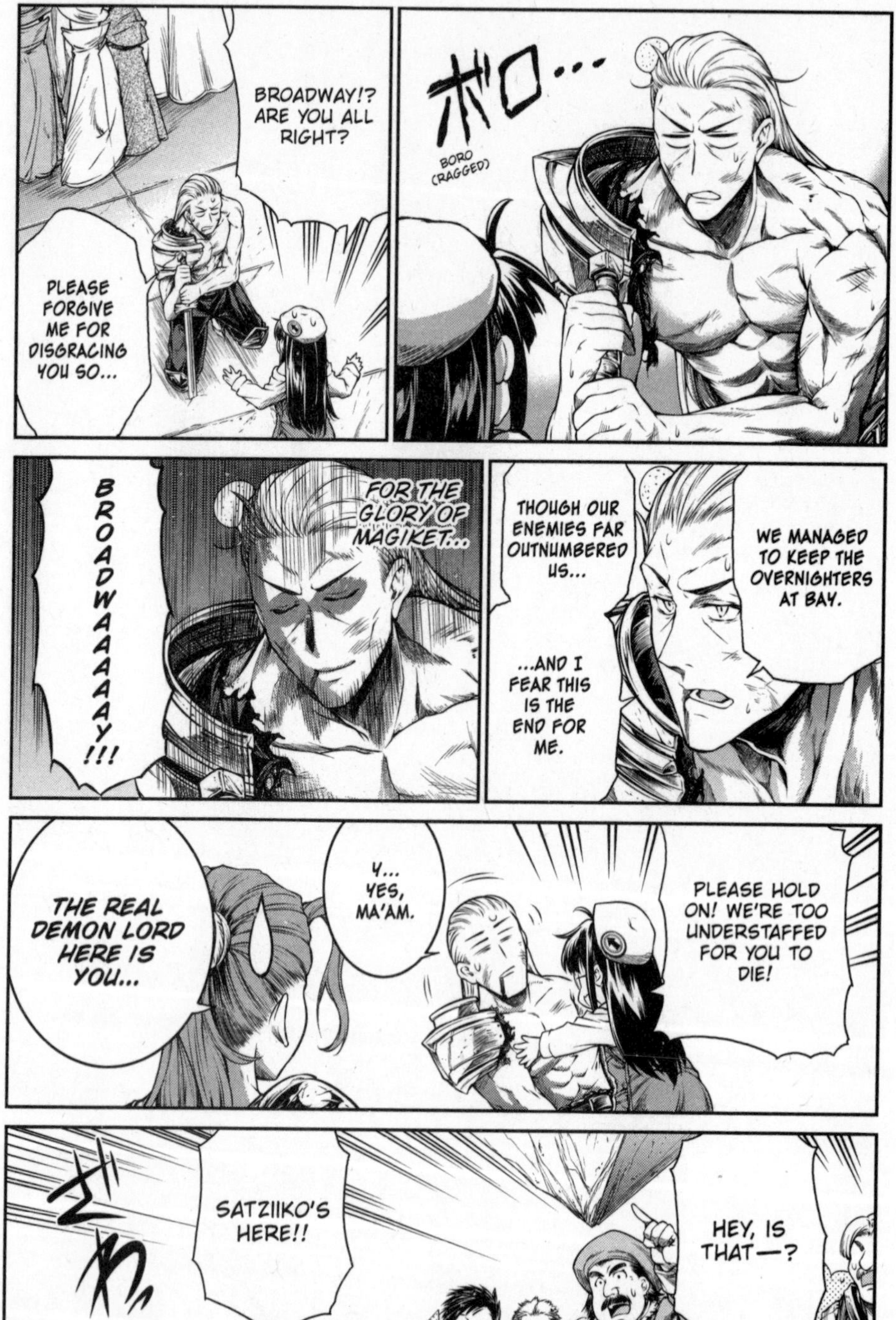
ボロ…
BORO (RAGGED)
BROADWAY!? ARE YOU ALL RIGHT?
PLEASE FORGIVE ME FOR DISGRACING YOU SO…
WE MANAGED TO KEEP THE OVERNIGHTERS AT BAY.
THOUGH OUR ENEMIES FAR OUTNUMBERED US…
…AND I FEAR THIS IS THE END FOR ME.
FOR THE GLORY OF MAGIKET…
BROADWAAAAAAAY!!!
PLEASE HOLD ON! WE'RE TOO UNDERSTAFFED FOR YOU TO DIE!
Y… YES, MA'AM.
THE REAL DEMON LORD HERE IS YOU…
HEY, IS THAT—?
SATZIIKO'S HERE!!
ざわ
ZAWA (THRUM)

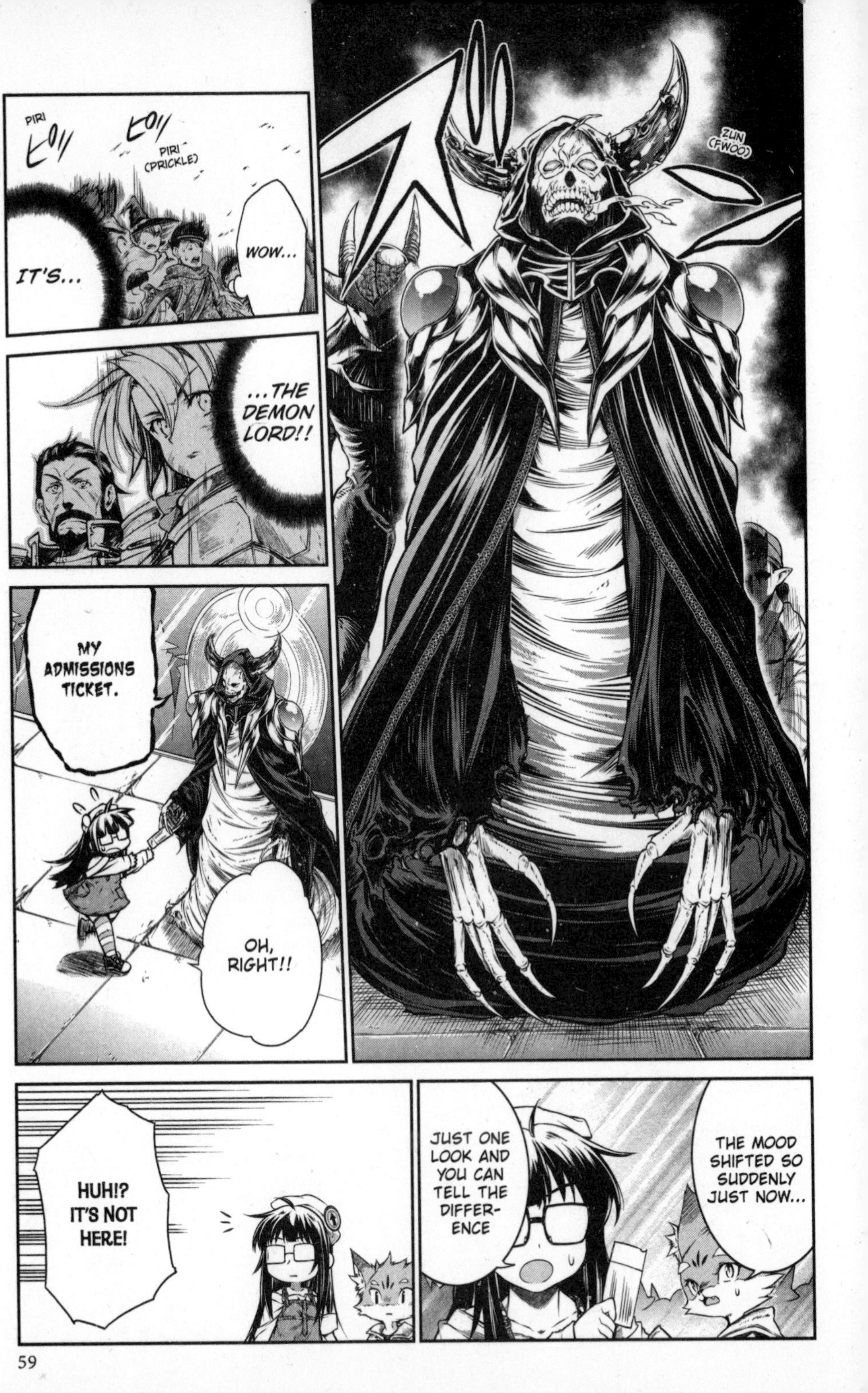
ZUN (FWOO)
PIRI (PRICKLE)
ピリ
PIRI
ピリ
WOW...
IT'S...
...THE DEMON LORD!!
MY ADMISSIONS TICKET.
OH, RIGHT!!
THE MOOD SHIFTED SO SUDDENLY JUST NOW...
JUST ONE LOOK AND YOU CAN TELL THE DIFFER-ENCE
HUH!? IT'S NOT HERE!

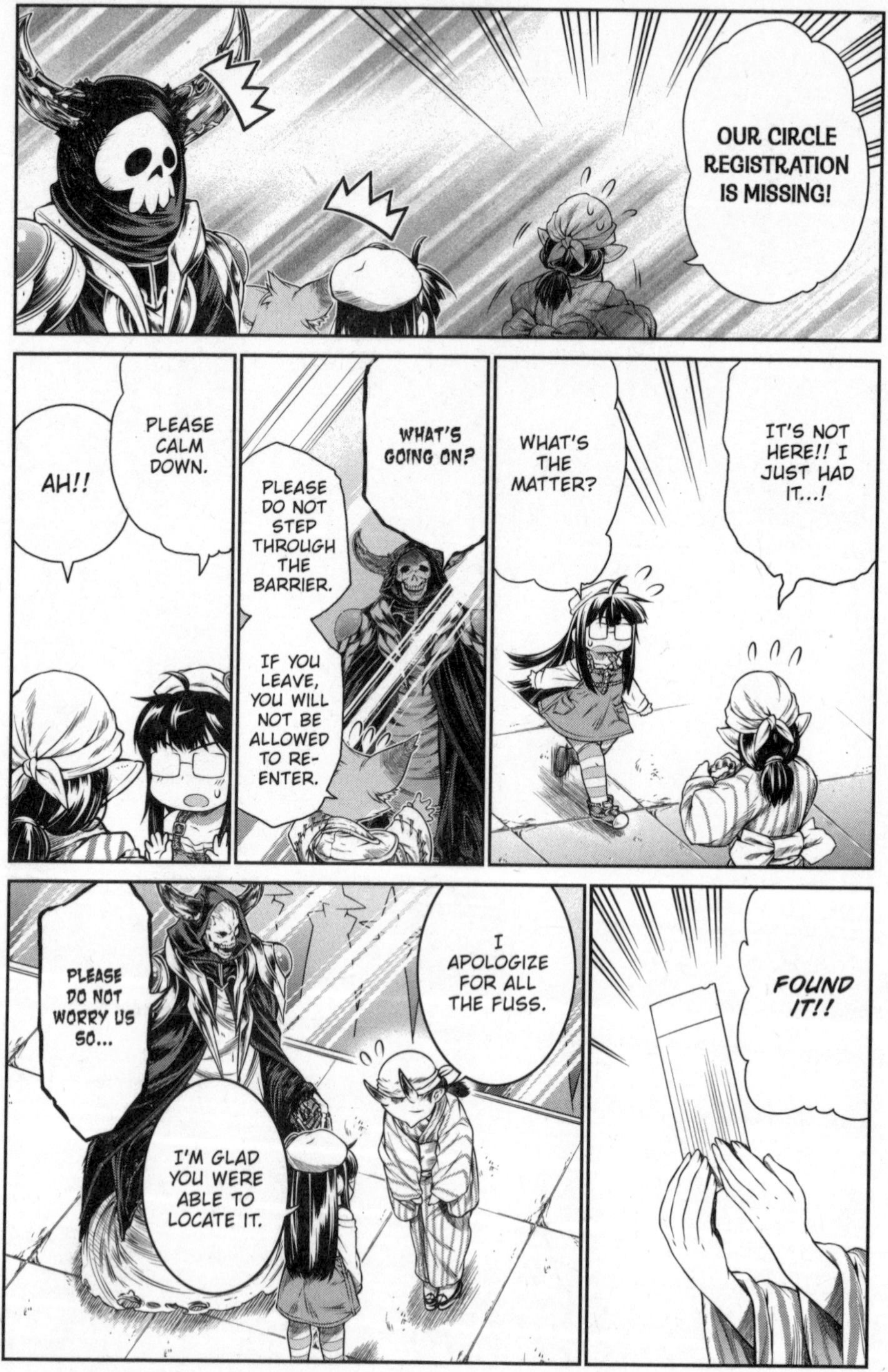
OUR CIRCLE REGISTRATION IS MISSING!
IT'S NOT HERE!! I JUST HAD IT...!
WHAT'S THE MATTER?
WHAT'S GOING ON?
PLEASE DO NOT STEP THROUGH THE BARRIER.
IF YOU LEAVE, YOU WILL NOT BE ALLOWED TO RE-ENTER.
PLEASE CALM DOWN.
AH!!
FOUND IT!!
I APOLOGIZE FOR ALL THE FUSS.
PLEASE DO NOT WORRY US SO...
I'M GLAD YOU WERE ABLE TO LOCATE IT.

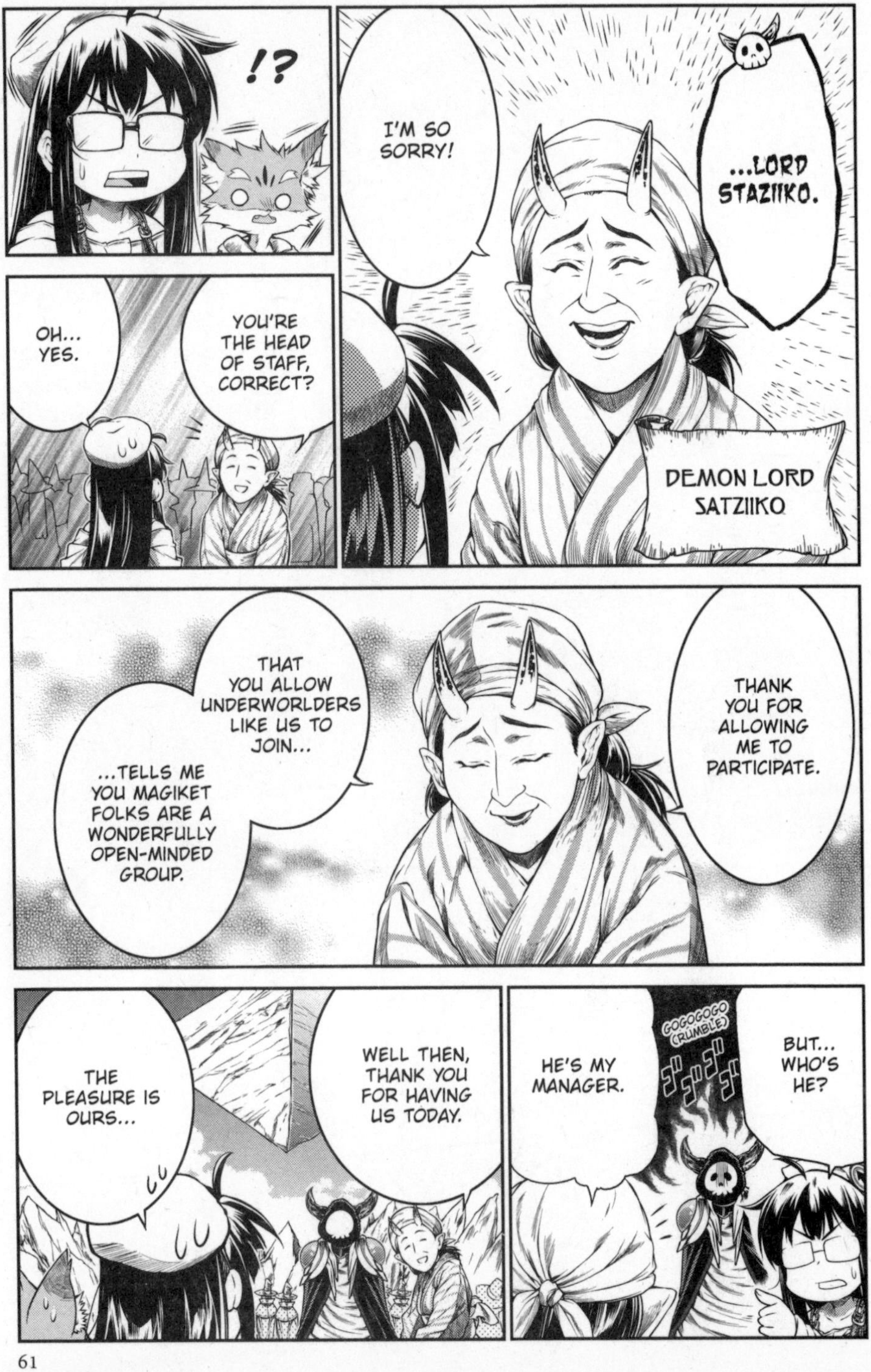
...LORD STAZIIKO.
I'M SO SORRY!
DEMON LORD SATZIIKO
!?
YOU'RE THE HEAD OF STAFF, CORRECT?
OH... YES.
THANK YOU FOR ALLOWING ME TO PARTICIPATE.
THAT YOU ALLOW UNDERWORLDERS LIKE US TO JOIN...
...TELLS ME YOU MAGIKET FOLKS ARE A WONDERFULLY OPEN-MINDED GROUP.
BUT... WHO'S HE?
GOGOGOGO (RUMBLE)
HE'S MY MANAGER.
WELL THEN, THANK YOU FOR HAVING US TODAY.
THE PLEASURE IS OURS...

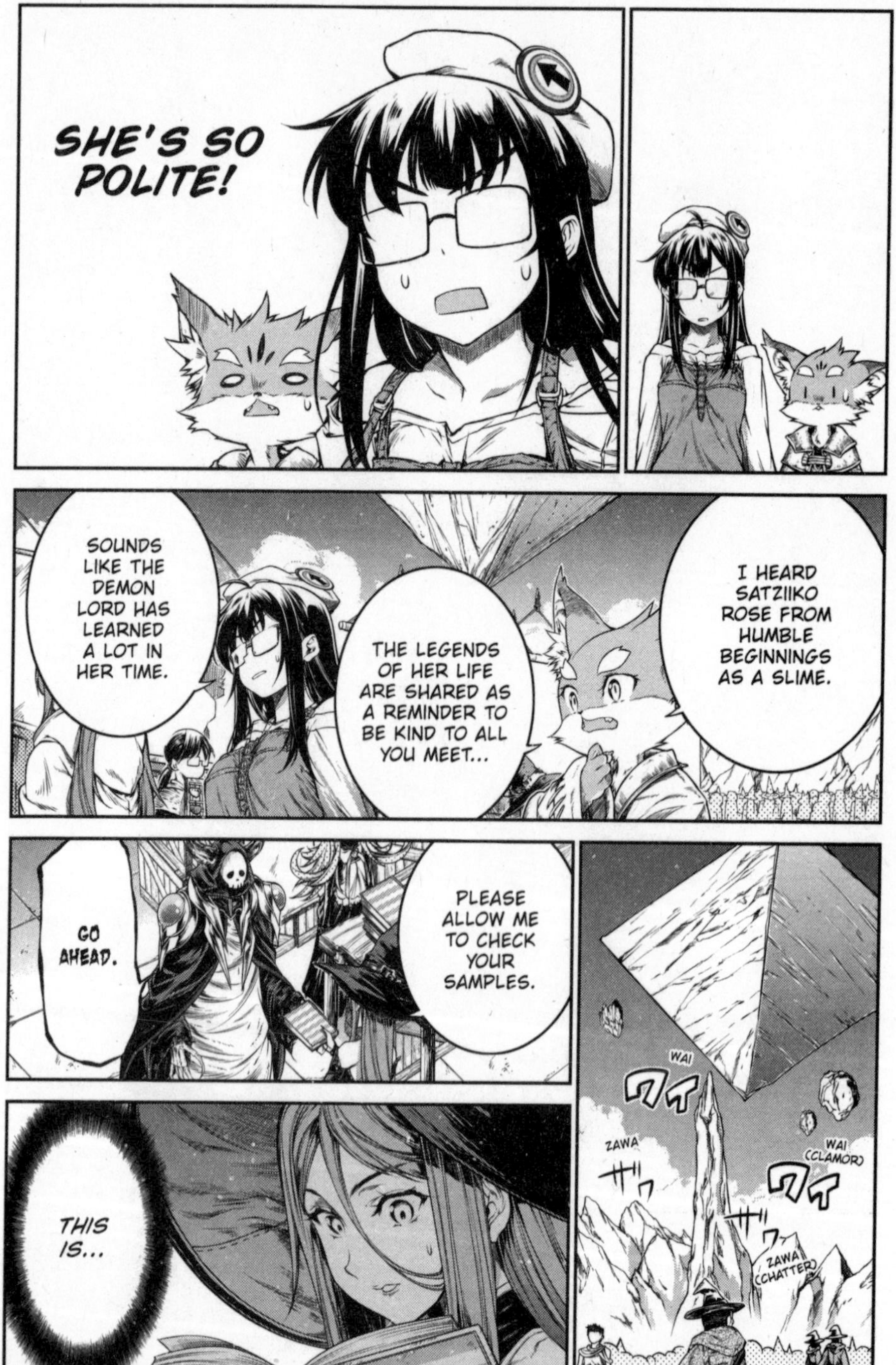
SHE'S SO POLITE!
I HEARD SATZIIKO ROSE FROM HUMBLE BEGINNINGS AS A SLIME.
THE LEGENDS OF HER LIFE ARE SHARED AS A REMINDER TO BE KIND TO ALL YOU MEET...
SOUNDS LIKE THE DEMON LORD HAS LEARNED A LOT IN HER TIME.
WAI
ワイ
ZAWA
ザワ
WAI (CLAMOR)
ワイ
ザワ
ZAWA (CHATTER)
PLEASE ALLOW ME TO CHECK YOUR SAMPLES.
GO AHEAD.
THIS IS...

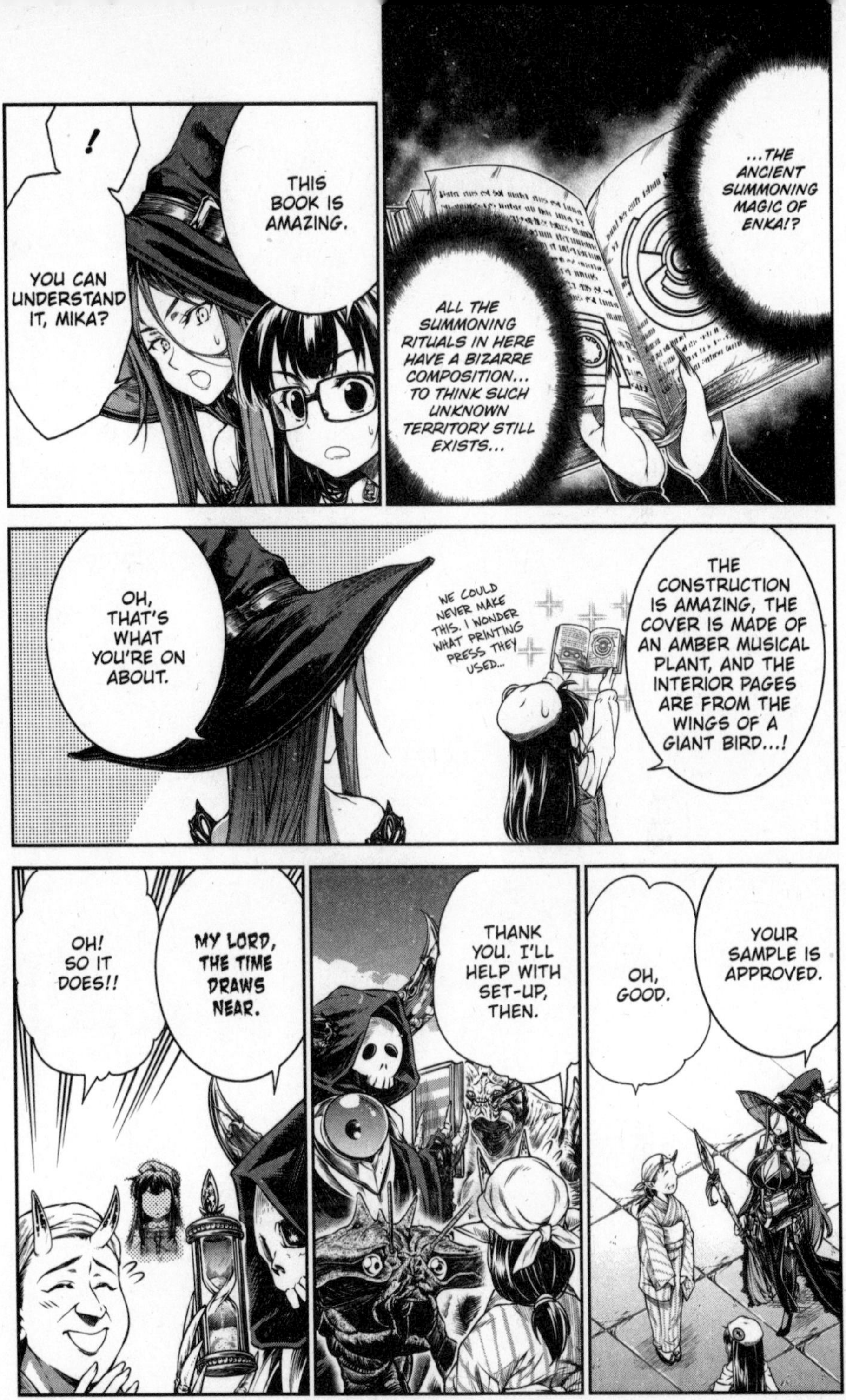
...THE ANCIENT SUMMONING MAGIC OF ENKA!?
ALL THE SUMMONING RITUALS IN HERE HAVE A BIZARRE COMPOSITION... TO THINK SUCH UNKNOWN TERRITORY STILL EXISTS...
THIS BOOK IS AMAZING.
!
YOU CAN UNDERSTAND IT, MIKA?
THE CONSTRUCTION IS AMAZING, THE COVER IS MADE OF AN AMBER MUSICAL PLANT, AND THE INTERIOR PAGES ARE FROM THE WINGS OF A GIANT BIRD...!
WE COULD NEVER MAKE THIS. I WONDER WHAT PRINTING PRESS THEY USED...
OH, THAT'S WHAT YOU'RE ON ABOUT.
YOUR SAMPLE IS APPROVED.
OH, GOOD.
THANK YOU. I'LL HELP WITH SET-UP, THEN.
MY LORD, THE TIME DRAWS NEAR.
OH! SO IT DOES!!

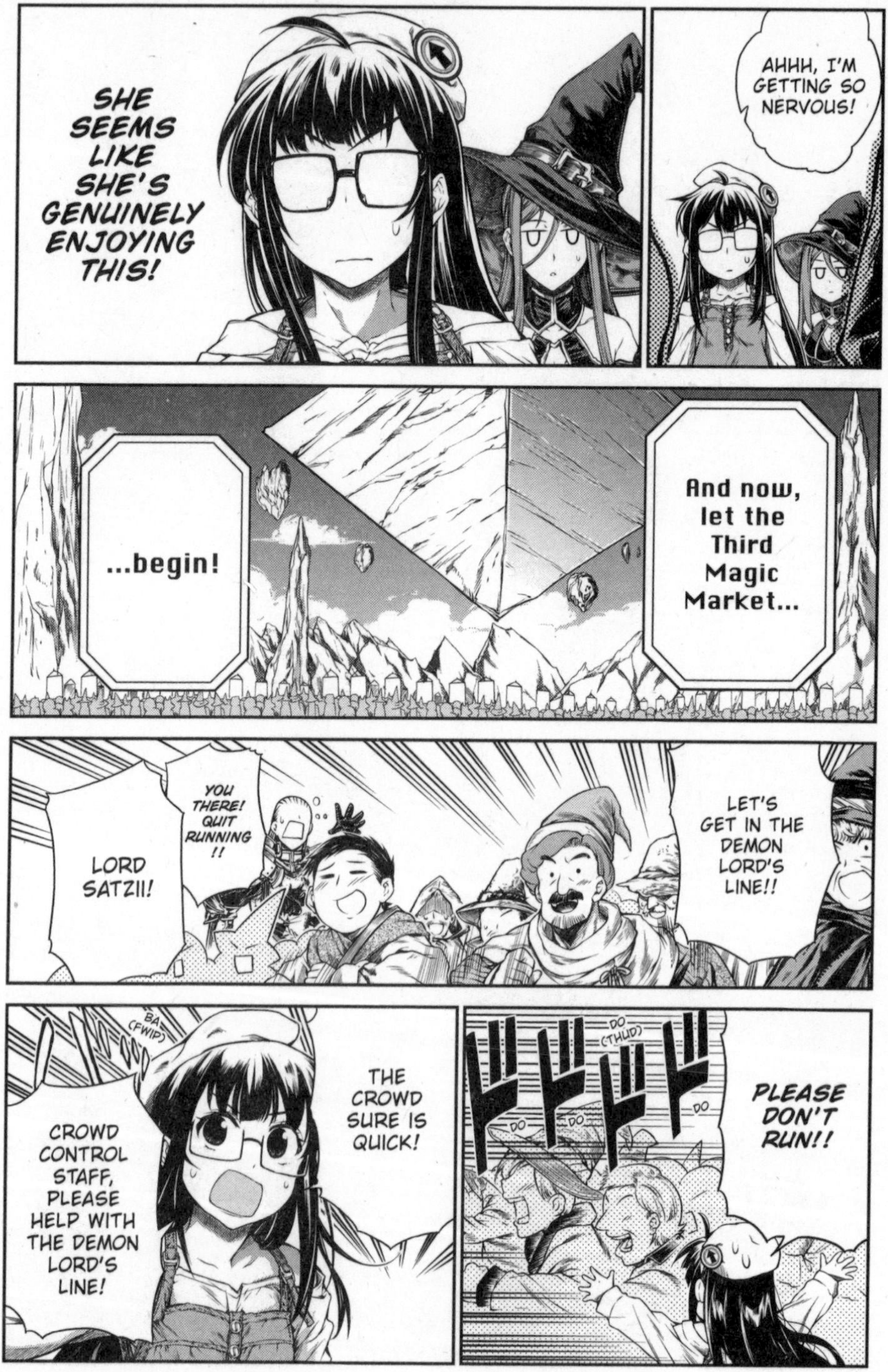
AHHH, I'M GETTING SO NERVOUS!
SHE SEEMS LIKE SHE'S GENUINELY ENJOYING THIS!
And now, let the Third Magic Market...
...begin!
LET'S GET IN THE DEMON LORD'S LINE!!
YOU THERE! QUIT RUNNING!!
LORD SATZII!
ドドドド
DO (THUD)
DO
DO
DO
PLEASE DON'T RUN!!
BA (FWIP)
THE CROWD SURE IS QUICK!
CROWD CONTROL STAFF, PLEASE HELP WITH THE DEMON LORD'S LINE!

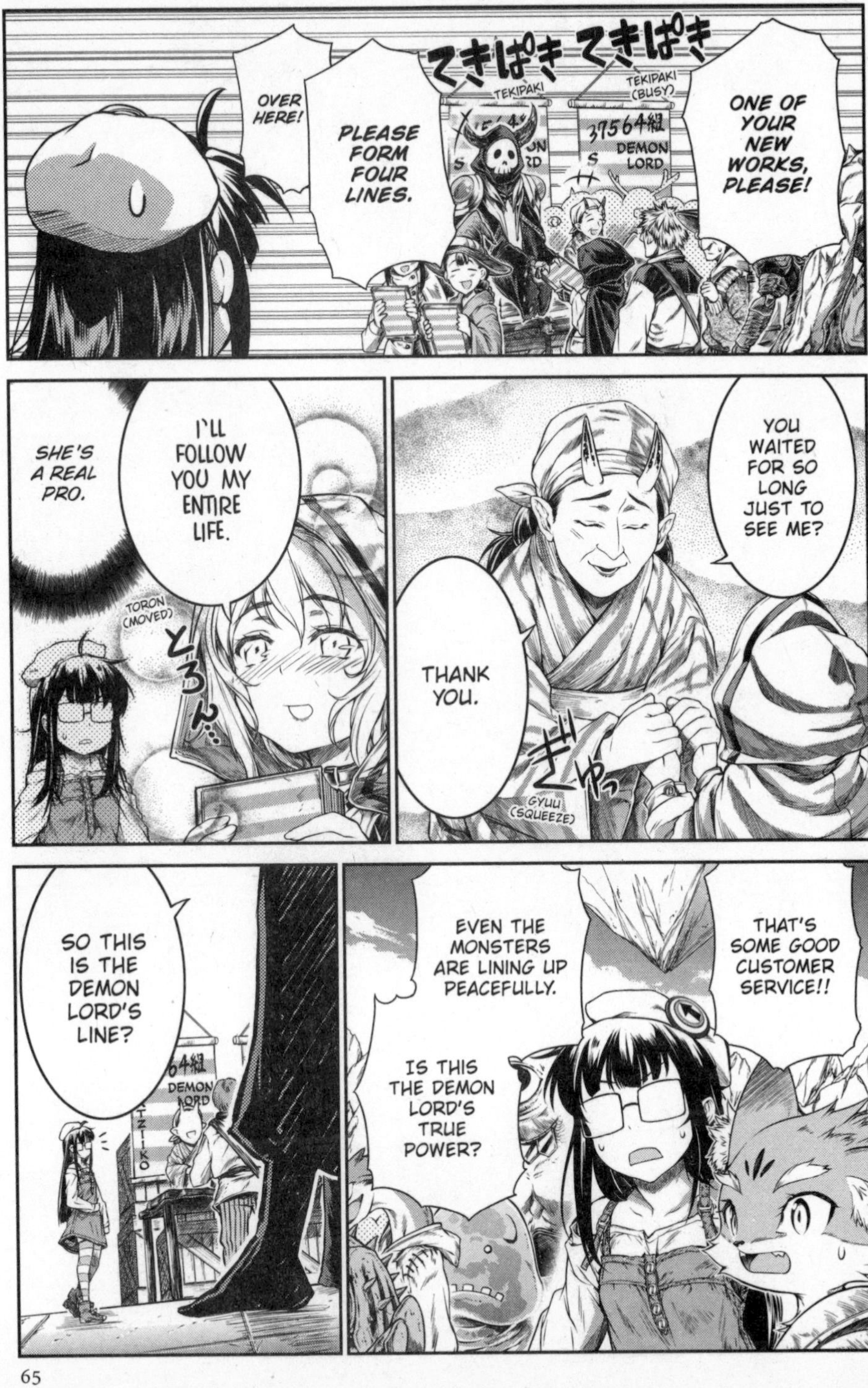
ONE OF YOUR NEW WORKS, PLEASE!
てきぱき てきぱき
TEKIPAKI (BUSY)
TEKIPAKI
37564組
DEMON LORD
PLEASE FORM FOUR LINES.
OVER HERE!
YOU WAITED FOR SO LONG JUST TO SEE ME?
THANK YOU.
ぎゅっ
GYUU (SQUEEZE)
I'LL FOLLOW YOU MY ENTIRE LIFE.
SHE'S A REAL PRO.
とろん…
TORON (MOVED)
THAT'S SOME GOOD CUSTOMER SERVICE!!
EVEN THE MONSTERS ARE LINING UP PEACEFULLY.
IS THIS THE DEMON LORD'S TRUE POWER?
SO THIS IS THE DEMON LORD'S LINE?
64組
DEMON LORD

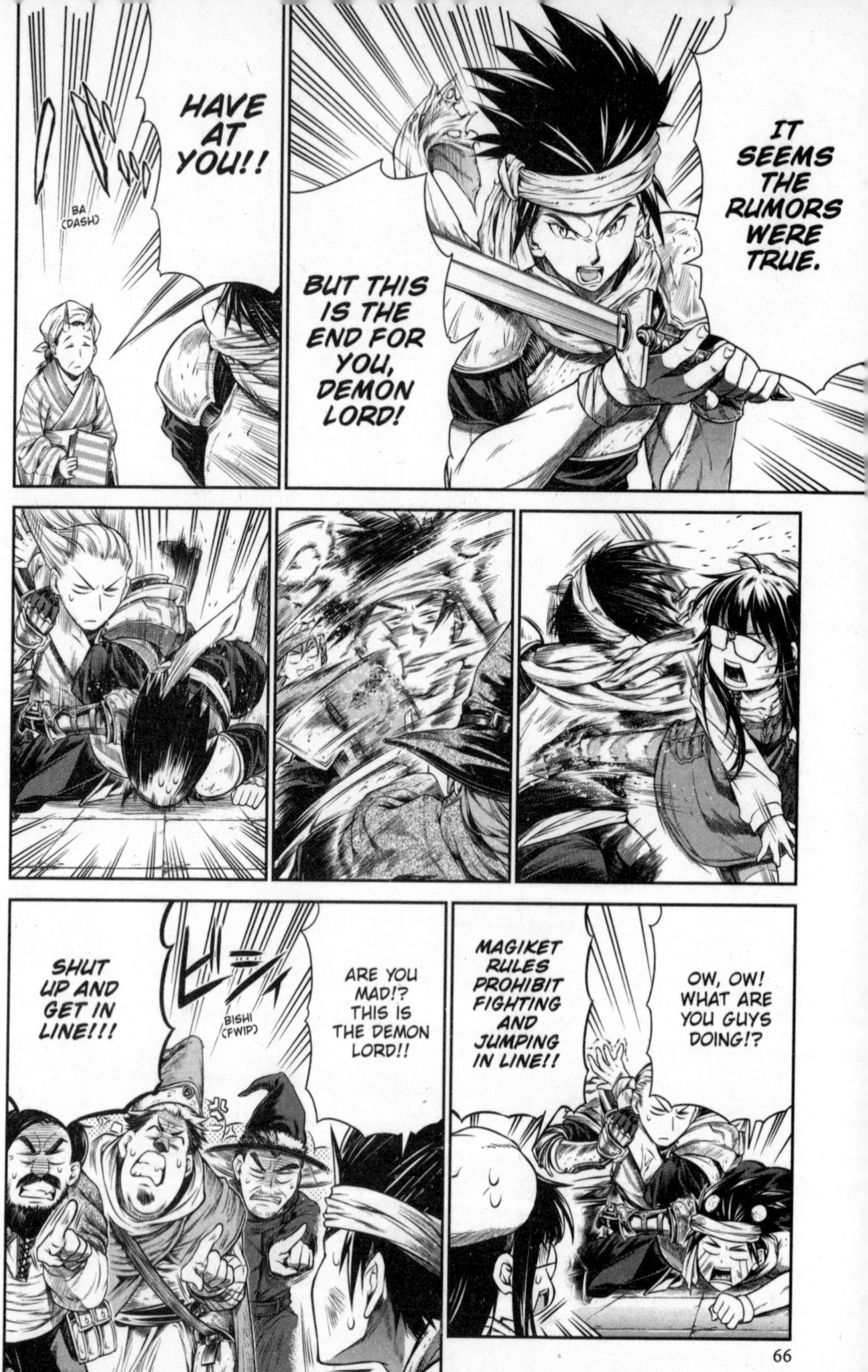
IT SEEMS THE RUMORS WERE TRUE.
BUT THIS IS THE END FOR YOU, DEMON LORD!
HAVE AT YOU!!
BA (DASH)
OW, OW! WHAT ARE YOU GUYS DOING!?
MAGIKET RULES PROHIBIT FIGHTING AND JUMPING IN LINE!!
ARE YOU MAD!? THIS IS THE DEMON LORD!!
BISHI (FWIP)
SHUT UP AND GET IN LINE!!!

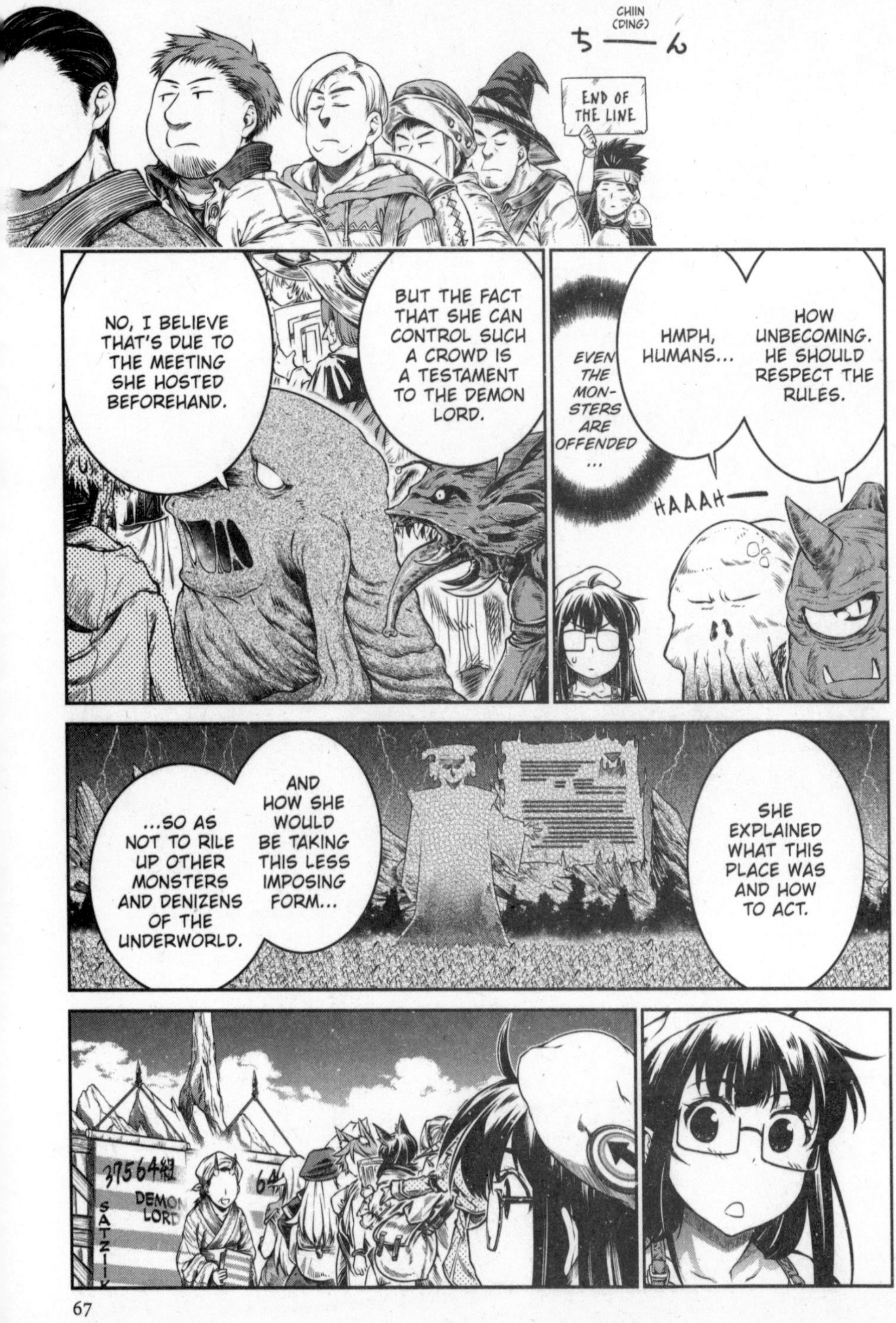
CHIIN (DING)
ちーん
END OF THE LINE
HOW UNBECOMING. HE SHOULD RESPECT THE RULES.
HMPH, HUMANS...
EVEN THE MONSTERS ARE OFFENDED...
HAAAH—
BUT THE FACT THAT SHE CAN CONTROL SUCH A CROWD IS A TESTAMENT TO THE DEMON LORD.
NO, I BELIEVE THAT'S DUE TO THE MEETING SHE HOSTED BEFOREHAND.
SHE EXPLAINED WHAT THIS PLACE WAS AND HOW TO ACT.
AND HOW SHE WOULD BE TAKING THIS LESS IMPOSING FORM...
...SO AS NOT TO RILE UP OTHER MONSTERS AND DENIZENS OF THE UNDERWORLD.
DEMON LORD

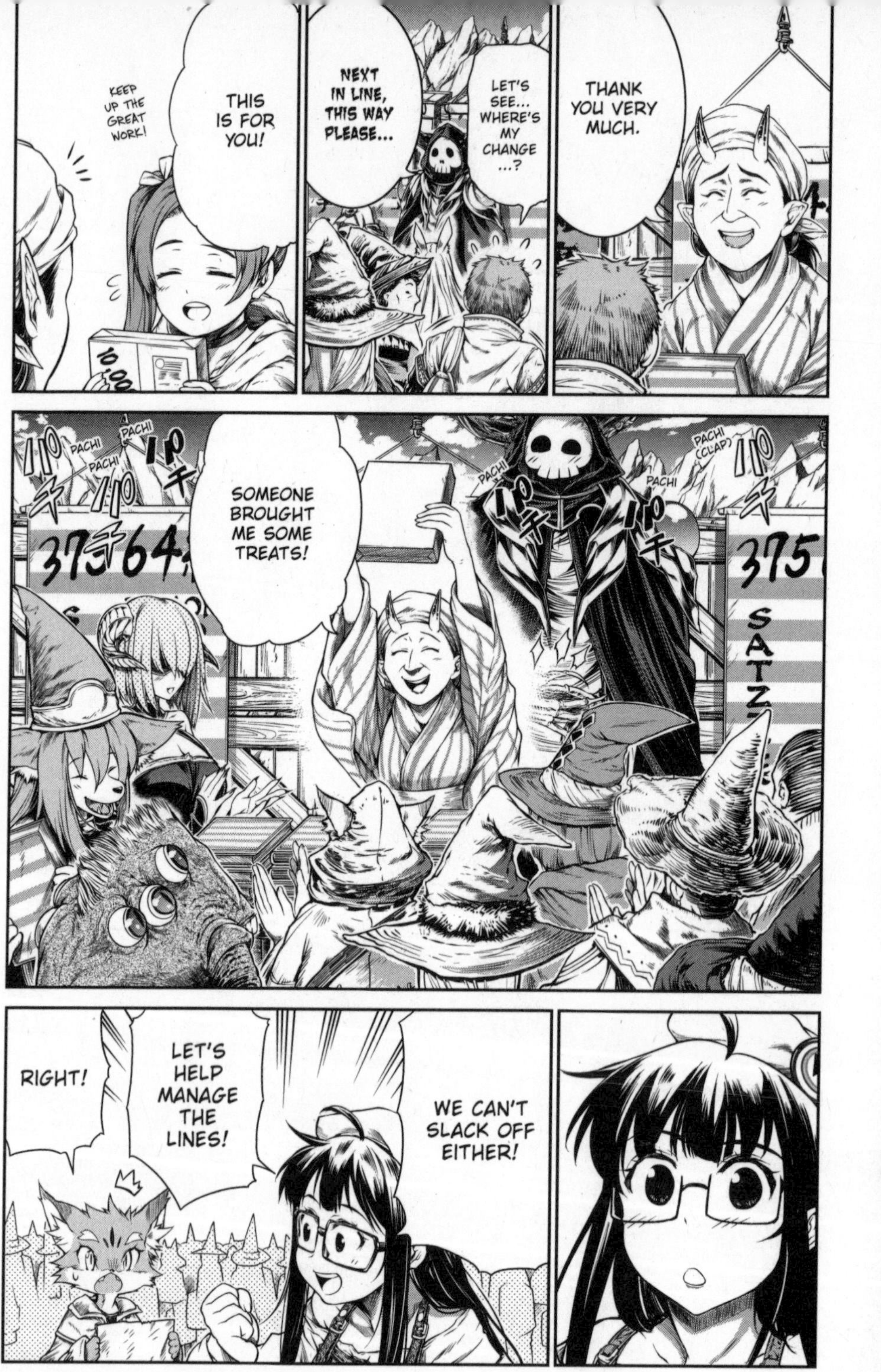
THANK YOU VERY MUCH.
LET'S SEE... WHERE'S MY CHANGE ...?
NEXT IN LINE, THIS WAY PLEASE...
THIS IS FOR YOU!
KEEP UP THE GREAT WORK!
PACHI (CLAP)
PACHI
PACHI
SOMEONE BROUGHT ME SOME TREATS!
PACHI
PACHI
PACHI
SATZ
WE CAN'T SLACK OFF EITHER!
LET'S HELP MANAGE THE LINES!
RIGHT!

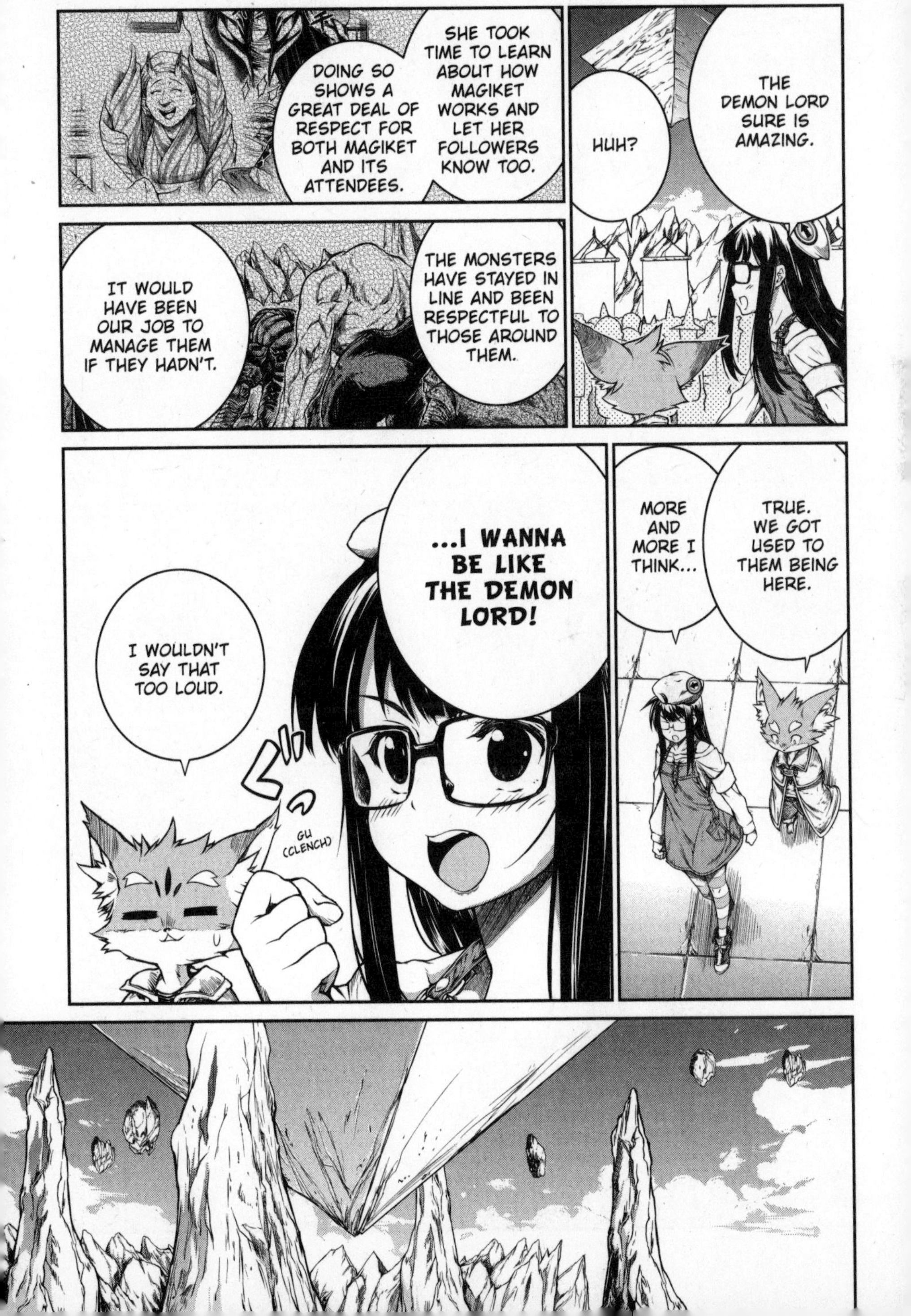
THE DEMON LORD SURE IS AMAZING.
HUH?
SHE TOOK TIME TO LEARN ABOUT HOW MAGIKET WORKS AND LET HER FOLLOWERS KNOW TOO.
DOING SO SHOWS A GREAT DEAL OF RESPECT FOR BOTH MAGIKET AND ITS ATTENDEES.
THE MONSTERS HAVE STAYED IN LINE AND BEEN RESPECTFUL TO THOSE AROUND THEM.
IT WOULD HAVE BEEN OUR JOB TO MANAGE THEM IF THEY HADN'T.
TRUE. WE GOT USED TO THEM BEING HERE.
MORE AND MORE I THINK...
...I WANNA BE LIKE THE DEMON LORD!
GU (CLENCH)
I WOULDN'T SAY THAT TOO LOUD.

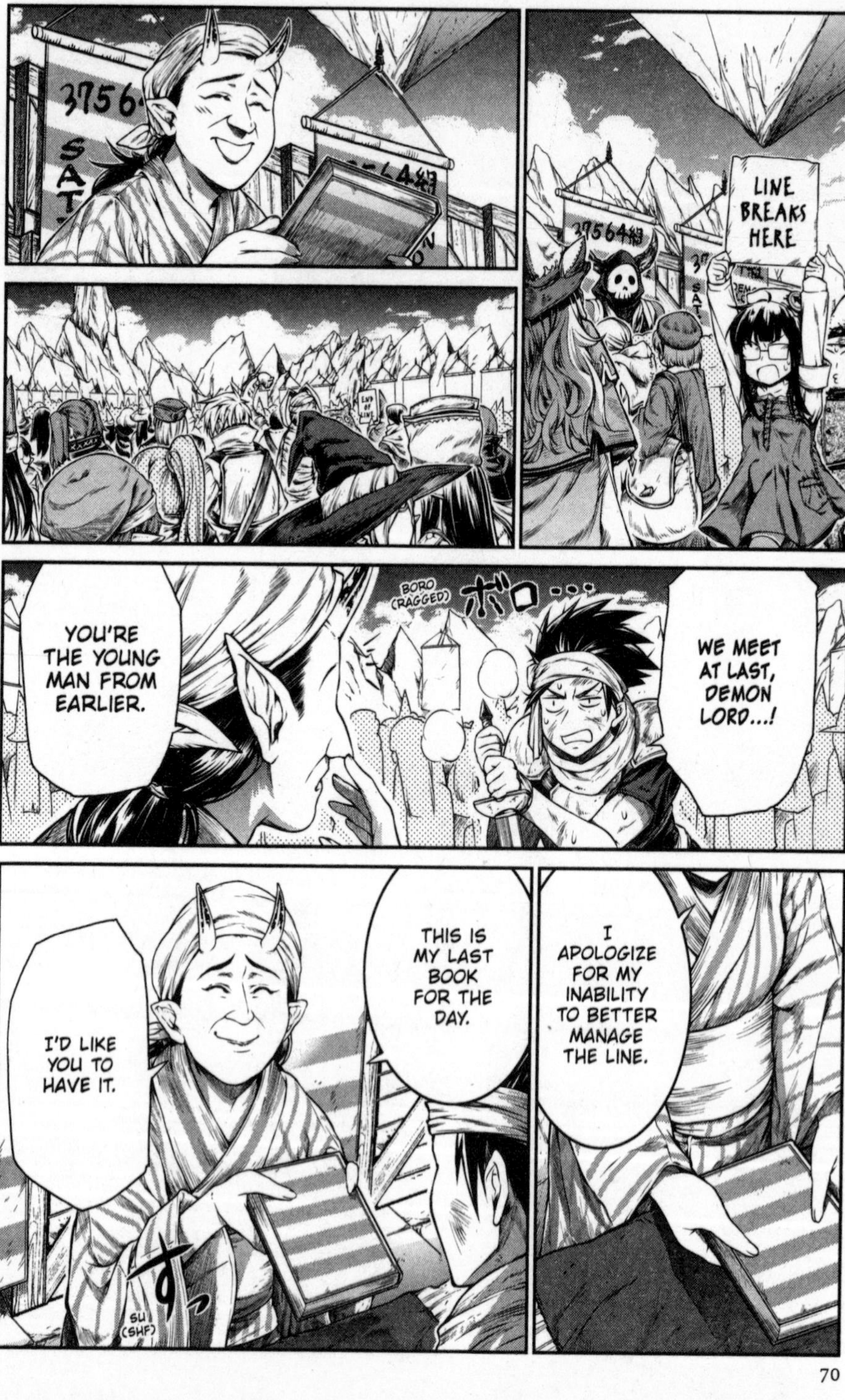
LINE BREAKS HERE
WE MEET AT LAST, DEMON LORD...!
BORO (RAGGED)
ボロ...
YOU'RE THE YOUNG MAN FROM EARLIER.
I APOLOGIZE FOR MY INABILITY TO BETTER MANAGE THE LINE.
THIS IS MY LAST BOOK FOR THE DAY.
I'D LIKE YOU TO HAVE IT.
す
SU (SHF)

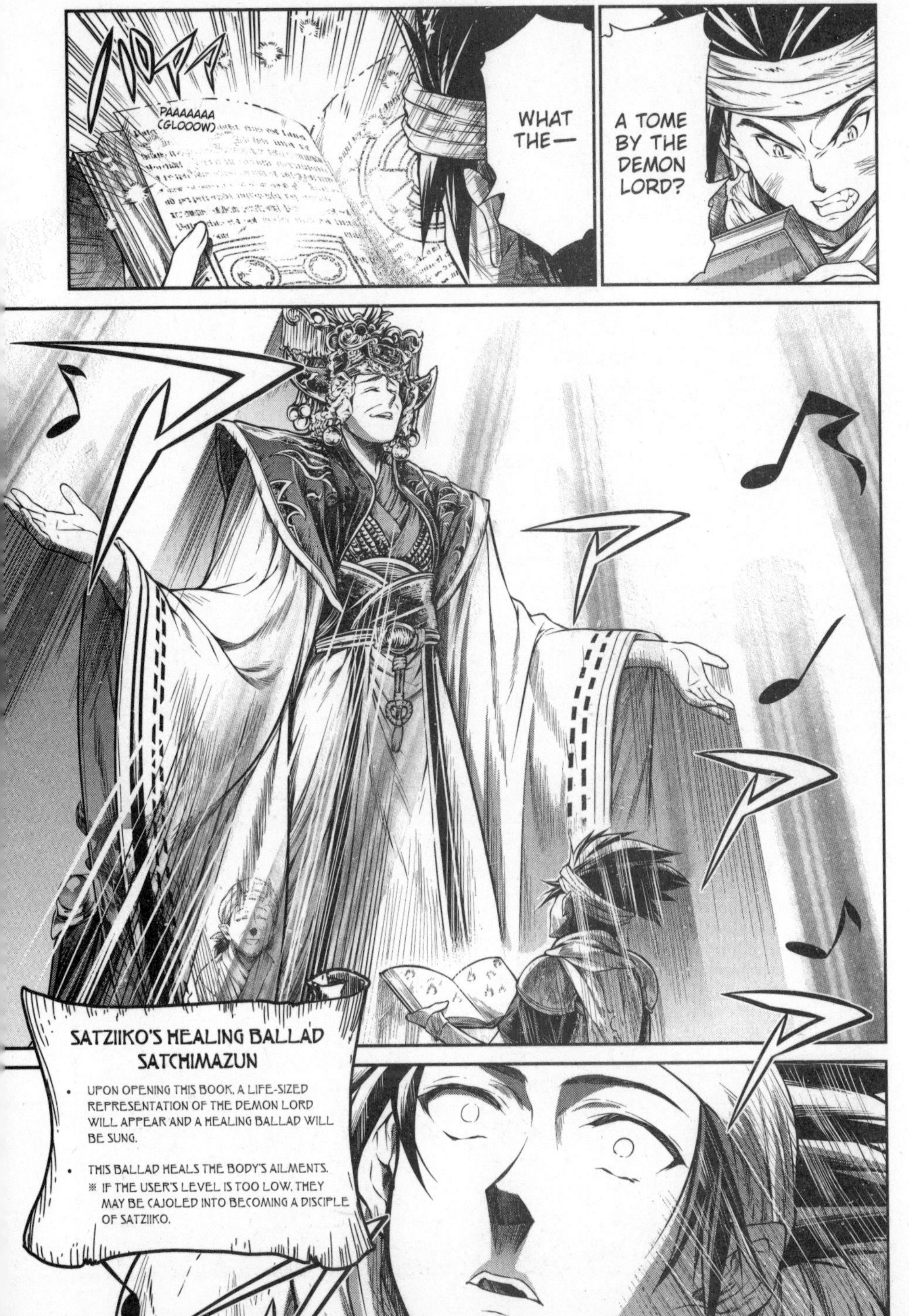
A TOME BY THE DEMON LORD?
WHAT THE—
PAAAAAAA (GLOOOW)
SATZIIKO'S HEALING BALLAD
SATCHIMAZUN
UPON OPENING THIS BOOK, A LIFE-SIZED REPRESENTATION OF THE DEMON LORD WILL APPEAR AND A HEALING BALLAD WILL BE SUNG.
THIS BALLAD HEALS THE BODY'S AILMENTS.
※ IF THE USER'S LEVEL IS TOO LOW, THEY MAY BE CAJOLED INTO BECOMING A DISCIPLE OF SATZIIKO.

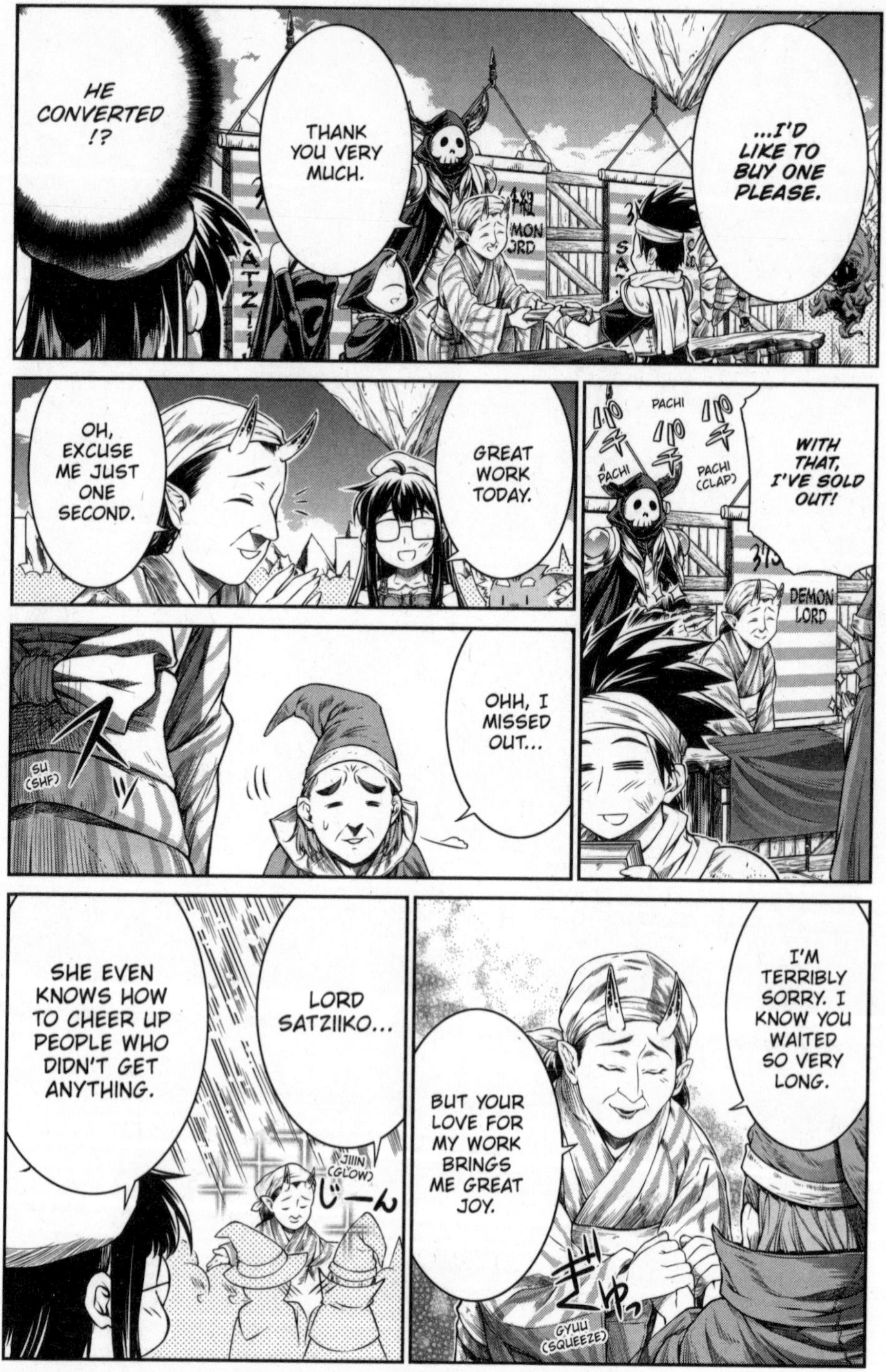
...I'D LIKE TO BUY ONE PLEASE.
THANK YOU VERY MUCH.
HE CONVERTED !?
WITH THAT, I'VE SOLD OUT!
PACHI PACHI PACHI (CLAP)
DEMON LORD
GREAT WORK TODAY.
OH, EXCUSE ME JUST ONE SECOND.
OHH, I MISSED OUT...
SU (SHF)
I'M TERRIBLY SORRY. I KNOW YOU WAITED SO VERY LONG.
BUT YOUR LOVE FOR MY WORK BRINGS ME GREAT JOY.
GYUU (SQUEEZE)
LORD SATZIIKO...
SHE EVEN KNOWS HOW TO CHEER UP PEOPLE WHO DIDN'T GET ANYTHING.
JIIIN (GLOW)

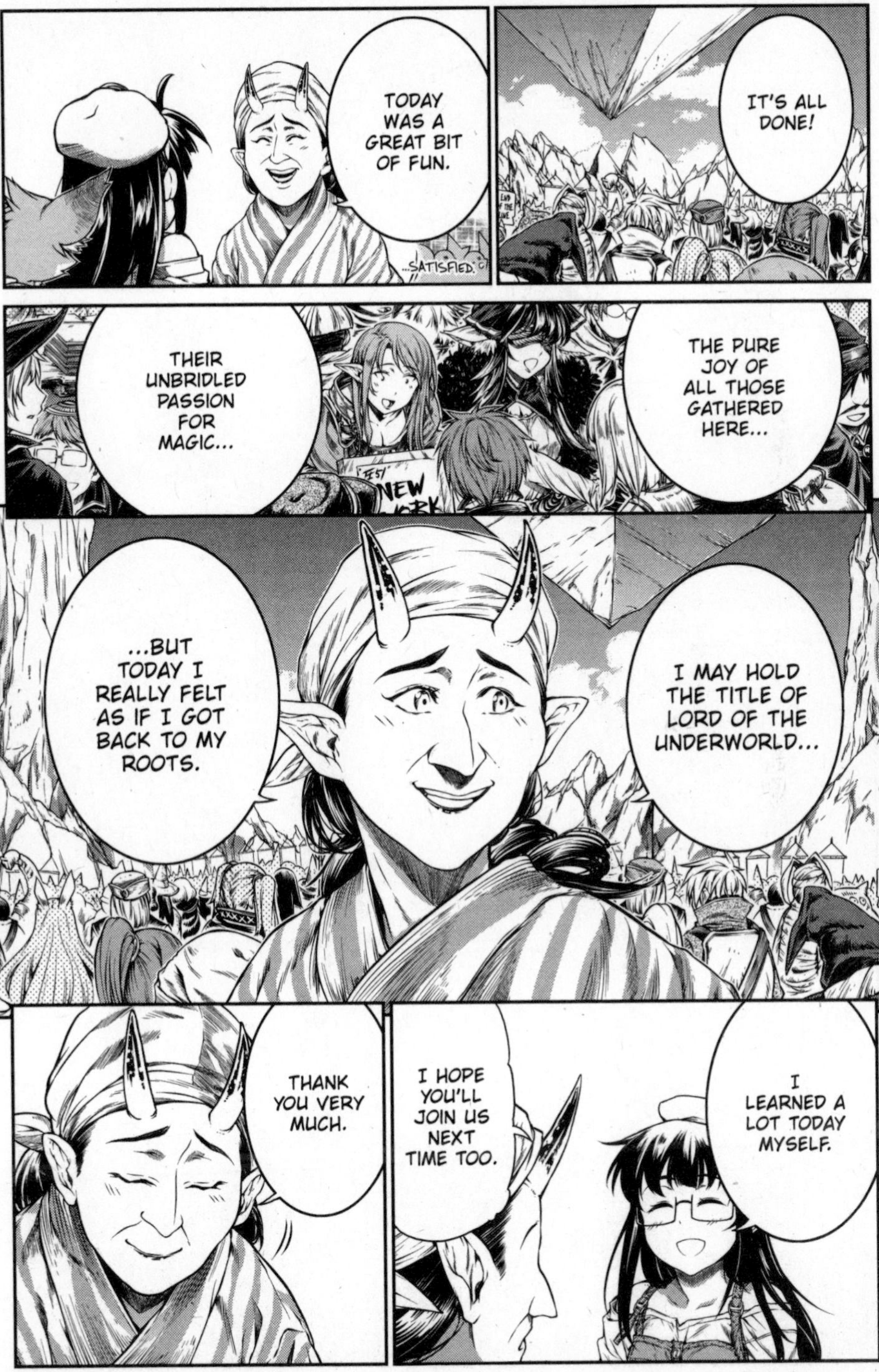
IT'S ALL DONE!
TODAY WAS A GREAT BIT OF FUN.
...SATISFIED.
THE PURE JOY OF ALL THOSE GATHERED HERE...
THEIR UNBRIDLED PASSION FOR MAGIC...
I MAY HOLD THE TITLE OF LORD OF THE UNDERWORLD...
...BUT TODAY I REALLY FELT AS IF I GOT BACK TO MY ROOTS.
I LEARNED A LOT TODAY MYSELF.
I HOPE YOU'LL JOIN US NEXT TIME TOO.
THANK YOU VERY MUCH.

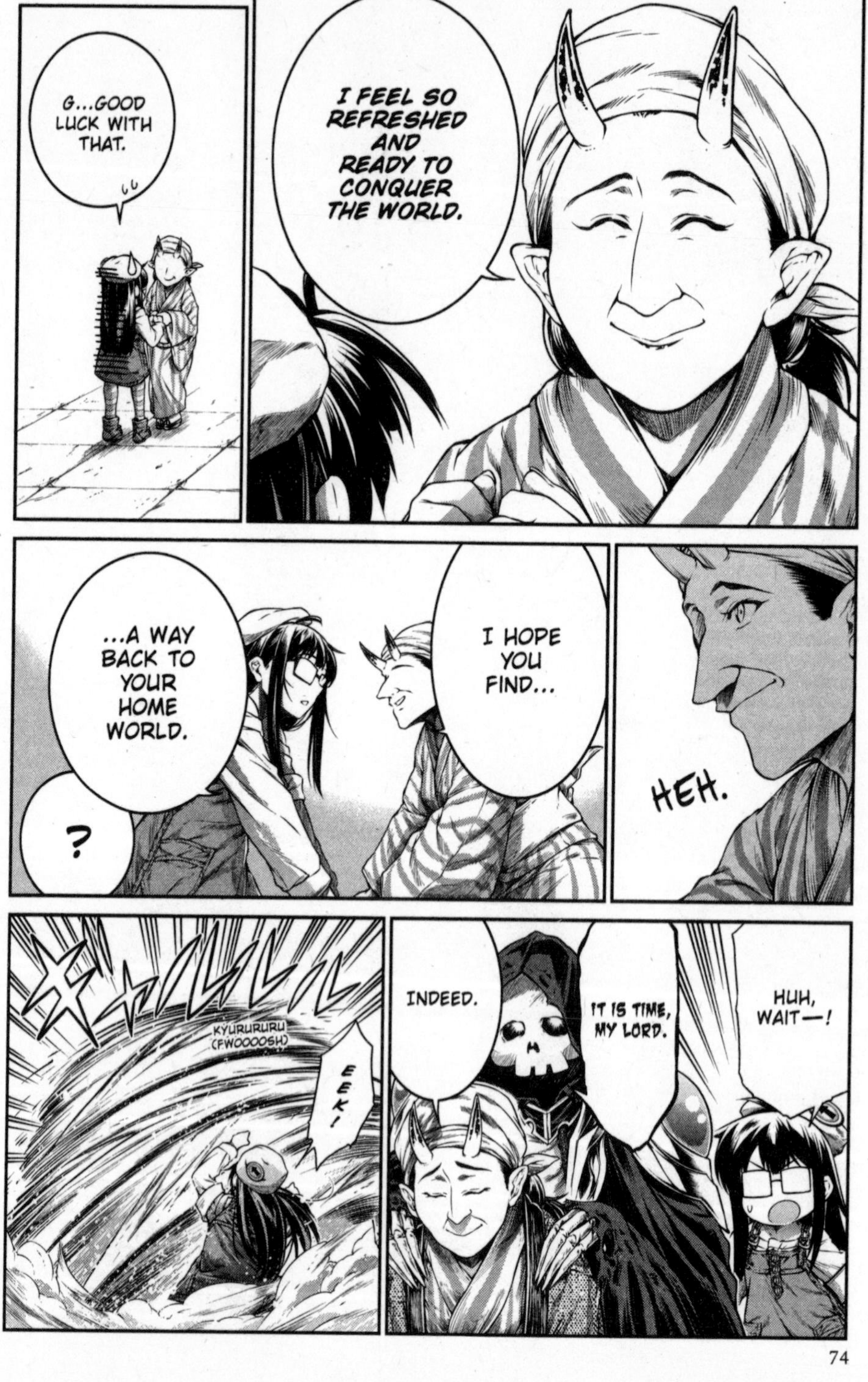
I FEEL SO REFRESHED AND READY TO CONQUER THE WORLD.
G...GOOD LUCK WITH THAT.
HEH.
I HOPE YOU FIND...
...A WAY BACK TO YOUR HOME WORLD.
?
IT IS TIME, MY LORD.
INDEED.
HUH, WAIT—!
KYURURURU (FWOOOOSH)
EEK!

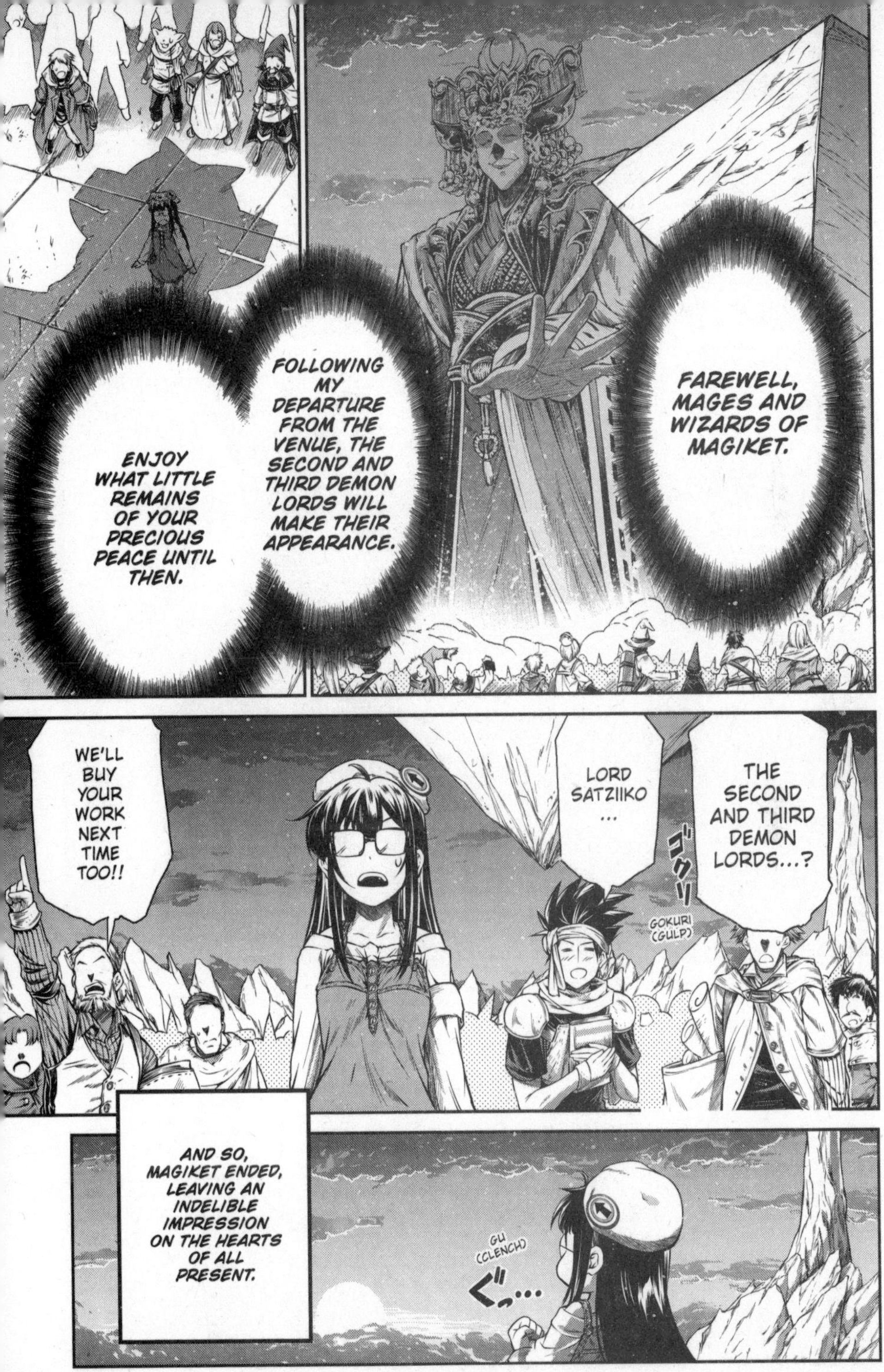
FAREWELL, MAGES AND WIZARDS OF MAGIKET.
FOLLOWING MY DEPARTURE FROM THE VENUE, THE SECOND AND THIRD DEMON LORDS WILL MAKE THEIR APPEARANCE.
ENJOY WHAT LITTLE REMAINS OF YOUR PRECIOUS PEACE UNTIL THEN.
THE SECOND AND THIRD DEMON LORDS...?
ゴクリ
GOKURI (GULP)
LORD SATZIIKO ...
WE'LL BUY YOUR WORK NEXT TIME TOO!!
AND SO, MAGIKET ENDED, LEAVING AN INDELIBLE IMPRESSION ON THE HEARTS OF ALL PRESENT.
GU (CLENCH)
ぐっ…

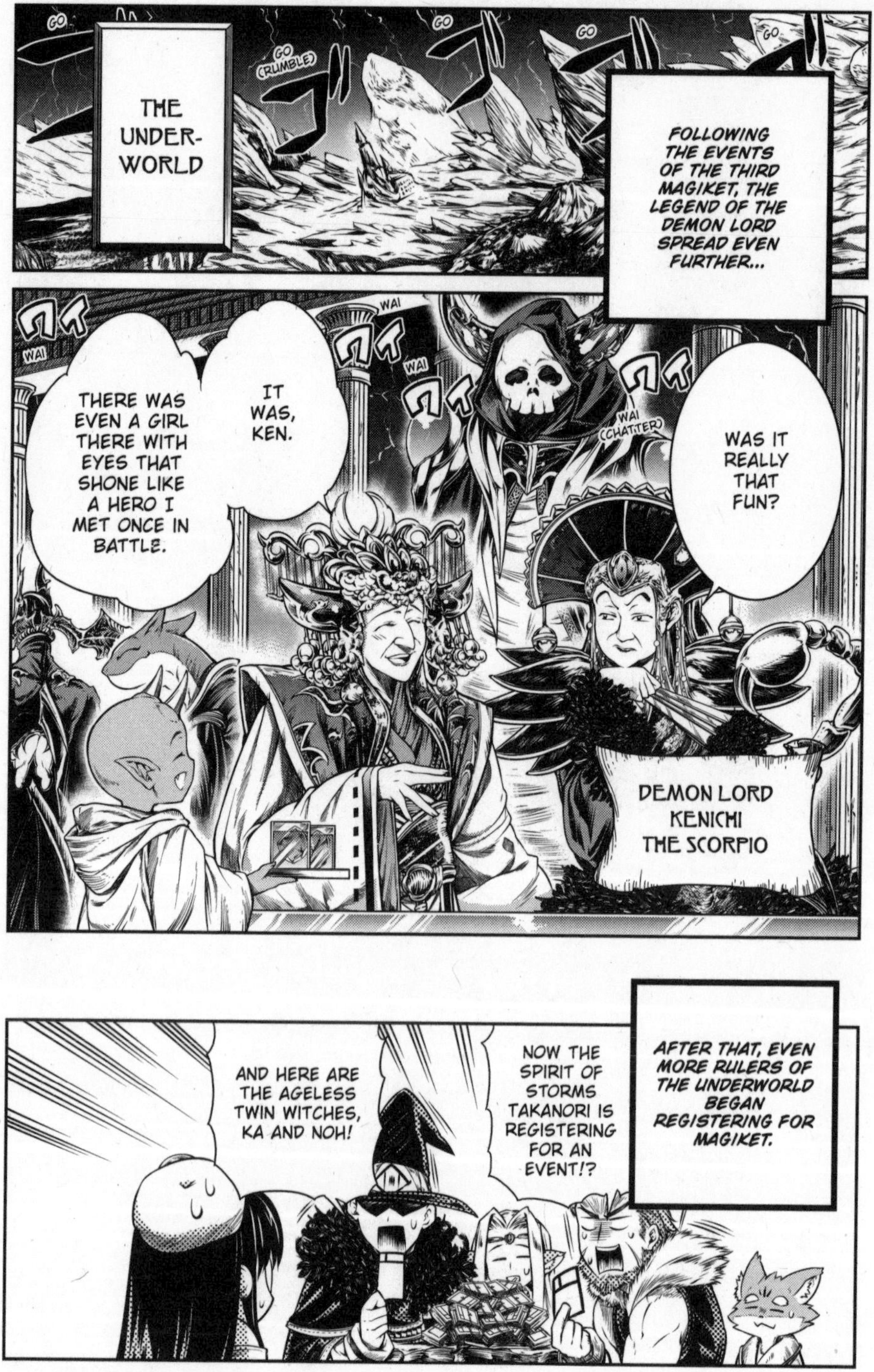
GO
GO
GO (RUMBLE)
GO
GO
THE UNDERWORLD
FOLLOWING THE EVENTS OF THE THIRD MAGIKET, THE LEGEND OF THE DEMON LORD SPREAD EVEN FURTHER...
WAI (CHATTER)
WAI
WAI
WAI
WAS IT REALLY THAT FUN?
IT WAS, KEN.
THERE WAS EVEN A GIRL THERE WITH EYES THAT SHONE LIKE A HERO I MET ONCE IN BATTLE.
DEMON LORD KENICHI THE SCORPIO
AFTER THAT, EVEN MORE RULERS OF THE UNDERWORLD BEGAN REGISTERING FOR MAGIKET.
NOW THE SPIRIT OF STORMS TAKANORI IS REGISTERING FOR AN EVENT!?
AND HERE ARE THE AGELESS TWIN WITCHES, KA AND NOH!

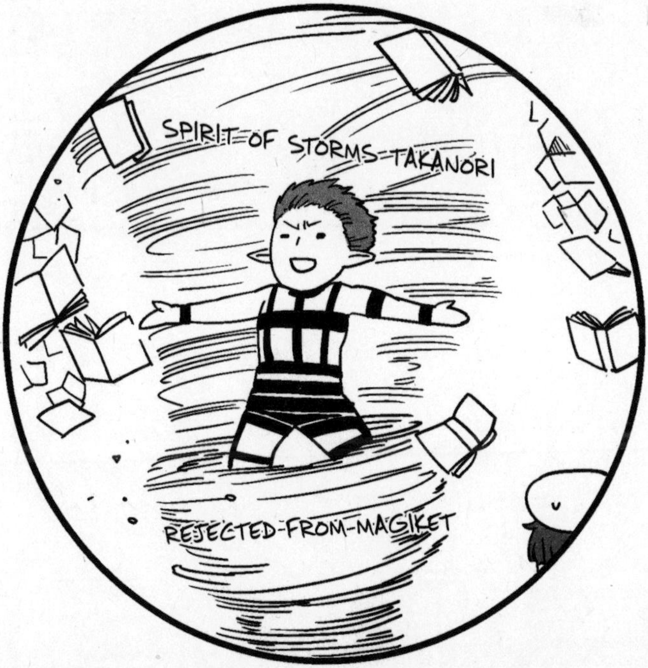
SPIRIT OF STORMS TAKANORI
REJECTED FROM MAGIKET

# A WITCH'S PRINTING OFFICE

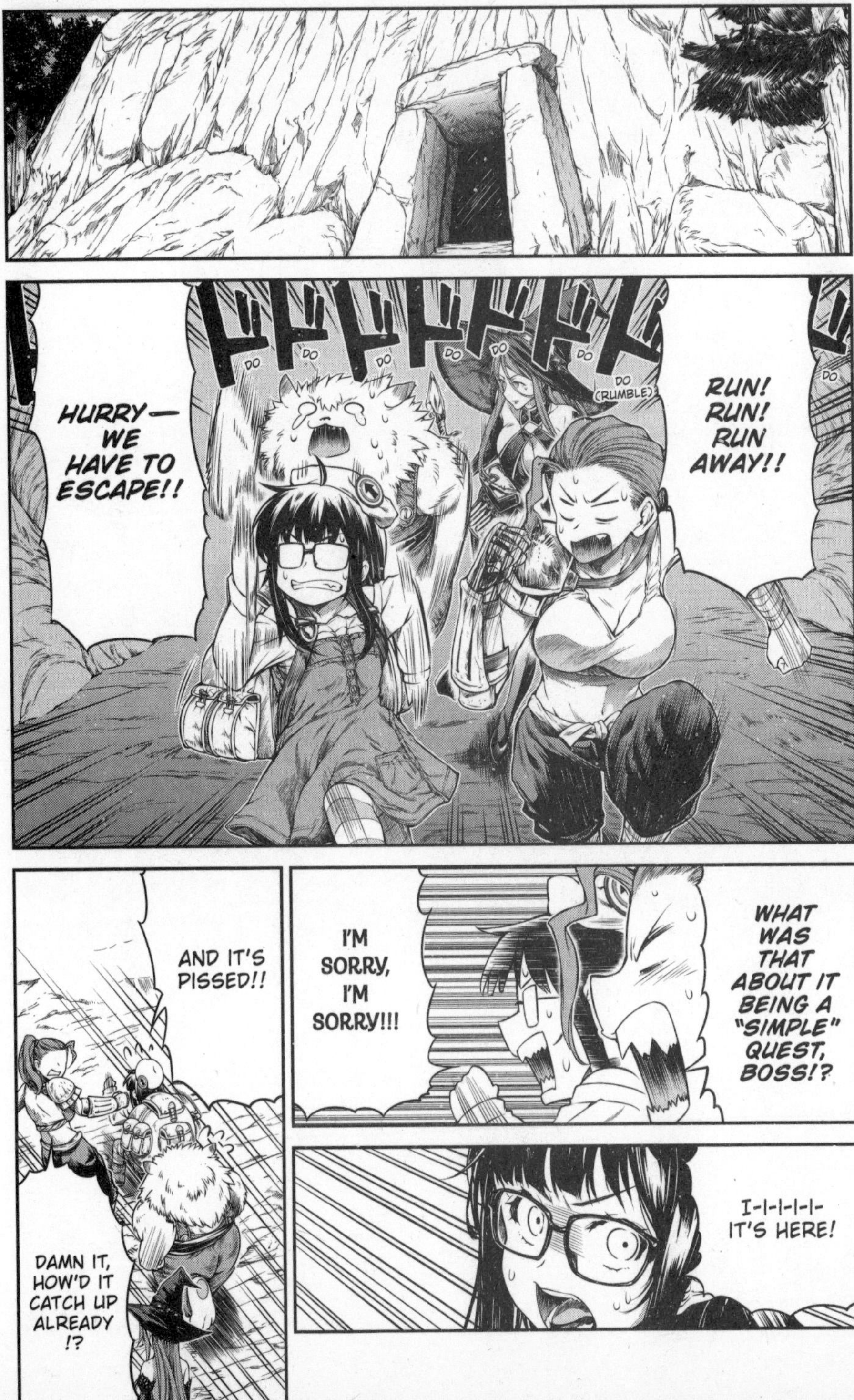
DO DO DO DO DO DO DO (RUMBLE) DO
RUN! RUN! RUN AWAY!!
HURRY— WE HAVE TO ESCAPE!!
WHAT WAS THAT ABOUT IT BEING A "SIMPLE" QUEST, BOSS!?
I'M SORRY, I'M SORRY!!!
I-I-I-I-I- IT'S HERE!
AND IT'S PISSED!!
DAMN IT, HOW'D IT CATCH UP ALREADY !?

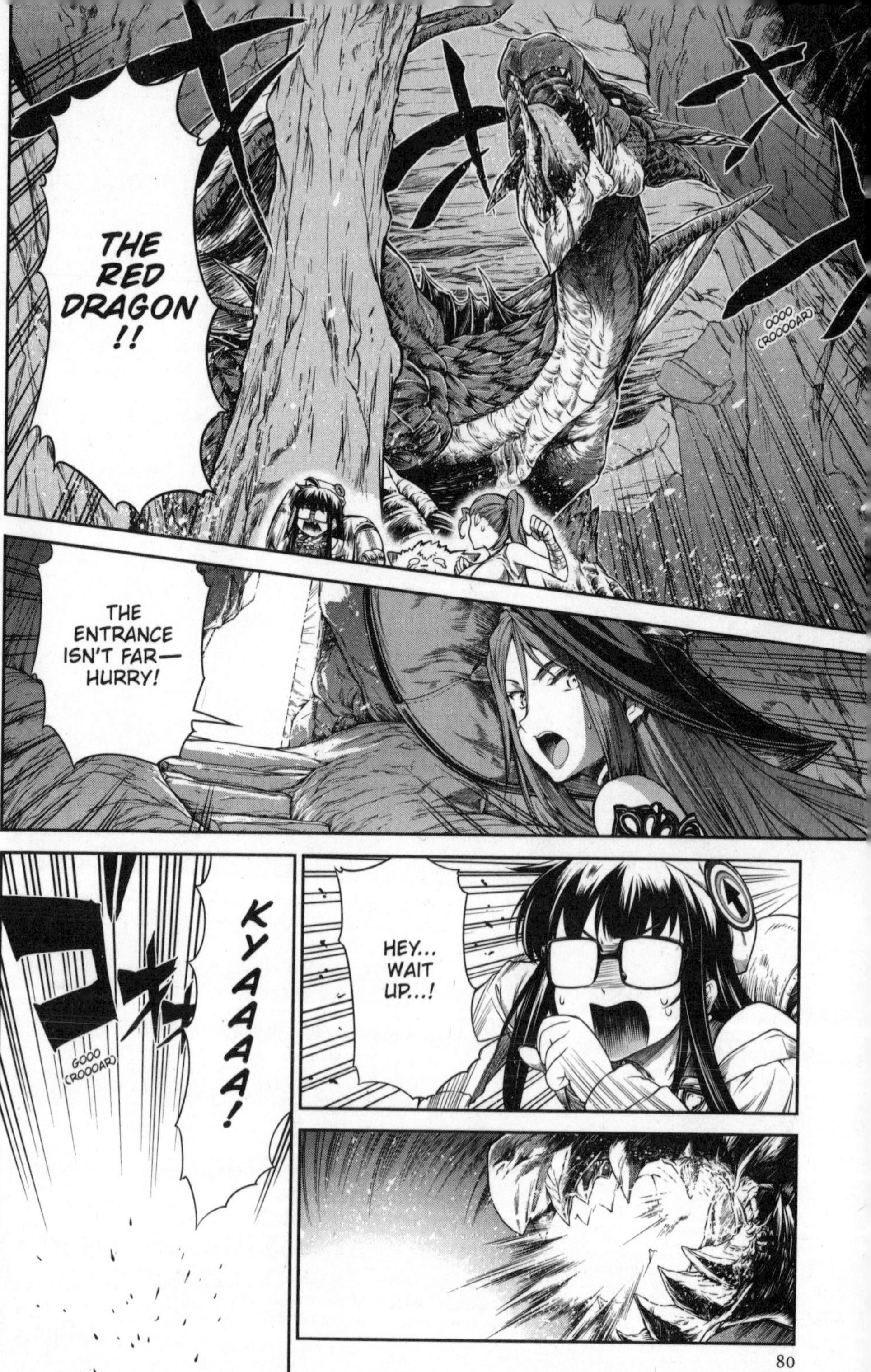

OOOO (ROOOOAR)
THE RED DRAGON!!
THE ENTRANCE ISN'T FAR—HURRY!
HEY... WAIT UP...!
KYAAAAA!
GOOO (ROOOAR)

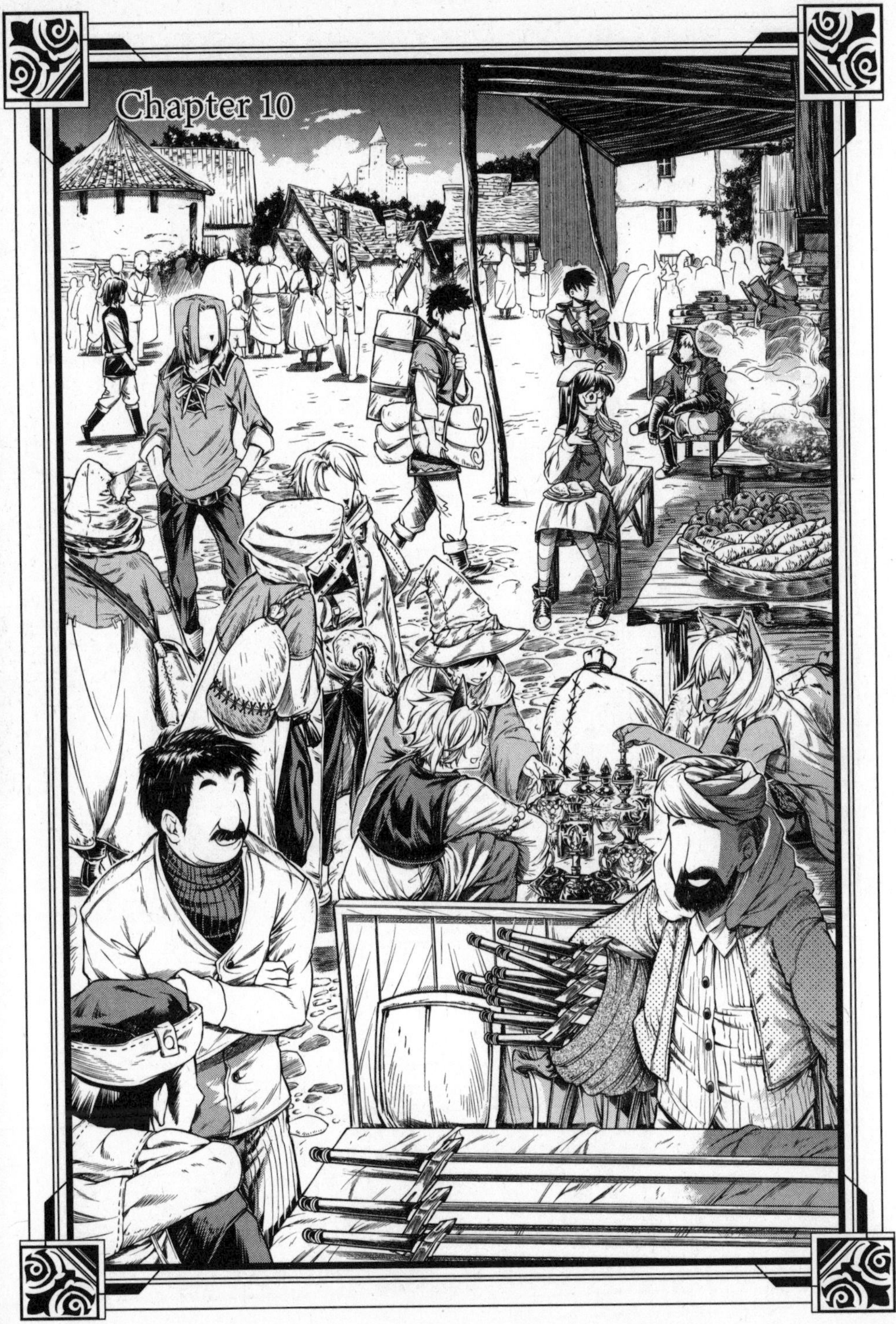
Chapter 10

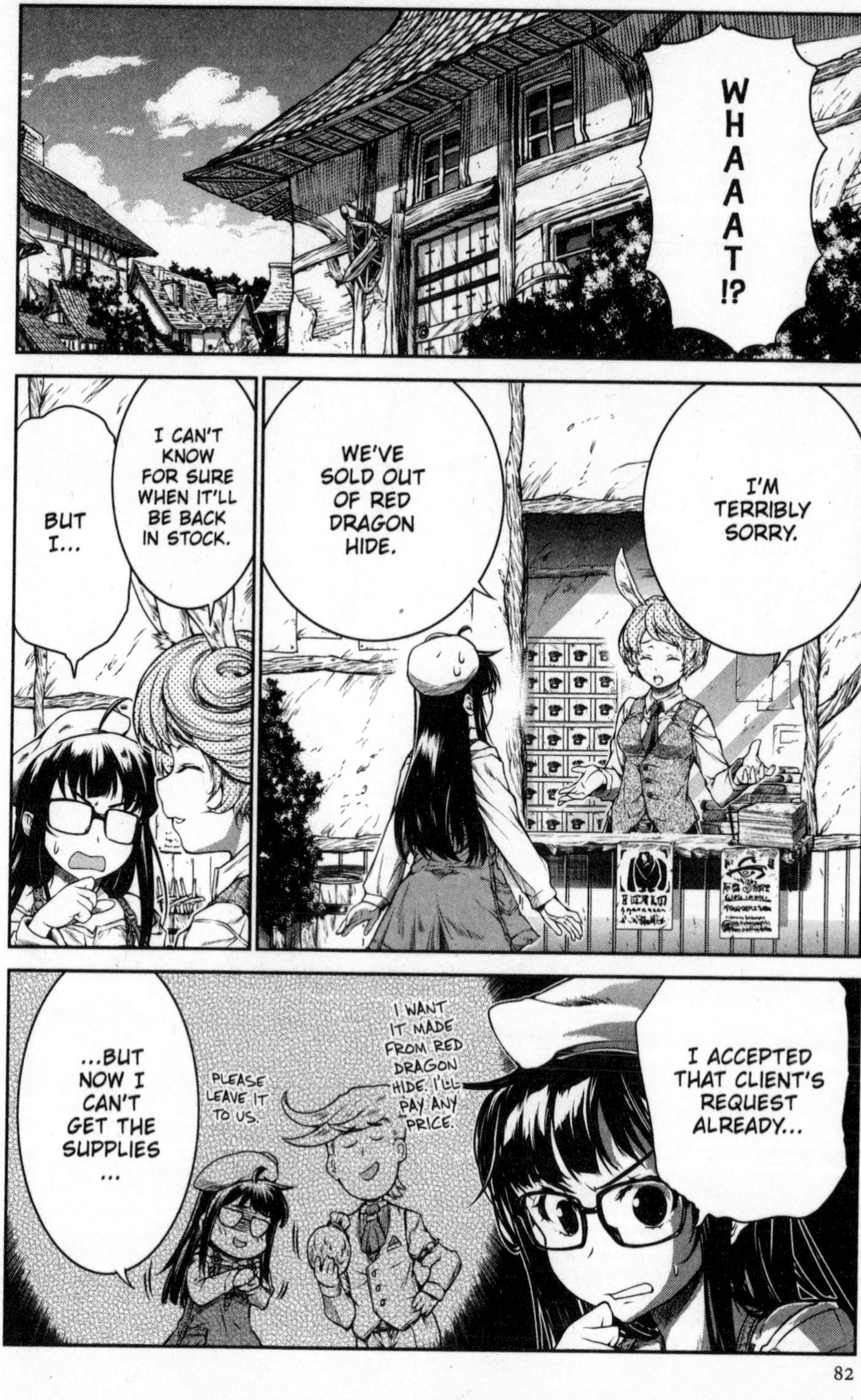
WHAAAT!?
I'M TERRIBLY SORRY.
WE'VE SOLD OUT OF RED DRAGON HIDE.
I CAN'T KNOW FOR SURE WHEN IT'LL BE BACK IN STOCK.
BUT I...
I ACCEPTED THAT CLIENT'S REQUEST ALREADY...
I WANT IT MADE FROM RED DRAGON HIDE. I'LL PAY ANY PRICE.
PLEASE LEAVE IT TO US.
...BUT NOW I CAN'T GET THE SUPPLIES...

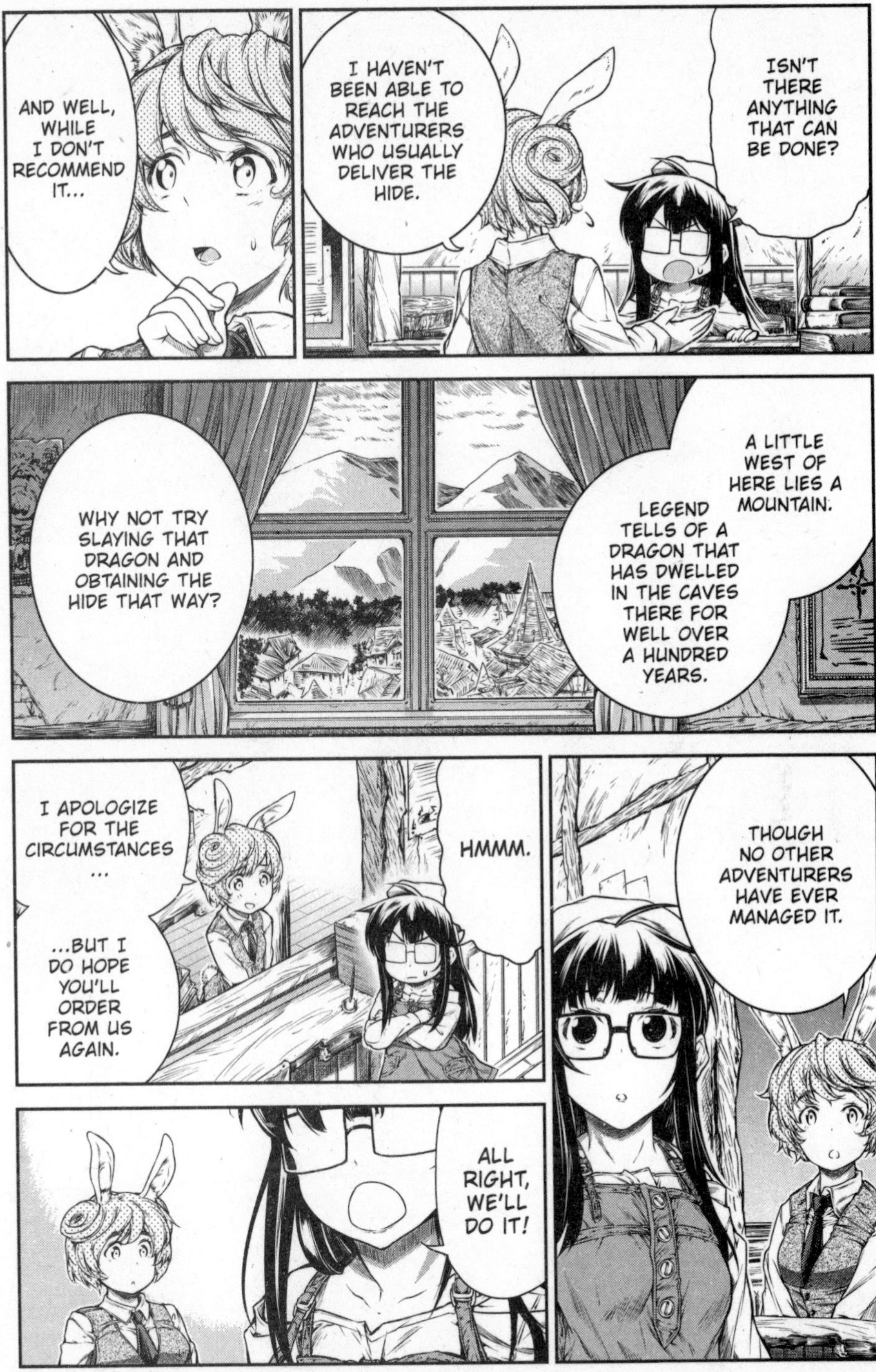
ISN'T THERE ANYTHING THAT CAN BE DONE?
I HAVEN'T BEEN ABLE TO REACH THE ADVENTURERS WHO USUALLY DELIVER THE HIDE.
AND WELL, WHILE I DON'T RECOMMEND IT...
A LITTLE WEST OF HERE LIES A MOUNTAIN.
LEGEND TELLS OF A DRAGON THAT HAS DWELLED IN THE CAVES THERE FOR WELL OVER A HUNDRED YEARS.
WHY NOT TRY SLAYING THAT DRAGON AND OBTAINING THE HIDE THAT WAY?
THOUGH NO OTHER ADVENTURERS HAVE EVER MANAGED IT.
HMMM.
I APOLOGIZE FOR THE CIRCUMSTANCES ...
...BUT I DO HOPE YOU'LL ORDER FROM US AGAIN.
ALL RIGHT, WE'LL DO IT!

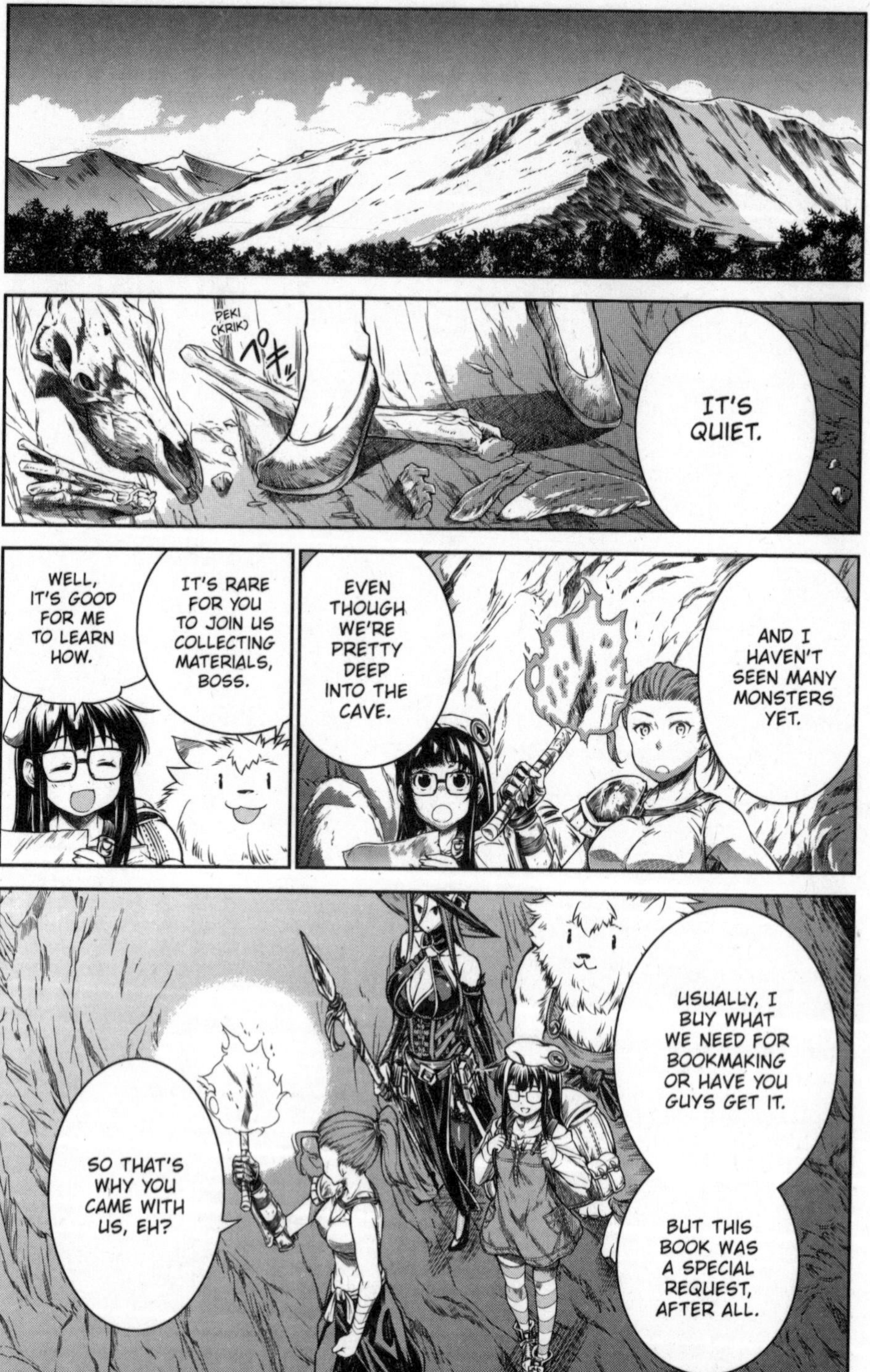
PEKI (KRIK)
IT'S QUIET.
AND I HAVEN'T SEEN MANY MONSTERS YET.
EVEN THOUGH WE'RE PRETTY DEEP INTO THE CAVE.
IT'S RARE FOR YOU TO JOIN US COLLECTING MATERIALS, BOSS.
WELL, IT'S GOOD FOR ME TO LEARN HOW.
USUALLY, I BUY WHAT WE NEED FOR BOOKMAKING OR HAVE YOU GUYS GET IT.
BUT THIS BOOK WAS A SPECIAL REQUEST, AFTER ALL.
SO THAT'S WHY YOU CAME WITH US, EH?

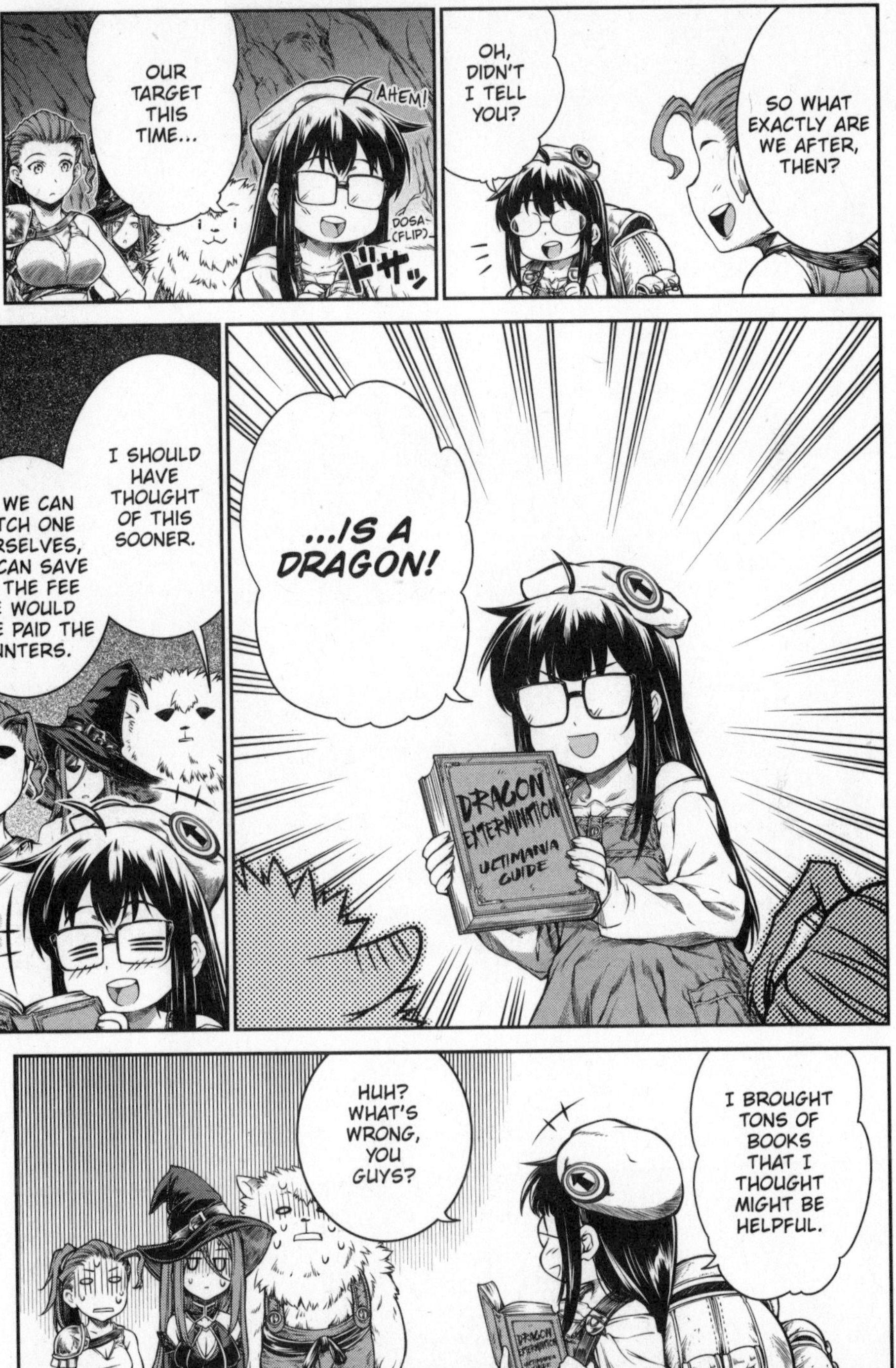
SO WHAT EXACTLY ARE WE AFTER, THEN?
OH, DIDN'T I TELL YOU?
AHEM!
OUR TARGET THIS TIME...
DOSA- (FLIP)
ドサッ
...IS A DRAGON!
DRAGON EXTERMINATION ULTIMANIA GUIDE
I SHOULD HAVE THOUGHT OF THIS SOONER.
IF WE CAN CATCH ONE OURSELVES, WE CAN SAVE ON THE FEE WE WOULD HAVE PAID THE HUNTERS.
I BROUGHT TONS OF BOOKS THAT I THOUGHT MIGHT BE HELPFUL.
HUH? WHAT'S WRONG, YOU GUYS?

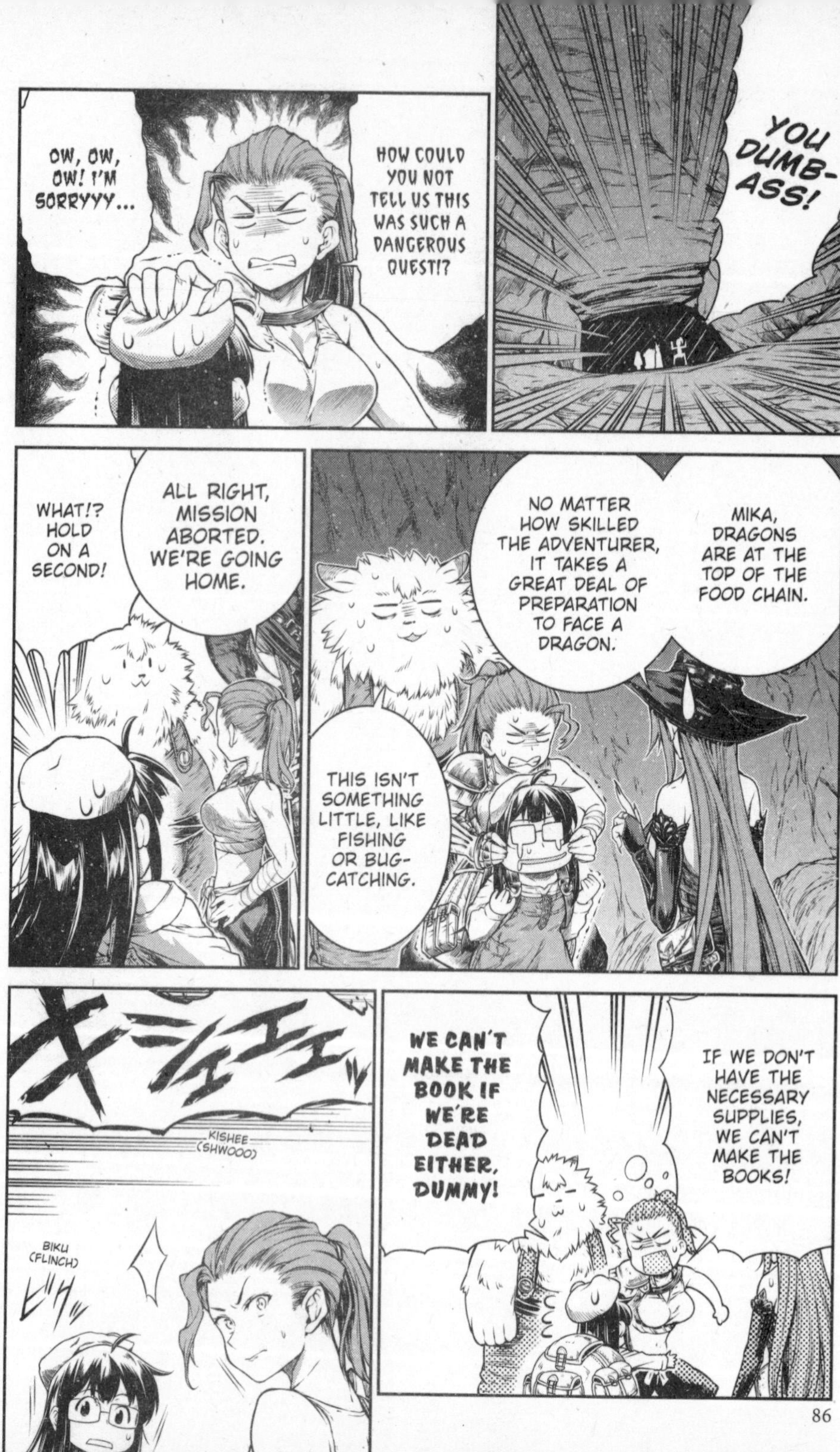
YOU DUMB-ASS!
HOW COULD YOU NOT TELL US THIS WAS SUCH A DANGEROUS QUEST!?
OW, OW, OW! I'M SORRYYY...
MIKA, DRAGONS ARE AT THE TOP OF THE FOOD CHAIN.
NO MATTER HOW SKILLED THE ADVENTURER, IT TAKES A GREAT DEAL OF PREPARATION TO FACE A DRAGON.
THIS ISN'T SOMETHING LITTLE, LIKE FISHING OR BUG-CATCHING.
ALL RIGHT, MISSION ABORTED. WE'RE GOING HOME.
WHAT!? HOLD ON A SECOND!
IF WE DON'T HAVE THE NECESSARY SUPPLIES, WE CAN'T MAKE THE BOOKS!
WE CAN'T MAKE THE BOOK IF WE'RE DEAD EITHER, DUMMY!
KISHEE (SHWOOO)
BIKU (FLINCH)

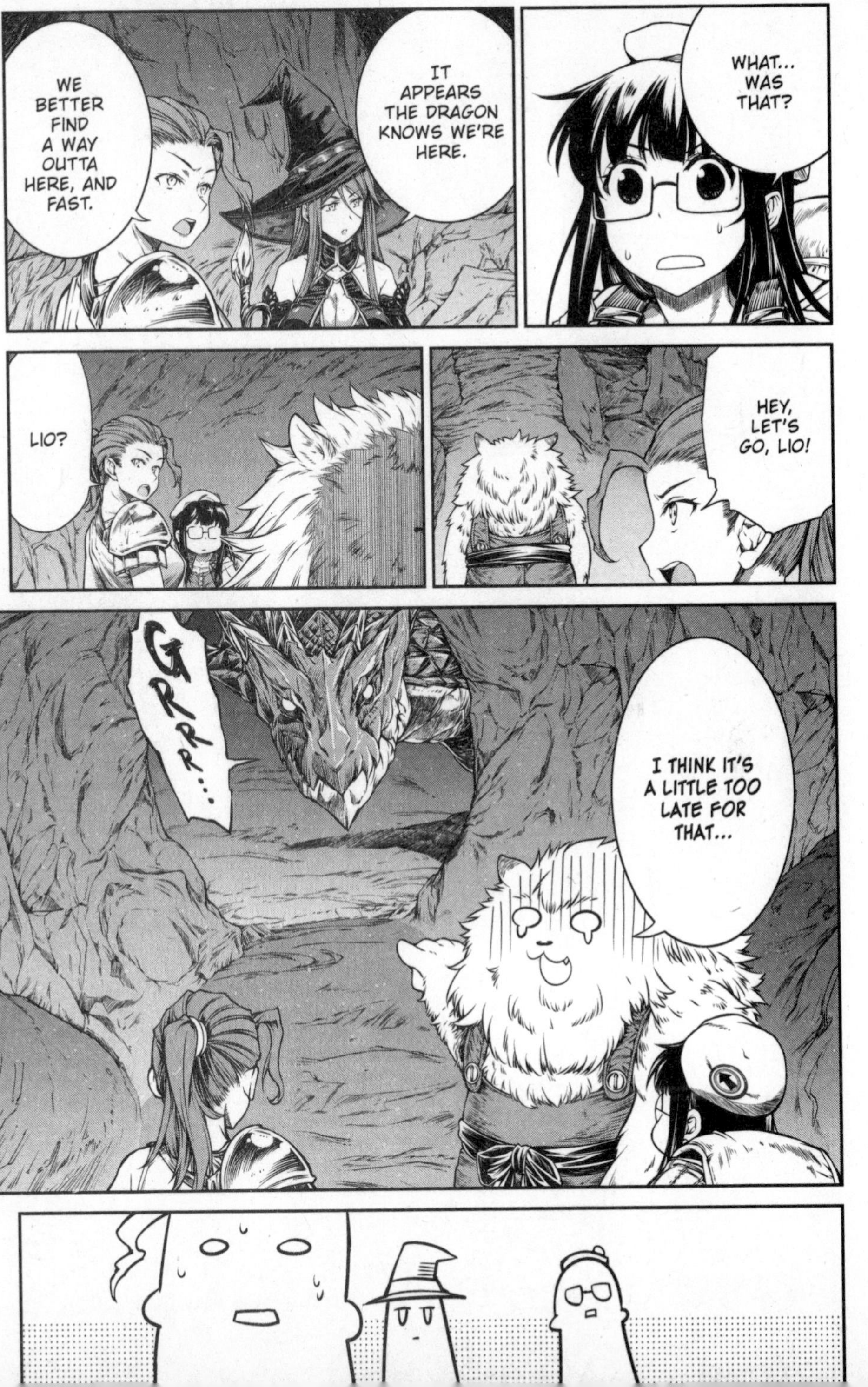
WHAT... WAS THAT?
IT APPEARS THE DRAGON KNOWS WE'RE HERE.
WE BETTER FIND A WAY OUTTA HERE, AND FAST.
HEY, LET'S GO, LIO!
LIO?
GRRR...
I THINK IT'S A LITTLE TOO LATE FOR THAT...

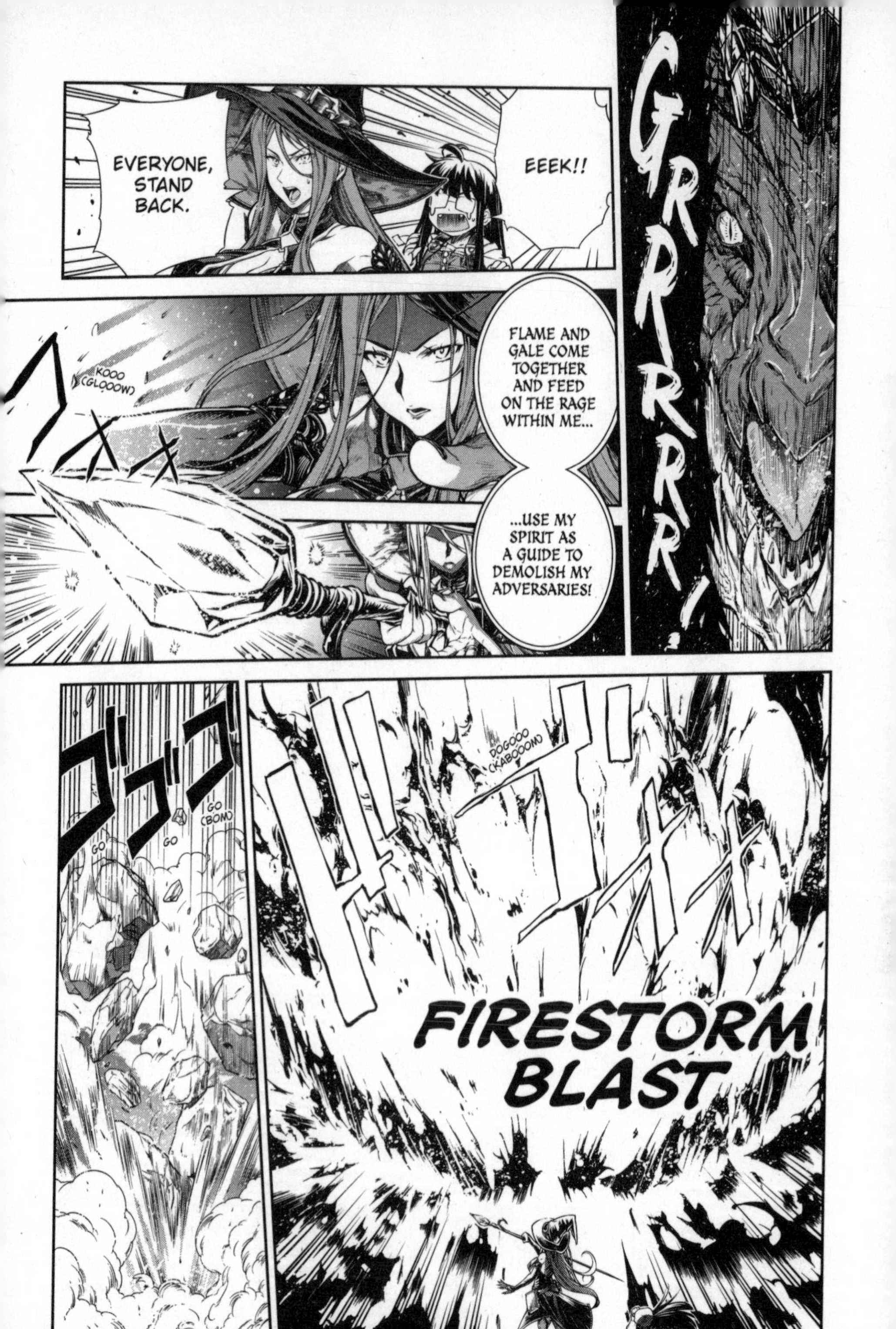
GRRRRR!
EEEK!!
EVERYONE, STAND BACK.
FLAME AND GALE COME TOGETHER AND FEED ON THE RAGE WITHIN ME...
...USE MY SPIRIT AS A GUIDE TO DEMOLISH MY ADVERSARIES!
KOOO (GLOOOW)
DOGOOO (KABOOOM)
FIRESTORM BLAST
GO (BOM)
GO
GO

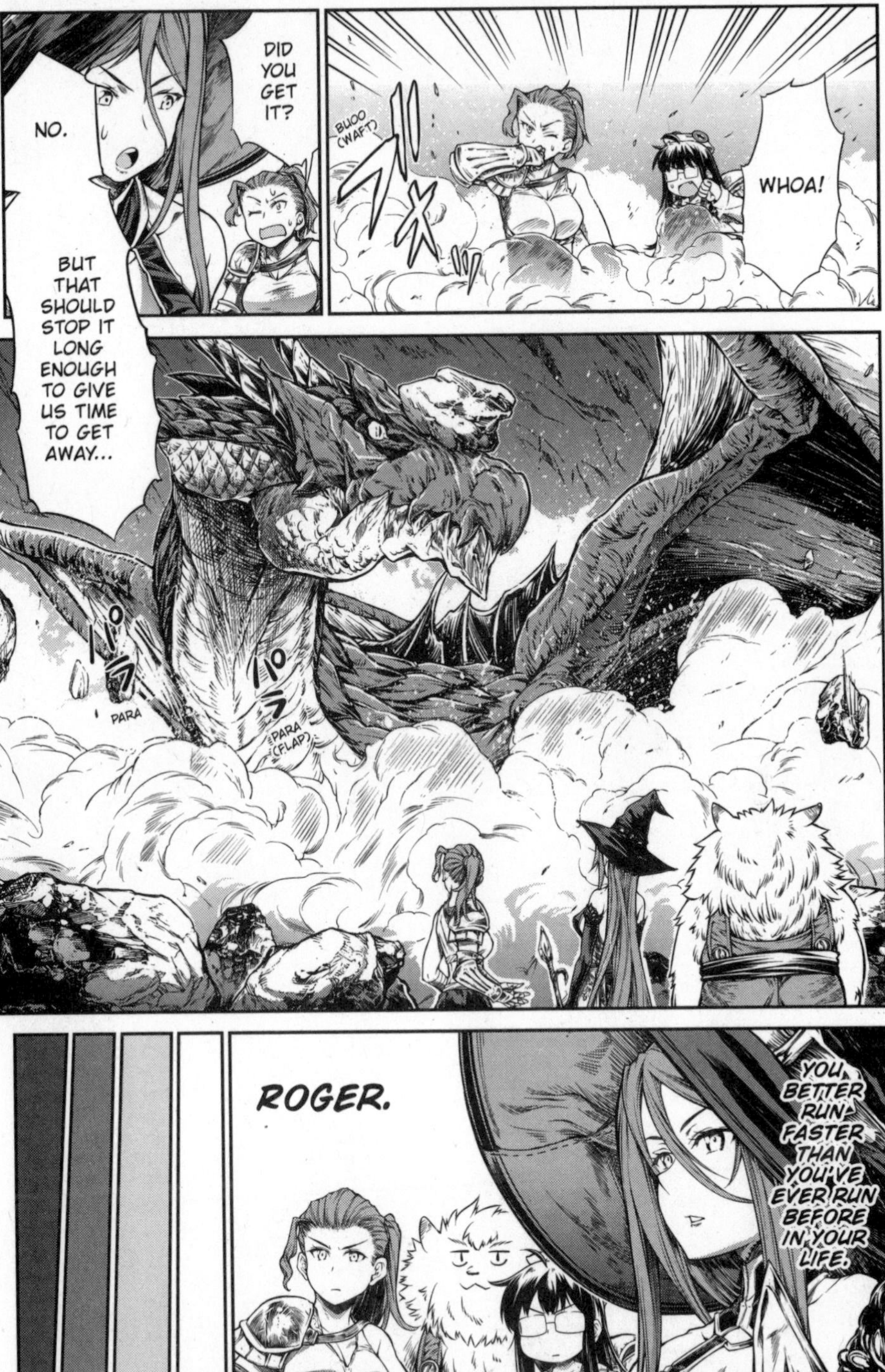
BUOO (WAFT)
WHOA!
DID YOU GET IT?
NO.
BUT THAT SHOULD STOP IT LONG ENOUGH TO GIVE US TIME TO GET AWAY...
PARA (FLAP)
PARA
YOU BETTER RUN FASTER THAN YOU'VE EVER RUN BEFORE IN YOUR LIFE.
ROGER.

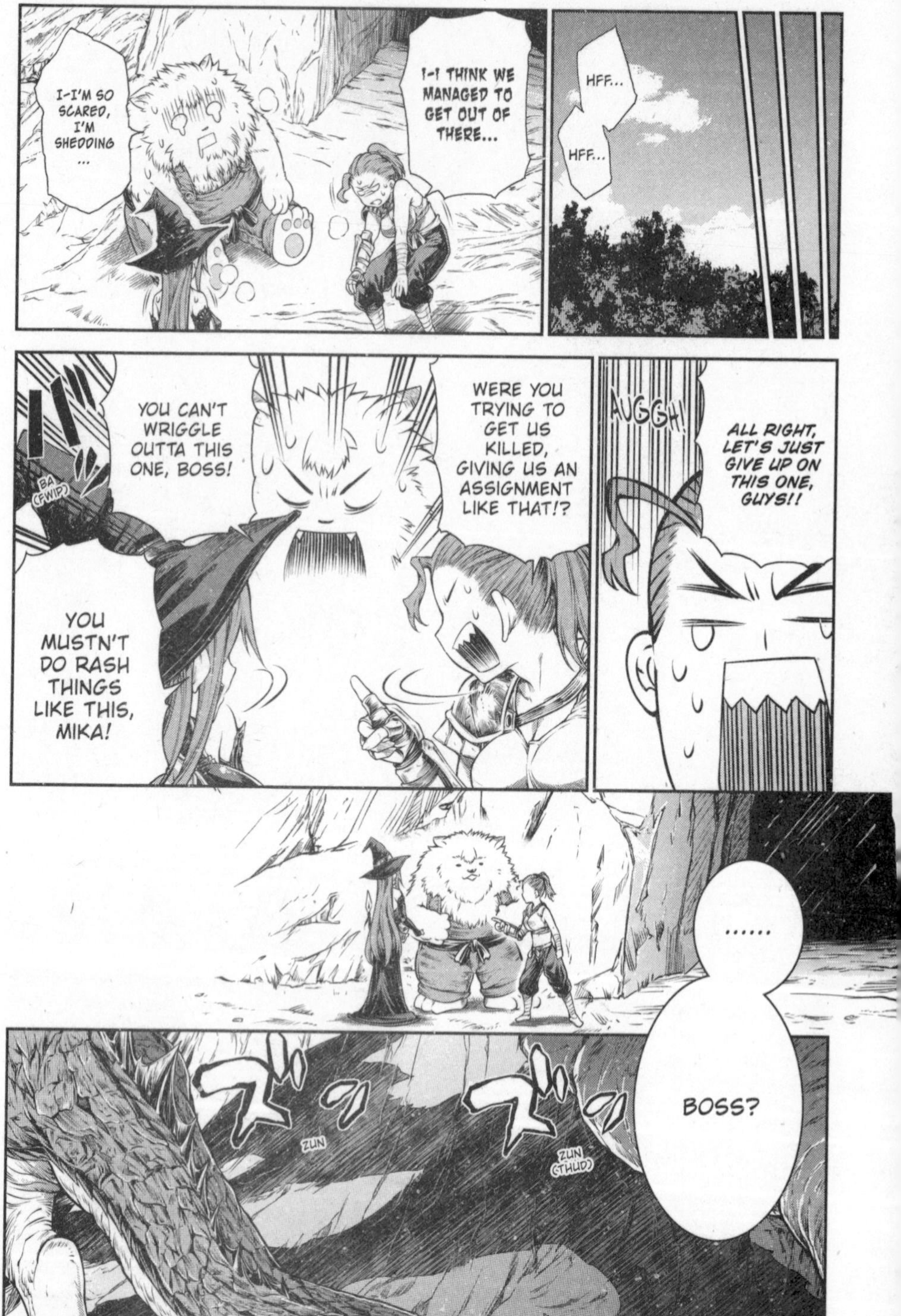
HFF...
HFF...
I-I THINK WE MANAGED TO GET OUT OF THERE...
I-I'M SO SCARED, I'M SHEDDING ...
AUGGH!
ALL RIGHT, LET'S JUST GIVE UP ON THIS ONE, GUYS!!
WERE YOU TRYING TO GET US KILLED, GIVING US AN ASSIGNMENT LIKE THAT!?
YOU CAN'T WRIGGLE OUTTA THIS ONE, BOSS!
BA (PWIP)
YOU MUSTN'T DO RASH THINGS LIKE THIS, MIKA!
......
BOSS?
ZUN (THUD)
ZUN

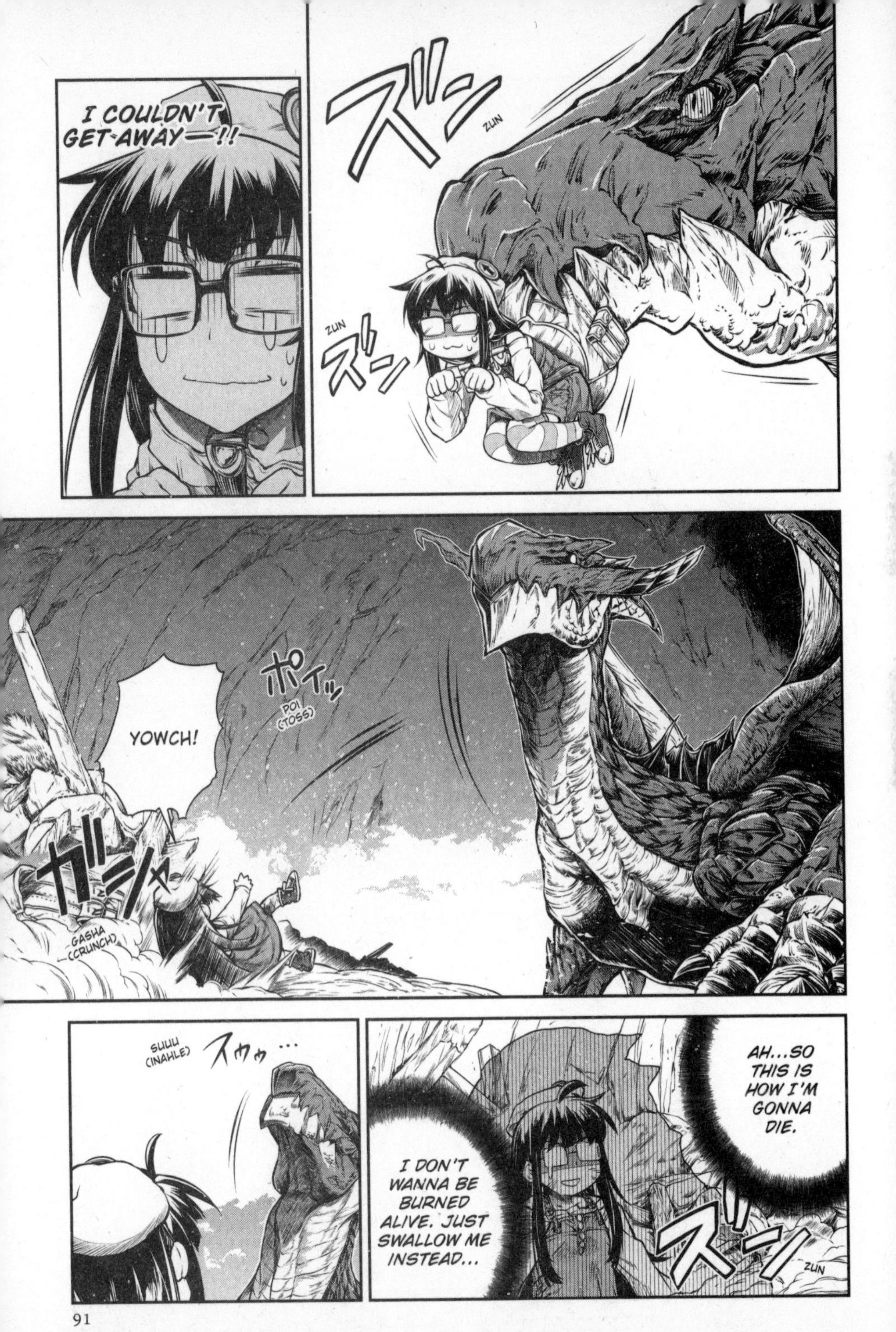
ZUN
ZUN
I COULDN'T GET AWAY—!!
ポイッ
POI (TOSS)
YOWCH!
GASHA (CRUNCH)
AH...SO THIS IS HOW I'M GONNA DIE.
I DON'T WANNA BE BURNED ALIVE. JUST SWALLOW ME INSTEAD...
ZUN
スゥ…
SUUU (INAHLE)

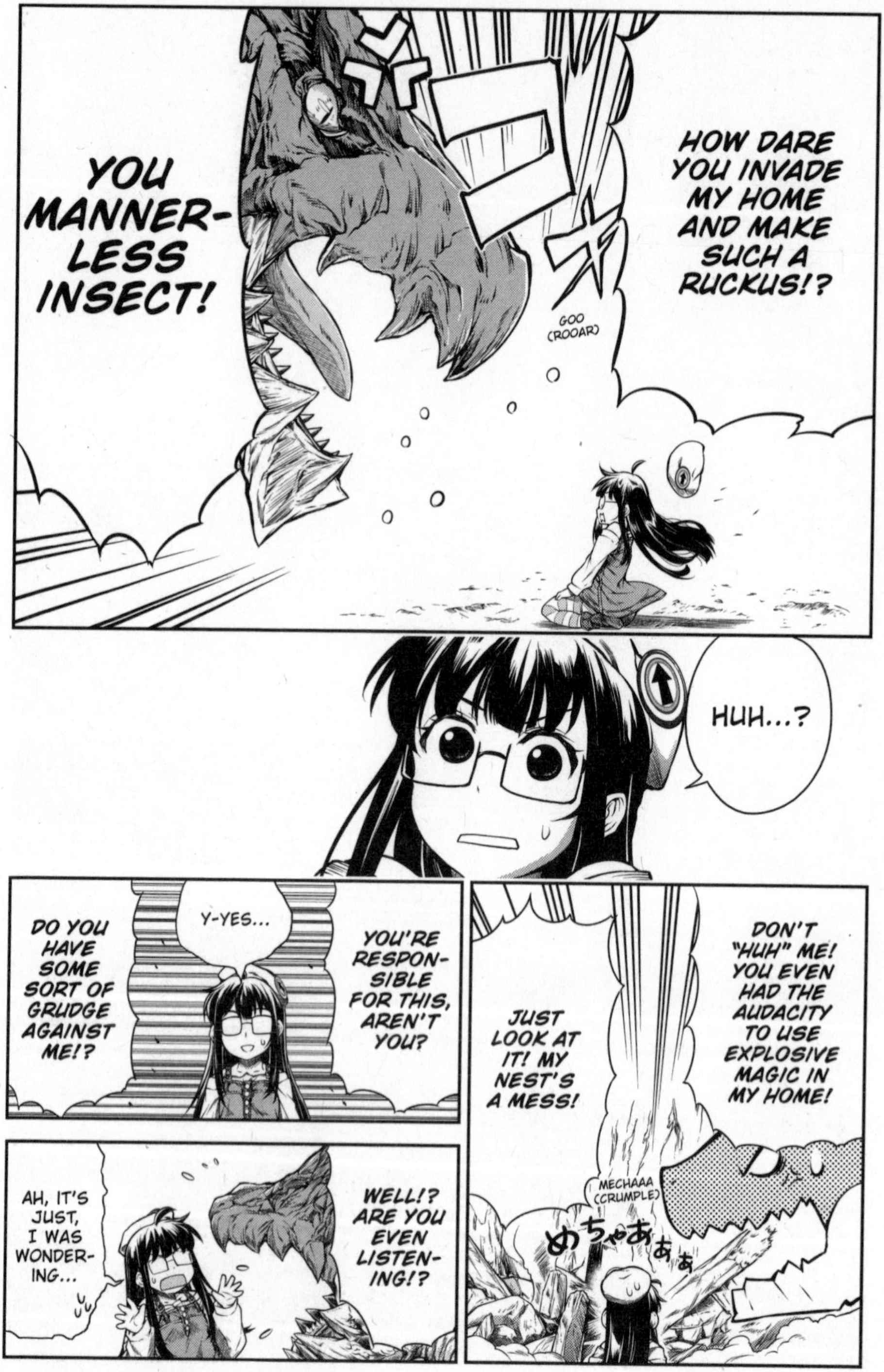
HOW DARE YOU INVADE MY HOME AND MAKE SUCH A RUCKUS!?
GOO (ROOAR)
YOU MANNER-LESS INSECT!
HUH...?
DON'T "HUH" ME! YOU EVEN HAD THE AUDACITY TO USE EXPLOSIVE MAGIC IN MY HOME!
JUST LOOK AT IT! MY NEST'S A MESS!
MECHAAA (CRUMPLE)
めちゃあぁぁ
YOU'RE RESPON-SIBLE FOR THIS, AREN'T YOU?
Y-YES...
DO YOU HAVE SOME SORT OF GRUDGE AGAINST ME!?
WELL!? ARE YOU EVEN LISTEN-ING!?
AH, IT'S JUST, I WAS WONDER-ING...

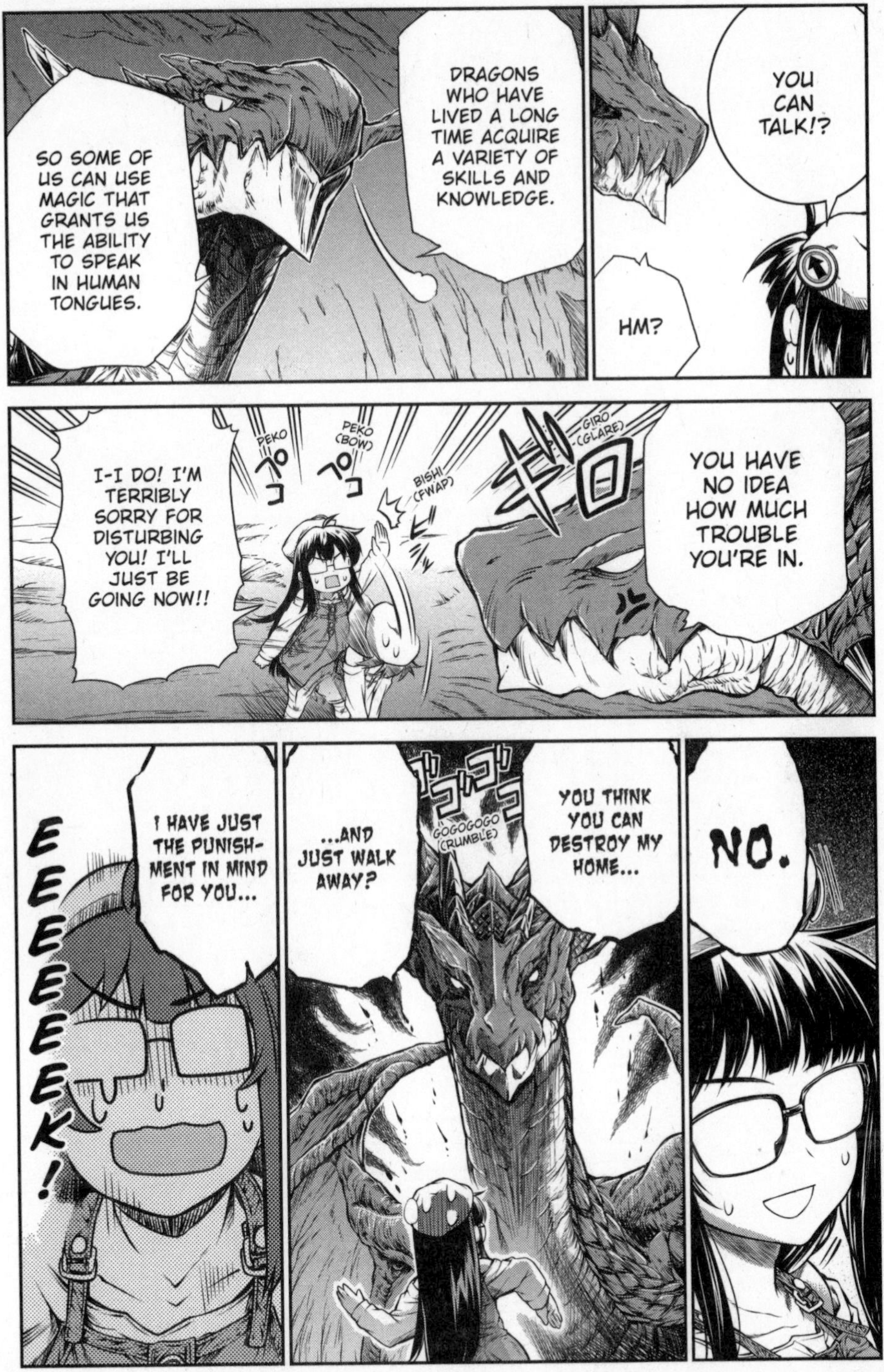

YOU CAN TALK!?
HM?
DRAGONS WHO HAVE LIVED A LONG TIME ACQUIRE A VARIETY OF SKILLS AND KNOWLEDGE.
SO SOME OF US CAN USE MAGIC THAT GRANTS US THE ABILITY TO SPEAK IN HUMAN TONGUES.
YOU HAVE NO IDEA HOW MUCH TROUBLE YOU'RE IN.
GIRO (GLARE)
BISHI (FWAP)
PEKO (BOW)
PEKO
I-I DO! I'M TERRIBLY SORRY FOR DISTURBING YOU! I'LL JUST BE GOING NOW!!
NO.
YOU THINK YOU CAN DESTROY MY HOME...
GOGOGOGO (CRUMBLE)
...AND JUST WALK AWAY?
I HAVE JUST THE PUNISHMENT IN MIND FOR YOU...
EEEEEEEK!

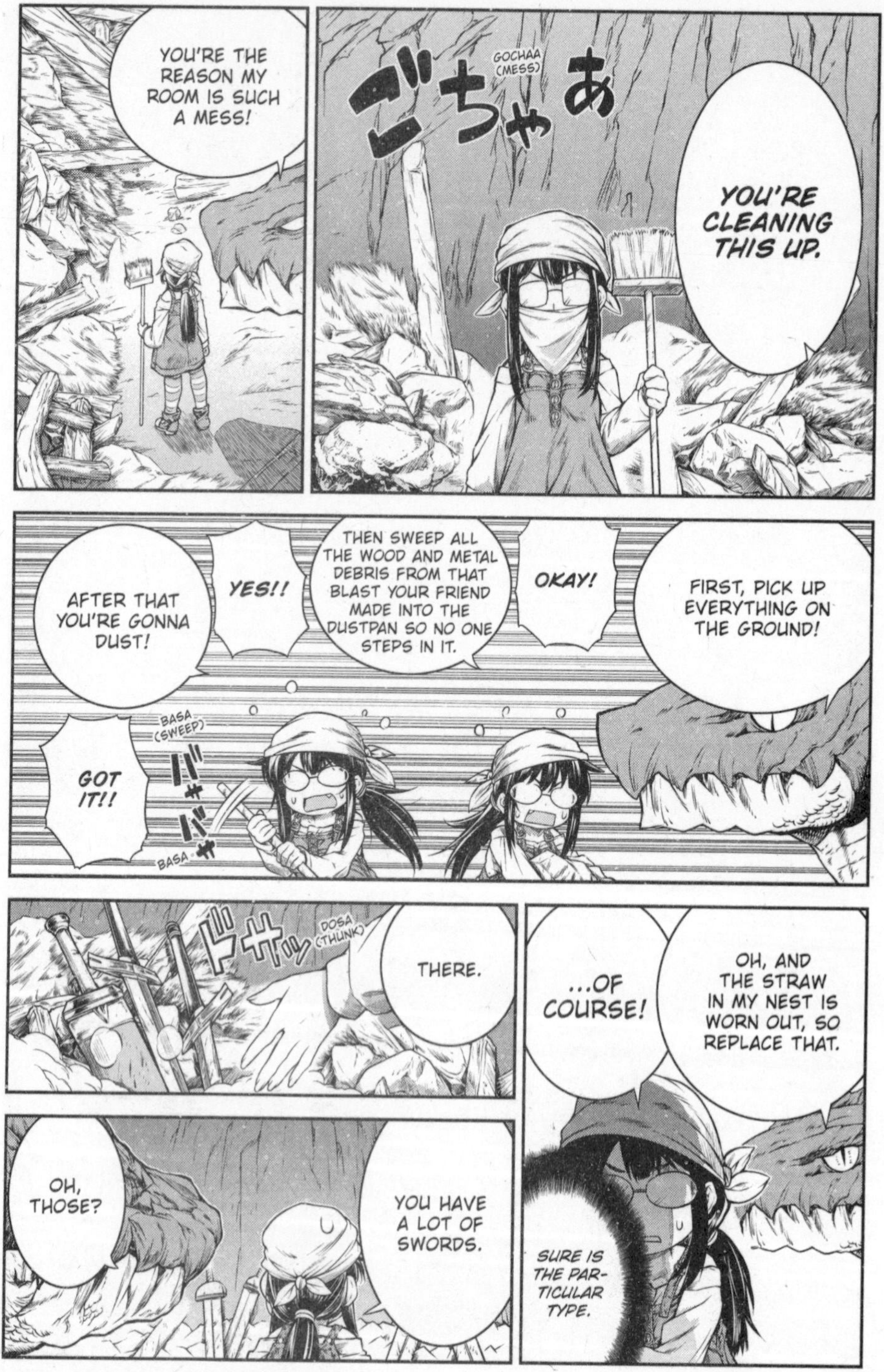
GOCHAA (MESS)
ごちゃあ
YOU'RE CLEANING THIS UP.
YOU'RE THE REASON MY ROOM IS SUCH A MESS!
FIRST, PICK UP EVERYTHING ON THE GROUND!
OKAY!
THEN SWEEP ALL THE WOOD AND METAL DEBRIS FROM THAT BLAST YOUR FRIEND MADE INTO THE DUSTPAN SO NO ONE STEPS IN IT.
YES!!
AFTER THAT YOU'RE GONNA DUST!
BASA (SWEEP)
バサバサ
BASA
GOT IT!!
OH, AND THE STRAW IN MY NEST IS WORN OUT, SO REPLACE THAT.
...OF COURSE!
SURE IS THE PARTICULAR TYPE.
DOSA (THUNK)
ドサッ
THERE.
YOU HAVE A LOT OF SWORDS.
OH, THOSE?

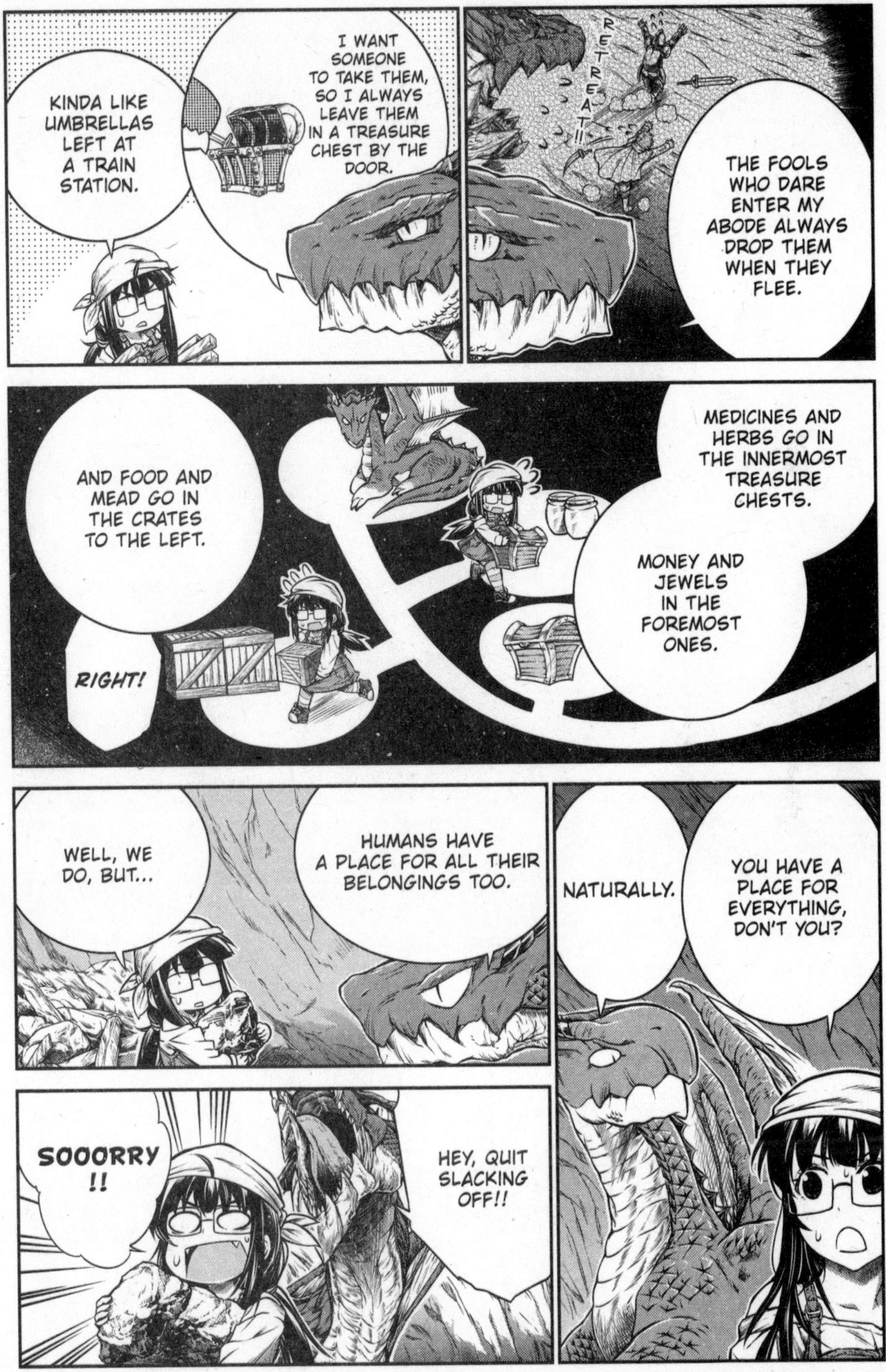
RETREAT!!
THE FOOLS WHO DARE ENTER MY ABODE ALWAYS DROP THEM WHEN THEY FLEE.
I WANT SOMEONE TO TAKE THEM, SO I ALWAYS LEAVE THEM IN A TREASURE CHEST BY THE DOOR.
KINDA LIKE UMBRELLAS LEFT AT A TRAIN STATION.
MEDICINES AND HERBS GO IN THE INNERMOST TREASURE CHESTS.
MONEY AND JEWELS IN THE FOREMOST ONES.
AND FOOD AND MEAD GO IN THE CRATES TO THE LEFT.
RIGHT!
YOU HAVE A PLACE FOR EVERYTHING, DON'T YOU?
NATURALLY.
HUMANS HAVE A PLACE FOR ALL THEIR BELONGINGS TOO.
WELL, WE DO, BUT...
HEY, QUIT SLACKING OFF!!
SOOORRY !!

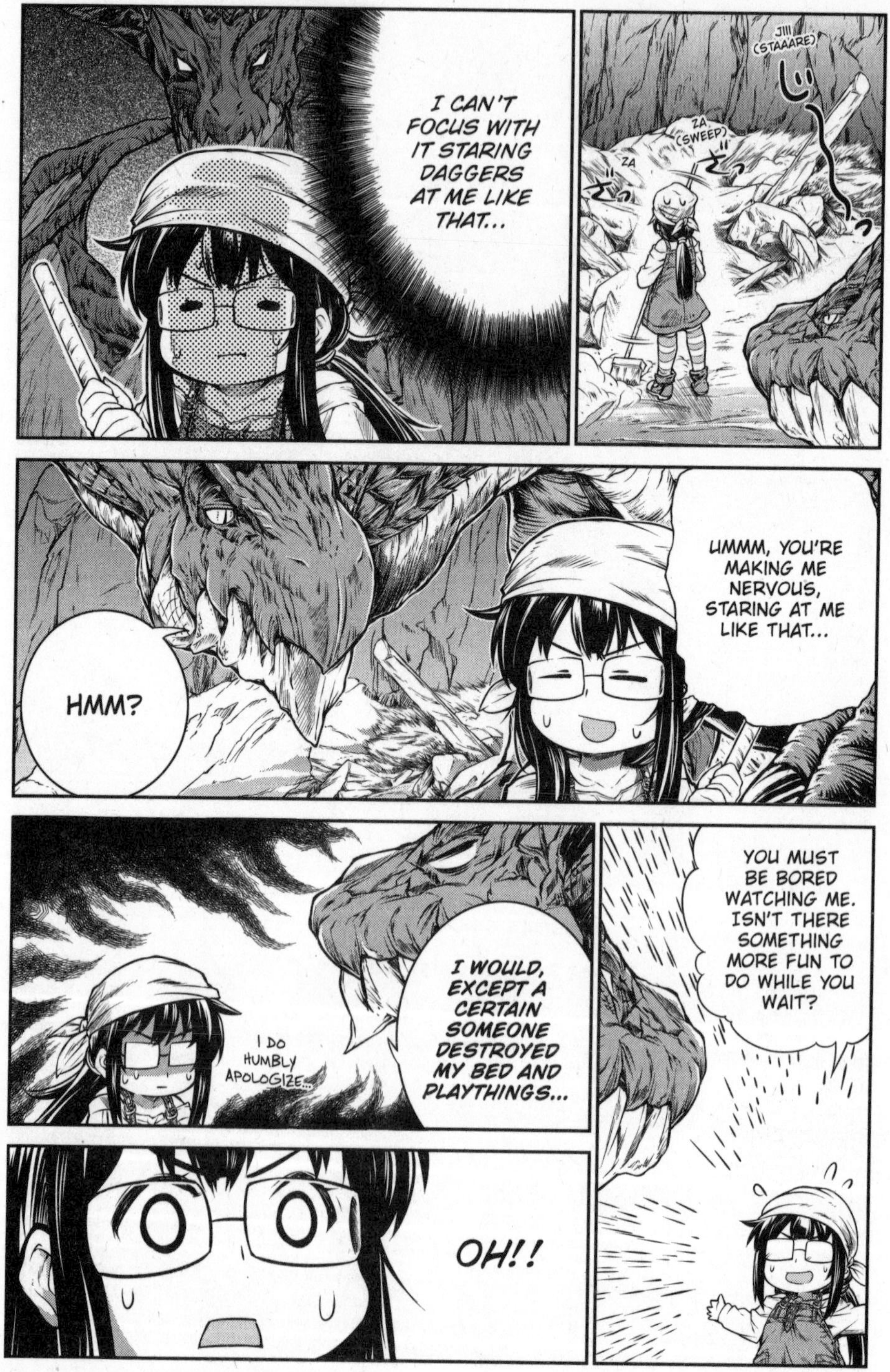
JIII (STAAARE)
ZA (SWEEP)
ZA
I CAN'T FOCUS WITH IT STARING DAGGERS AT ME LIKE THAT...
UMMM, YOU'RE MAKING ME NERVOUS, STARING AT ME LIKE THAT...
HMM?
YOU MUST BE BORED WATCHING ME. ISN'T THERE SOMETHING MORE FUN TO DO WHILE YOU WAIT?
I WOULD, EXCEPT A CERTAIN SOMEONE DESTROYED MY BED AND PLAYTHINGS...
I DO HUMBLY APOLOGIZE...
OH!!

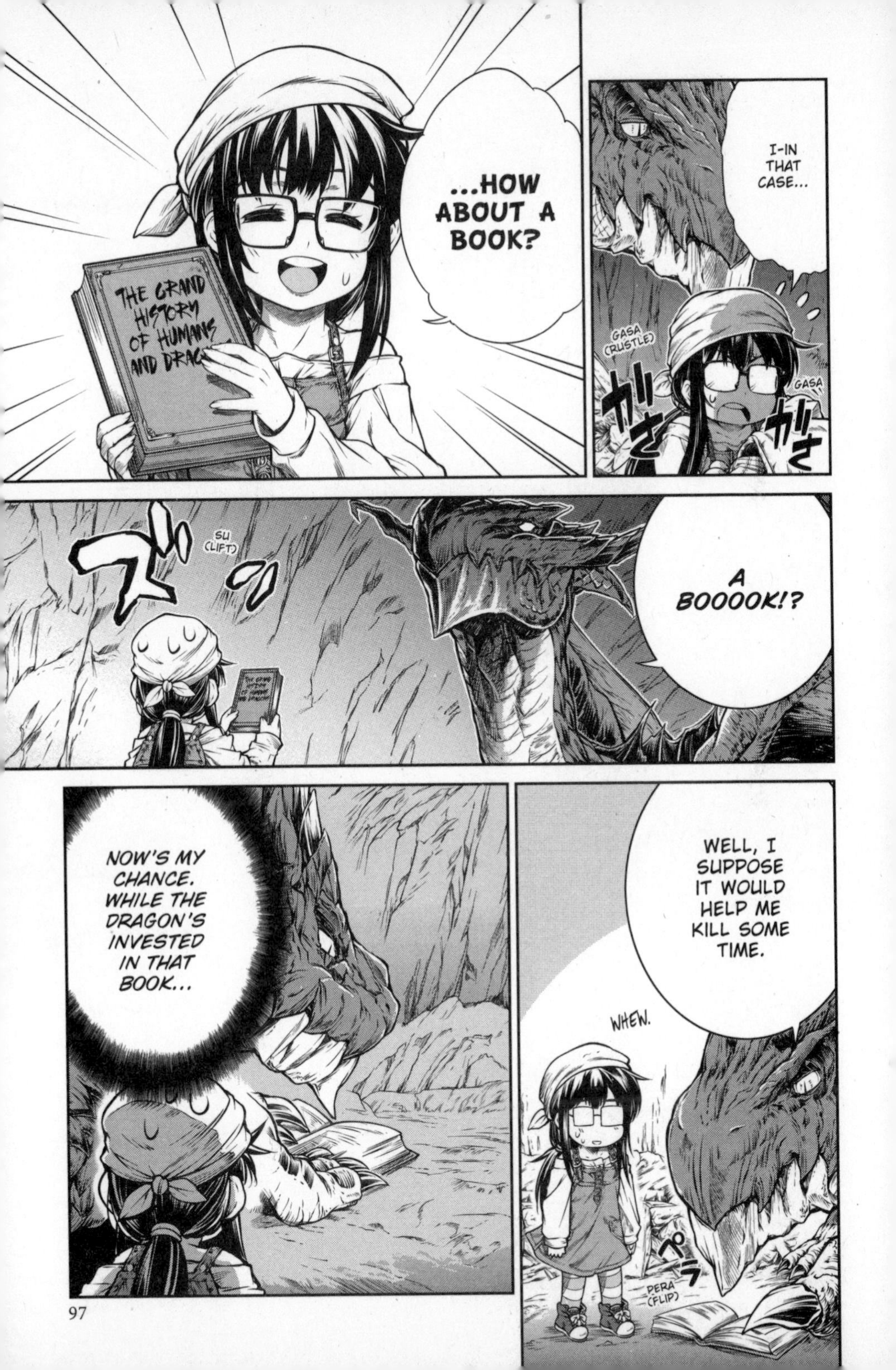

I-IN THAT CASE...
GASA (RUSTLE)
GASA
...HOW ABOUT A BOOK?
THE GRAND HISTORY OF HUMANS AND DRAG
A BOOOOK!?
SU (LIFT)
WELL, I SUPPOSE IT WOULD HELP ME KILL SOME TIME.
WHEW.
PERA (FLIP)
NOW'S MY CHANCE. WHILE THE DRAGON'S INVESTED IN THAT BOOK...

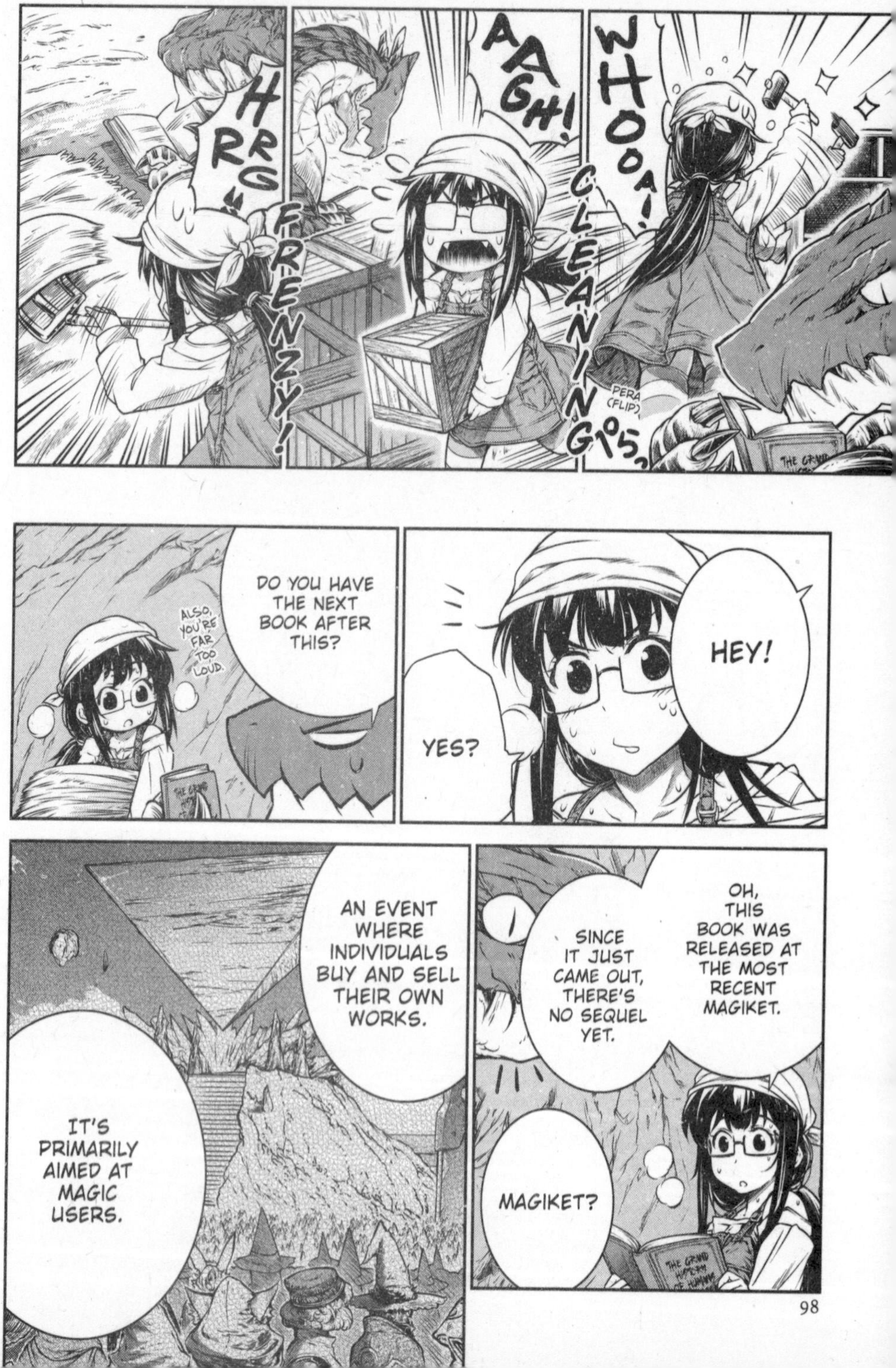
WHOOA!
PERA (FLIP)
AAGH!
CLEANING
HRRG
FRENZY!
HEY!
YES?
DO YOU HAVE THE NEXT BOOK AFTER THIS?
ALSO, YOU'RE FAR TOO LOUD.
OH, THIS BOOK WAS RELEASED AT THE MOST RECENT MAGIKET.
SINCE IT JUST CAME OUT, THERE'S NO SEQUEL YET.
MAGIKET?
AN EVENT WHERE INDIVIDUALS BUY AND SELL THEIR OWN WORKS.
IT'S PRIMARILY AIMED AT MAGIC USERS.

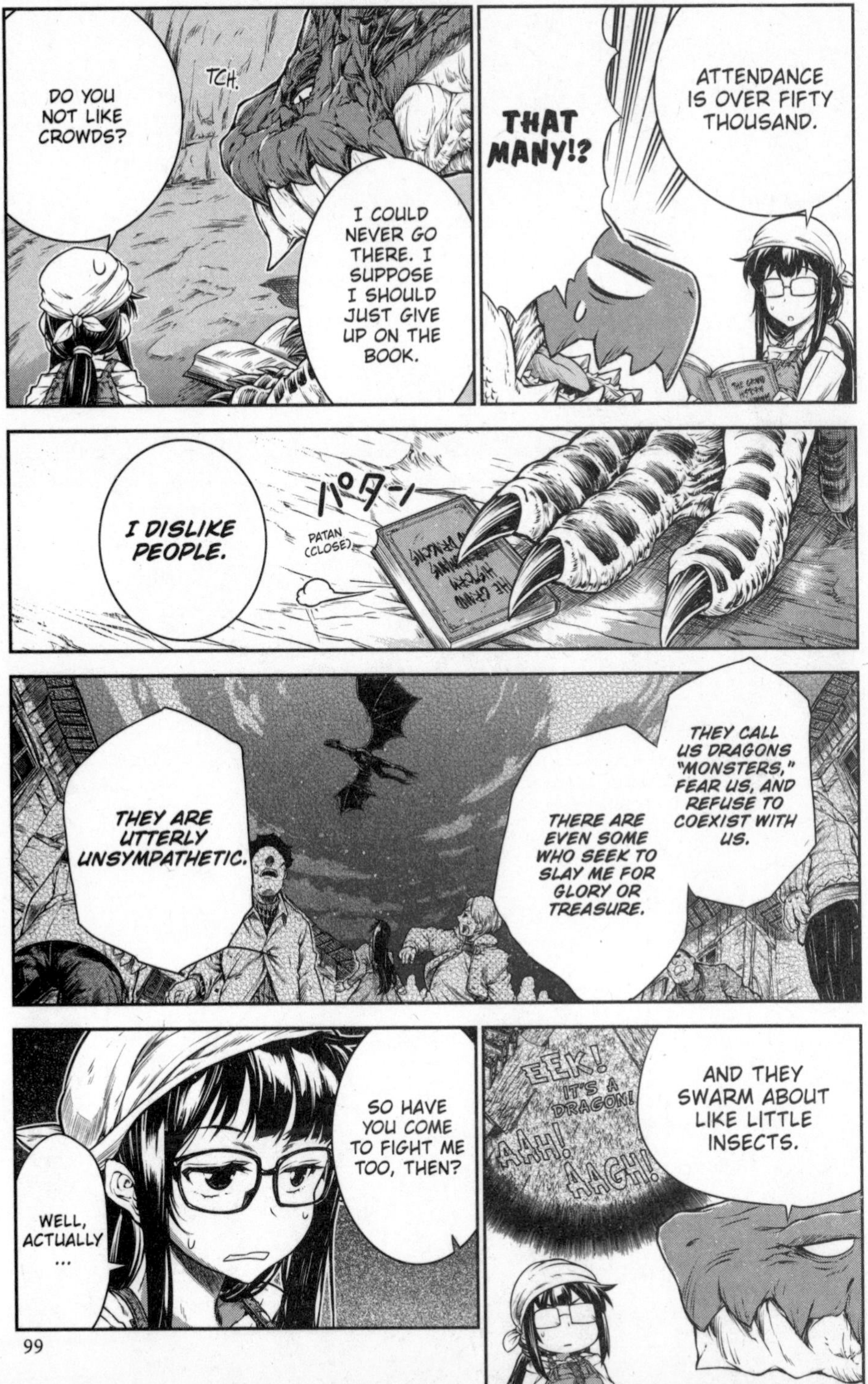
ATTENDANCE IS OVER FIFTY THOUSAND.
THAT MANY!?
DO YOU NOT LIKE CROWDS?
TCH.
I COULD NEVER GO THERE. I SUPPOSE I SHOULD JUST GIVE UP ON THE BOOK.
パタン
PATAN (CLOSE)
I DISLIKE PEOPLE.
THEY CALL US DRAGONS "MONSTERS," FEAR US, AND REFUSE TO COEXIST WITH US.
THERE ARE EVEN SOME WHO SEEK TO SLAY ME FOR GLORY OR TREASURE.
THEY ARE UTTERLY UNSYMPATHETIC.
AND THEY SWARM ABOUT LIKE LITTLE INSECTS.
EEK!
IT'S A DRAGON!
AAH!
AAGH!
SO HAVE YOU COME TO FIGHT ME TOO, THEN?
WELL, ACTUALLY ...

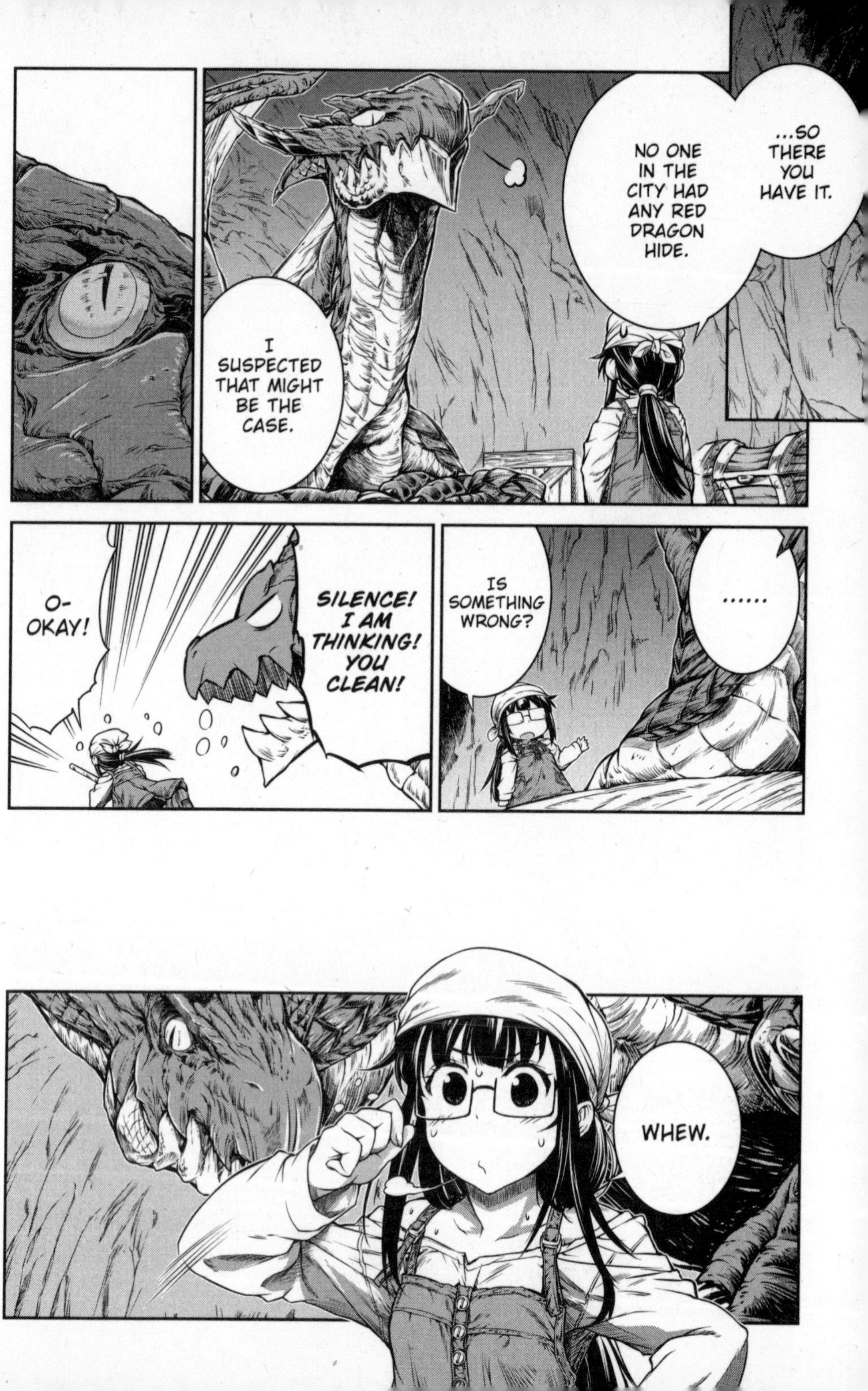
...SO THERE YOU HAVE IT.
NO ONE IN THE CITY HAD ANY RED DRAGON HIDE.
I SUSPECTED THAT MIGHT BE THE CASE.
......
IS SOMETHING WRONG?
SILENCE! I AM THINKING! YOU CLEAN!
O-OKAY!
WHEW.

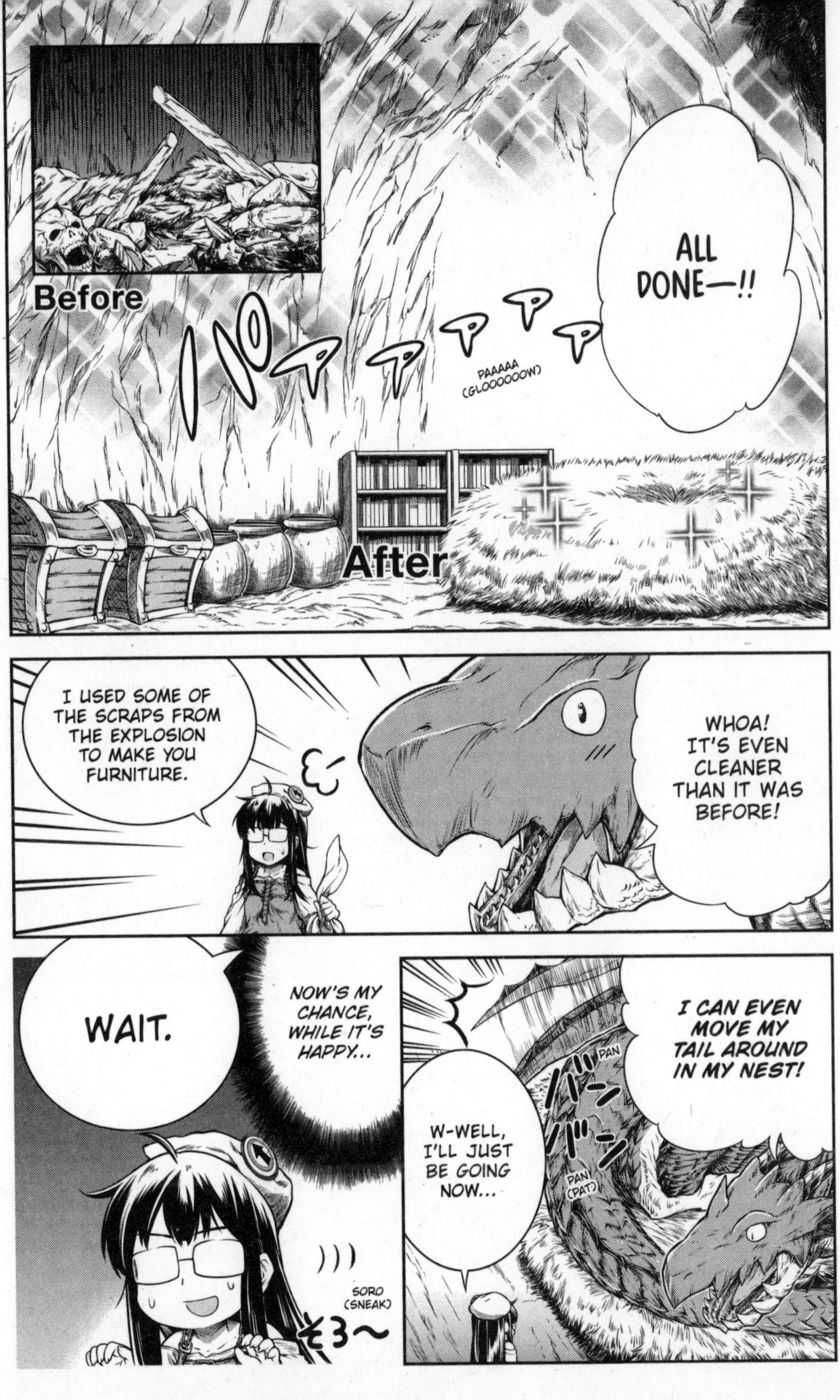
Before
ALL DONE—!!
PAAAAA (GLOOOOOOW)
After
WHOA! IT'S EVEN CLEANER THAN IT WAS BEFORE!
I USED SOME OF THE SCRAPS FROM THE EXPLOSION TO MAKE YOU FURNITURE.
I CAN EVEN MOVE MY TAIL AROUND IN MY NEST!
PAN
PAN (PAT)
W-WELL, I'LL JUST BE GOING NOW...
NOW'S MY CHANCE, WHILE IT'S HAPPY...
WAIT.
SORO (SNEAK)

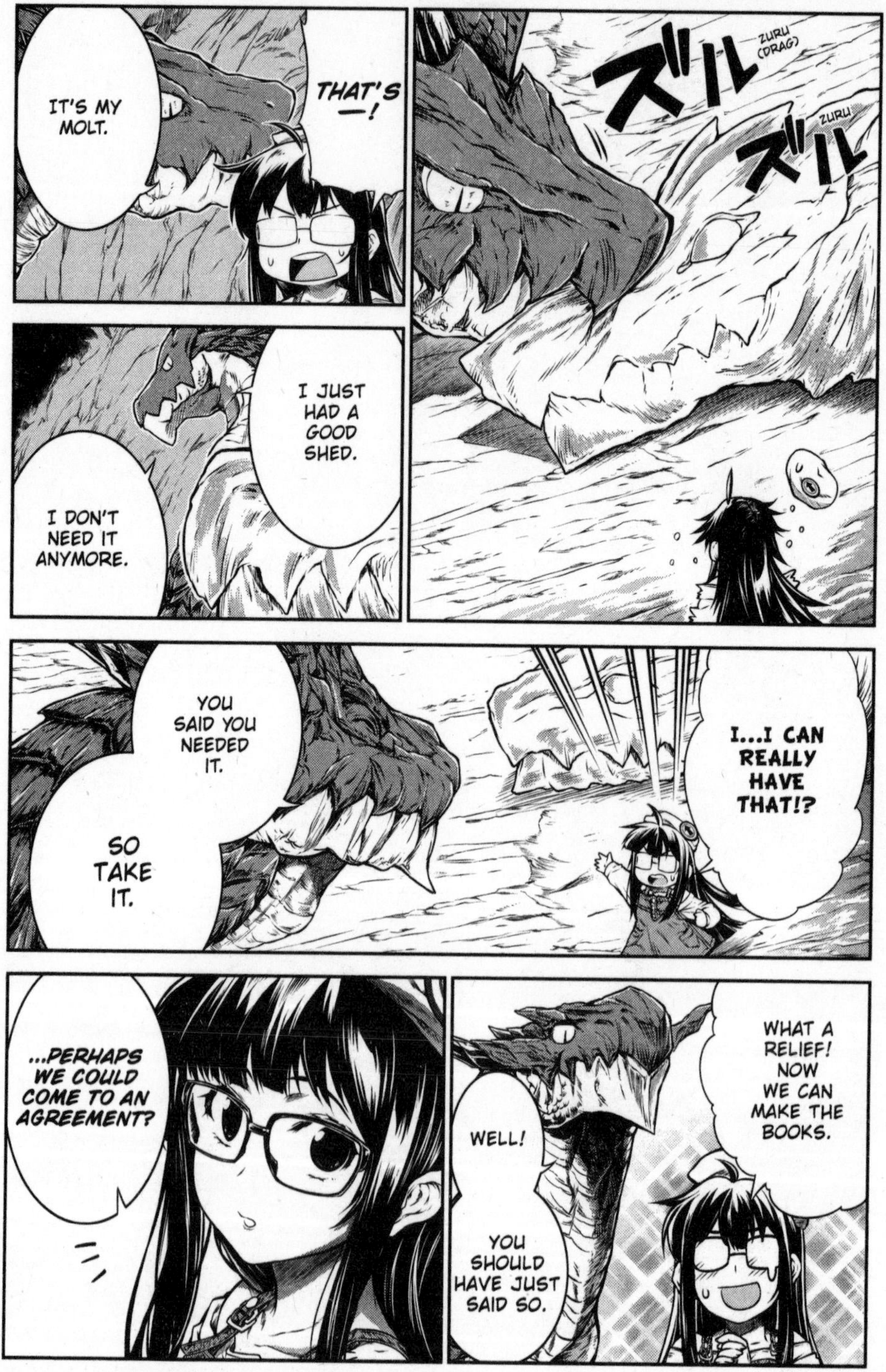
ズル
ZURU (DRAG)
ズル
ZURU
THAT'S—!
IT'S MY MOLT.
I JUST HAD A GOOD SHED.
I DON'T NEED IT ANYMORE.
I...I CAN REALLY HAVE THAT!?
YOU SAID YOU NEEDED IT.
SO TAKE IT.
WHAT A RELIEF! NOW WE CAN MAKE THE BOOKS.
WELL!
YOU SHOULD HAVE JUST SAID SO.
...PERHAPS WE COULD COME TO AN AGREEMENT?

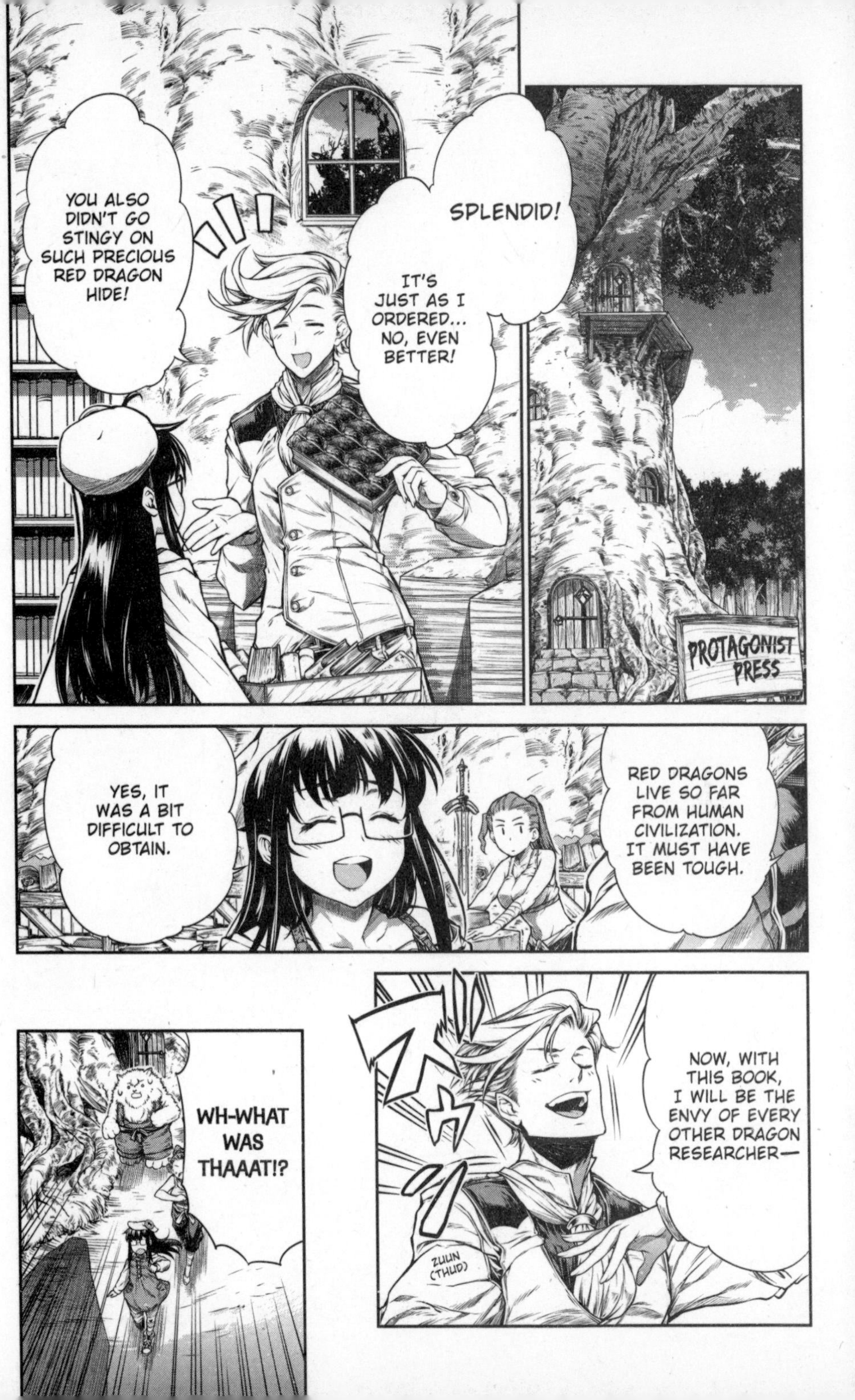
PROTAGONIST PRESS
SPLENDID!
IT'S JUST AS I ORDERED... NO, EVEN BETTER!
YOU ALSO DIDN'T GO STINGY ON SUCH PRECIOUS RED DRAGON HIDE!
RED DRAGONS LIVE SO FAR FROM HUMAN CIVILIZATION. IT MUST HAVE BEEN TOUGH.
YES, IT WAS A BIT DIFFICULT TO OBTAIN.
NOW, WITH THIS BOOK, I WILL BE THE ENVY OF EVERY OTHER DRAGON RESEARCHER—
ZUUN (THUD)
WH-WHAT WAS THAAAT!?

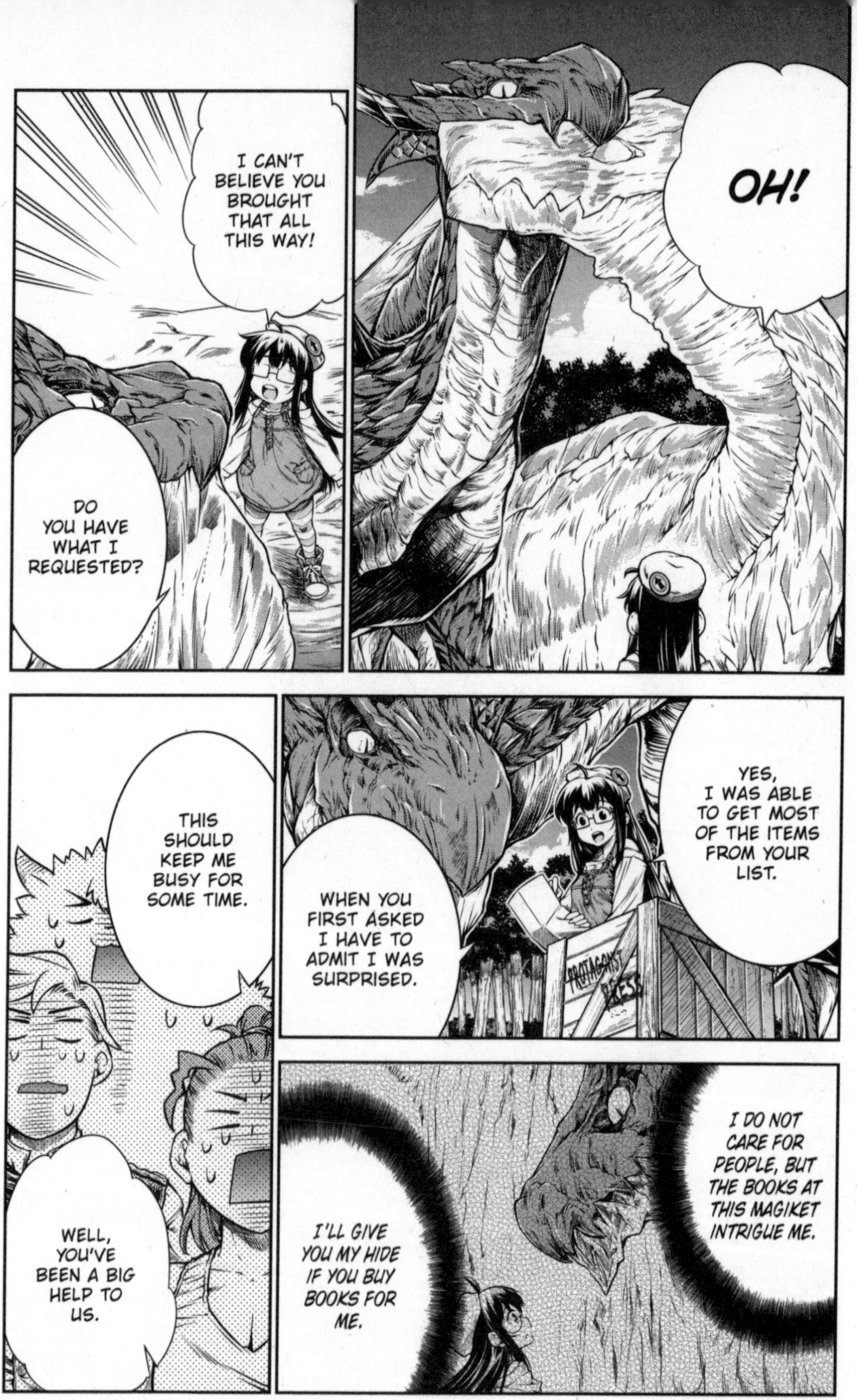
OH!
I CAN'T BELIEVE YOU BROUGHT THAT ALL THIS WAY!
DO YOU HAVE WHAT I REQUESTED?
YES, I WAS ABLE TO GET MOST OF THE ITEMS FROM YOUR LIST.
WHEN YOU FIRST ASKED I HAVE TO ADMIT I WAS SURPRISED.
I DO NOT CARE FOR PEOPLE, BUT THE BOOKS AT THIS MAGIKET INTRIGUE ME.
I'LL GIVE YOU MY HIDE IF YOU BUY BOOKS FOR ME.
THIS SHOULD KEEP ME BUSY FOR SOME TIME.
WELL, YOU'VE BEEN A BIG HELP TO US.

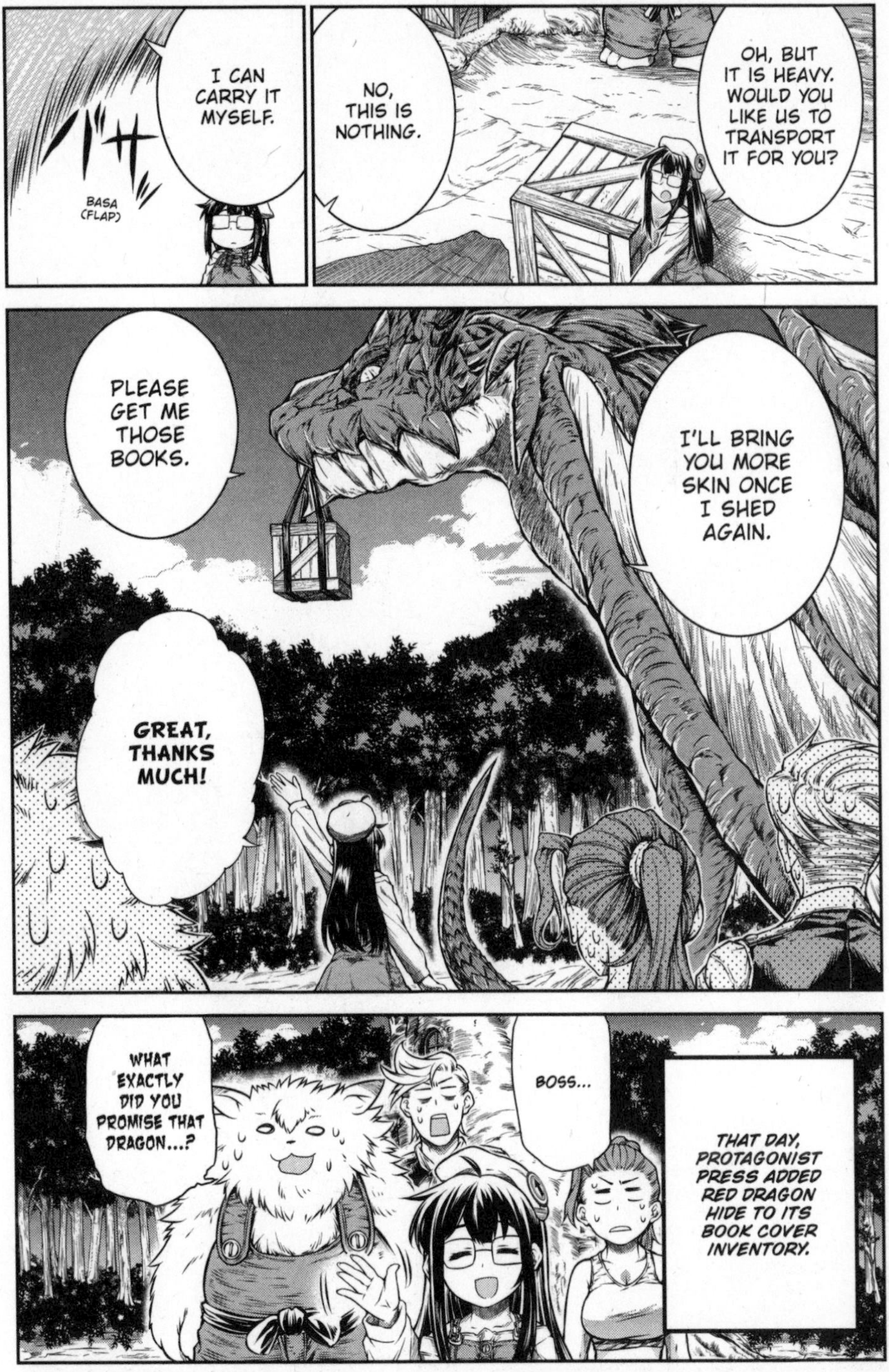
OH, BUT IT IS HEAVY. WOULD YOU LIKE US TO TRANSPORT IT FOR YOU?
NO, THIS IS NOTHING.
I CAN CARRY IT MYSELF.
BASA (FLAP)
I'LL BRING YOU MORE SKIN ONCE I SHED AGAIN.
PLEASE GET ME THOSE BOOKS.
GREAT, THANKS MUCH!
THAT DAY, PROTAGONIST PRESS ADDED RED DRAGON HIDE TO ITS BOOK COVER INVENTORY.
BOSS...
WHAT EXACTLY DID YOU PROMISE THAT DRAGON...?

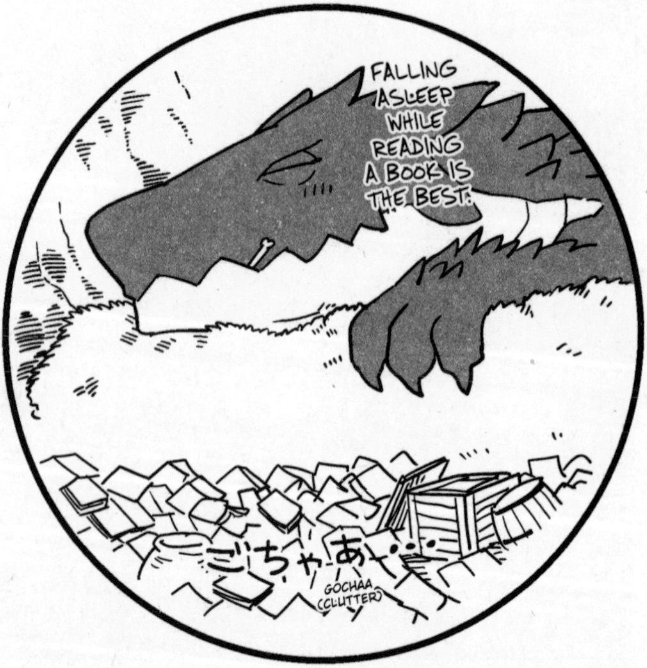
FALLING ASLEEP WHILE READING A BOOK IS THE BEST.
ごちゃあ…
GOCHAA (CLUTTER)

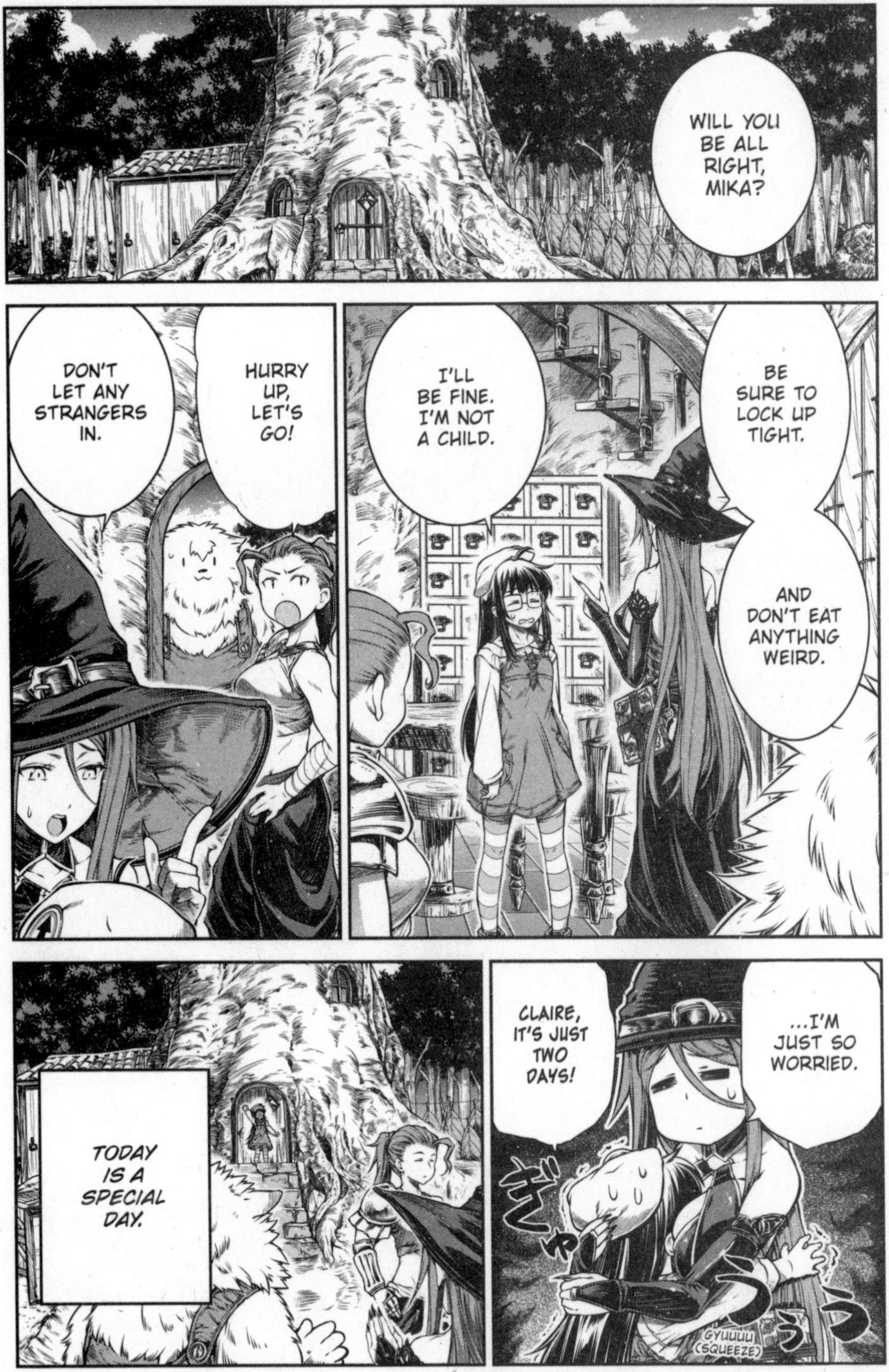
WILL YOU BE ALL RIGHT, MIKA?
BE SURE TO LOCK UP TIGHT.
AND DON'T EAT ANYTHING WEIRD.
I'LL BE FINE. I'M NOT A CHILD.
HURRY UP, LET'S GO!
DON'T LET ANY STRANGERS IN.
...I'M JUST SO WORRIED.
CLAIRE, IT'S JUST TWO DAYS!
Gyuuuu (SQUEEZE)
TODAY IS A SPECIAL DAY.

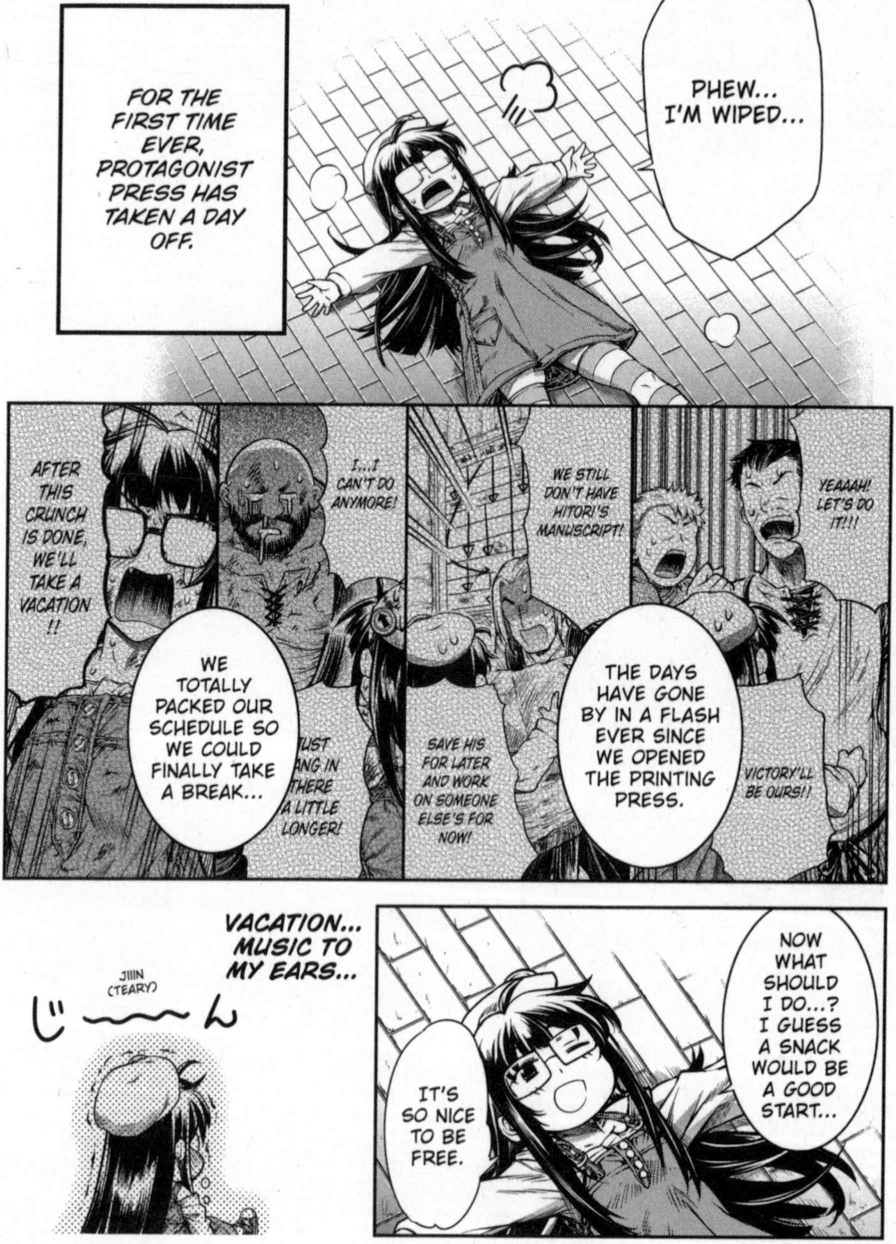
PHEW... I'M WIPED...
FOR THE FIRST TIME EVER, PROTAGONIST PRESS HAS TAKEN A DAY OFF.
YEAAAH! LET'S DO IT!!!
THE DAYS HAVE GONE BY IN A FLASH EVER SINCE WE OPENED THE PRINTING PRESS.
VICTORY'LL BE OURS!!
WE STILL DON'T HAVE HITORI'S MANUSCRIPT!
SAVE HIS FOR LATER AND WORK ON SOMEONE ELSE'S FOR NOW!
I...I CAN'T DO ANYMORE!
JUST HANG IN THERE A LITTLE LONGER!
WE TOTALLY PACKED OUR SCHEDULE SO WE COULD FINALLY TAKE A BREAK...
AFTER THIS CRUNCH IS DONE, WE'LL TAKE A VACATION!!
NOW WHAT SHOULD I DO...? I GUESS A SNACK WOULD BE A GOOD START...
IT'S SO NICE TO BE FREE.
VACATION... MUSIC TO MY EARS...
JIIIN (TEARY)
じ〜〜ん

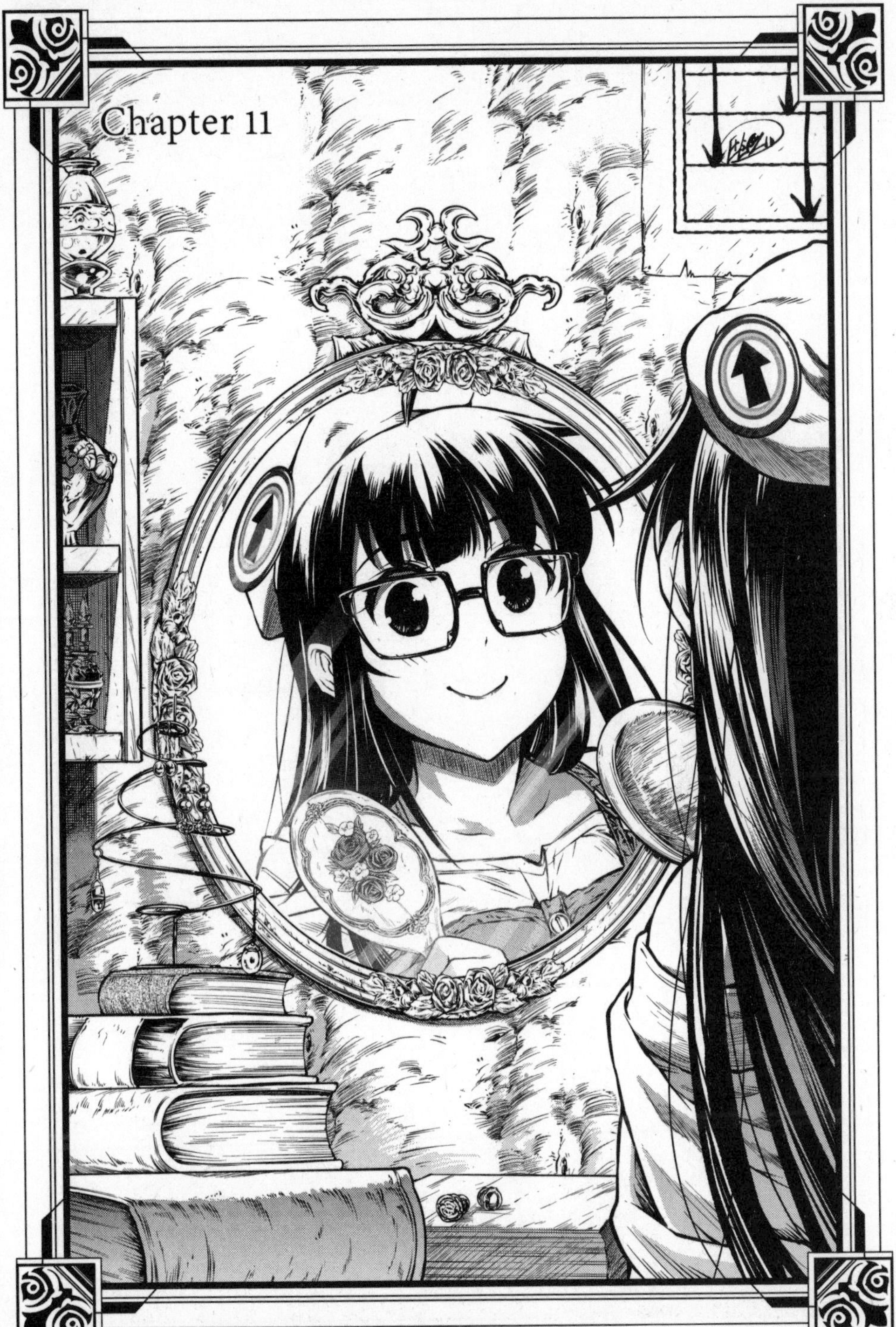
Chapter 11

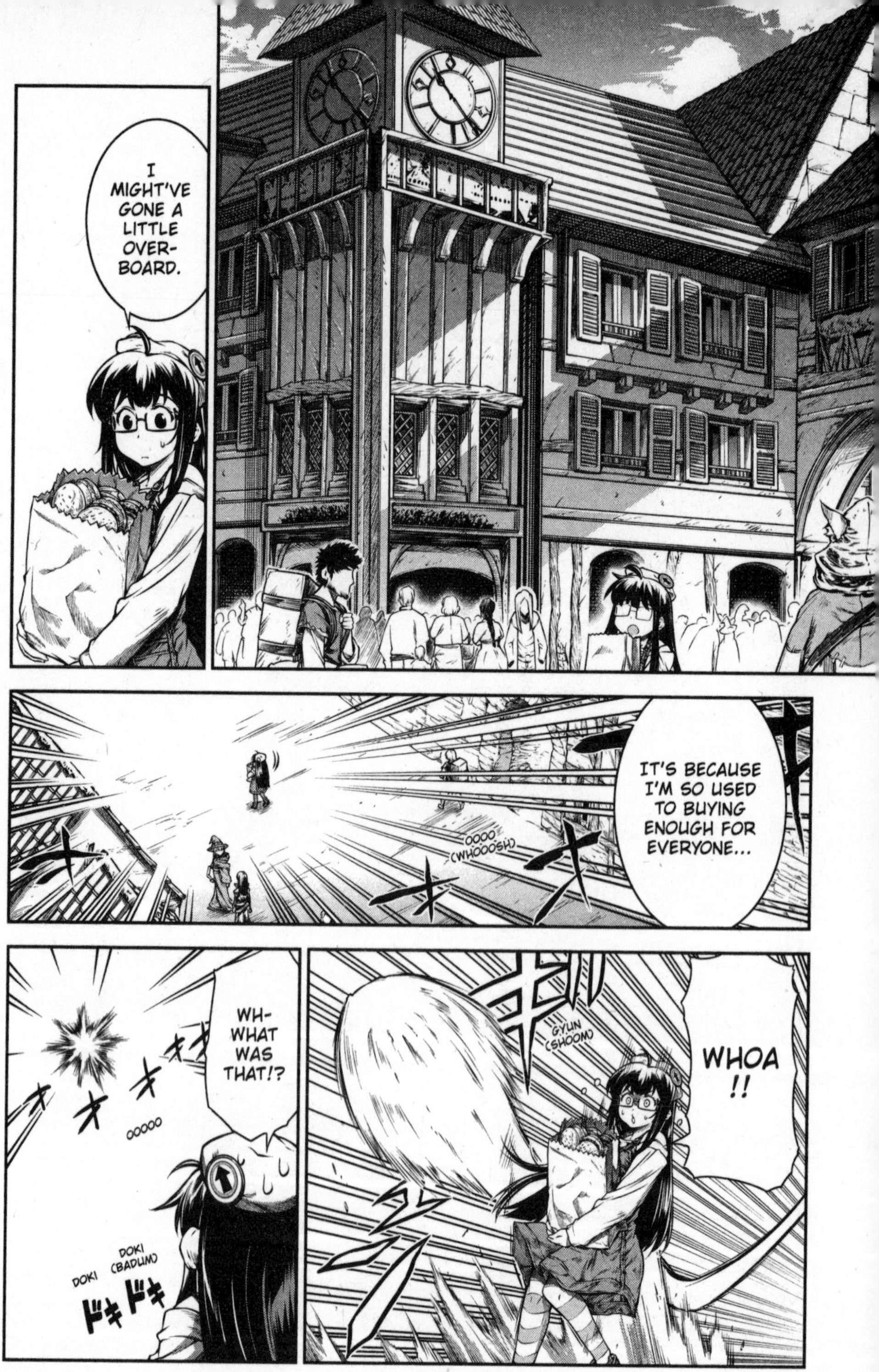
I MIGHT'VE GONE A LITTLE OVER-BOARD.
IT'S BECAUSE I'M SO USED TO BUYING ENOUGH FOR EVERYONE...
OOOO (WHOOOSH)
GYUN (SHOOM)
WHOA!!
WH-WHAT WAS THAT!?
OOOOO
DOKI DOKI (BADUM)
ドキドキ

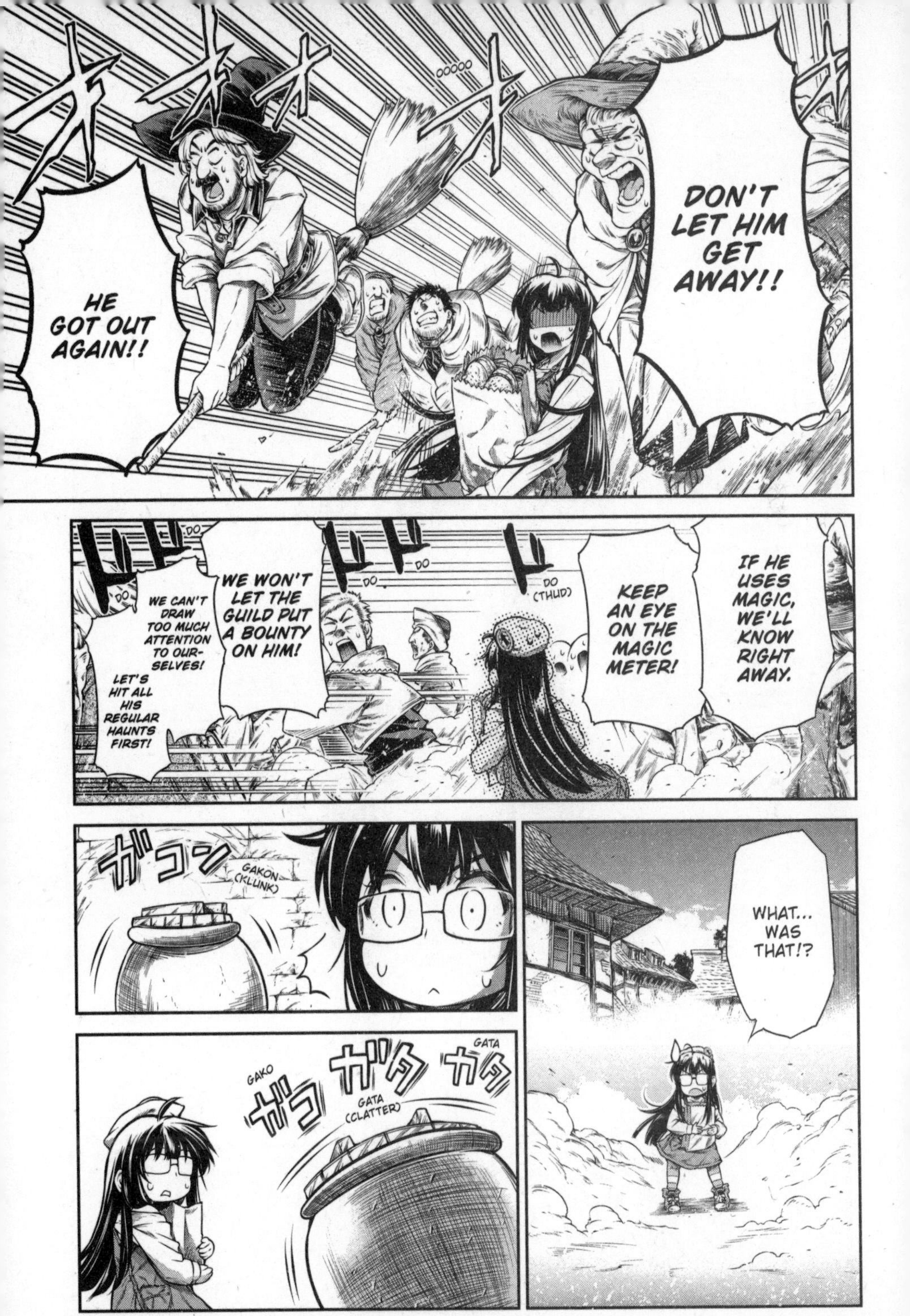
OOOOO
DON'T LET HIM GET AWAY!!
HE GOT OUT AGAIN!!
IF HE USES MAGIC, WE'LL KNOW RIGHT AWAY.
KEEP AN EYE ON THE MAGIC METER!
DO (THUD)
DO
DO
WE WON'T LET THE GUILD PUT A BOUNTY ON HIM!
WE CAN'T DRAW TOO MUCH ATTENTION TO OURSELVES!
LET'S HIT ALL HIS REGULAR HAUNTS FIRST!
DO
DO
WHAT... WAS THAT!?
GAKON (KLUNK)
GATA
GATA (CLATTER)
GAKO

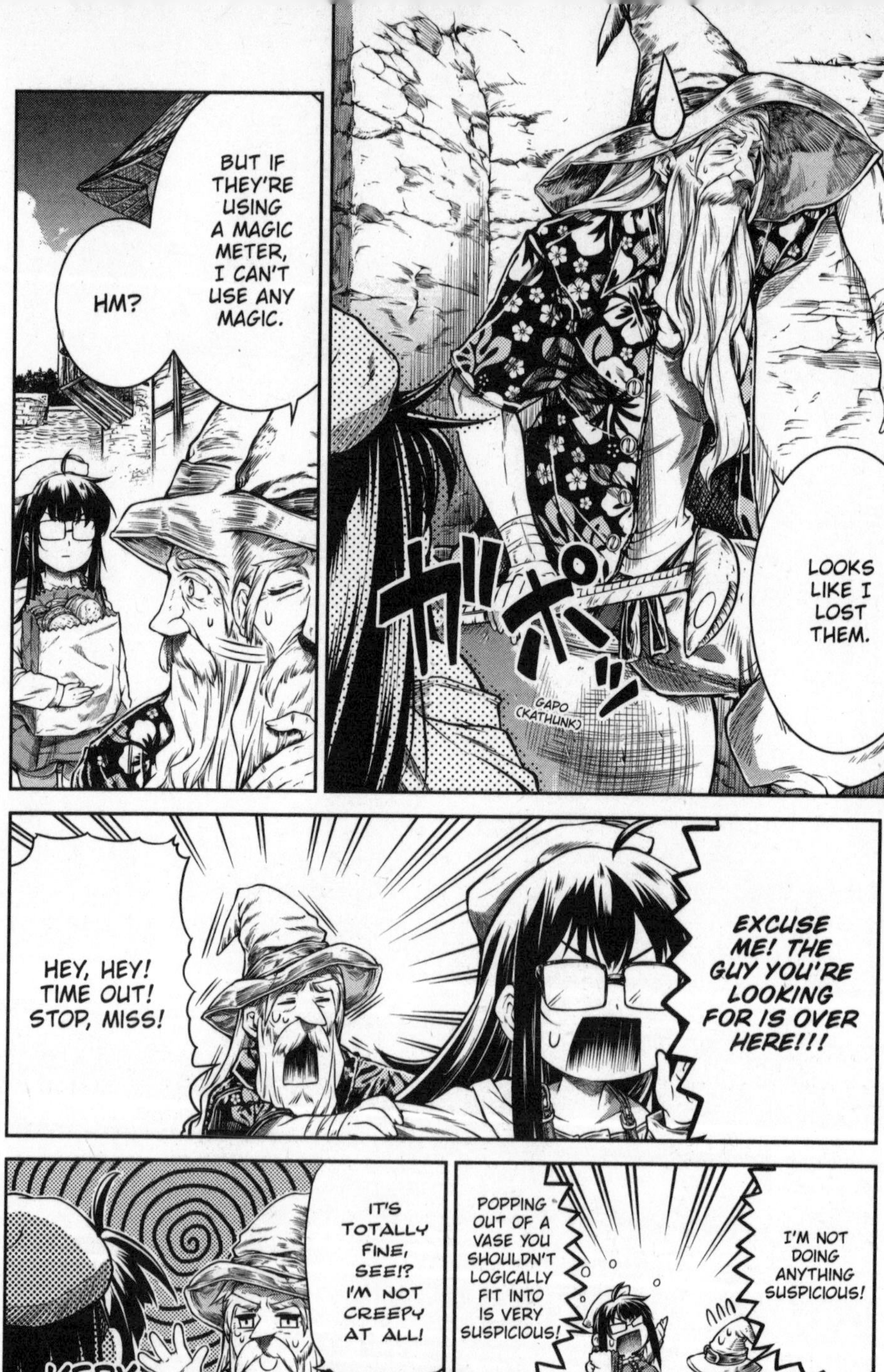
ガポッ
GAPO (KATHUNK)
LOOKS LIKE I LOST THEM.
BUT IF THEY'RE USING A MAGIC METER, I CAN'T USE ANY MAGIC.
HM?
EXCUSE ME! THE GUY YOU'RE LOOKING FOR IS OVER HERE!!!
HEY, HEY! TIME OUT! STOP, MISS!
I'M NOT DOING ANYTHING SUSPICIOUS!
POPPING OUT OF A VASE YOU SHOULDN'T LOGICALLY FIT INTO IS VERY SUSPICIOUS!
IT'S TOTALLY FINE, SEE!? I'M NOT CREEPY AT ALL!
VERY CREEPY.

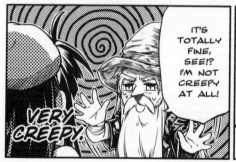

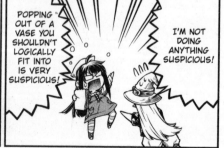

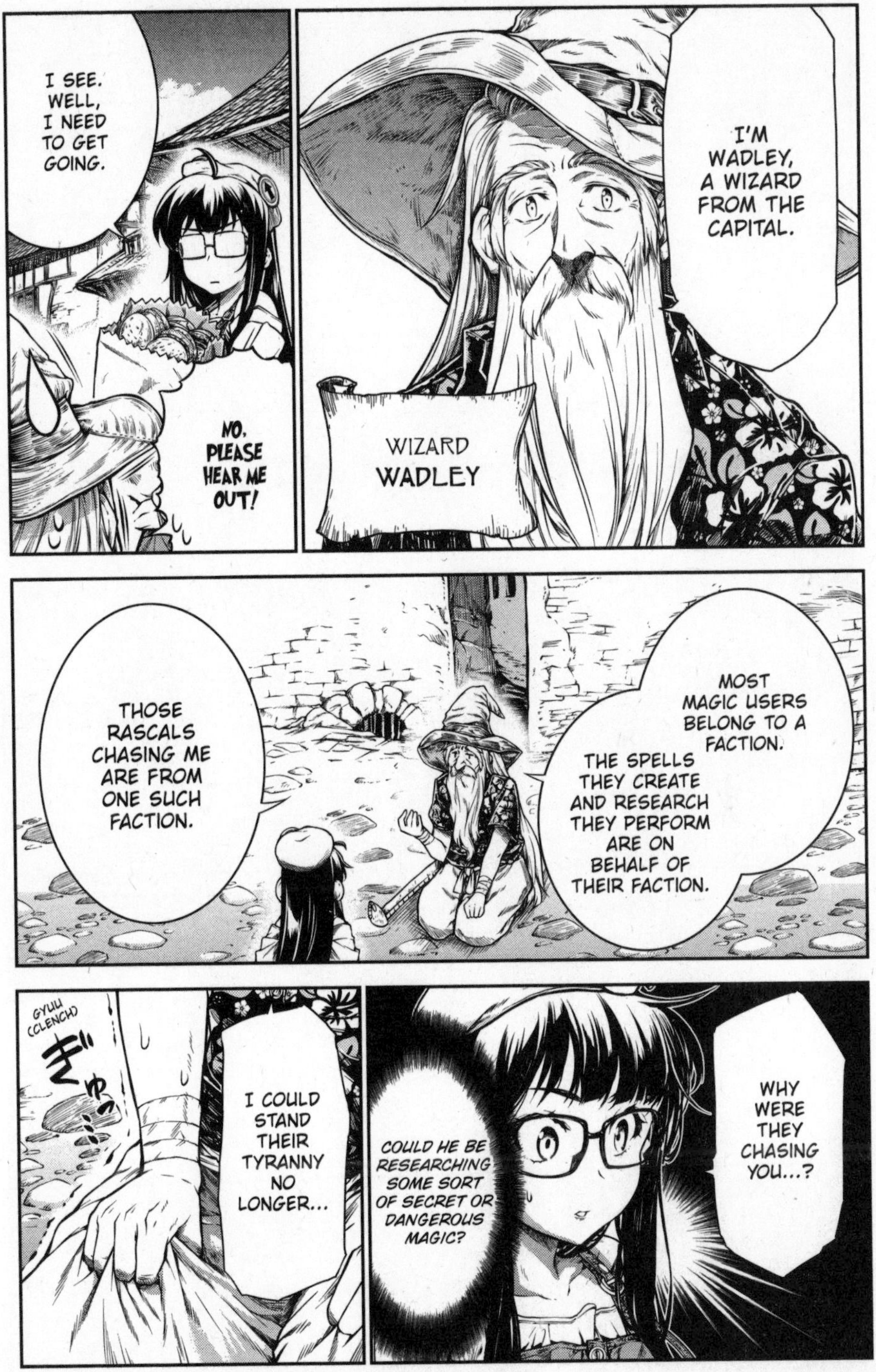
I'M WADLEY, A WIZARD FROM THE CAPITAL.
WIZARD WADLEY
I SEE. WELL, I NEED TO GET GOING.
NO. PLEASE HEAR ME OUT!
MOST MAGIC USERS BELONG TO A FACTION.
THE SPELLS THEY CREATE AND RESEARCH THEY PERFORM ARE ON BEHALF OF THEIR FACTION.
THOSE RASCALS CHASING ME ARE FROM ONE SUCH FACTION.
WHY WERE THEY CHASING YOU...?
COULD HE BE RESEARCHING SOME SORT OF SECRET OR DANGEROUS MAGIC?
I COULD STAND THEIR TYRANNY NO LONGER...
GYUU (CLENCH)

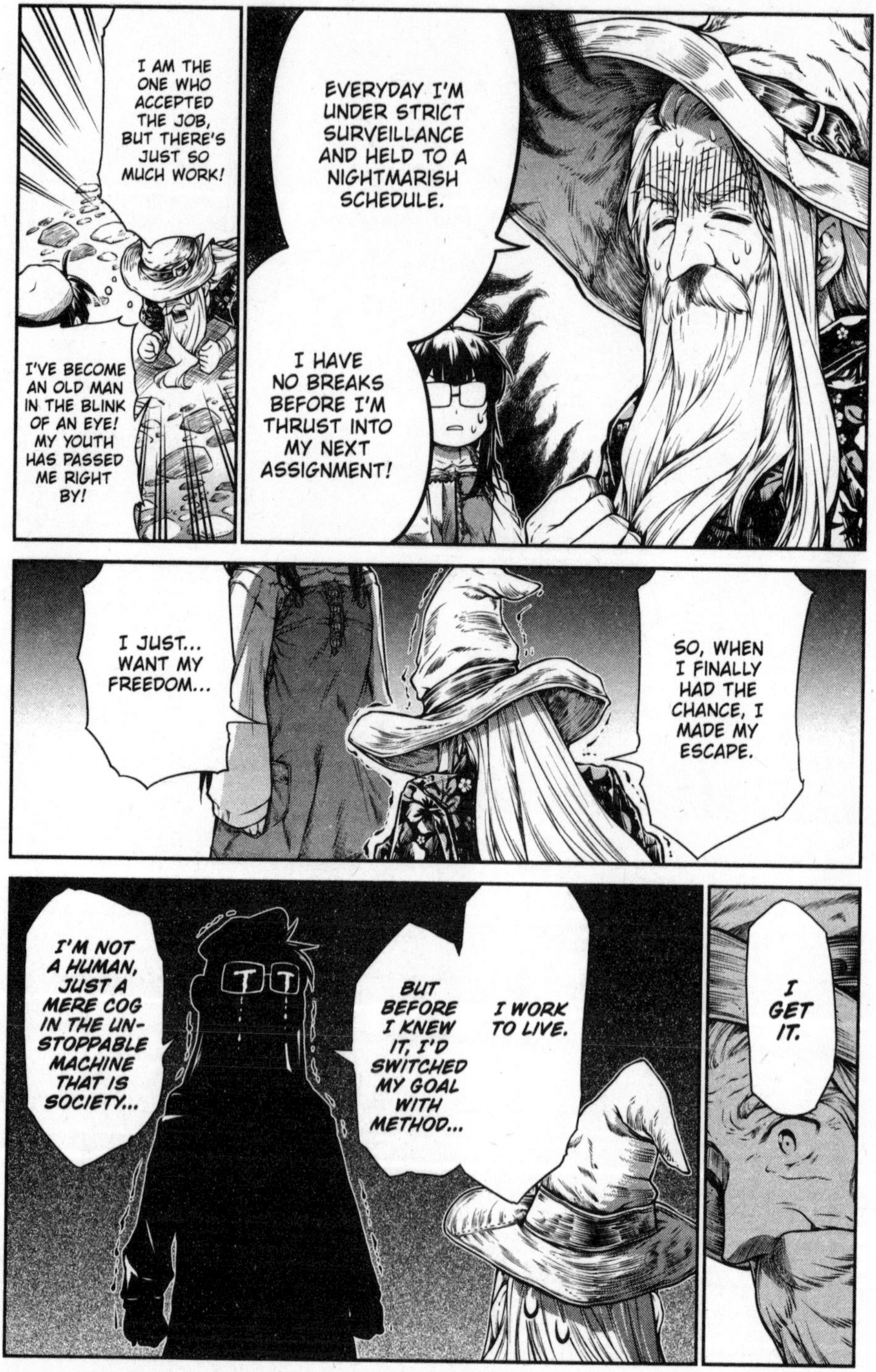
EVERYDAY I'M UNDER STRICT SURVEILLANCE AND HELD TO A NIGHTMARISH SCHEDULE.
I HAVE NO BREAKS BEFORE I'M THRUST INTO MY NEXT ASSIGNMENT!
I AM THE ONE WHO ACCEPTED THE JOB, BUT THERE'S JUST SO MUCH WORK!
I'VE BECOME AN OLD MAN IN THE BLINK OF AN EYE! MY YOUTH HAS PASSED ME RIGHT BY!
SO, WHEN I FINALLY HAD THE CHANCE, I MADE MY ESCAPE.
I JUST... WANT MY FREEDOM...
I GET IT.
I WORK TO LIVE.
BUT BEFORE I KNEW IT, I'D SWITCHED MY GOAL WITH METHOD...
I'M NOT A HUMAN, JUST A MERE COG IN THE UN-STOPPABLE MACHINE THAT IS SOCIETY...

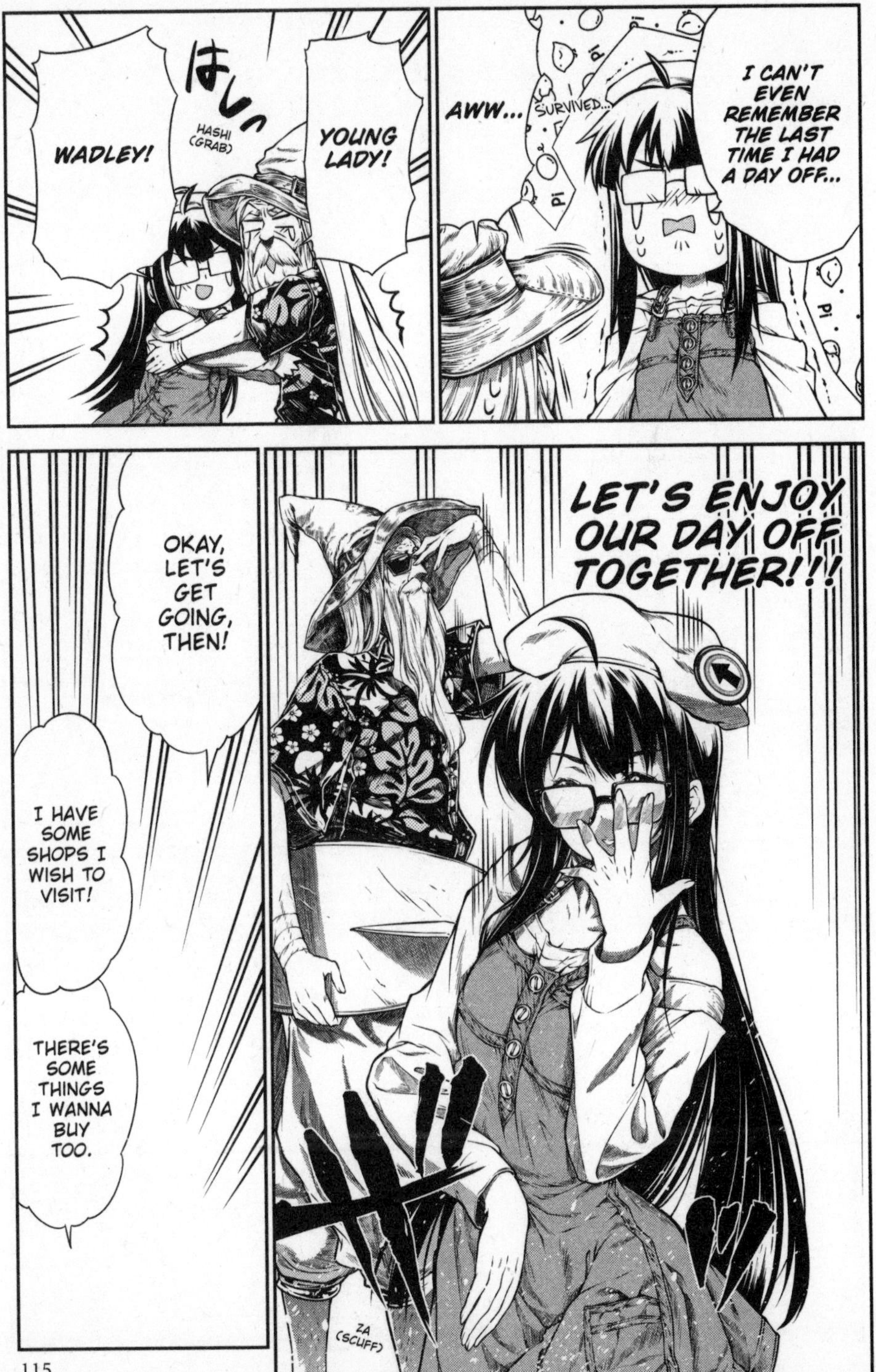
I CAN'T EVEN REMEMBER THE LAST TIME I HAD A DAY OFF...
PI
PI
SURVIVED...
PI
AWW...
YOUNG LADY!
はしっ
HASHI (GRAB)
WADLEY!
LET'S ENJOY OUR DAY OFF TOGETHER!!!
ZA (SCUFF)
OKAY, LET'S GET GOING, THEN!
I HAVE SOME SHOPS I WISH TO VISIT!
THERE'S SOME THINGS I WANNA BUY TOO.

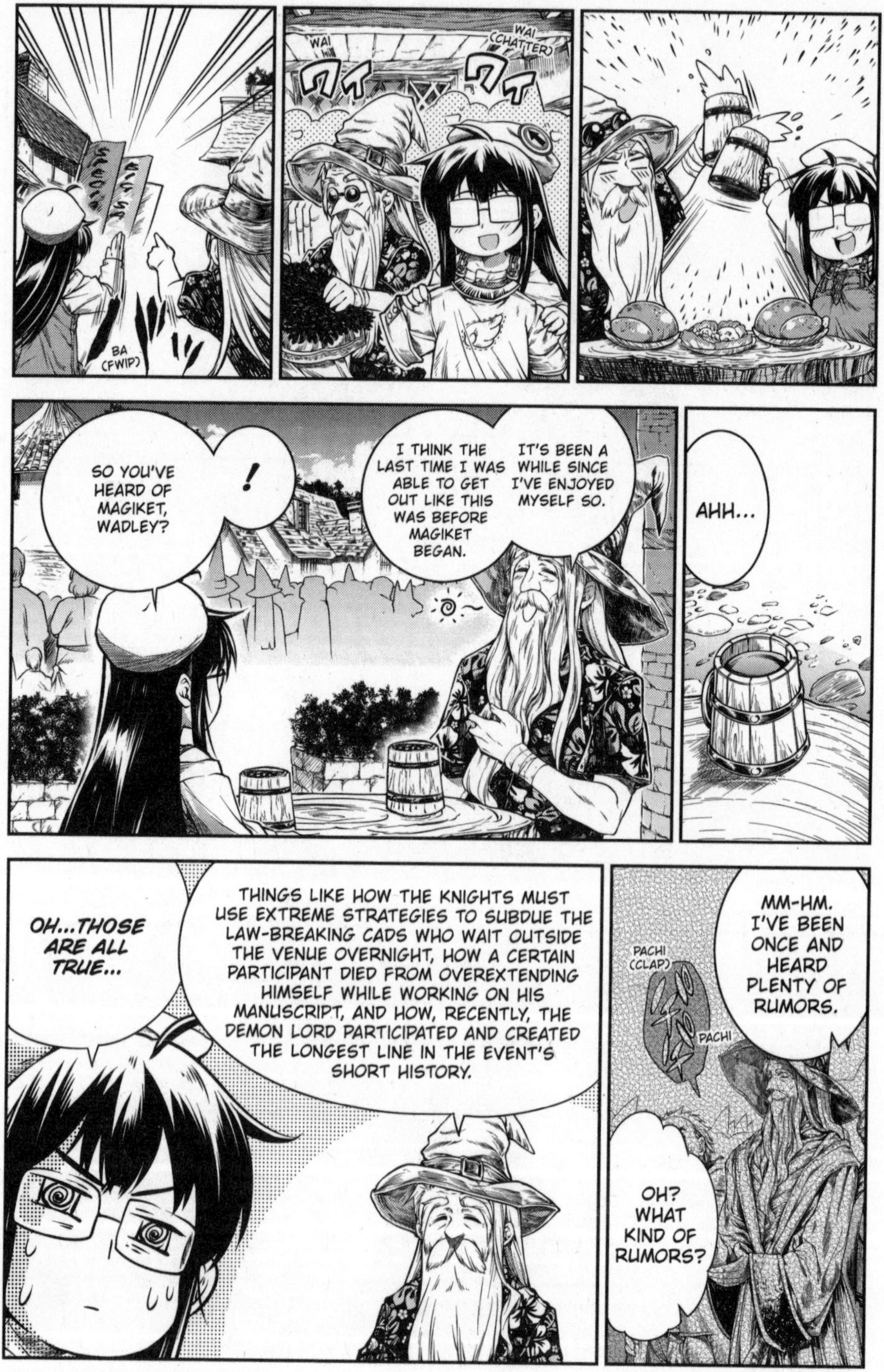
WAI (CHATTER)
ワイ
WAI
ワイ
BA (FWIP)
AHH...
IT'S BEEN A WHILE SINCE I'VE ENJOYED MYSELF SO.
I THINK THE LAST TIME I WAS ABLE TO GET OUT LIKE THIS WAS BEFORE MAGIKET BEGAN.
!
SO YOU'VE HEARD OF MAGIKET, WADLEY?
MM-HM. I'VE BEEN ONCE AND HEARD PLENTY OF RUMORS.
PACHI (CLAP)
PACHI
OH? WHAT KIND OF RUMORS?
THINGS LIKE HOW THE KNIGHTS MUST USE EXTREME STRATEGIES TO SUBDUE THE LAW-BREAKING CADS WHO WAIT OUTSIDE THE VENUE OVERNIGHT, HOW A CERTAIN PARTICIPANT DIED FROM OVEREXTENDING HIMSELF WHILE WORKING ON HIS MANUSCRIPT, AND HOW, RECENTLY, THE DEMON LORD PARTICIPATED AND CREATED THE LONGEST LINE IN THE EVENT'S SHORT HISTORY.
OH...THOSE ARE ALL TRUE...

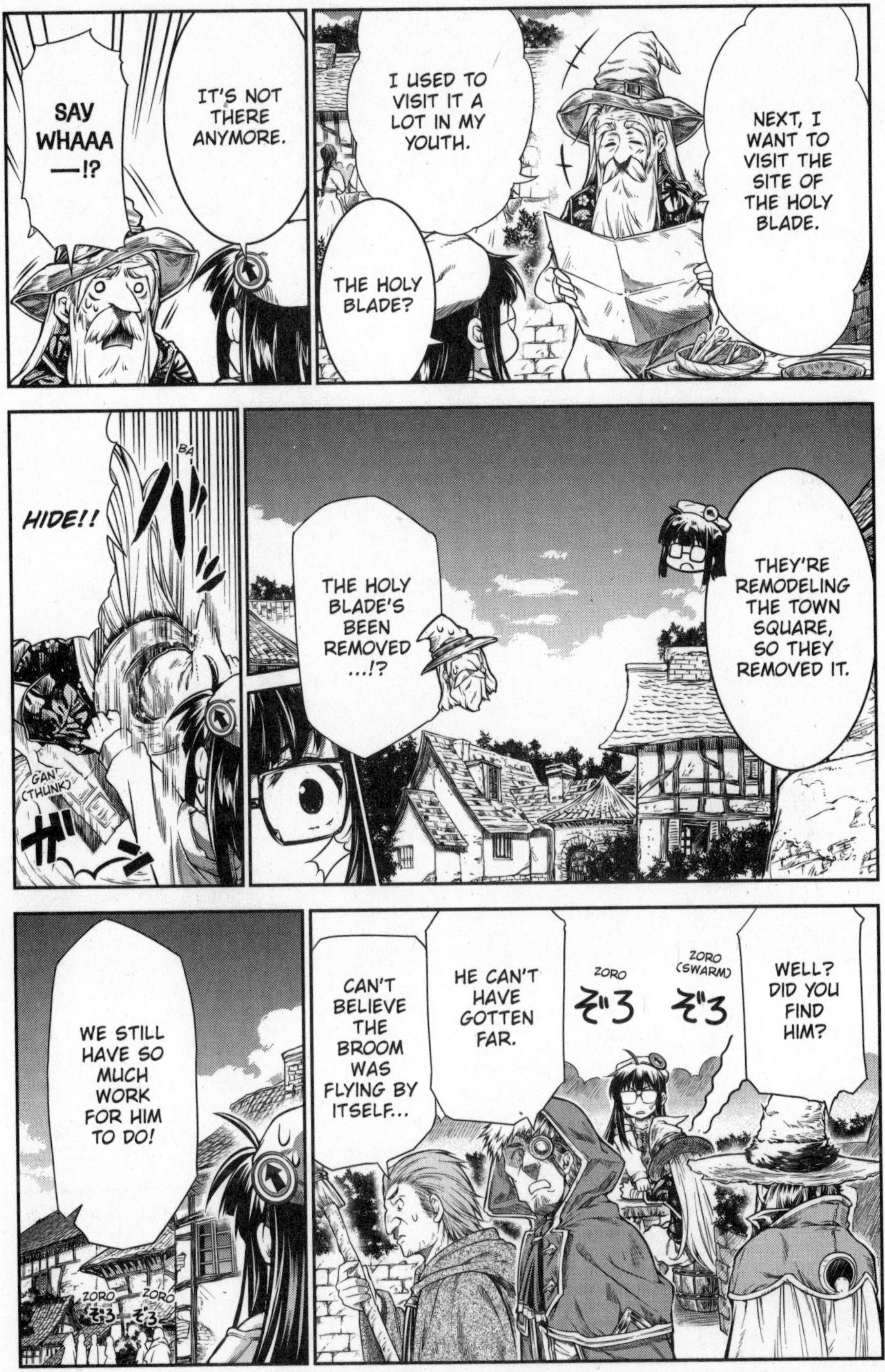
NEXT, I WANT TO VISIT THE SITE OF THE HOLY BLADE.
I USED TO VISIT IT A LOT IN MY YOUTH.
THE HOLY BLADE?
IT'S NOT THERE ANYMORE.
SAY WHAAA—!?
THEY'RE REMODELING THE TOWN SQUARE, SO THEY REMOVED IT.
THE HOLY BLADE'S BEEN REMOVED ...!?
BA
HIDE!!
GAN (THUNK)
WELL? DID YOU FIND HIM?
ZORO (SWARM)
ぞろ
ZORO
ぞろ
HE CAN'T HAVE GOTTEN FAR.
CAN'T BELIEVE THE BROOM WAS FLYING BY ITSELF...
WE STILL HAVE SO MUCH WORK FOR HIM TO DO!
ZORO
ぞろ
ZORO
ぞろ

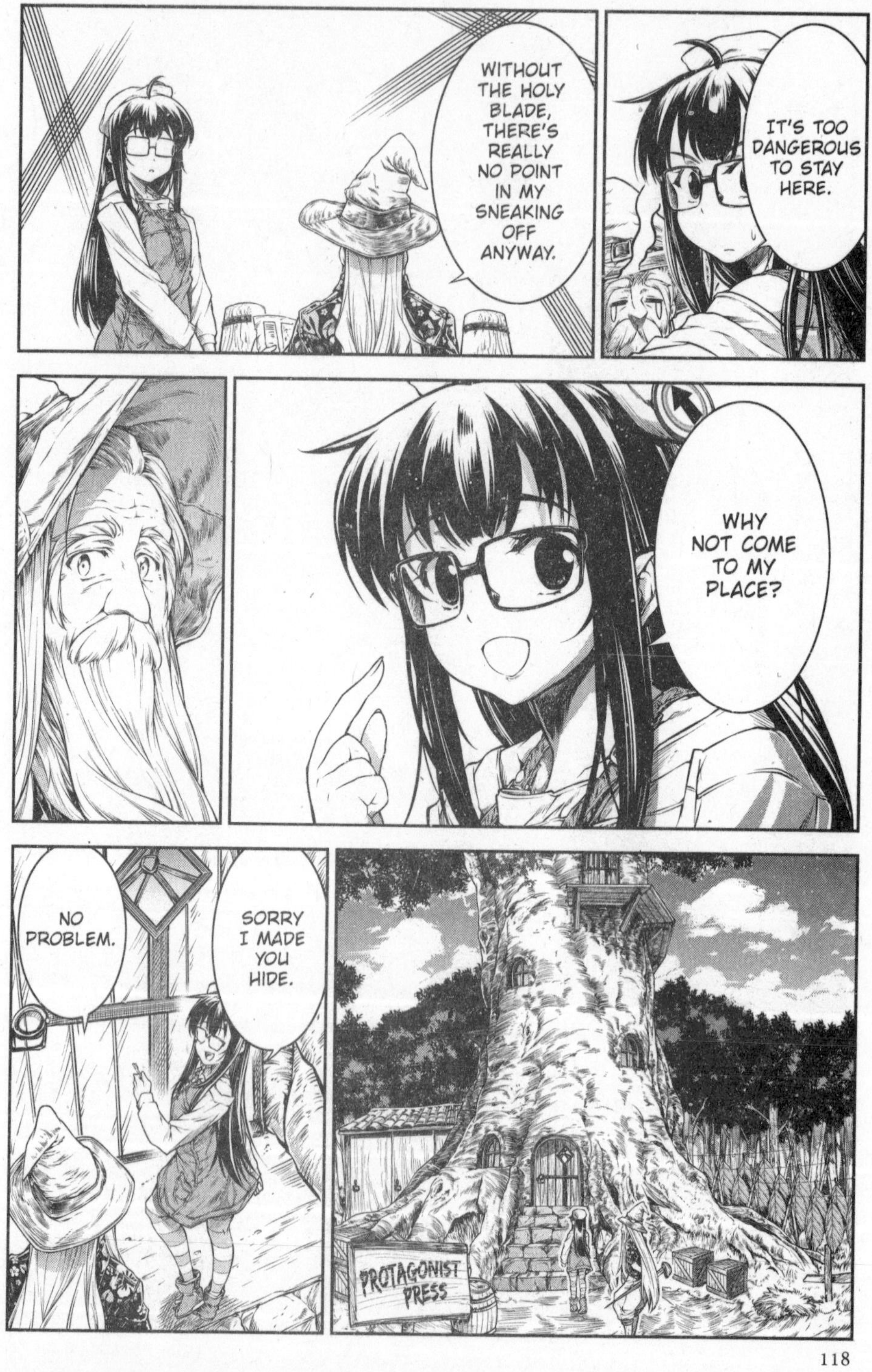
IT'S TOO DANGEROUS TO STAY HERE.
WITHOUT THE HOLY BLADE, THERE'S REALLY NO POINT IN MY SNEAKING OFF ANYWAY.
WHY NOT COME TO MY PLACE?
PROTAGONIST PRESS
SORRY I MADE YOU HIDE.
NO PROBLEM.

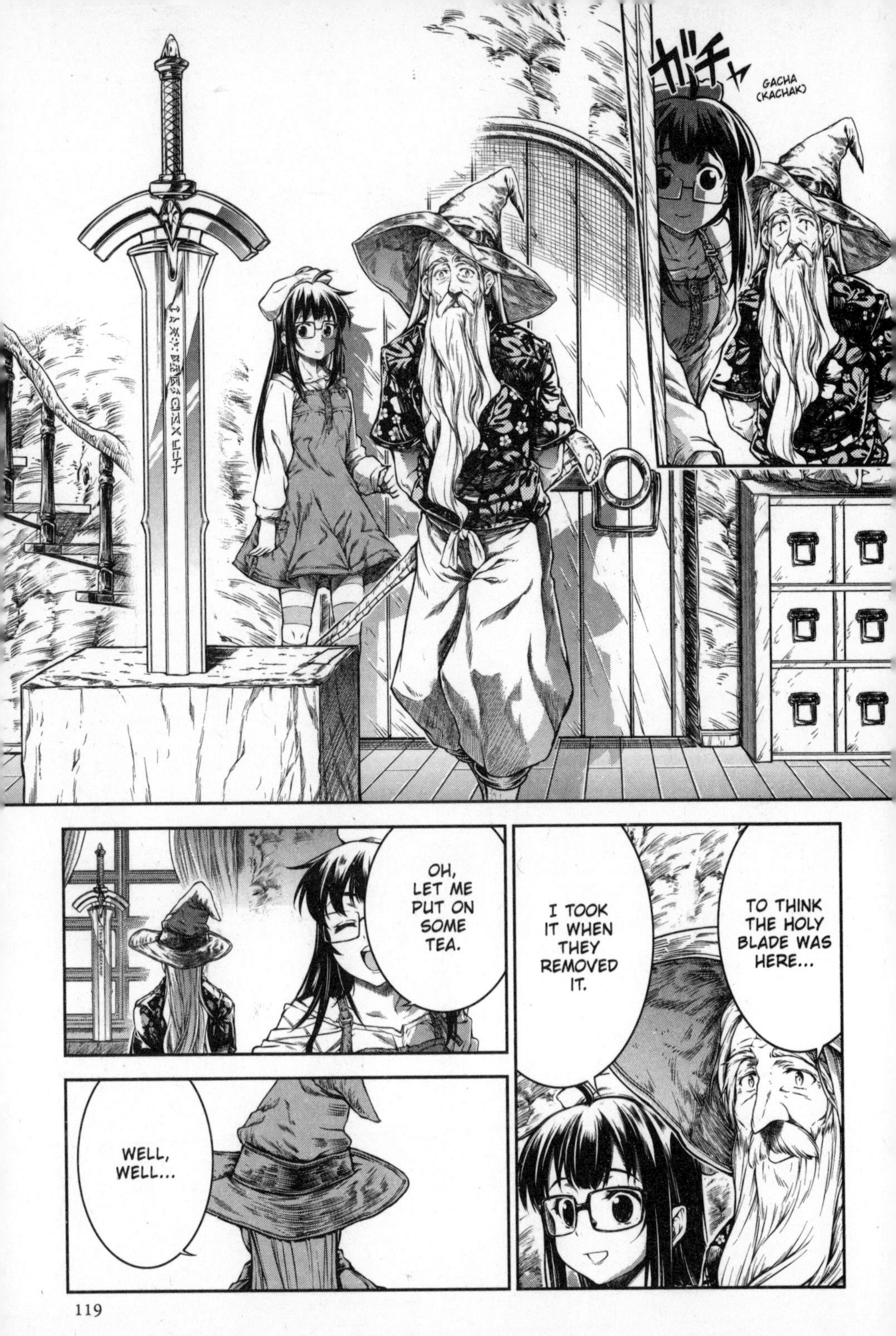
ガチャ
GACHA (KACHAK)
TO THINK THE HOLY BLADE WAS HERE...
I TOOK IT WHEN THEY REMOVED IT.
OH, LET ME PUT ON SOME TEA.
WELL, WELL...

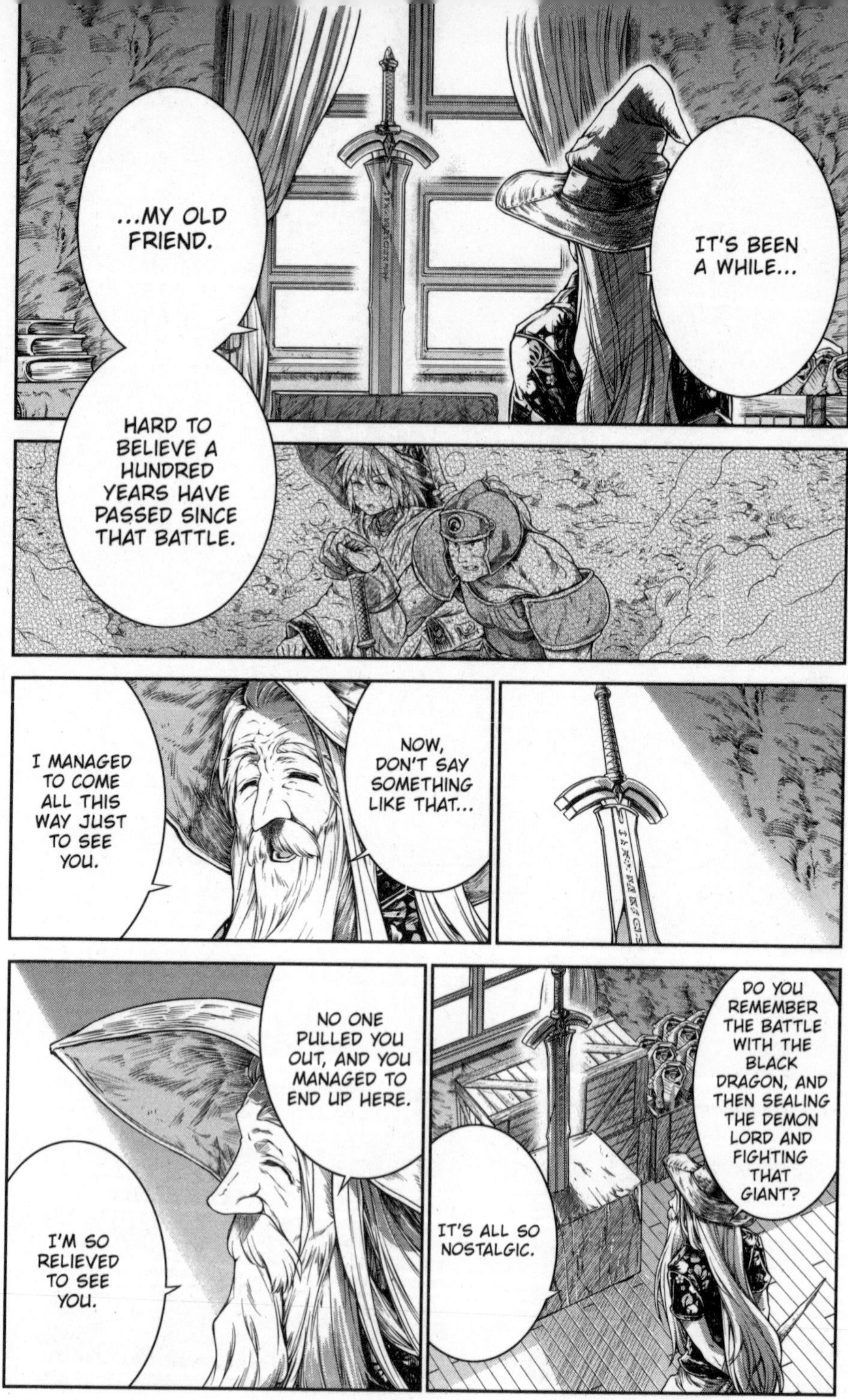
IT'S BEEN A WHILE...
...MY OLD FRIEND.
HARD TO BELIEVE A HUNDRED YEARS HAVE PASSED SINCE THAT BATTLE.
NOW, DON'T SAY SOMETHING LIKE THAT...
I MANAGED TO COME ALL THIS WAY JUST TO SEE YOU.
DO YOU REMEMBER THE BATTLE WITH THE BLACK DRAGON, AND THEN SEALING THE DEMON LORD AND FIGHTING THAT GIANT?
IT'S ALL SO NOSTALGIC.
NO ONE PULLED YOU OUT, AND YOU MANAGED TO END UP HERE.
I'M SO RELIEVED TO SEE YOU.

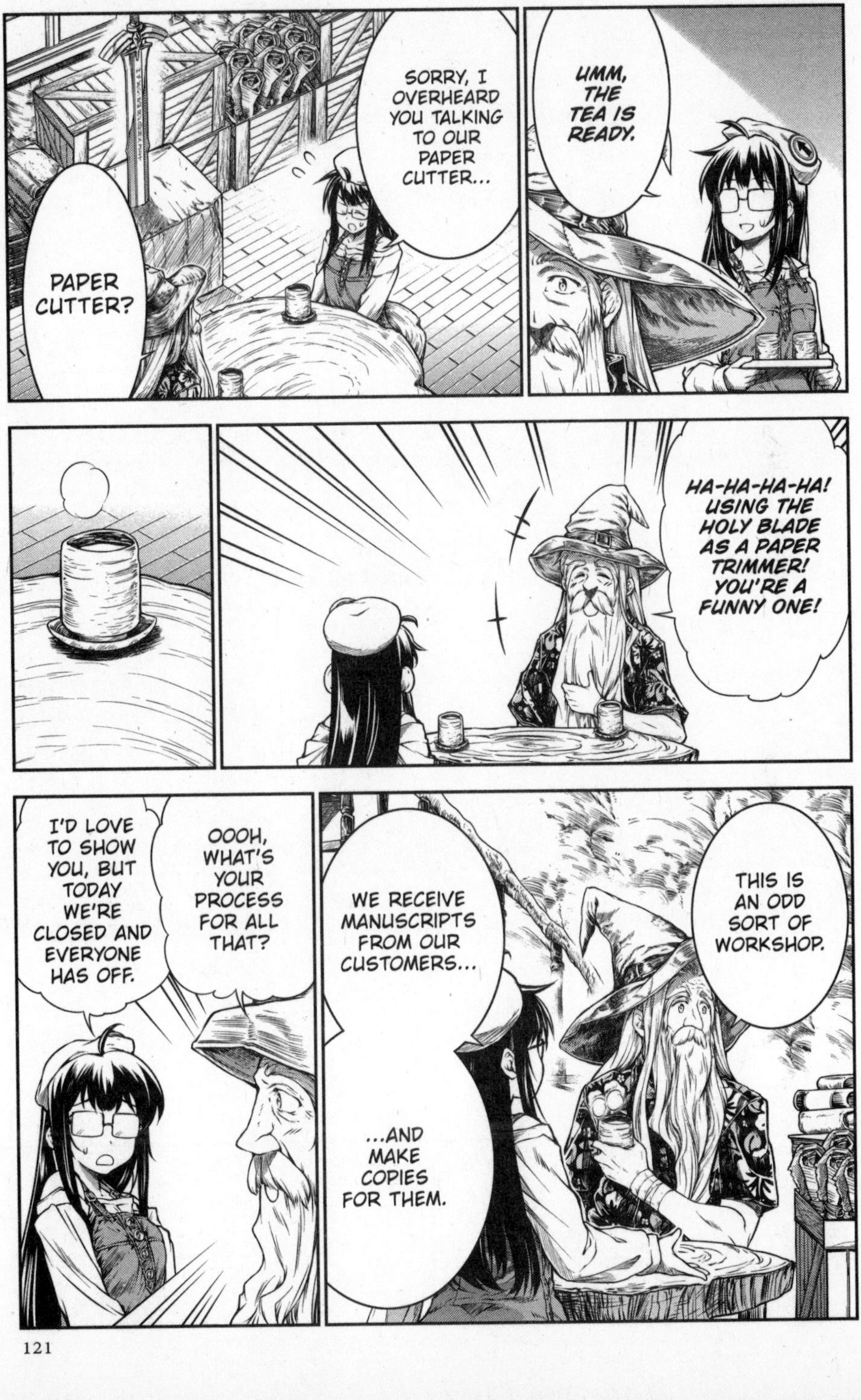
UMM, THE TEA IS READY.
SORRY, I OVERHEARD YOU TALKING TO OUR PAPER CUTTER...
PAPER CUTTER?
HA-HA-HA-HA! USING THE HOLY BLADE AS A PAPER TRIMMER! YOU'RE A FUNNY ONE!
THIS IS AN ODD SORT OF WORKSHOP.
WE RECEIVE MANUSCRIPTS FROM OUR CUSTOMERS...
...AND MAKE COPIES FOR THEM.
OOOH, WHAT'S YOUR PROCESS FOR ALL THAT?
I'D LOVE TO SHOW YOU, BUT TODAY WE'RE CLOSED AND EVERYONE HAS OFF.

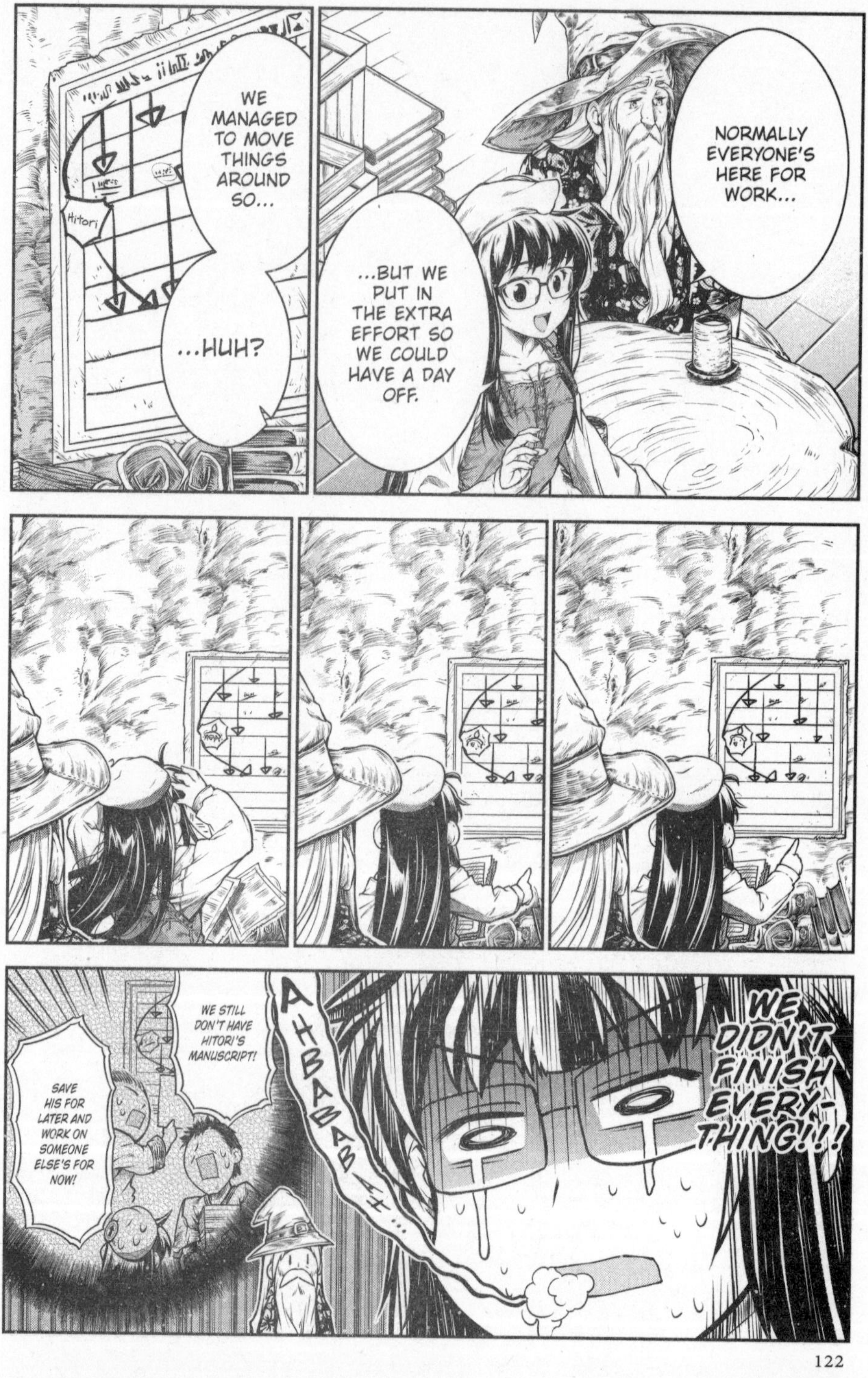
NORMALLY EVERYONE'S HERE FOR WORK...
...BUT WE PUT IN THE EXTRA EFFORT SO WE COULD HAVE A DAY OFF.
WE MANAGED TO MOVE THINGS AROUND SO...
Hitori
...HUH?
WE DIDN'T FINISH EVERY-THING!!!
AHBABABAH...
WE STILL DON'T HAVE HITORI'S MANUSCRIPT!
SAVE HIS FOR LATER AND WORK ON SOMEONE ELSE'S FOR NOW!

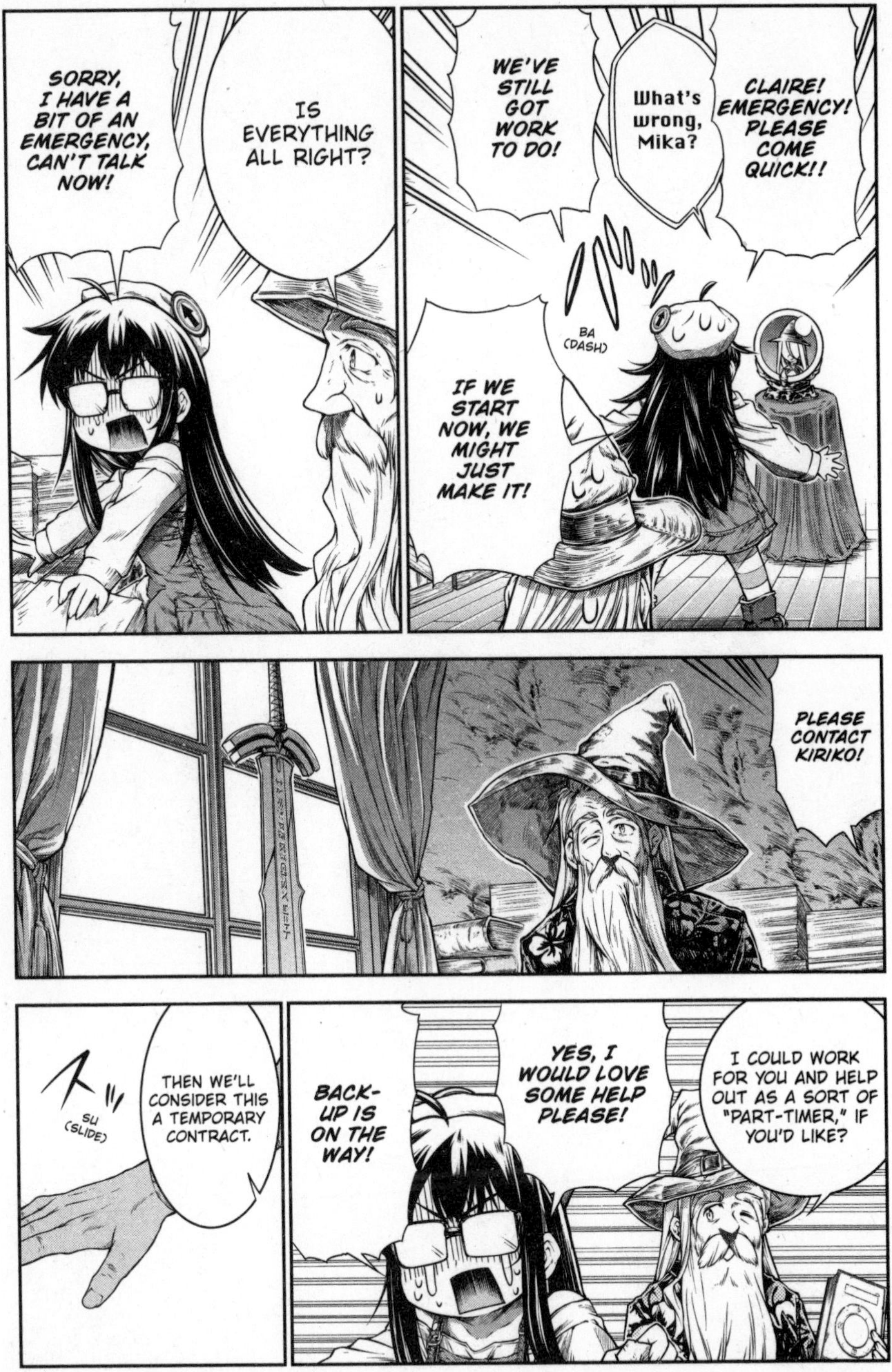
CLAIRE! EMERGENCY! PLEASE COME QUICK!!
What's wrong, Mika?
WE'VE STILL GOT WORK TO DO!
BA (DASH)
IF WE START NOW, WE MIGHT JUST MAKE IT!
IS EVERYTHING ALL RIGHT?
SORRY, I HAVE A BIT OF AN EMERGENCY, CAN'T TALK NOW!
PLEASE CONTACT KIRIKO!
I COULD WORK FOR YOU AND HELP OUT AS A SORT OF "PART-TIMER," IF YOU'D LIKE?
YES, I WOULD LOVE SOME HELP PLEASE!
BACK-UP IS ON THE WAY!
THEN WE'LL CONSIDER THIS A TEMPORARY CONTRACT.
SU (SLIDE)

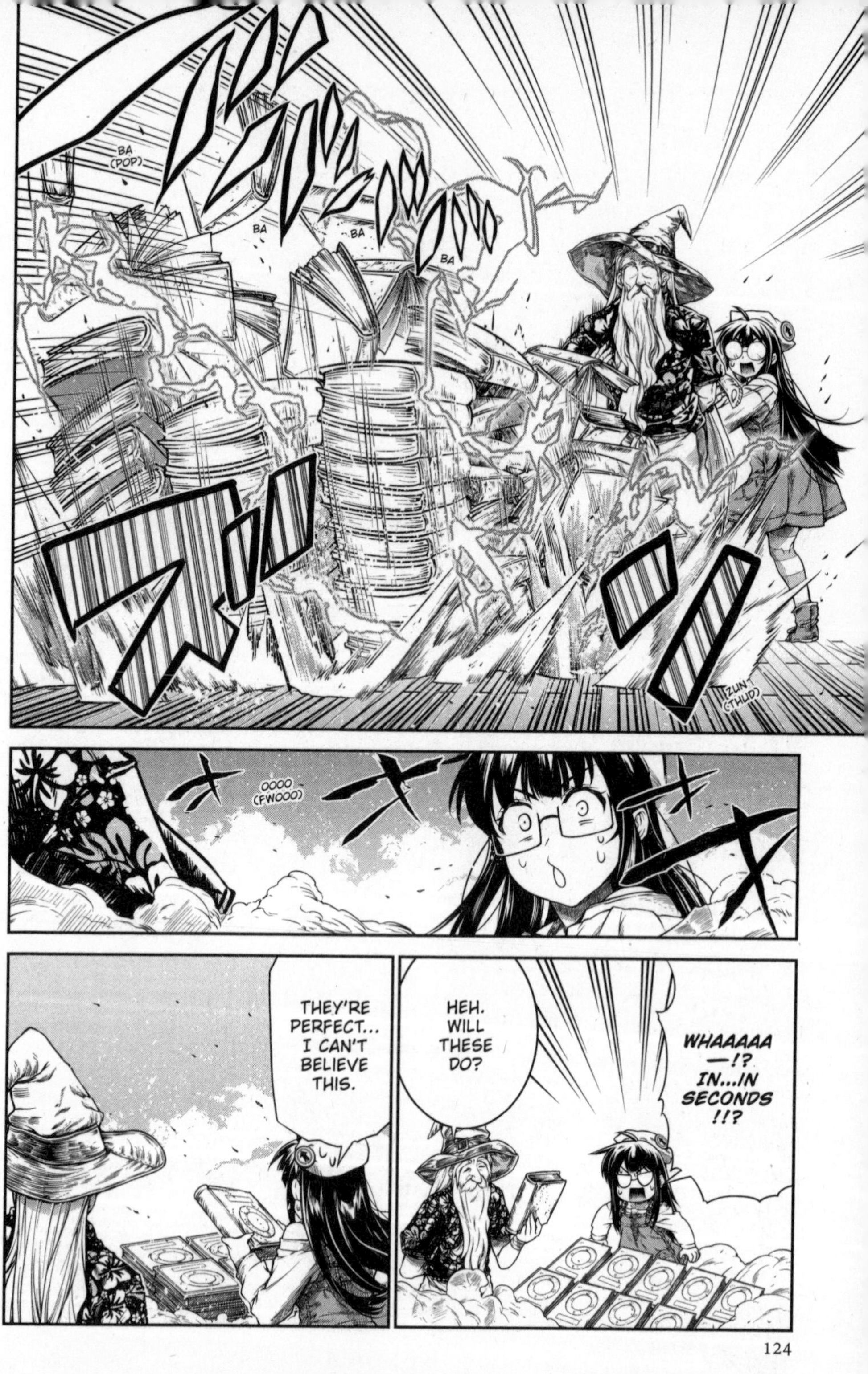
BA
(POP)
BA
BA
BA
ZUNT
(THUD)
OOOO
(FWOOO)
WHAAAAA—!? IN...IN SECONDS!!?
HEH. WILL THESE DO?
THEY'RE PERFECT... I CAN'T BELIEVE THIS.

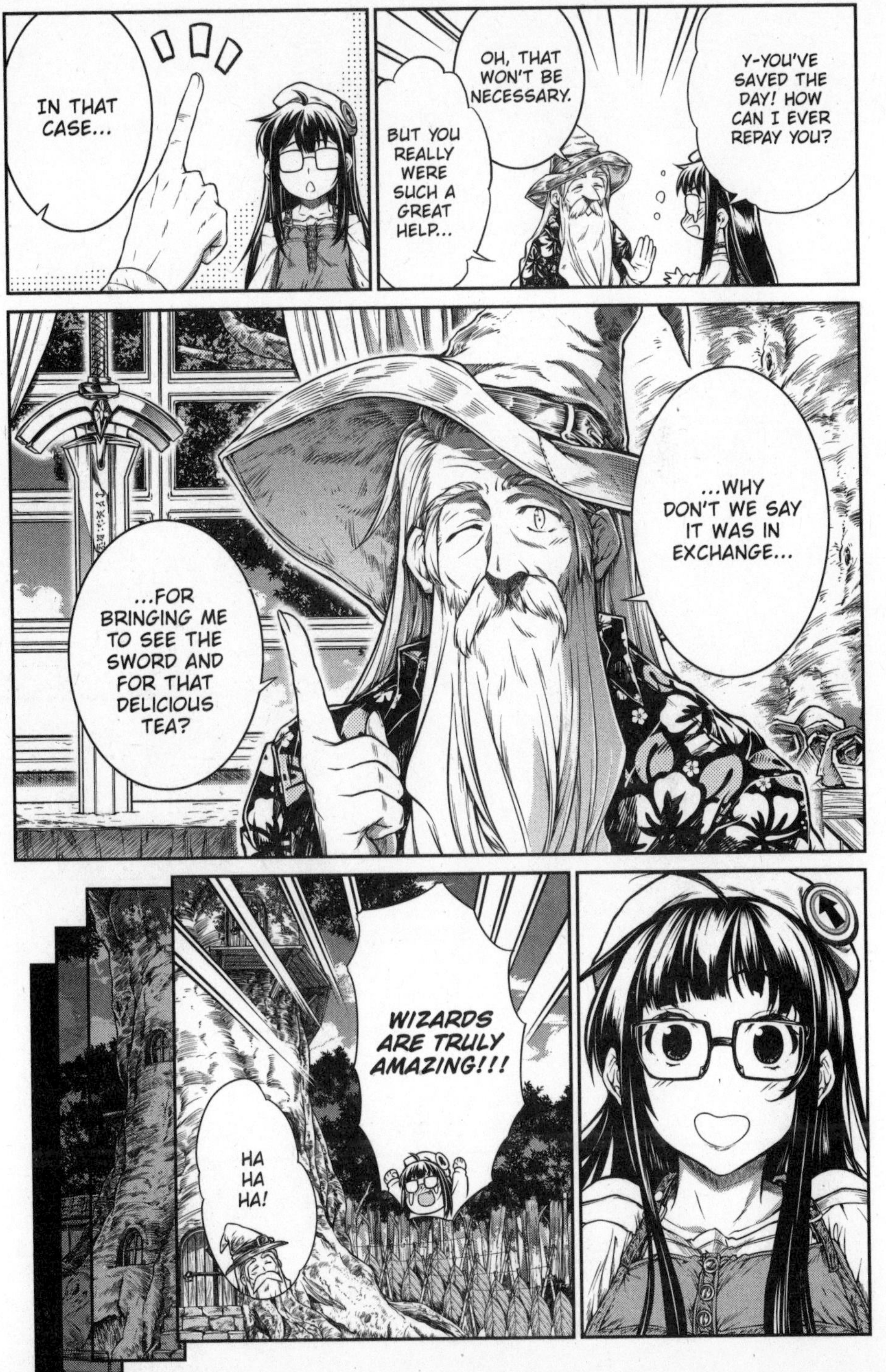
Y-YOU'VE SAVED THE DAY! HOW CAN I EVER REPAY YOU?
OH, THAT WON'T BE NECESSARY.
BUT YOU REALLY WERE SUCH A GREAT HELP...
IN THAT CASE...
...WHY DON'T WE SAY IT WAS IN EXCHANGE...
...FOR BRINGING ME TO SEE THE SWORD AND FOR THAT DELICIOUS TEA?
WIZARDS ARE TRULY AMAZING!!!
HA HA HA!

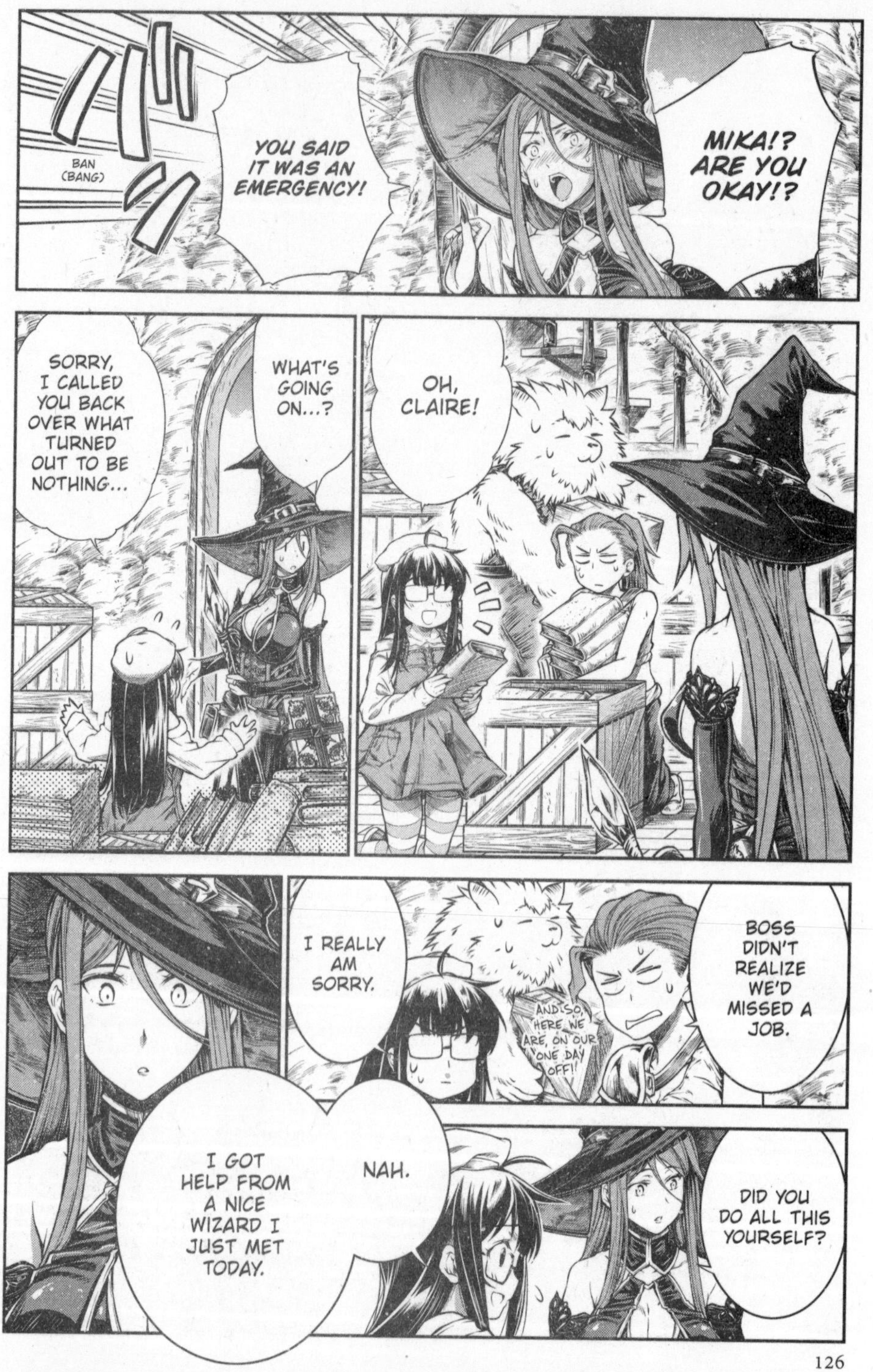
MIKA!? ARE YOU OKAY!?
YOU SAID IT WAS AN EMERGENCY!
BAN (BANG)
OH, CLAIRE!
WHAT'S GOING ON...?
SORRY, I CALLED YOU BACK OVER WHAT TURNED OUT TO BE NOTHING...
BOSS DIDN'T REALIZE WE'D MISSED A JOB.
AND SO, HERE WE ARE, ON OUR ONE DAY OFF!
I REALLY AM SORRY.
DID YOU DO ALL THIS YOURSELF?
NAH.
I GOT HELP FROM A NICE WIZARD I JUST MET TODAY.

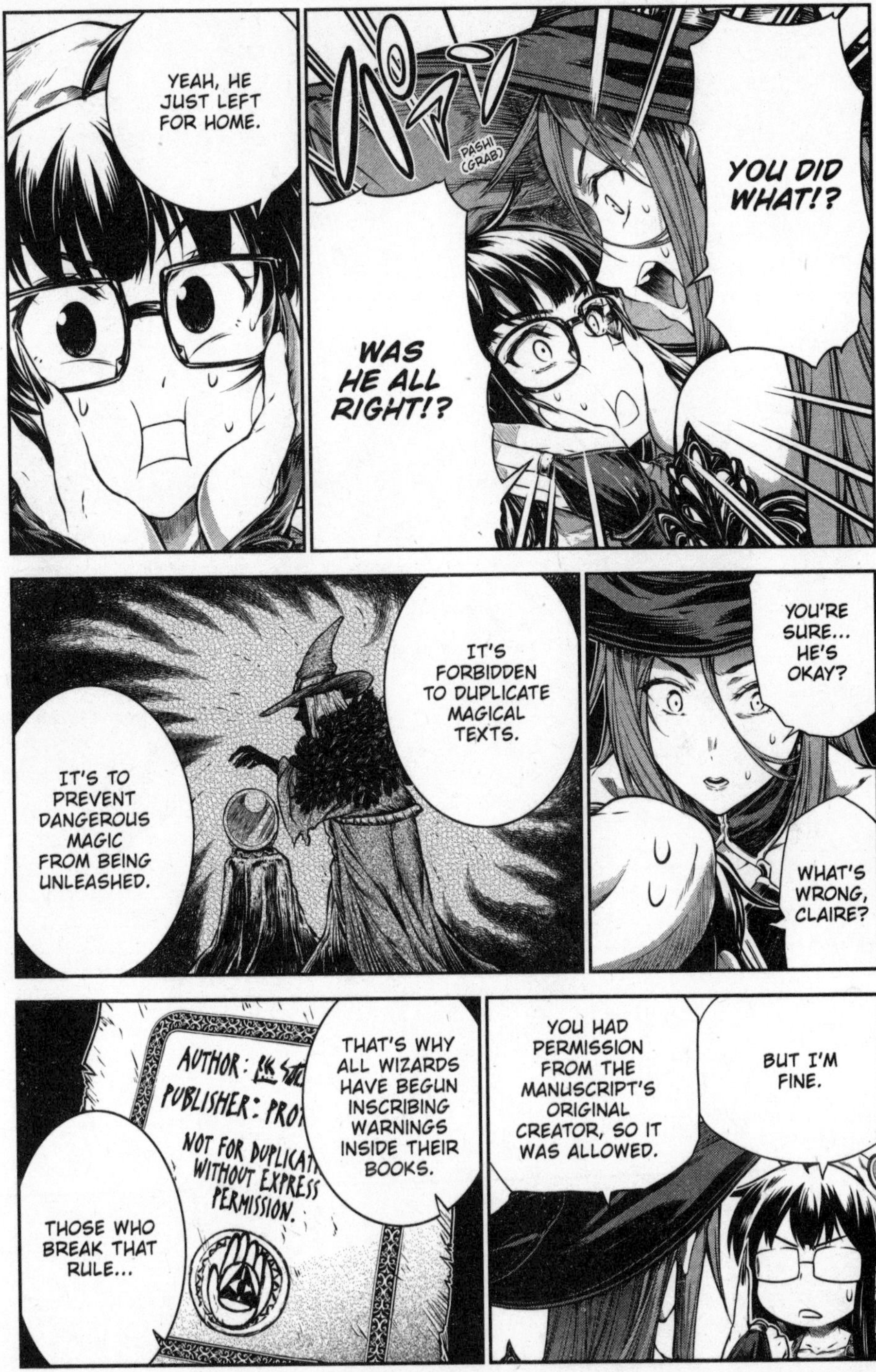
PASHI (GRAB)
YOU DID WHAT!?
WAS HE ALL RIGHT!?
YEAH, HE JUST LEFT FOR HOME.
YOU'RE SURE... HE'S OKAY?
WHAT'S WRONG, CLAIRE?
IT'S FORBIDDEN TO DUPLICATE MAGICAL TEXTS.
IT'S TO PREVENT DANGEROUS MAGIC FROM BEING UNLEASHED.
BUT I'M FINE.
YOU HAD PERMISSION FROM THE MANUSCRIPT'S ORIGINAL CREATOR, SO IT WAS ALLOWED.
THAT'S WHY ALL WIZARDS HAVE BEGUN INSCRIBING WARNINGS INSIDE THEIR BOOKS.
AUTHOR :
PUBLISHER : PRO
NOT FOR DUPLICAT
WITHOUT EXPRESS PERMISSION.
THOSE WHO BREAK THAT RULE...

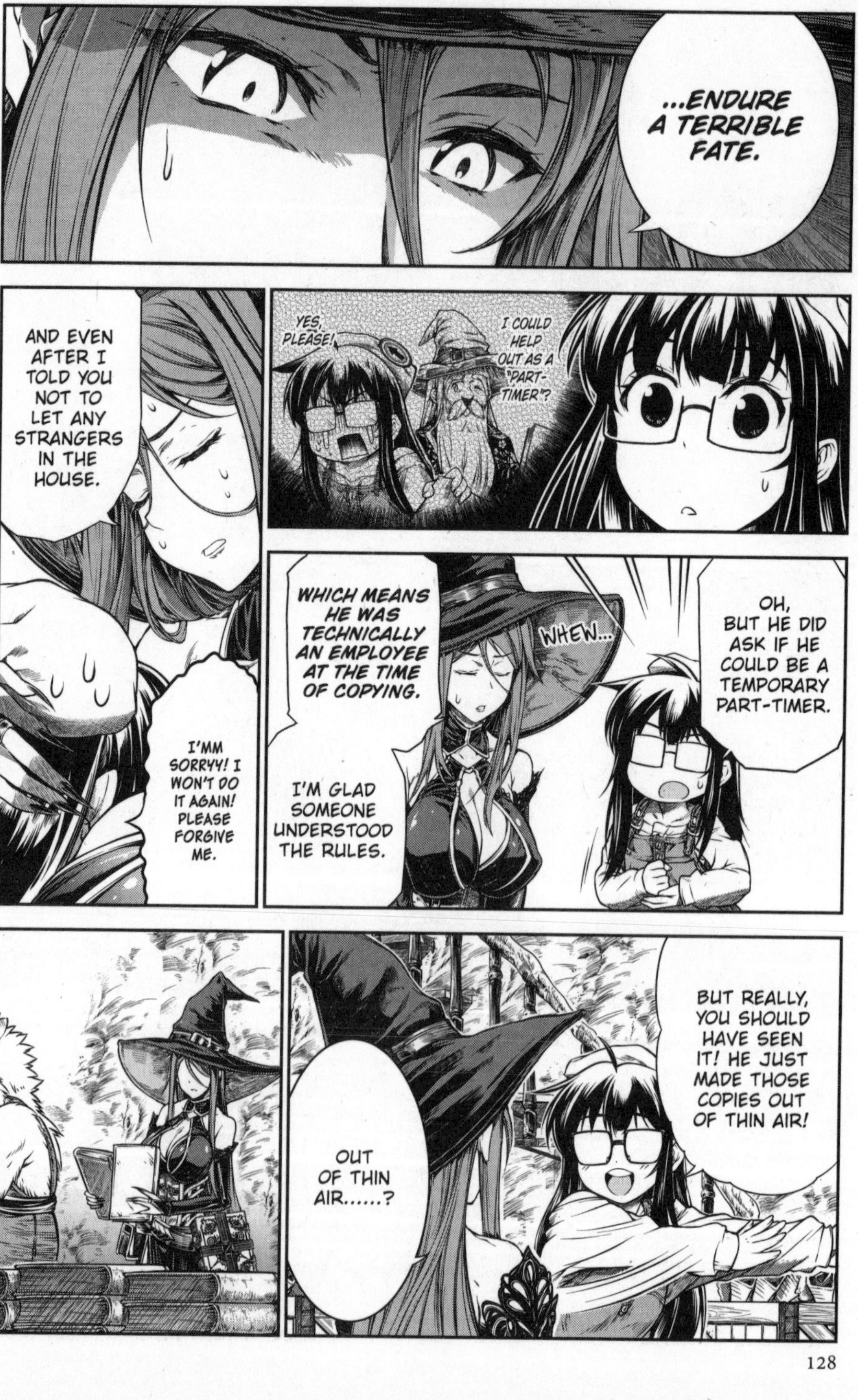
...ENDURE A TERRIBLE FATE.
I COULD HELP OUT AS A "PART-TIMER"?
YES, PLEASE!
OH, BUT HE DID ASK IF HE COULD BE A TEMPORARY PART-TIMER.
WHEW...
WHICH MEANS HE WAS TECHNICALLY AN EMPLOYEE AT THE TIME OF COPYING.
I'M GLAD SOMEONE UNDERSTOOD THE RULES.
AND EVEN AFTER I TOLD YOU NOT TO LET ANY STRANGERS IN THE HOUSE.
I'MM SORRYY! I WON'T DO IT AGAIN! PLEASE FORGIVE ME.
BUT REALLY, YOU SHOULD HAVE SEEN IT! HE JUST MADE THOSE COPIES OUT OF THIN AIR!
OUT OF THIN AIR......?

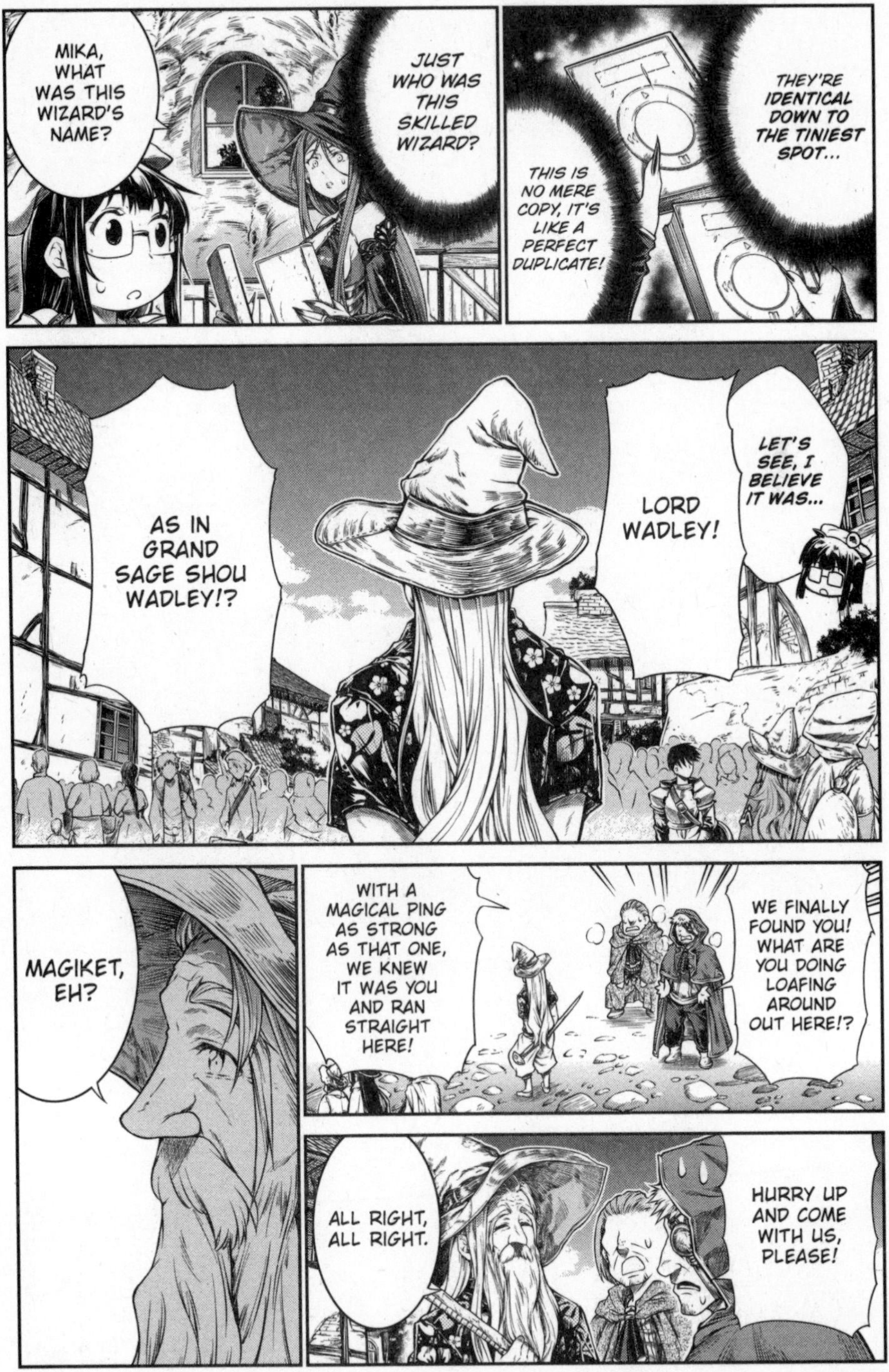
THEY'RE IDENTICAL DOWN TO THE TINIEST SPOT...
THIS IS NO MERE COPY, IT'S LIKE A PERFECT DUPLICATE!
JUST WHO WAS THIS SKILLED WIZARD?
MIKA, WHAT WAS THIS WIZARD'S NAME?
LET'S SEE, I BELIEVE IT WAS...
LORD WADLEY!
AS IN GRAND SAGE SHOU WADLEY!?
WE FINALLY FOUND YOU! WHAT ARE YOU DOING LOAFING AROUND OUT HERE!?
WITH A MAGICAL PING AS STRONG AS THAT ONE, WE KNEW IT WAS YOU AND RAN STRAIGHT HERE!
HURRY UP AND COME WITH US, PLEASE!
ALL RIGHT, ALL RIGHT.
MAGIKET, EH?

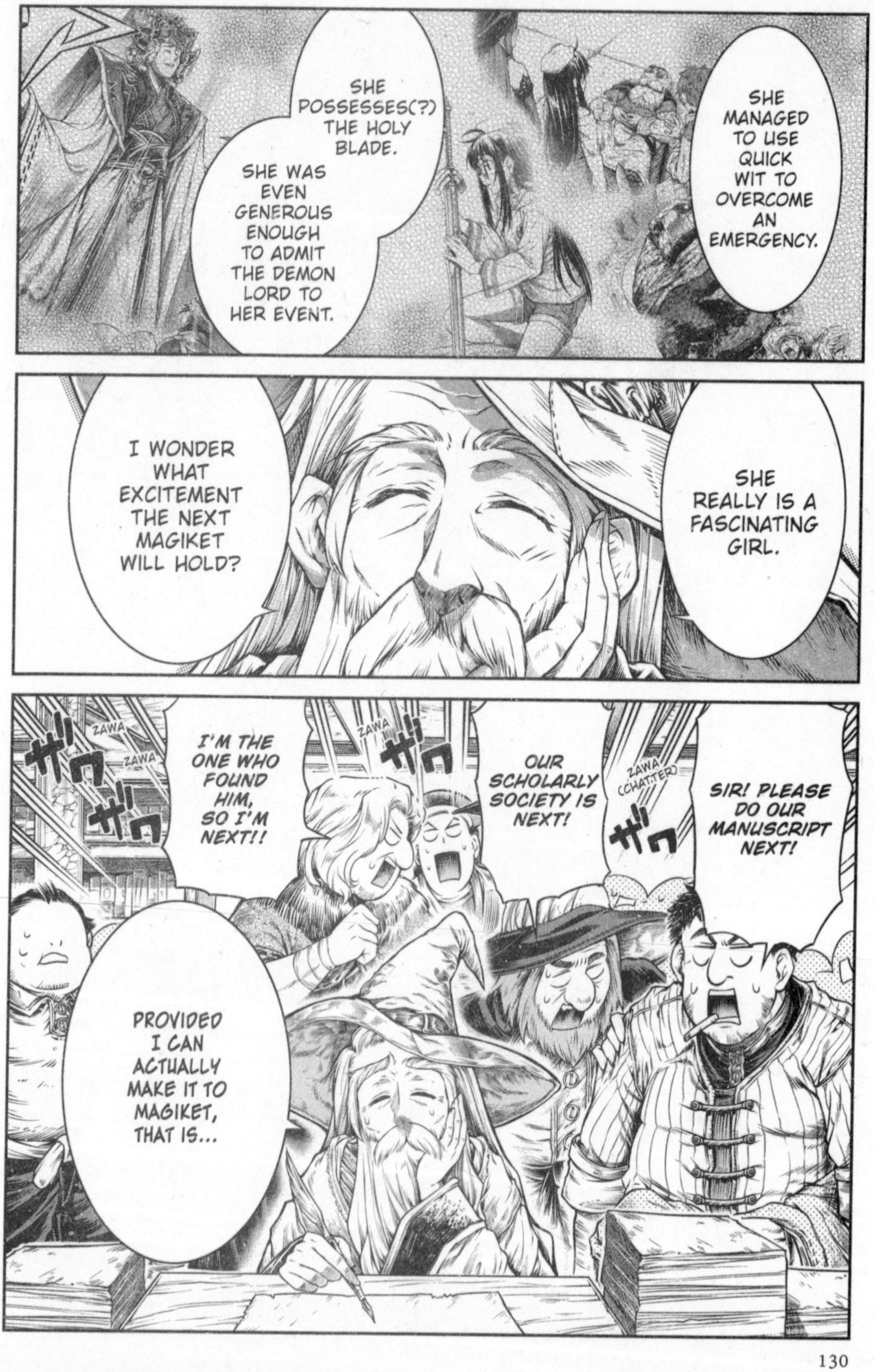
SHE MANAGED TO USE QUICK WIT TO OVERCOME AN EMERGENCY.
SHE POSSESSES(?) THE HOLY BLADE.
SHE WAS EVEN GENEROUS ENOUGH TO ADMIT THE DEMON LORD TO HER EVENT.
SHE REALLY IS A FASCINATING GIRL.
I WONDER WHAT EXCITEMENT THE NEXT MAGIKET WILL HOLD?
SIR! PLEASE DO OUR MANUSCRIPT NEXT!
ZAWA (CHATTER)
OUR SCHOLARLY SOCIETY IS NEXT!
ZAWA
I'M THE ONE WHO FOUND HIM, SO I'M NEXT!!
ZAWA
ZAWA
PROVIDED I CAN ACTUALLY MAKE IT TO MAGIKET, THAT IS...

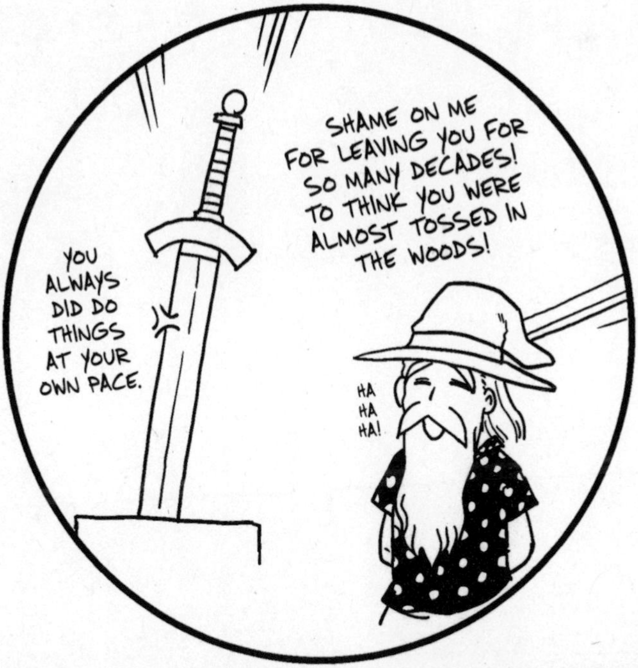
SHAME ON ME FOR LEAVING YOU FOR SO MANY DECADES! TO THINK YOU WERE ALMOST TOSSED IN THE WOODS!
YOU ALWAYS DID DO THINGS AT YOUR OWN PACE.
HA HA HA!

# A WITCH'S PRINTING OFFICE

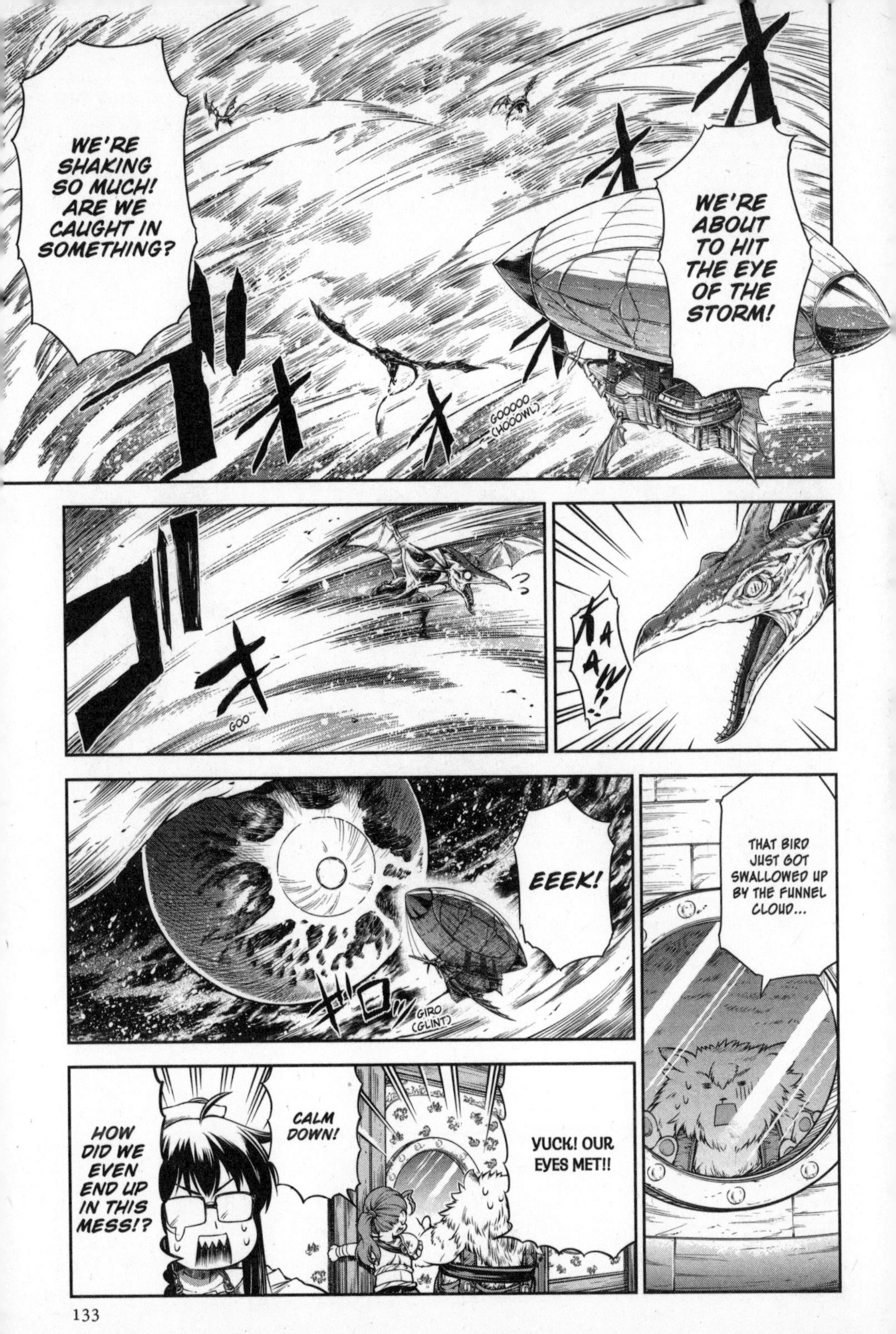
WE'RE ABOUT TO HIT THE EYE OF THE STORM!
WE'RE SHAKING SO MUCH! ARE WE CAUGHT IN SOMETHING?
GOOOOO (HOOOWL)
KAAAW!!
GOO
THAT BIRD JUST GOT SWALLOWED UP BY THE FUNNEL CLOUD...
EEEK!
GIRO (GLINT)
YUCK! OUR EYES MET!!
CALM DOWN!
HOW DID WE EVEN END UP IN THIS MESS!?

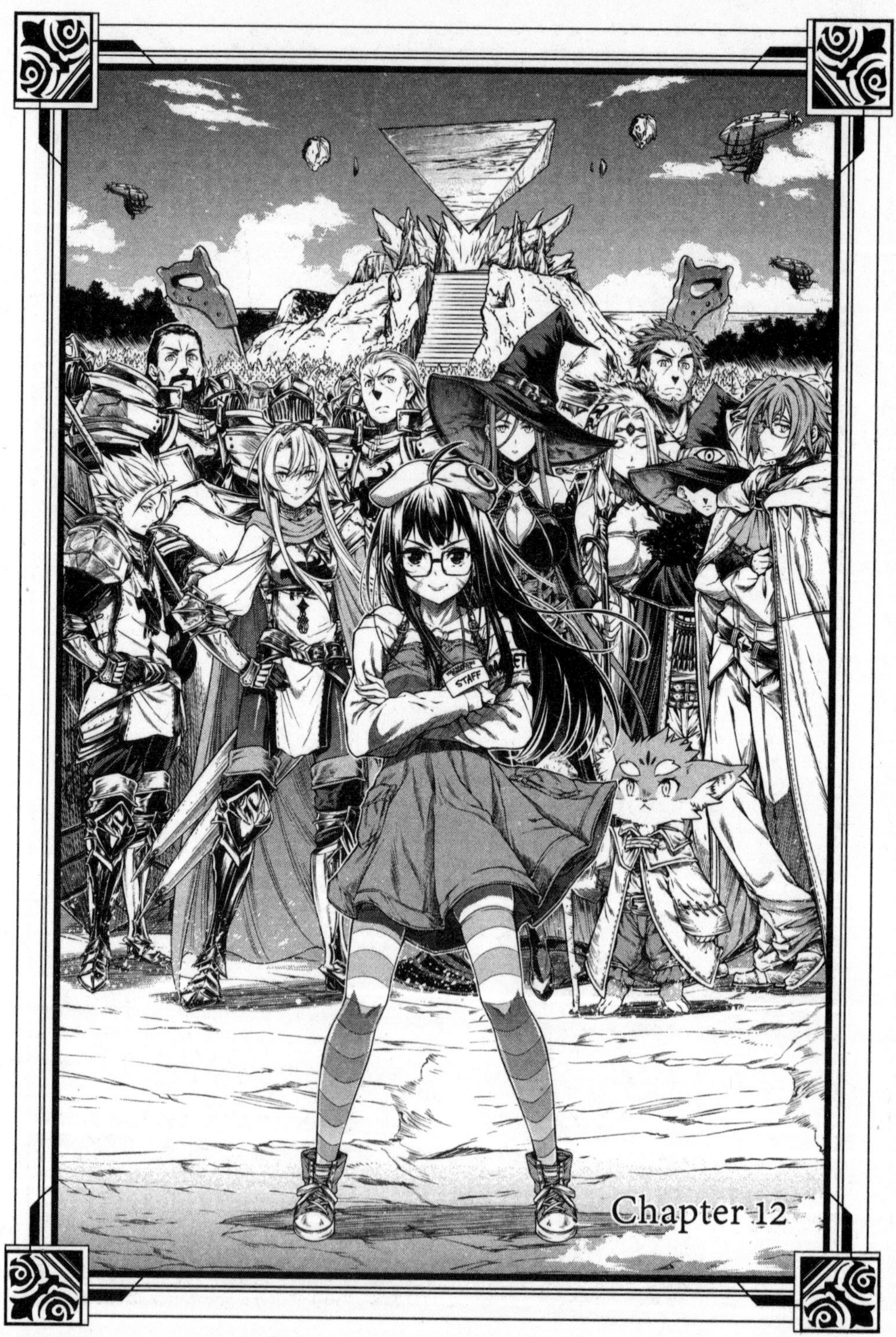
STAFF
Chapter 12

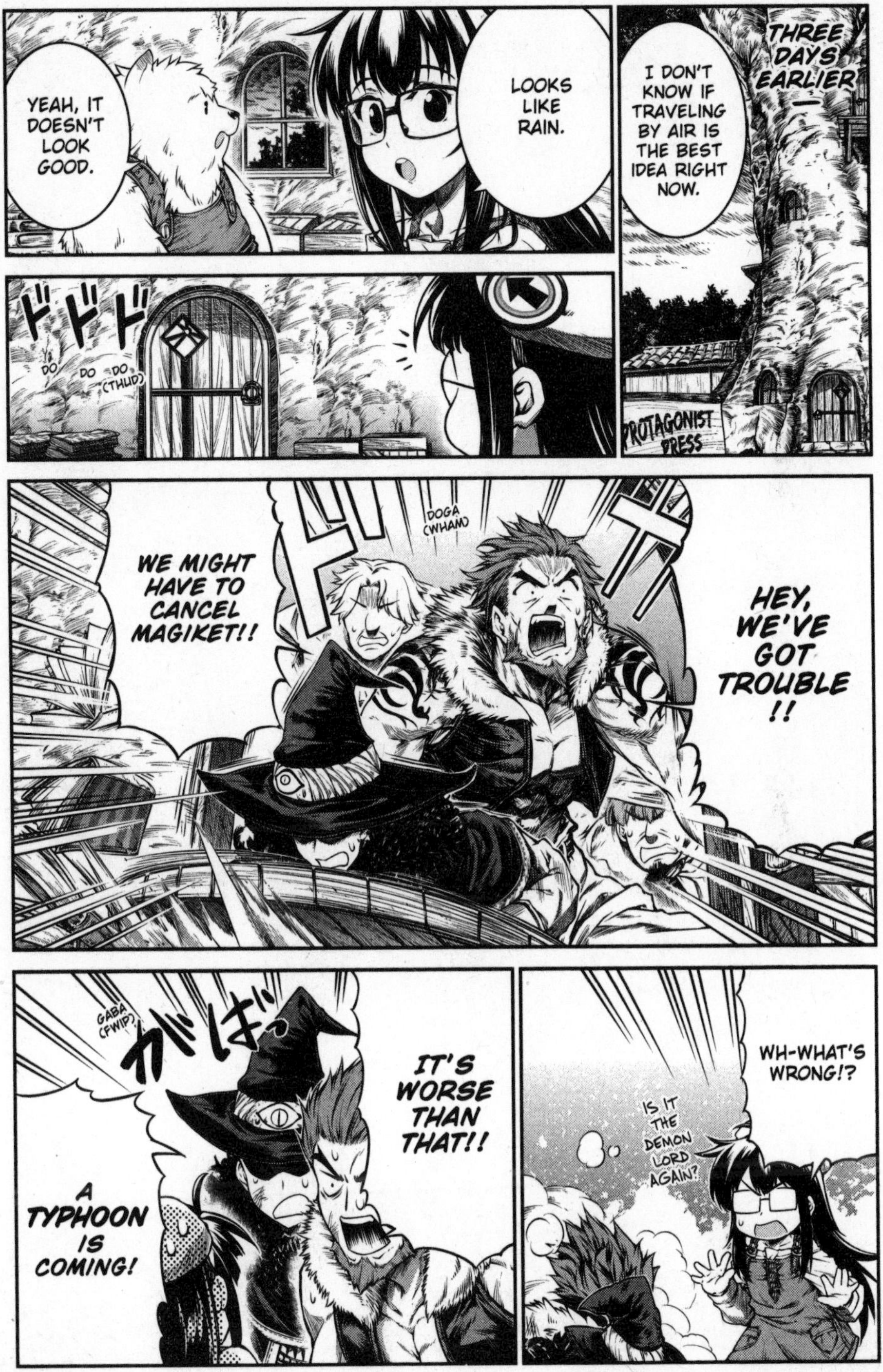
THREE DAYS EARLIER —
I DON'T KNOW IF TRAVELING BY AIR IS THE BEST IDEA RIGHT NOW.
PROTAGONIST PRESS
LOOKS LIKE RAIN.
YEAH, IT DOESN'T LOOK GOOD.
ドドド
DO DO DO (THUD)
HEY, WE'VE GOT TROUBLE!!
DOGA (WHAM)
WE MIGHT HAVE TO CANCEL MAGIKET!!
WH-WHAT'S WRONG!?
IS IT THE DEMON LORD AGAIN?
IT'S WORSE THAN THAT!!
がばっ
GABA (FWIP)
A TYPHOON IS COMING!

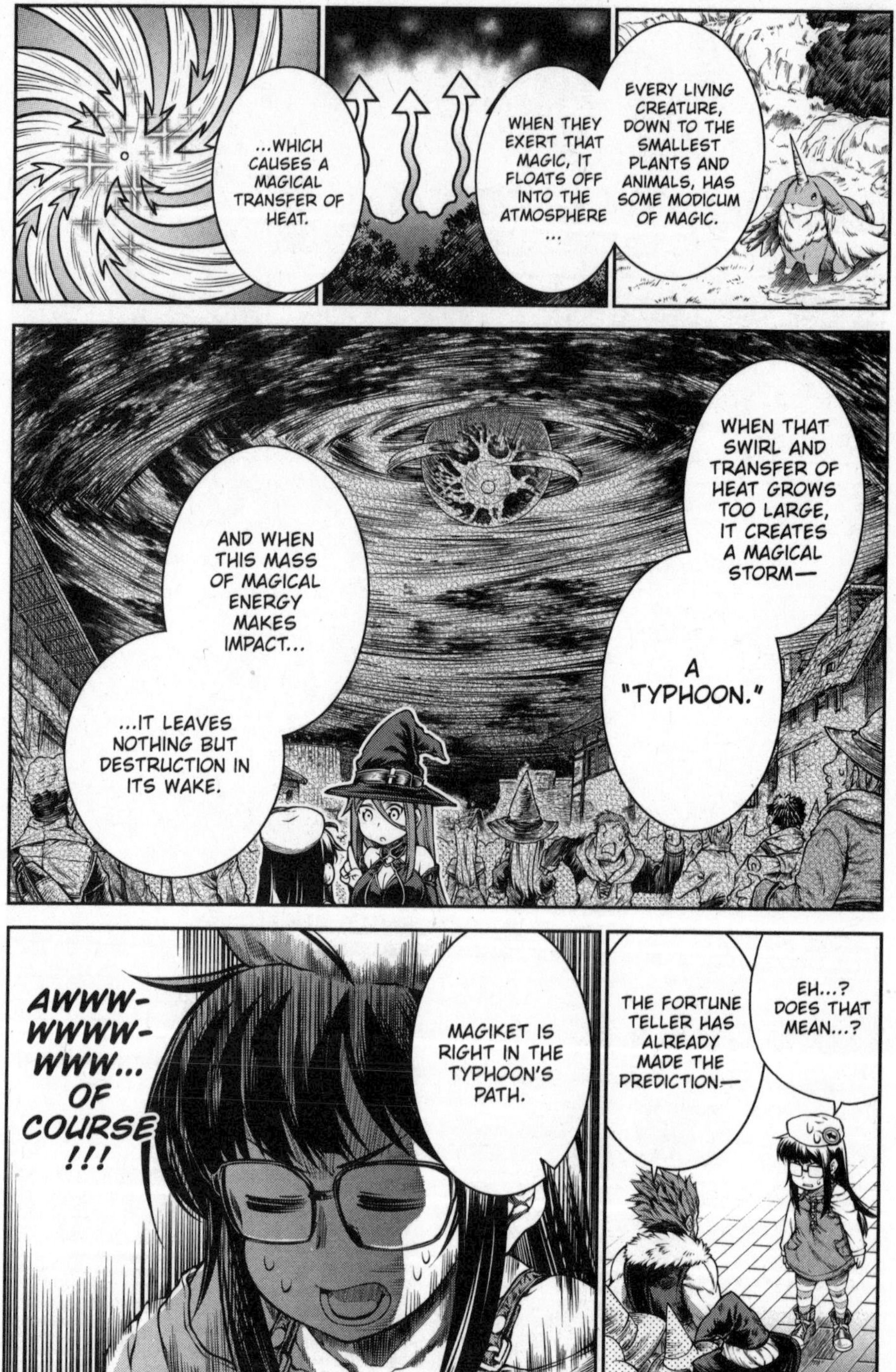
EVERY LIVING CREATURE, DOWN TO THE SMALLEST PLANTS AND ANIMALS, HAS SOME MODICUM OF MAGIC.
WHEN THEY EXERT THAT MAGIC, IT FLOATS OFF INTO THE ATMOSPHERE...
...WHICH CAUSES A MAGICAL TRANSFER OF HEAT.
WHEN THAT SWIRL AND TRANSFER OF HEAT GROWS TOO LARGE, IT CREATES A MAGICAL STORM—
A "TYPHOON."
AND WHEN THIS MASS OF MAGICAL ENERGY MAKES IMPACT...
...IT LEAVES NOTHING BUT DESTRUCTION IN ITS WAKE.
EH...? DOES THAT MEAN...?
THE FORTUNE TELLER HAS ALREADY MADE THE PREDICTION—
MAGIKET IS RIGHT IN THE TYPHOON'S PATH.
AWWW-WWWW-WWW... OF COURSE!!!

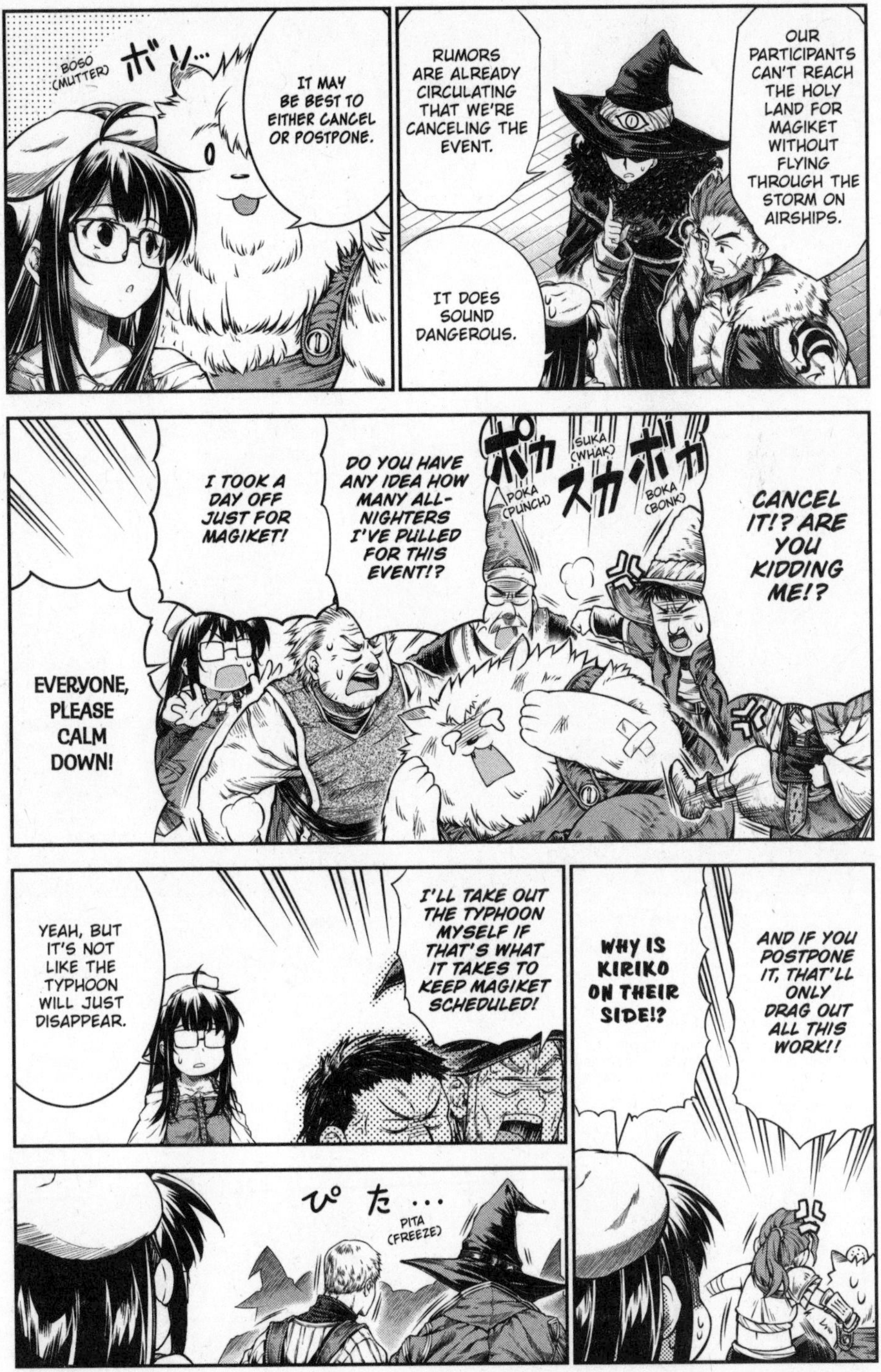
OUR PARTICIPANTS CAN'T REACH THE HOLY LAND FOR MAGIKET WITHOUT FLYING THROUGH THE STORM ON AIRSHIPS.
RUMORS ARE ALREADY CIRCULATING THAT WE'RE CANCELING THE EVENT.
IT DOES SOUND DANGEROUS.
IT MAY BE BEST TO EITHER CANCEL OR POSTPONE.
ボソ…
BOSO (MUTTER)
CANCEL IT!? ARE YOU KIDDING ME!?
ポカ
POKA (PUNCH)
スカ
SUKA (WHAK)
ボカ
BOKA (BONK)
DO YOU HAVE ANY IDEA HOW MANY ALL-NIGHTERS I'VE PULLED FOR THIS EVENT!?
I TOOK A DAY OFF JUST FOR MAGIKET!
EVERYONE, PLEASE CALM DOWN!
AND IF YOU POSTPONE IT, THAT'LL ONLY DRAG OUT ALL THIS WORK!!
WHY IS KIRIKO ON THEIR SIDE!?
I'LL TAKE OUT THE TYPHOON MYSELF IF THAT'S WHAT IT TAKES TO KEEP MAGIKET SCHEDULED!
YEAH, BUT IT'S NOT LIKE THE TYPHOON WILL JUST DISAPPEAR.
ぴた…
PITA (FREEZE)

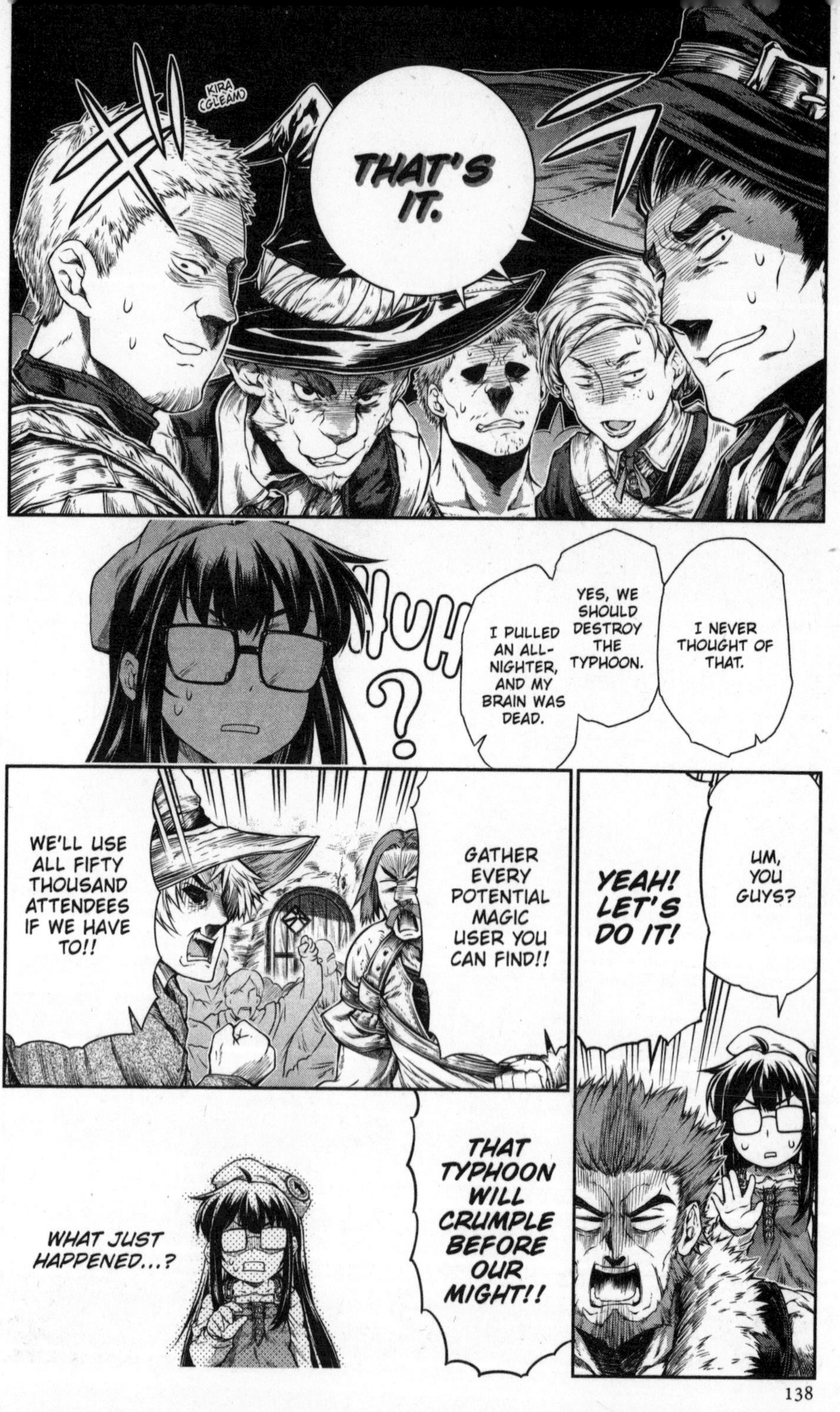
KIRA (GLEAM)
THAT'S IT.
I NEVER THOUGHT OF THAT.
YES, WE SHOULD DESTROY THE TYPHOON.
I PULLED AN ALL-NIGHTER, AND MY BRAIN WAS DEAD.
HUH?
UM, YOU GUYS?
YEAH! LET'S DO IT!
GATHER EVERY POTENTIAL MAGIC USER YOU CAN FIND!!
WE'LL USE ALL FIFTY THOUSAND ATTENDEES IF WE HAVE TO!!
THAT TYPHOON WILL CRUMPLE BEFORE OUR MIGHT!!
WHAT JUST HAPPENED...?

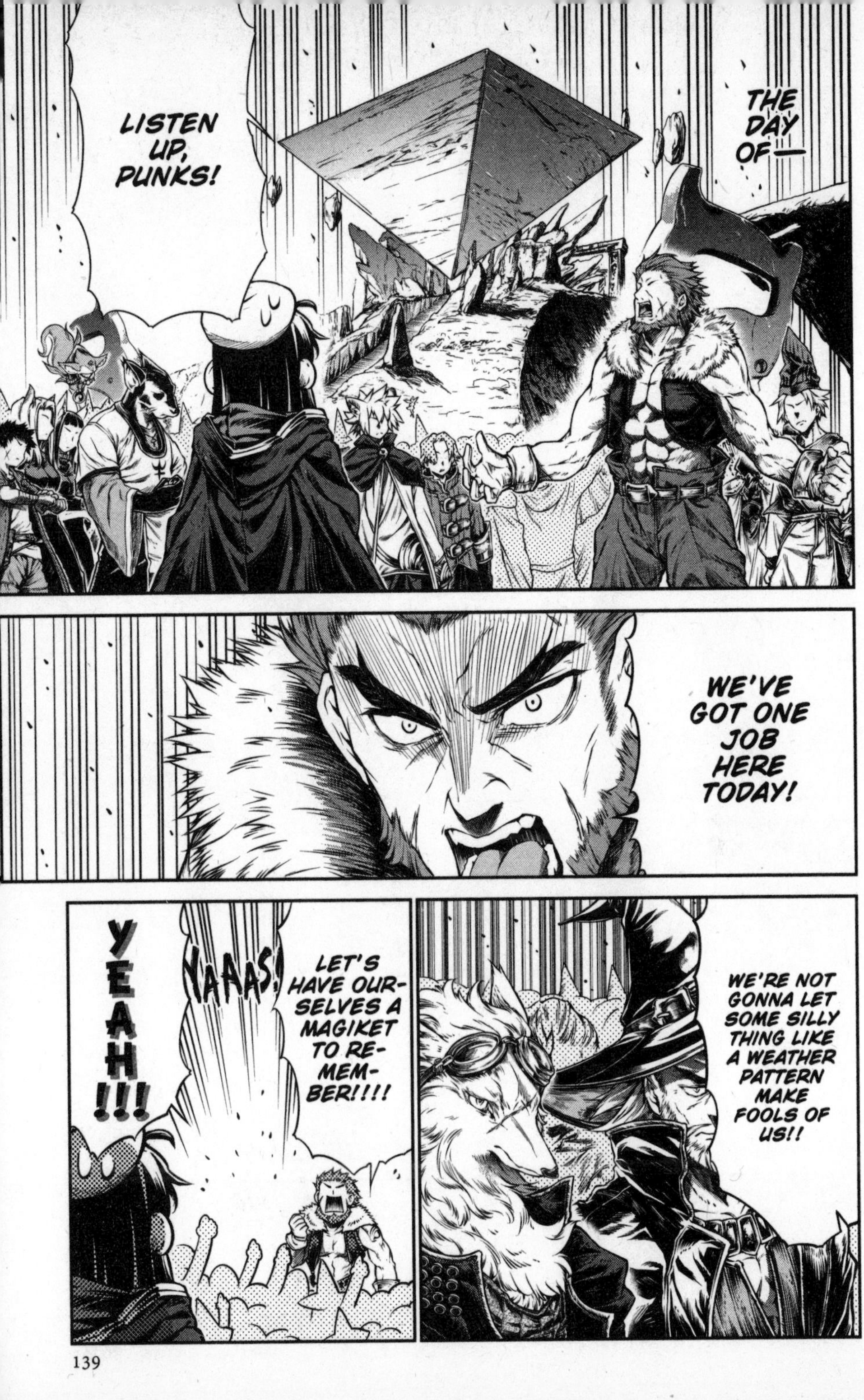
THE DAY OF—
LISTEN UP, PUNKS!
WE'VE GOT ONE JOB HERE TODAY!
WE'RE NOT GONNA LET SOME SILLY THING LIKE A WEATHER PATTERN MAKE FOOLS OF US!!
LET'S HAVE OURSELVES A MAGIKET TO RE-MEM-BER!!!!
YAAAS!
YEAH!!!

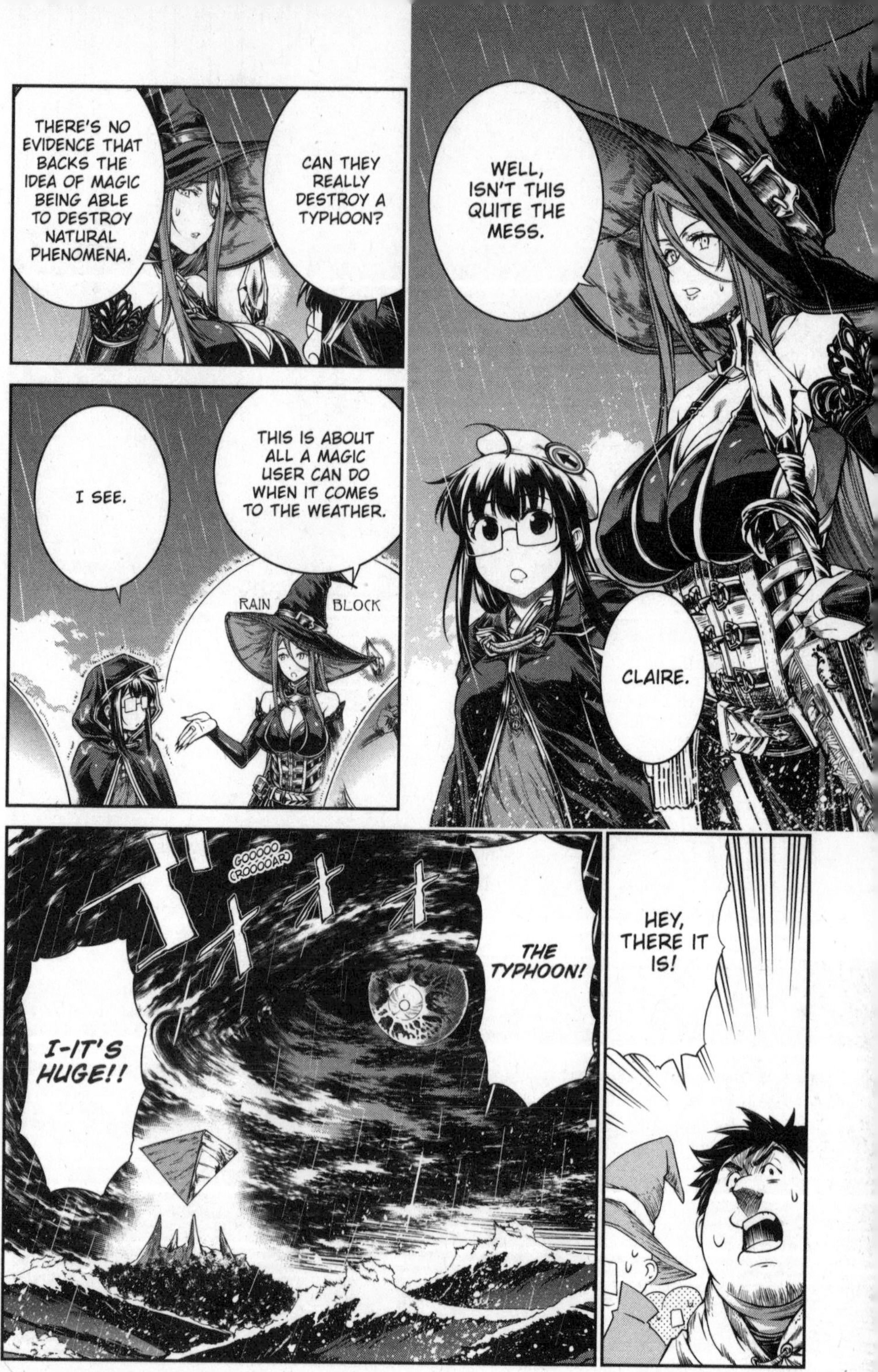
WELL, ISN'T THIS QUITE THE MESS.
CLAIRE.
CAN THEY REALLY DESTROY A TYPHOON?
THERE'S NO EVIDENCE THAT BACKS THE IDEA OF MAGIC BEING ABLE TO DESTROY NATURAL PHENOMENA.
THIS IS ABOUT ALL A MAGIC USER CAN DO WHEN IT COMES TO THE WEATHER.
RAIN BLOCK
I SEE.
HEY, THERE IT IS!
GOOOOO (ROOOOAR)
THE TYPHOON!
I-IT'S HUGE!!

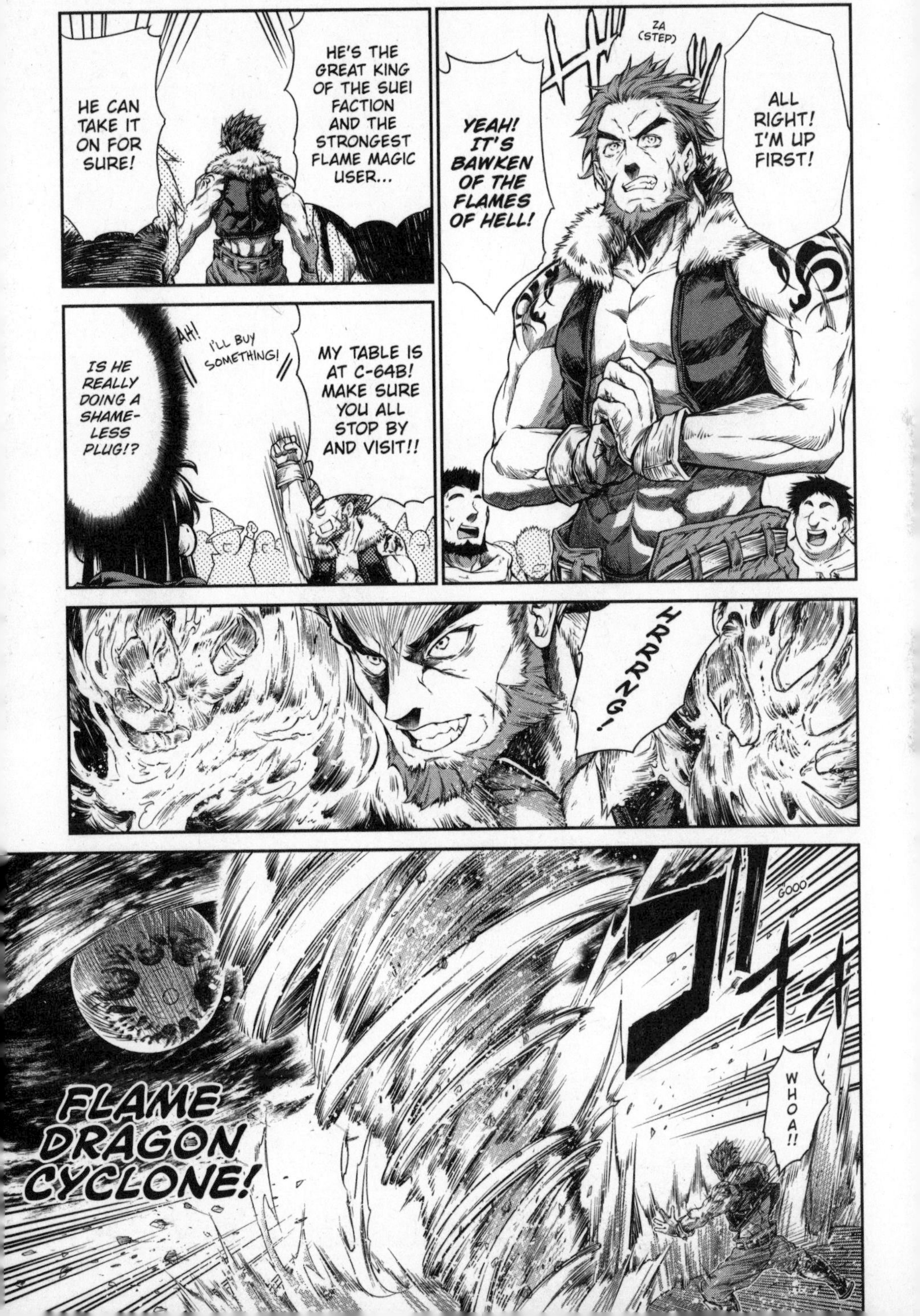
ALL RIGHT! I'M UP FIRST!
ZA (STEP)
YEAH! IT'S BAWKEN OF THE FLAMES OF HELL!
HE'S THE GREAT KING OF THE SUEI FACTION AND THE STRONGEST FLAME MAGIC USER...
HE CAN TAKE IT ON FOR SURE!
MY TABLE IS AT C-64B! MAKE SURE YOU ALL STOP BY AND VISIT!!
I'LL BUY SOMETHING!
IS HE REALLY DOING A SHAME-LESS PLUG!?
HRRRNG!
GOOO
WHOA!!
FLAME DRAGON CYCLONE!

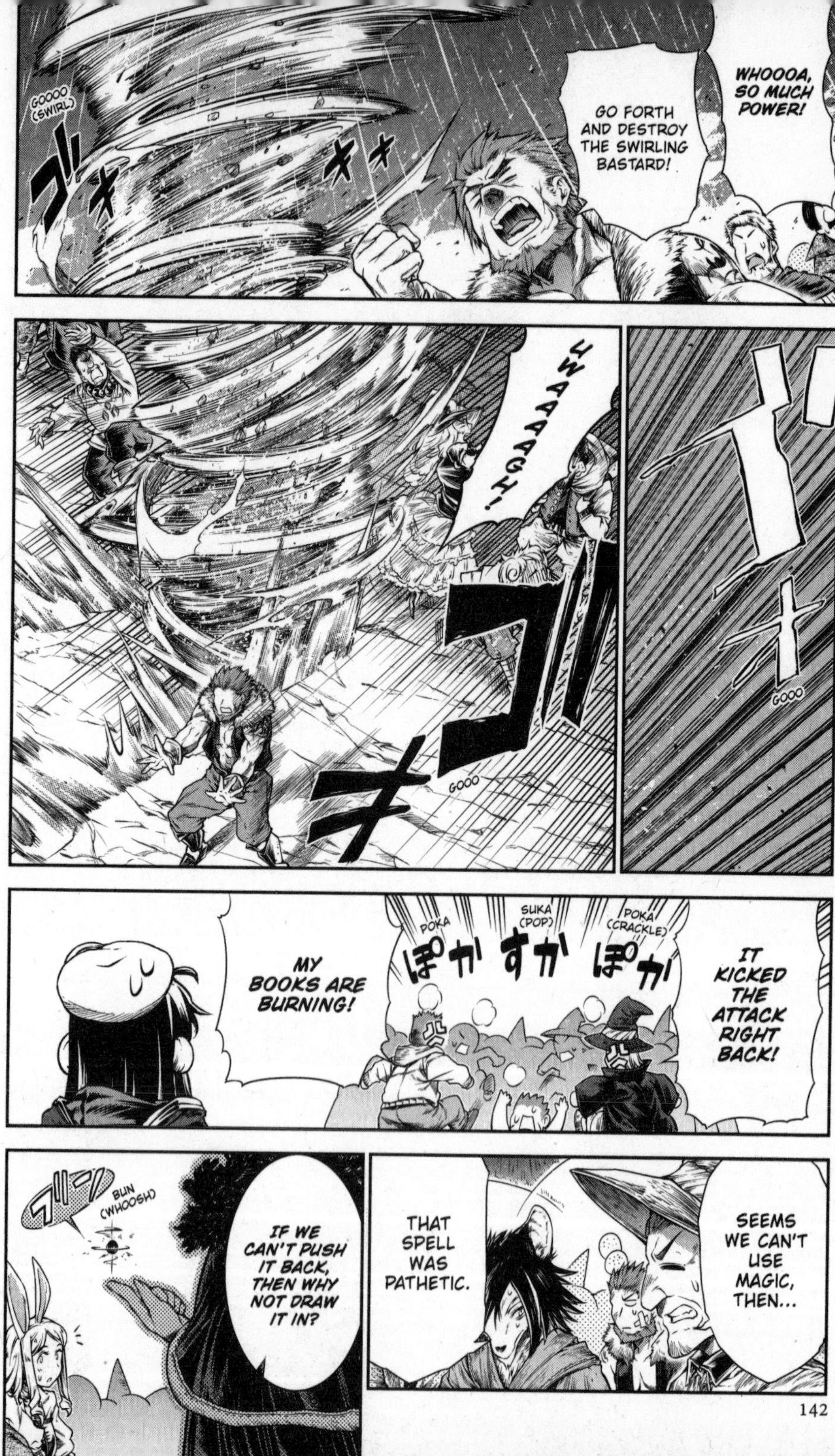
WHOOOA, SO MUCH POWER!
GO FORTH AND DESTROY THE SWIRLING BASTARD!
GOOOO (SWIRL)
GOOO
UWAAAAAGH!
GOOO
IT KICKED THE ATTACK RIGHT BACK!
POKA (CRACKLE)
SUKA (POP)
POKA
ぽか すか ぽか
MY BOOKS ARE BURNING!
SEEMS WE CAN'T USE MAGIC, THEN...
THAT SPELL WAS PATHETIC.
IF WE CAN'T PUSH IT BACK, THEN WHY NOT DRAW IT IN?
BUN (WHOOSH)

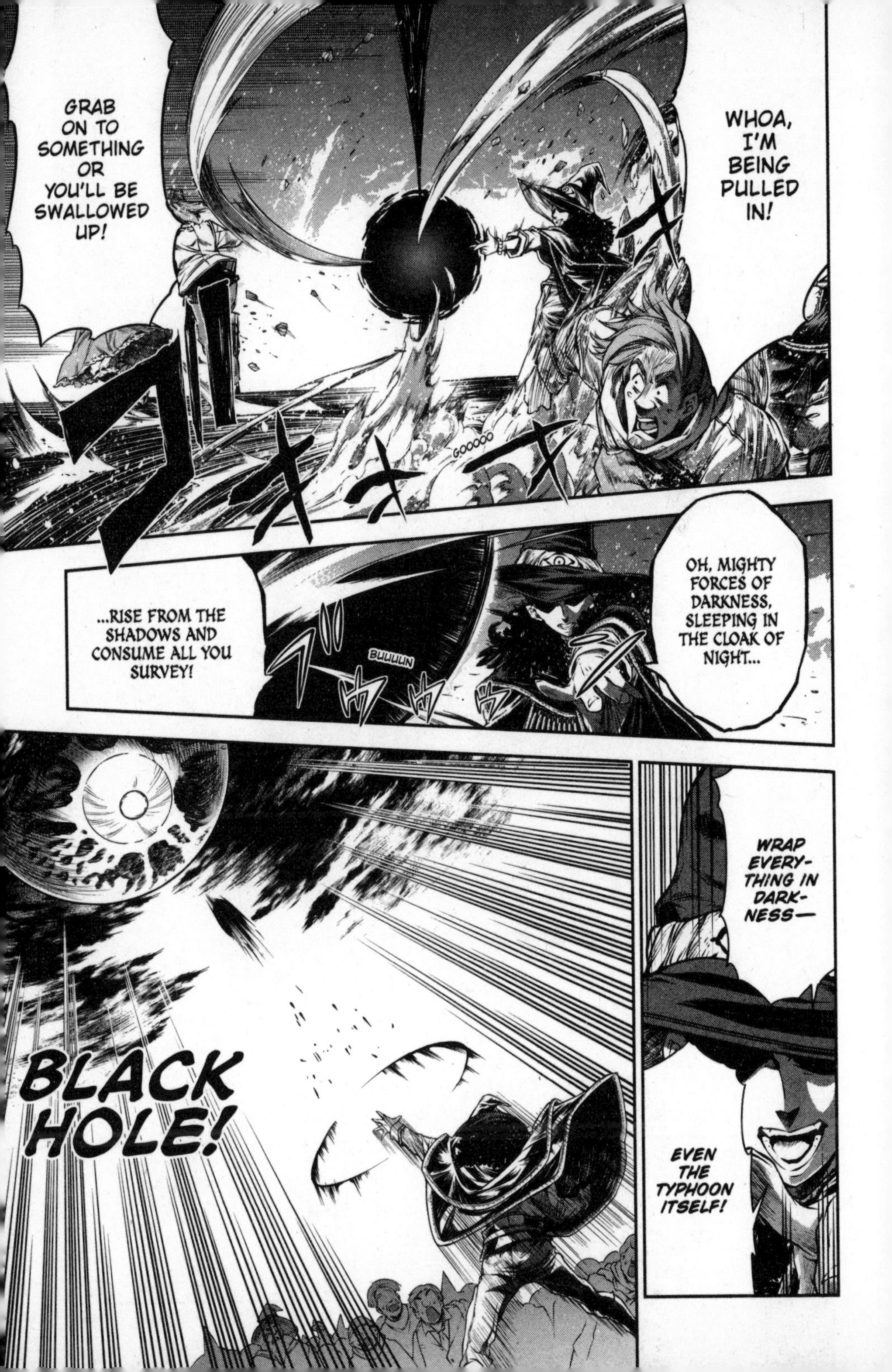
WHOA, I'M BEING PULLED IN!
GRAB ON TO SOMETHING OR YOU'LL BE SWALLOWED UP!
GOOOOO
OH, MIGHTY FORCES OF DARKNESS, SLEEPING IN THE CLOAK OF NIGHT...
...RISE FROM THE SHADOWS AND CONSUME ALL YOU SURVEY!
BUUUUN
WRAP EVERY-THING IN DARK-NESS—
EVEN THE TYPHOON ITSELF!
BLACK HOLE!

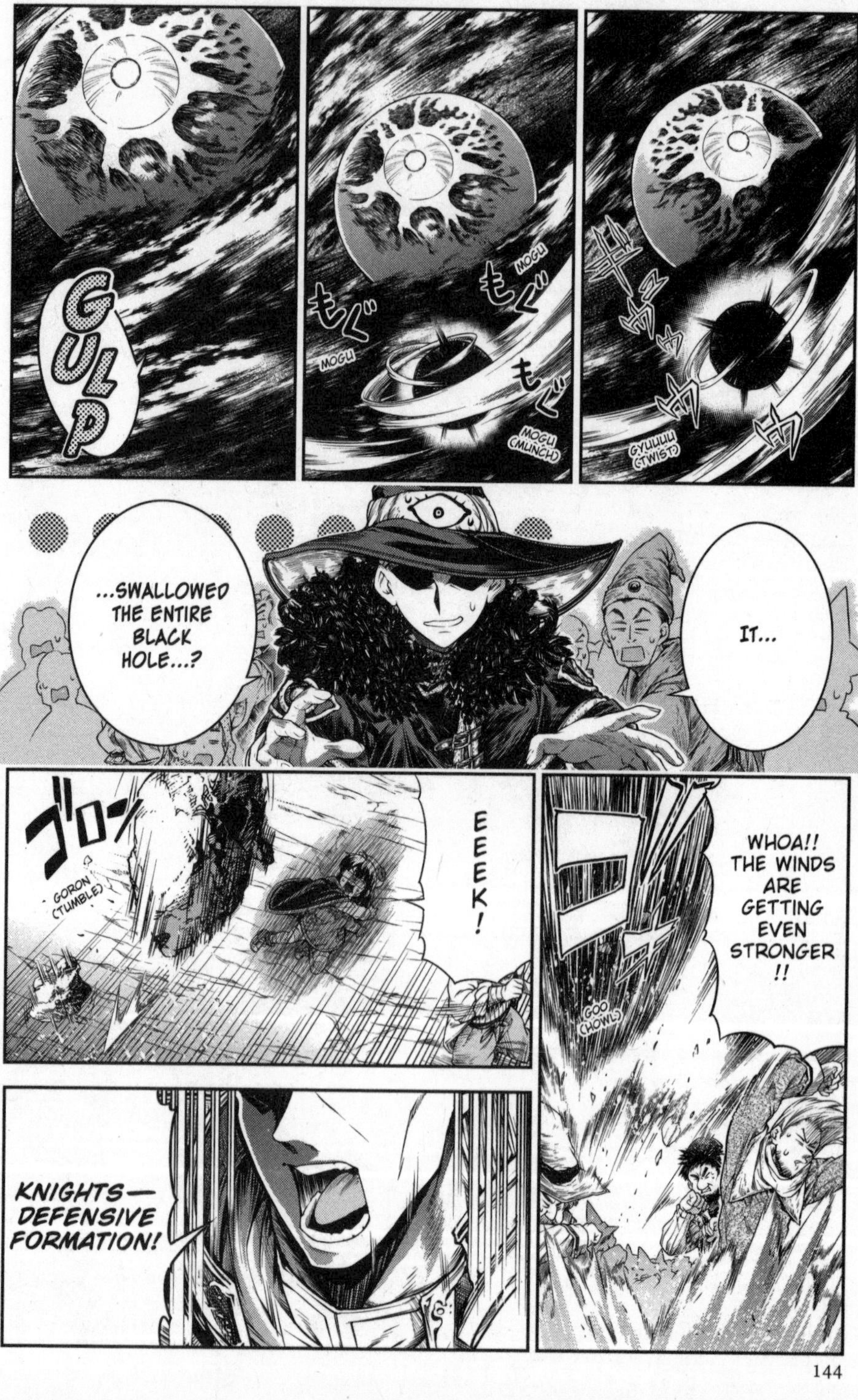
GYUUUU (TWIST)
MOGU
もぐ
MOGU
もぐ
もぐ
MOGU (MUNCH)
GULP
IT...
...SWALLOWED THE ENTIRE BLACK HOLE...?
WHOA!! THE WINDS ARE GETTING EVEN STRONGER!!
GOO (HOWL)
EEEEK!
GORON (TUMBLE)
KNIGHTS—DEFENSIVE FORMATION!

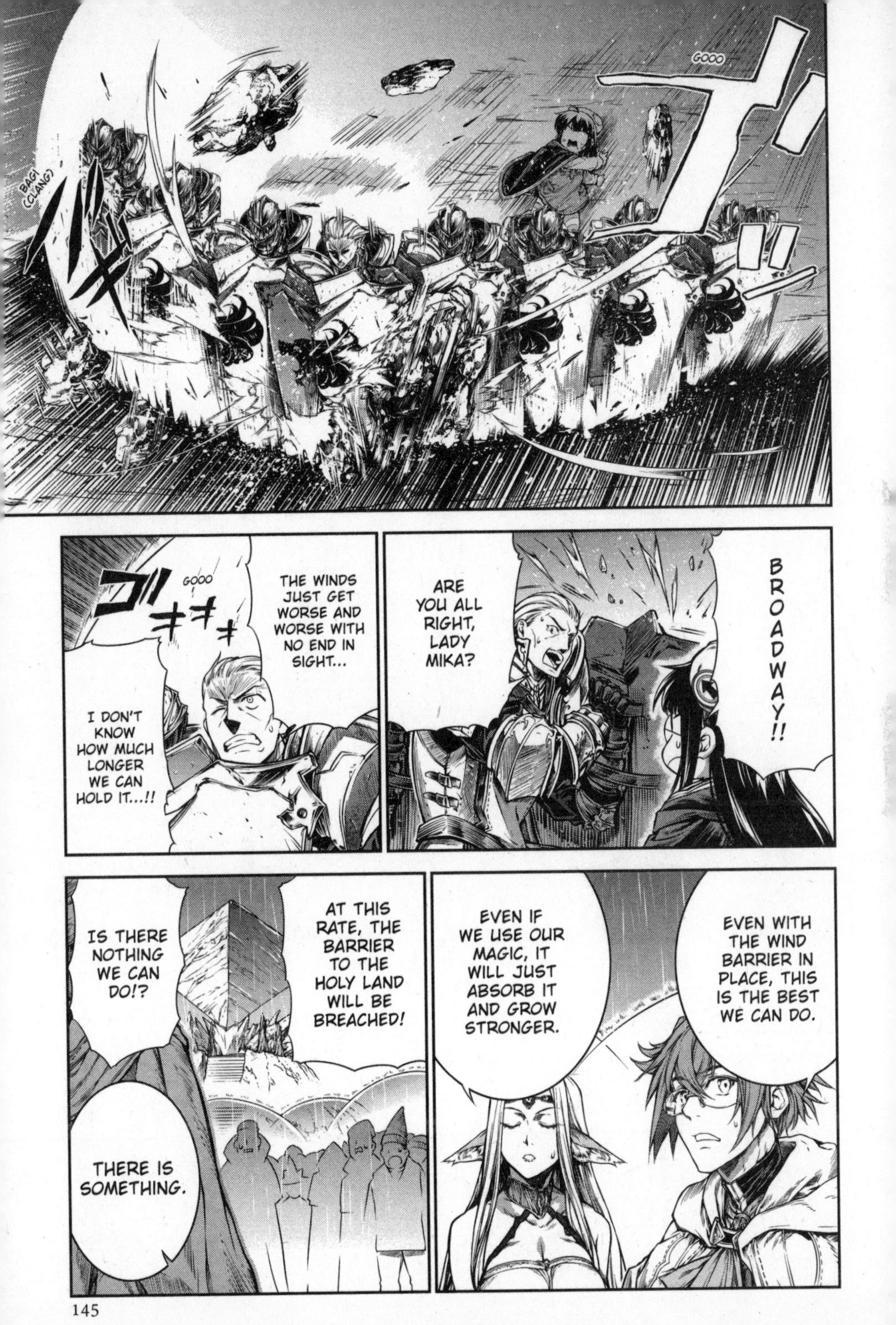
GOOO
BAGI (CLANG)
BROADWAY!!
ARE YOU ALL RIGHT, LADY MIKA?
THE WINDS JUST GET WORSE AND WORSE WITH NO END IN SIGHT...
GOOO
I DON'T KNOW HOW MUCH LONGER WE CAN HOLD IT...!!
EVEN WITH THE WIND BARRIER IN PLACE, THIS IS THE BEST WE CAN DO.
EVEN IF WE USE OUR MAGIC, IT WILL JUST ABSORB IT AND GROW STRONGER.
AT THIS RATE, THE BARRIER TO THE HOLY LAND WILL BE BREACHED!
IS THERE NOTHING WE CAN DO!?
THERE IS SOMETHING.

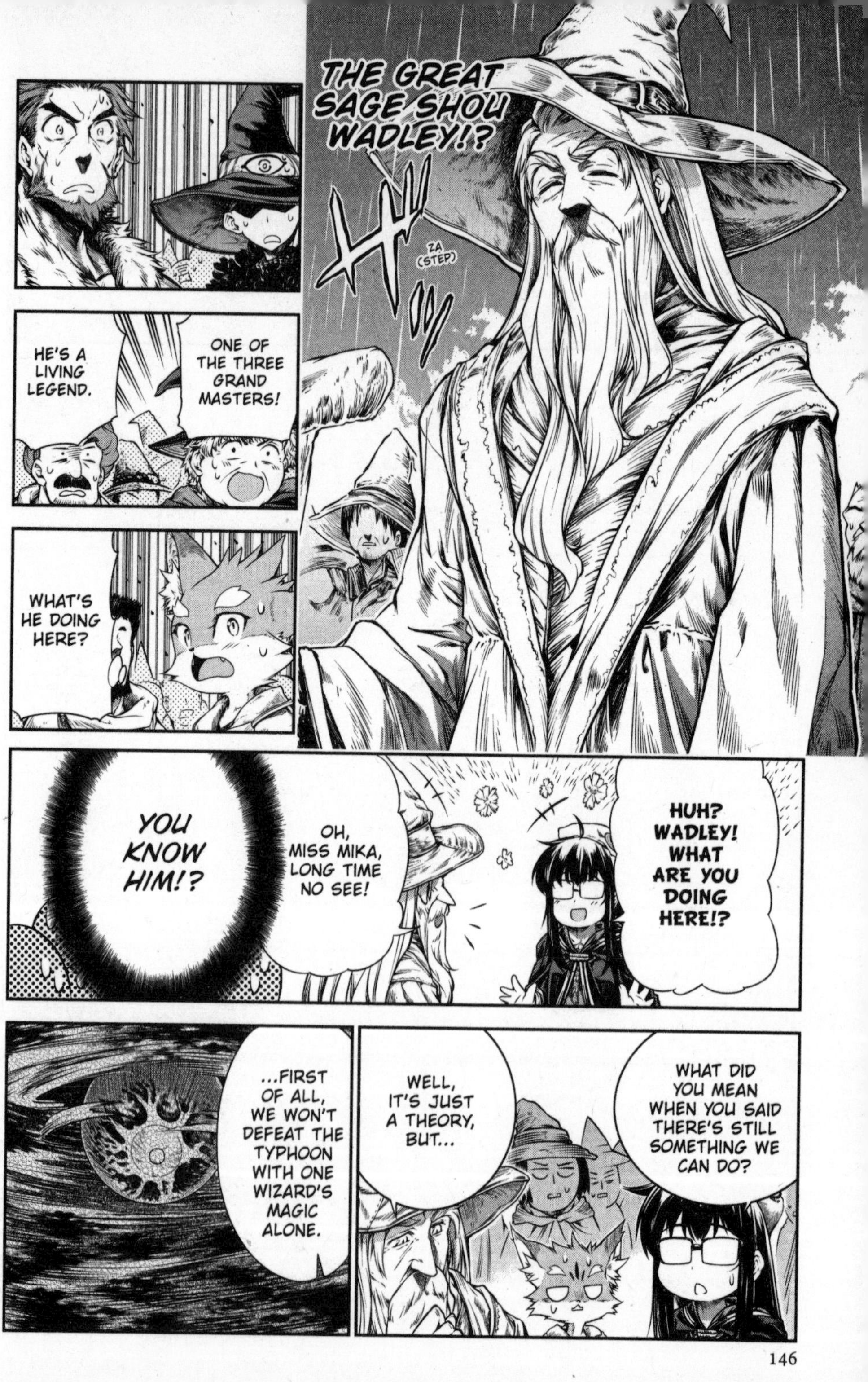
THE GREAT SAGE SHOU WADLEY!?
ZA (STEP)
ONE OF THE THREE GRAND MASTERS!
HE'S A LIVING LEGEND.
WHAT'S HE DOING HERE?
HUH? WADLEY! WHAT ARE YOU DOING HERE!?
OH, MISS MIKA, LONG TIME NO SEE!
YOU KNOW HIM!?
WHAT DID YOU MEAN WHEN YOU SAID THERE'S STILL SOMETHING WE CAN DO?
WELL, IT'S JUST A THEORY, BUT...
...FIRST OF ALL, WE WON'T DEFEAT THE TYPHOON WITH ONE WIZARD'S MAGIC ALONE.

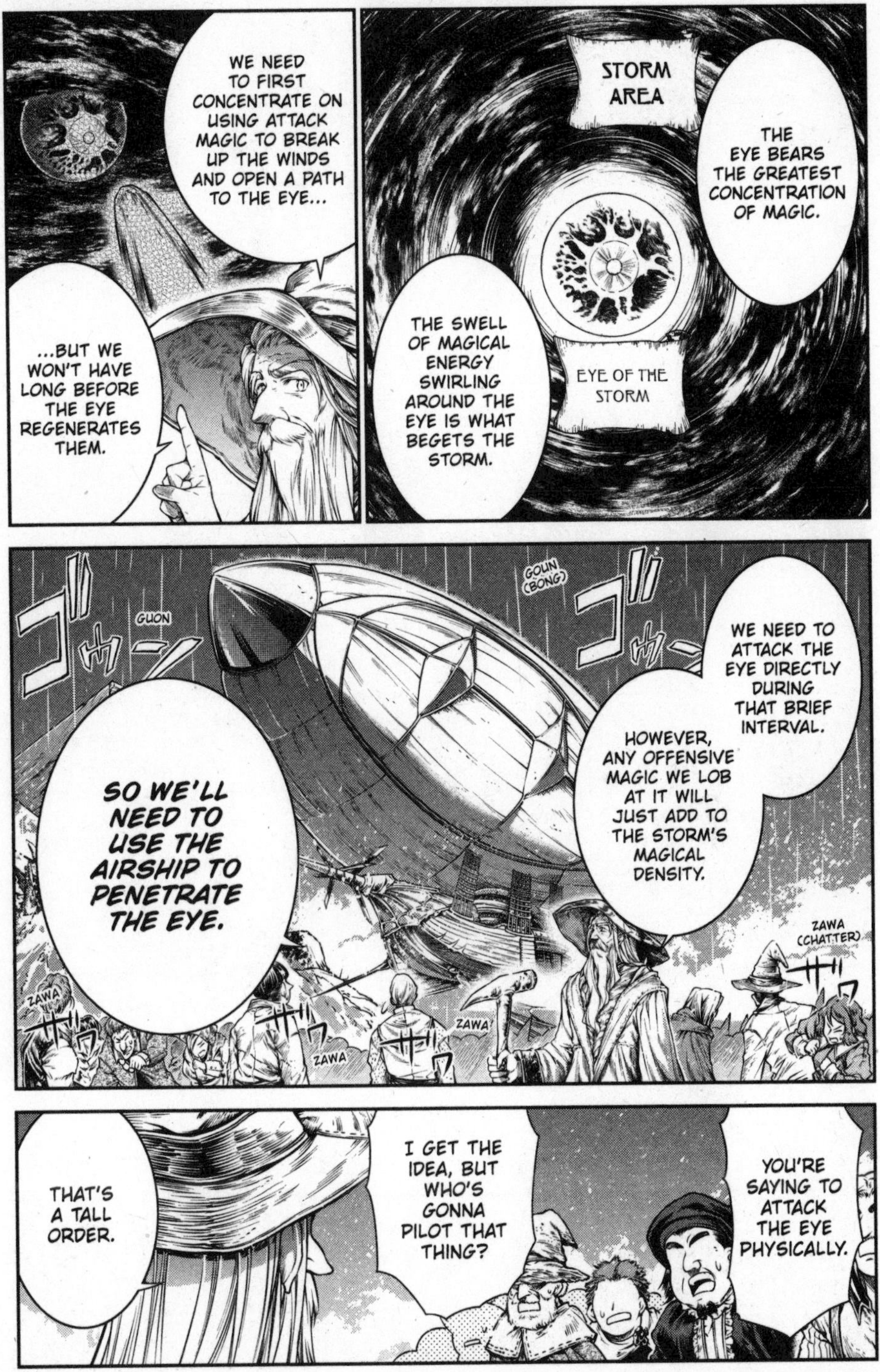
STORM AREA
THE EYE BEARS THE GREATEST CONCENTRATION OF MAGIC.
EYE OF THE STORM
THE SWELL OF MAGICAL ENERGY SWIRLING AROUND THE EYE IS WHAT BEGETS THE STORM.
WE NEED TO FIRST CONCENTRATE ON USING ATTACK MAGIC TO BREAK UP THE WINDS AND OPEN A PATH TO THE EYE...
...BUT WE WON'T HAVE LONG BEFORE THE EYE REGENERATES THEM.
GOUN (BONG)
WE NEED TO ATTACK THE EYE DIRECTLY DURING THAT BRIEF INTERVAL.
HOWEVER, ANY OFFENSIVE MAGIC WE LOB AT IT WILL JUST ADD TO THE STORM'S MAGICAL DENSITY.
GUON
SO WE'LL NEED TO USE THE AIRSHIP TO PENETRATE THE EYE.
ZAWA (CHATTER)
ZAWA
ZAWA
ZAWA
YOU'RE SAYING TO ATTACK THE EYE PHYSICALLY.
I GET THE IDEA, BUT WHO'S GONNA PILOT THAT THING?
THAT'S A TALL ORDER.

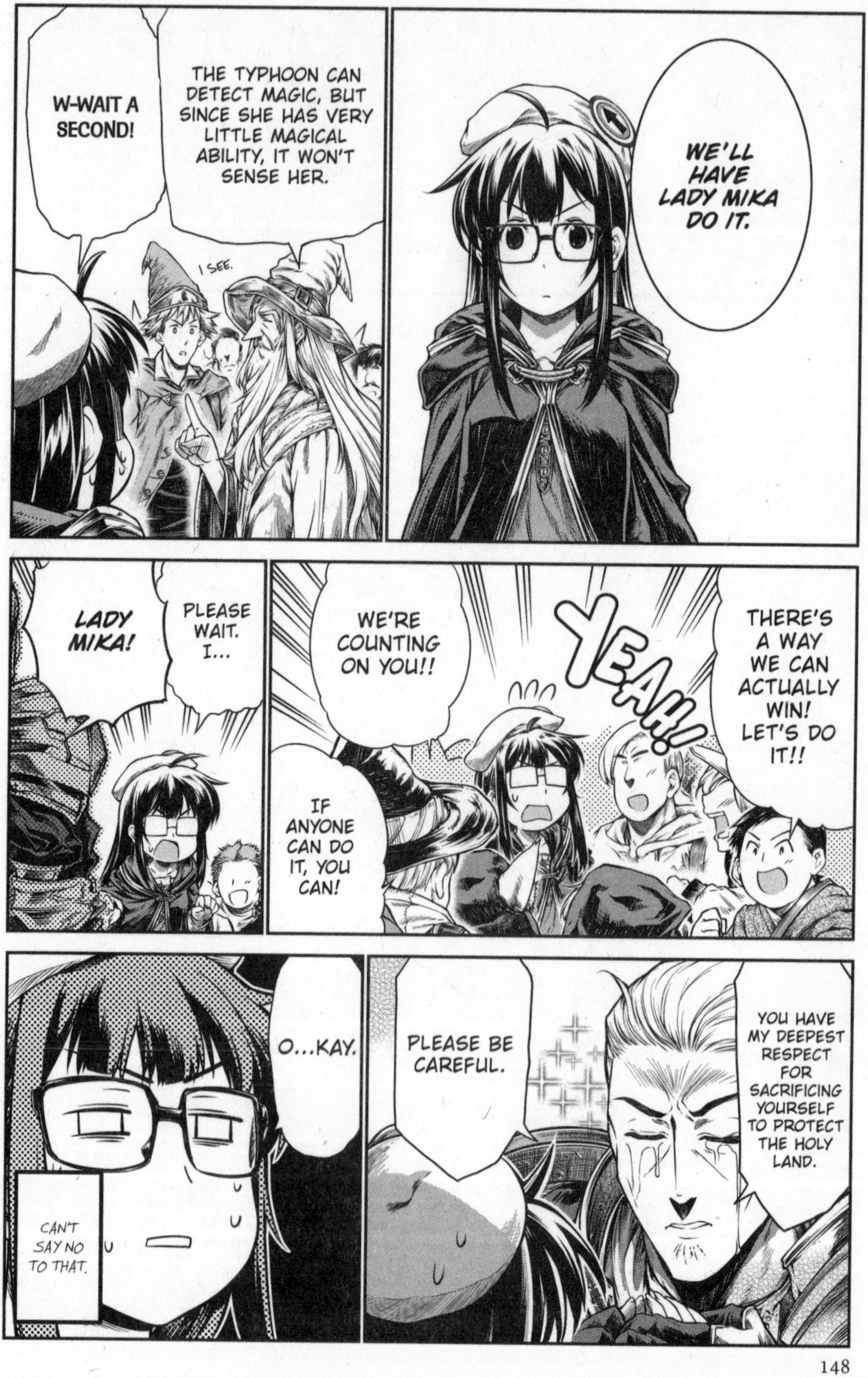
WE'LL HAVE LADY MIKA DO IT.
THE TYPHOON CAN DETECT MAGIC, BUT SINCE SHE HAS VERY LITTLE MAGICAL ABILITY, IT WON'T SENSE HER.
W-WAIT A SECOND!
I SEE.
THERE'S A WAY WE CAN ACTUALLY WIN! LET'S DO IT!!
YEAH!
WE'RE COUNTING ON YOU!!
IF ANYONE CAN DO IT, YOU CAN!
PLEASE WAIT. I...
LADY MIKA!
YOU HAVE MY DEEPEST RESPECT FOR SACRIFICING YOURSELF TO PROTECT THE HOLY LAND.
PLEASE BE CAREFUL.
O...KAY.
CAN'T SAY NO TO THAT.

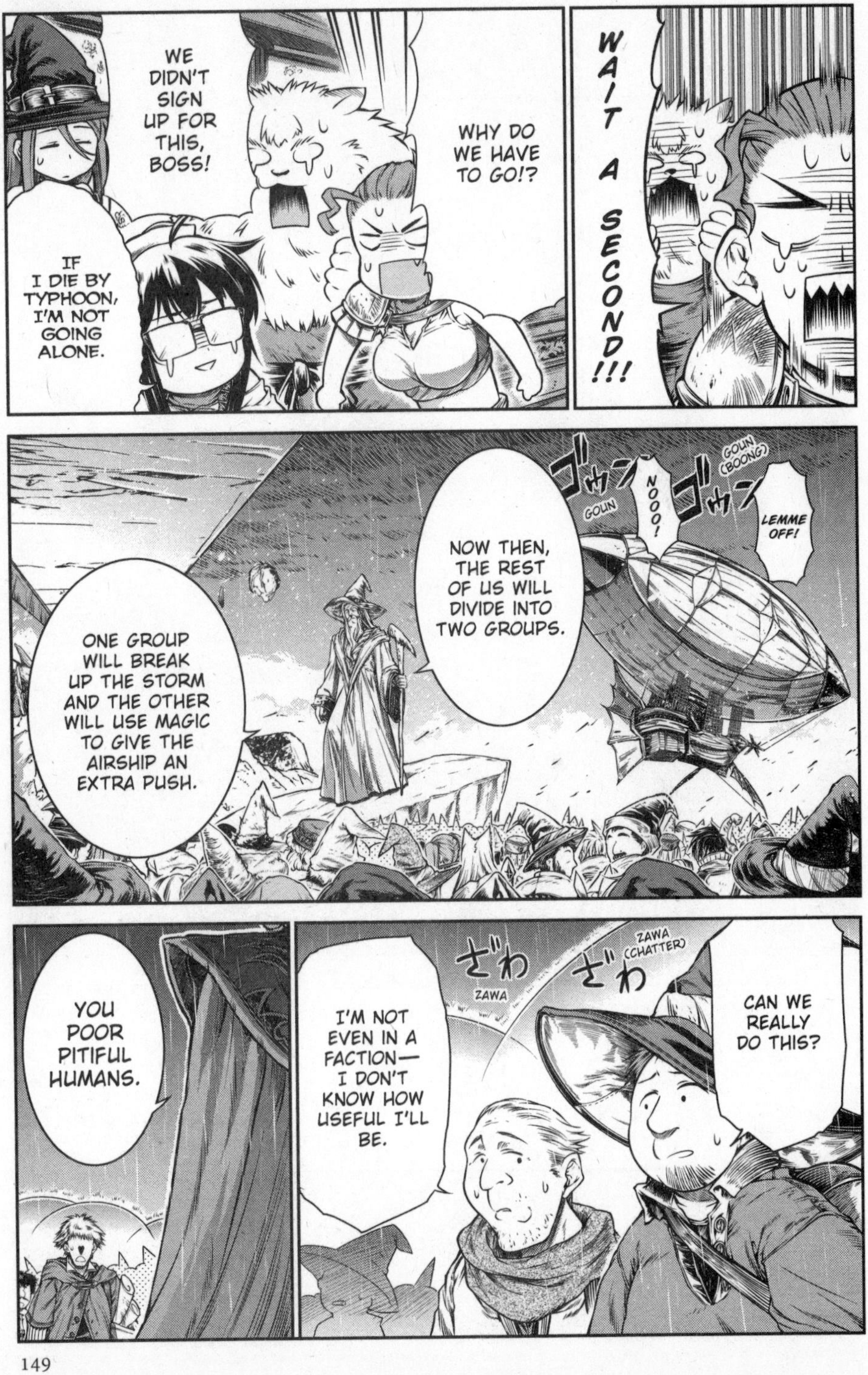
WAIT A SECOND!!!
WHY DO WE HAVE TO GO!?
WE DIDN'T SIGN UP FOR THIS, BOSS!
IF I DIE BY TYPHOON, I'M NOT GOING ALONE.
ゴゥン
GOUN (BOONG)
LEMME OFF!
ゴゥン
NOOOO!
GOUN
NOW THEN, THE REST OF US WILL DIVIDE INTO TWO GROUPS.
ONE GROUP WILL BREAK UP THE STORM AND THE OTHER WILL USE MAGIC TO GIVE THE AIRSHIP AN EXTRA PUSH.
CAN WE REALLY DO THIS?
ざわ
ZAWA (CHATTER)
ざわ
ZAWA
I'M NOT EVEN IN A FACTION— I DON'T KNOW HOW USEFUL I'LL BE.
YOU POOR PITIFUL HUMANS.

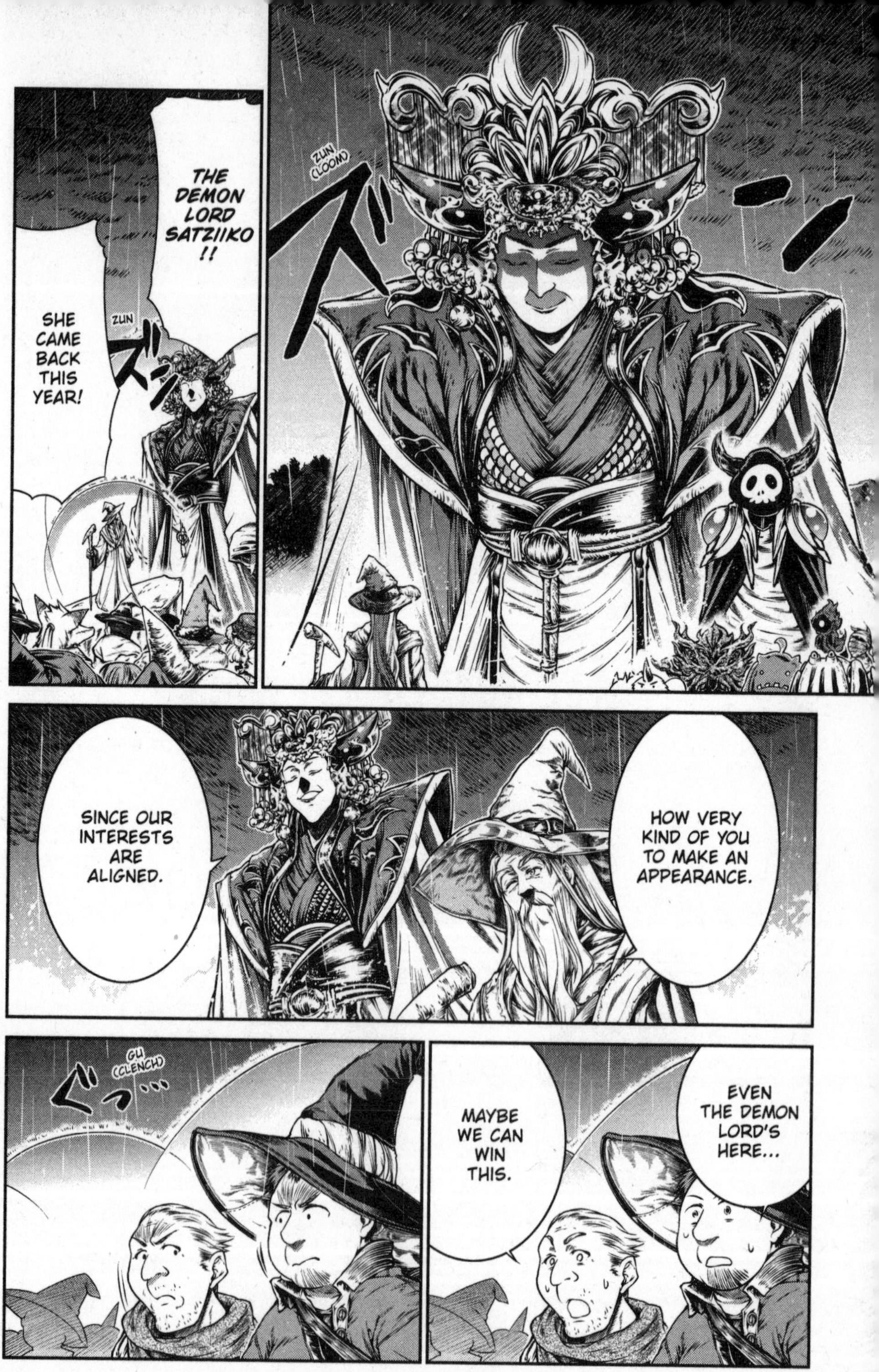
ZUN (LOOM)
THE DEMON LORD SATZIIKO!!
ZUN
SHE CAME BACK THIS YEAR!
HOW VERY KIND OF YOU TO MAKE AN APPEARANCE.
SINCE OUR INTERESTS ARE ALIGNED.
EVEN THE DEMON LORD'S HERE...
MAYBE WE CAN WIN THIS.
GU (CLENCH)

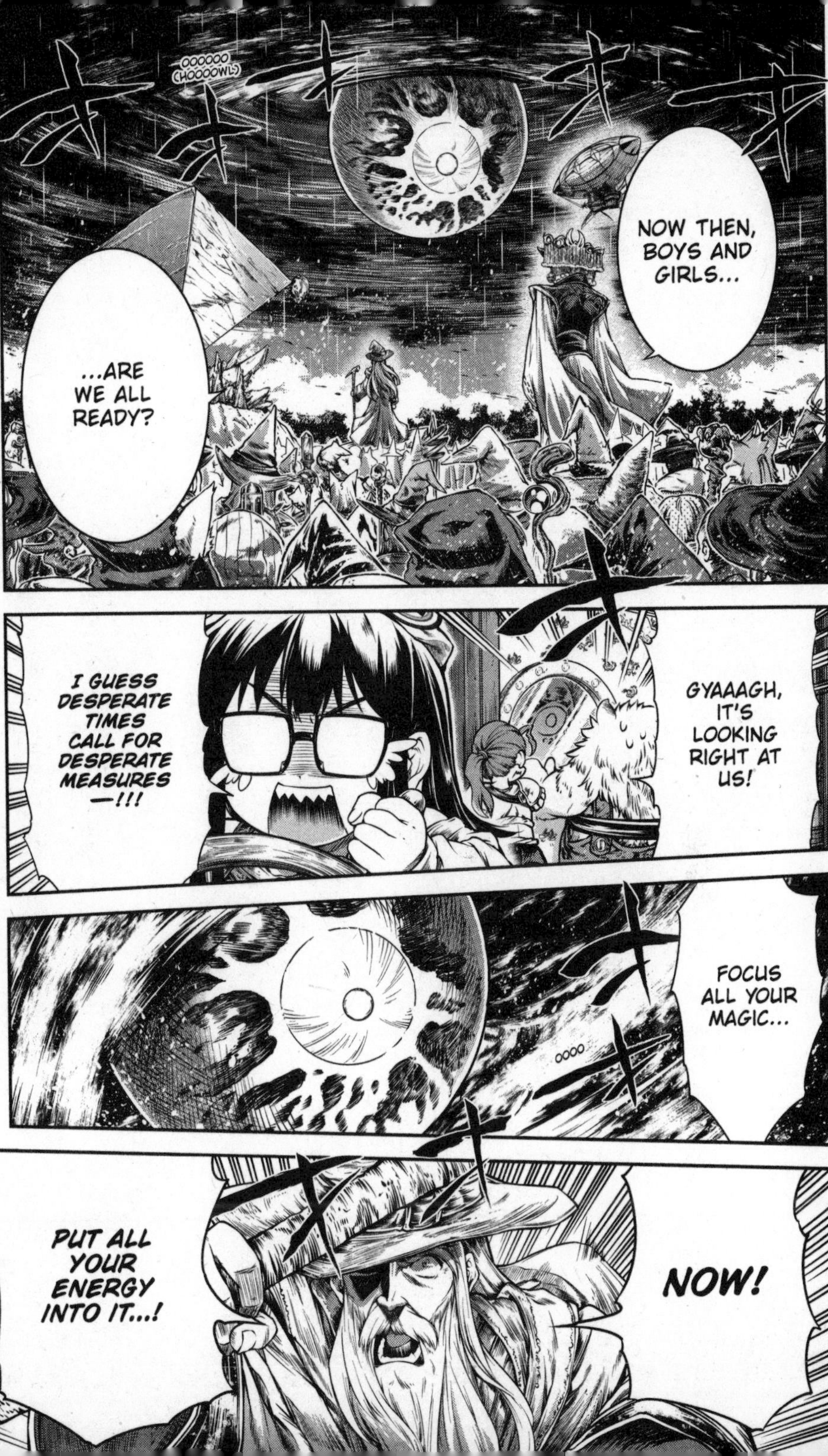
NOW THEN, BOYS AND GIRLS...
OOOOOO (HOOOOWL)
...ARE WE ALL READY?
GYAAAGH, IT'S LOOKING RIGHT AT US!
I GUESS DESPERATE TIMES CALL FOR DESPERATE MEASURES—!!!
FOCUS ALL YOUR MAGIC...
OOOO
NOW!
PUT ALL YOUR ENERGY INTO IT...!

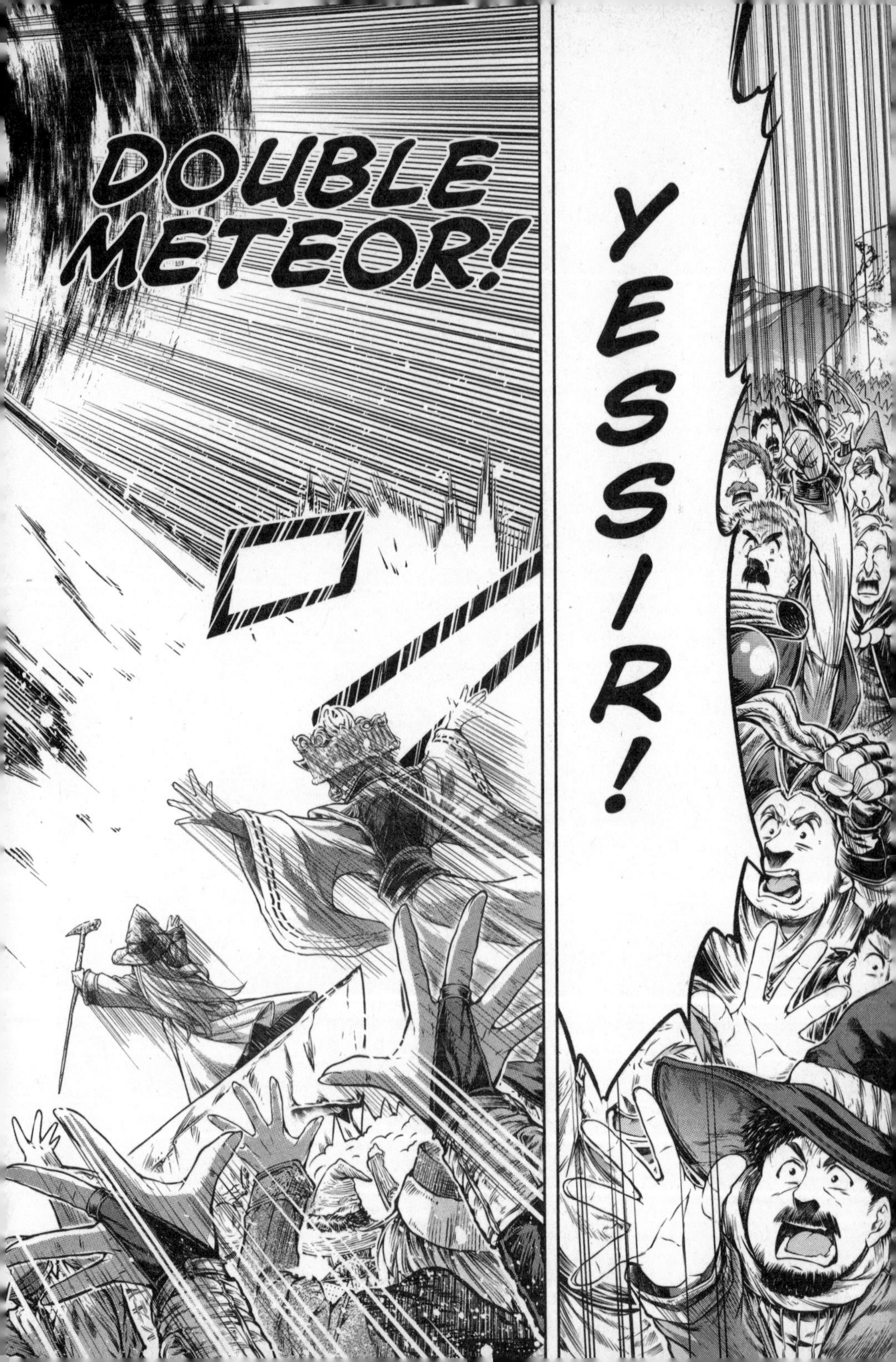
YESSIR!
DOUBLE METEOR!

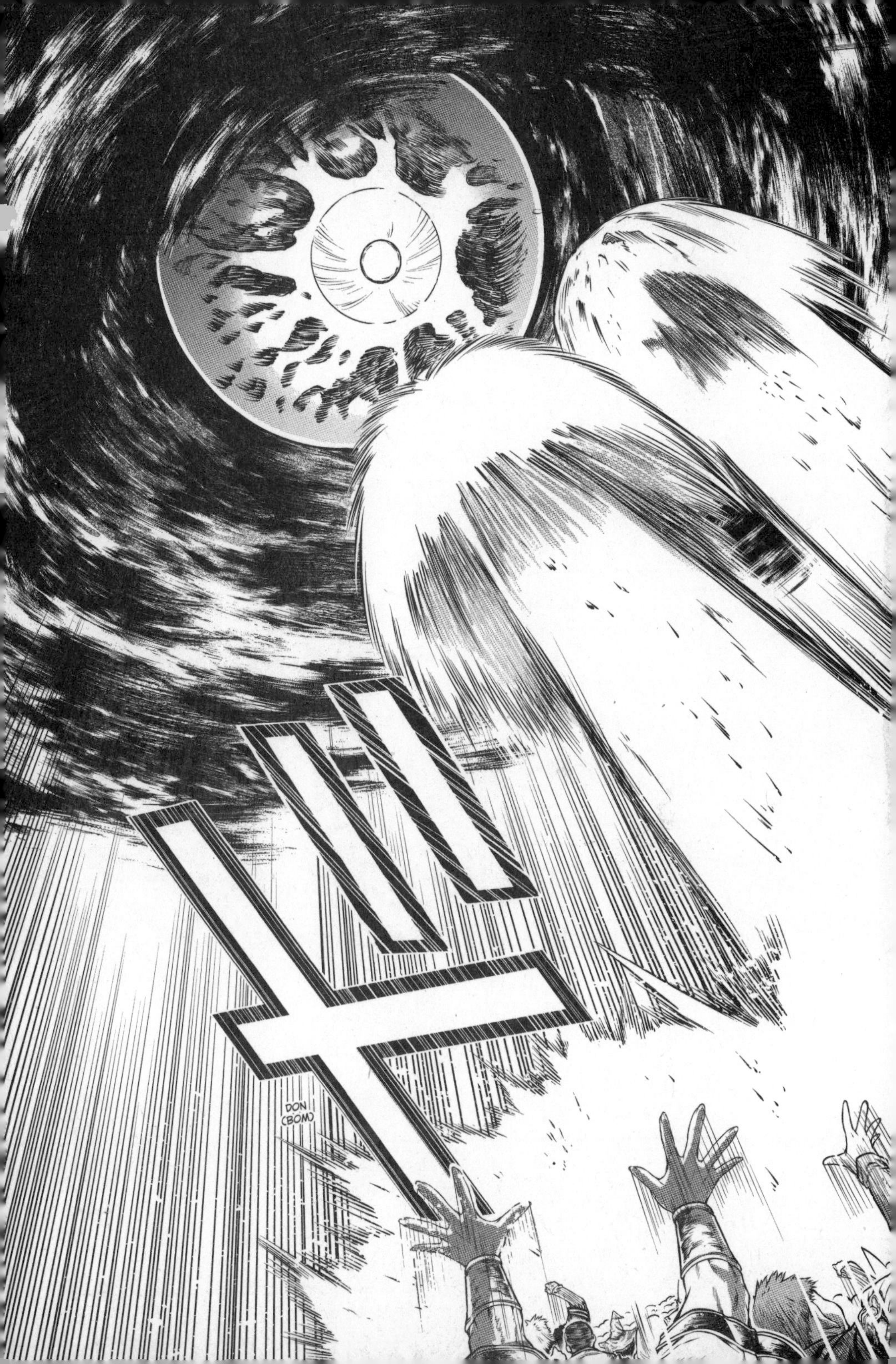

ドン
DON
(BOM)

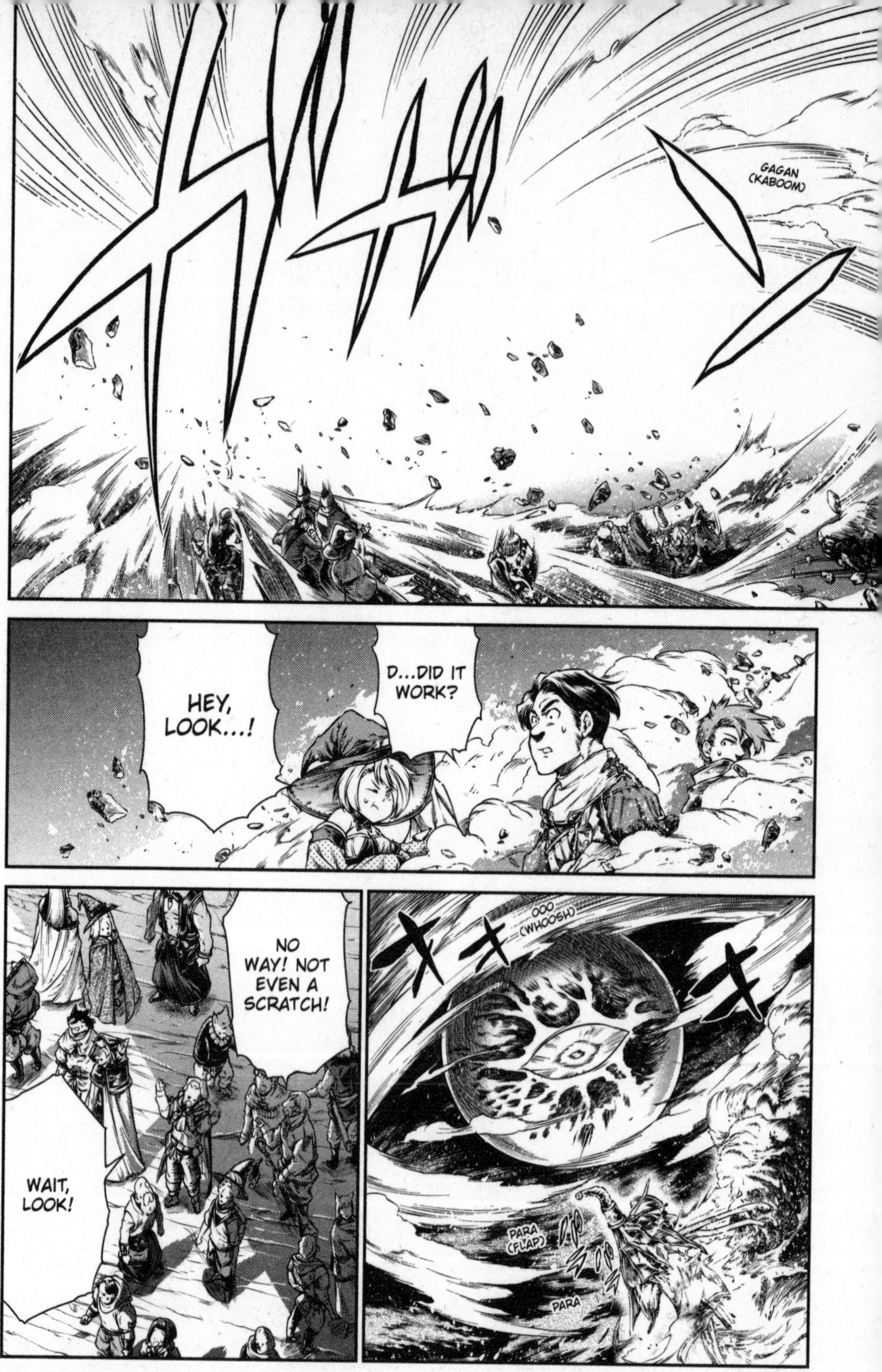
GAGAN
(KABOOM)
D...DID IT WORK?
HEY, LOOK...!
OOO
(WHOOSH)
PARA
(FLAP)
PARA
NO WAY! NOT EVEN A SCRATCH!
WAIT, LOOK!

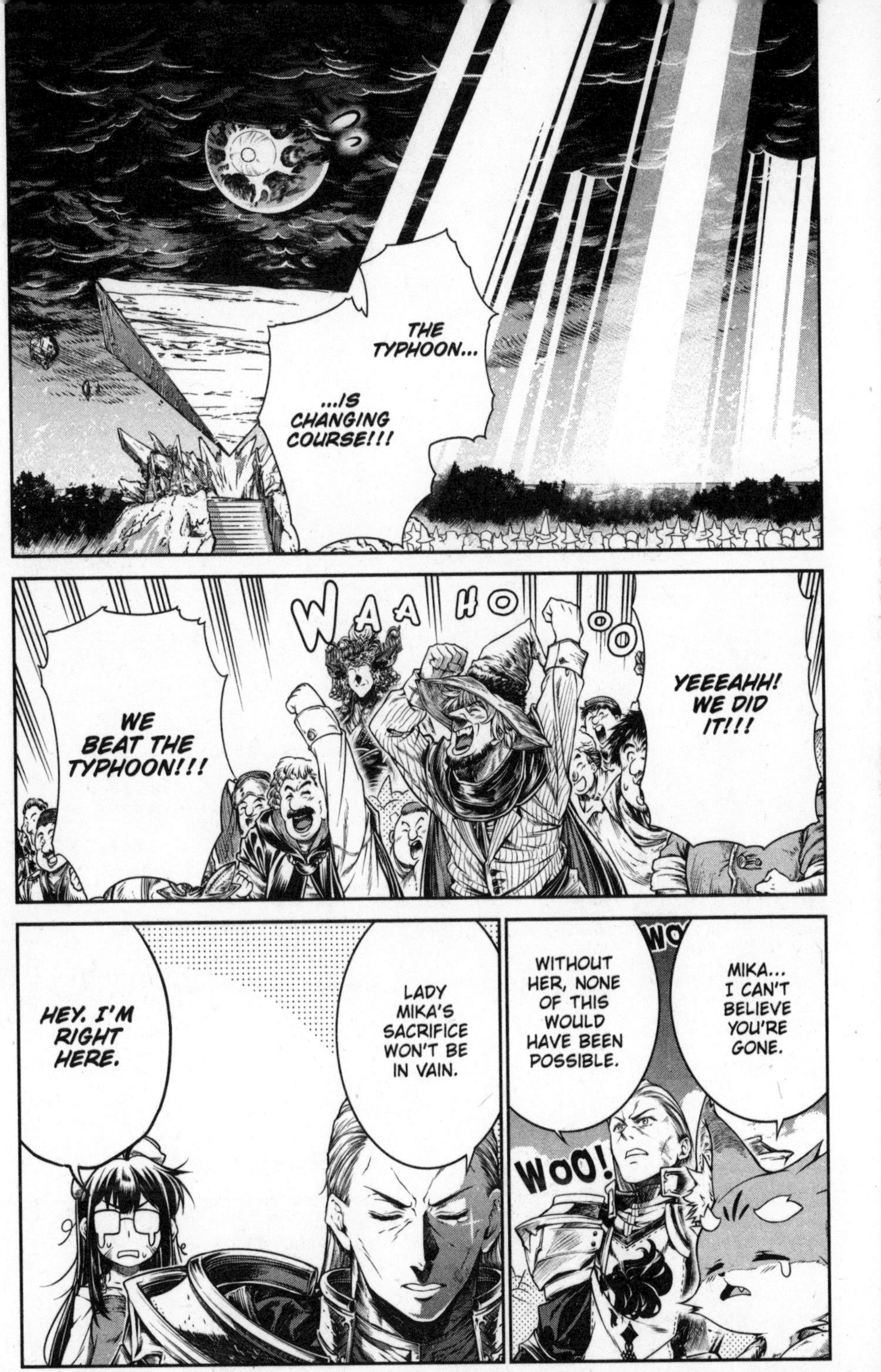
THE TYPHOON...
...IS CHANGING COURSE!!!
WAA HOOO
YEEEAHH! WE DID IT!!!
WE BEAT THE TYPHOON!!!
WOO
MIKA... I CAN'T BELIEVE YOU'RE GONE.
WITHOUT HER, NONE OF THIS WOULD HAVE BEEN POSSIBLE.
WOO!
LADY MIKA'S SACRIFICE WON'T BE IN VAIN.
HEY. I'M RIGHT HERE.

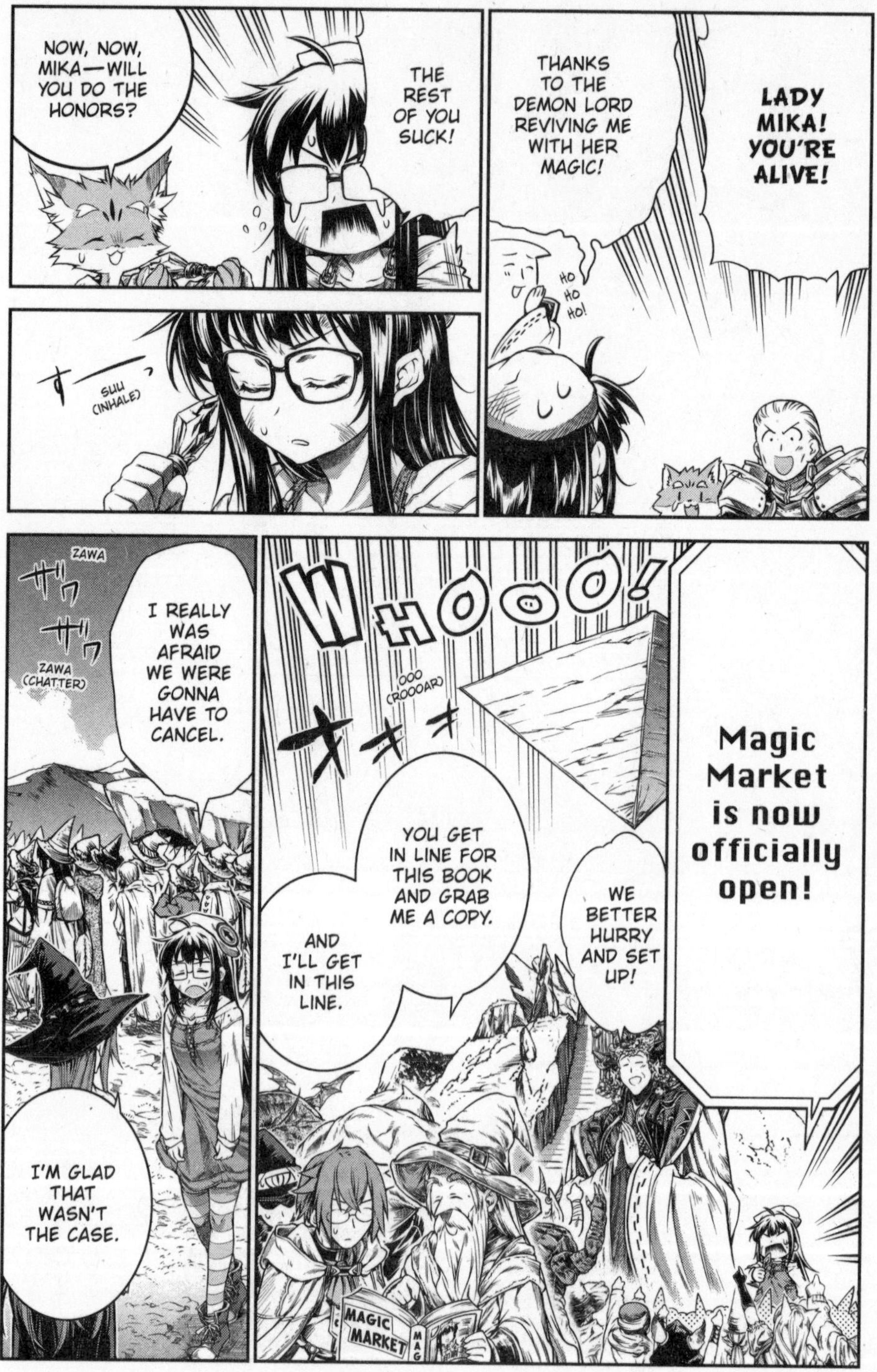
LADY MIKA! YOU'RE ALIVE!
THANKS TO THE DEMON LORD REVIVING ME WITH HER MAGIC!
HO HO HO!
THE REST OF YOU SUCK!
NOW, NOW, MIKA—WILL YOU DO THE HONORS?
SUU (INHALE)
Magic Market is now officially open!
WHOOO!
OOO (ROOOAR)
WE BETTER HURRY AND SET UP!
YOU GET IN LINE FOR THIS BOOK AND GRAB ME A COPY.
AND I'LL GET IN THIS LINE.
MAGIC MARKET
MAG
ZAWA
ZAWA (CHATTER)
I REALLY WAS AFRAID WE WERE GONNA HAVE TO CANCEL.
I'M GLAD THAT WASN'T THE CASE.

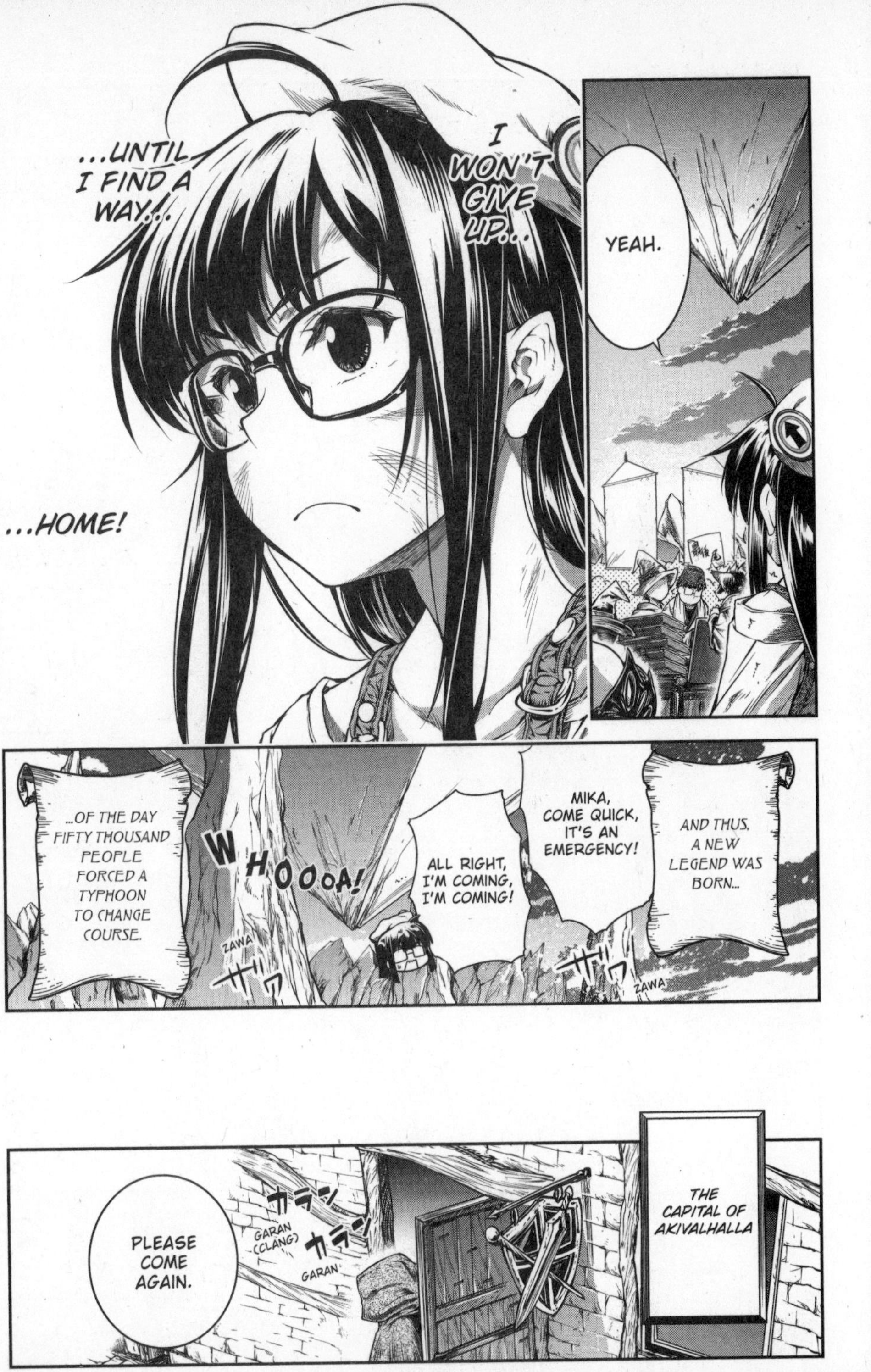

YEAH.
I WON'T GIVE UP...
...UNTIL I FIND A WAY...
...HOME!
AND THUS, A NEW LEGEND WAS BORN...
MIKA, COME QUICK, IT'S AN EMERGENCY!
ZAWA
ザワ
ALL RIGHT, I'M COMING, I'M COMING!
WHOOOOA!
...OF THE DAY FIFTY THOUSAND PEOPLE FORCED A TYPHOON TO CHANGE COURSE.
ZAWA
ザワ
THE CAPITAL OF AKIVALHALLA
カラン
GARAN (CLANG)
カラン
GARAN
PLEASE COME AGAIN.

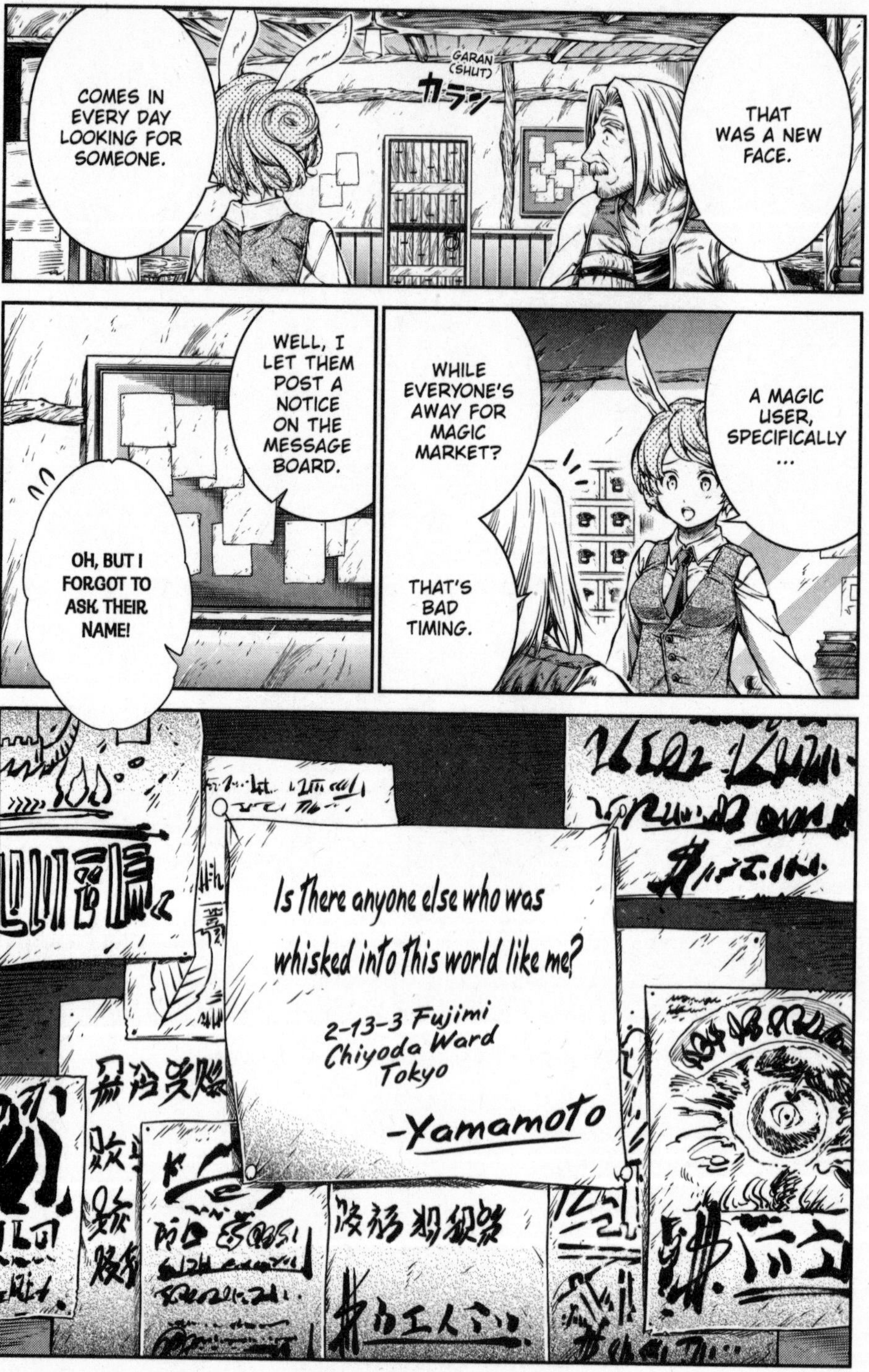

THAT WAS A NEW FACE.
GARAN (SHUT)
カラン
COMES IN EVERY DAY LOOKING FOR SOMEONE.
A MAGIC USER, SPECIFICALLY...
WHILE EVERYONE'S AWAY FOR MAGIC MARKET?
THAT'S BAD TIMING.
WELL, I LET THEM POST A NOTICE ON THE MESSAGE BOARD.
OH, BUT I FORGOT TO ASK THEIR NAME!
Is There anyone else who was whisked into This world like me?
2-13-3 Fujimi
Chiyoda Ward
Tokyo
-Yamamoto


TO BE CONTINUED IN VOLUME 3...

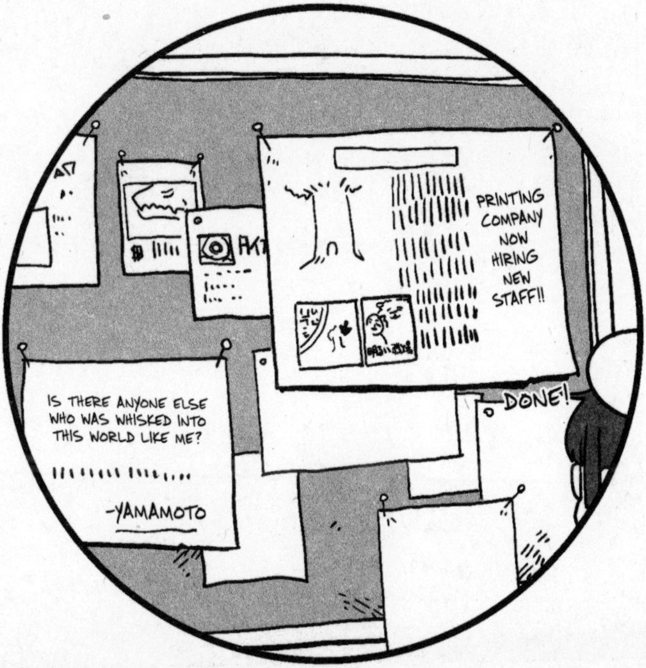
PRINTING COMPANY NOW HIRING NEW STAFF!!
DONE!
IS THERE ANYONE ELSE WHO WAS WHISKED INTO THIS WORLD LIKE ME?
-YAMAMOTO

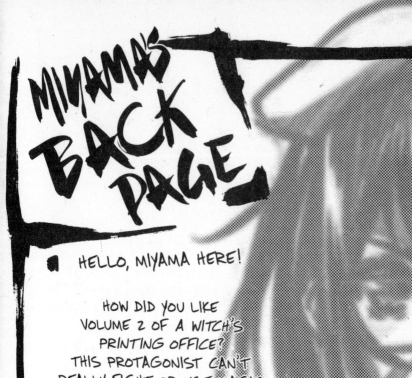

# MIYAMA'S BACK PAGE

HELLO, MIYAMA HERE!

HOW DID YOU LIKE VOLUME 2 OF A WITCH'S PRINTING OFFICE? THIS PROTAGONIST CAN'T REALLY FIGHT OR USE MAGIC AND WILL DO ANYTHING TO ACHIEVE HER GOAL. BUT SHE'S STILL LIVING LIFE IN A FANTASY WORLD JUST LIKE AN RPG HERO. EACH VOLUME, NO MATTER WHAT HARDSHIP THE WORLD FACES, MIKA FINDS HER OWN UNIQUE WAY TO HANDLE IT. THAT'S A TESTAMENT TO MOCHINCHI'S QUALITY WRITING STYLE.

THANKS AGAIN TO EVERYONE WHO PICKED UP THIS VOLUME!

HANKYUVEYMUH—!

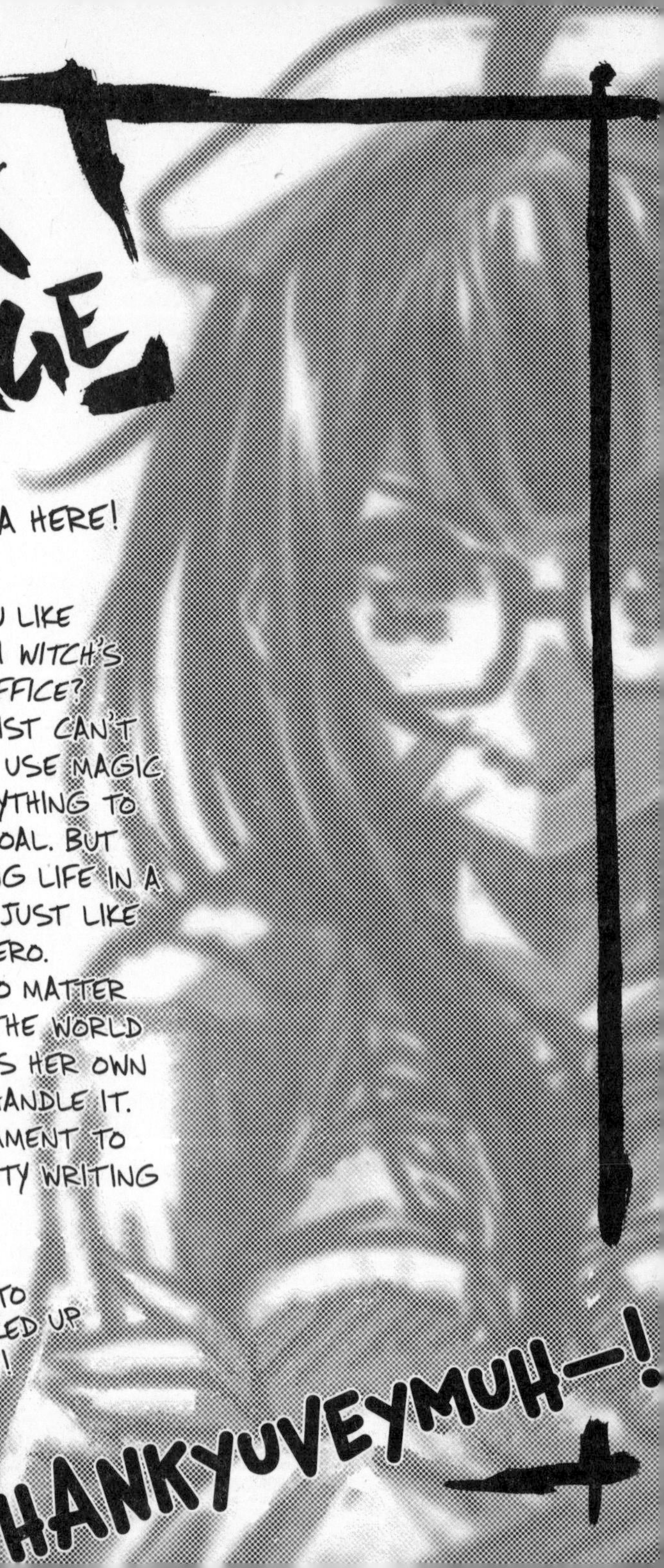

# A Witch's Printing Office

STORY
## MOCHINCHI

ART
## YASUHIRO MIYAMA

✦

ORIGINAL COVER DESIGN

## SAVA DESIGN

COVER PAINTING
## KICHIROKU

EDITOR IN CHARGE
## KENTAROU OGINO

# A WITCH'S PRINTING OFFICE ② story Mochinchi art Yasuhiro Miyama

TRANSLATION: AMBER TAMOSAITIS
LETTERING: ERIN HICKMAN

MAHOTSUKAI NO INSATSUJO Vol. 2
©Mochinchi 2018
©Yasuhiro Miyama 2018
First published in Japan in 2018 by KADOKAWA CORPORATION, Tokyo.
English translation rights arranged with KADOKAWA CORPORATION, Tokyo
through Tuttle-Mori Agency, Inc., Tokyo.

Yen Press
150 West 30th Street, 19th Floor
New York, NY 10001

Visit us at yenpress.com
facebook.com/yenpress
twitter.com/yenpress

yenpress.tumblr.com
instagram.com/yenpress

First Yen Press Edition: April 2020

Yen Press is an imprint of Yen Press, LLC.
The Yen Press name and logo are trademarks of Yen Press, LLC.

Library of Congress Control Number: 2019947774

ISBNs: 978-1-9753-9934-4 (paperback)
978-1-9753-0996-1 (ebook)

10 9 8 7 6 5 4 3 2 1

WOR

Printed in the United States of America